Your past has led you here.
Without your past you could not
face the future. And what you do here today and
in the near future is what you were always meant
to do.

Mantle

WINTER BOOK FOUR

KEVEN NEWSOME

Mantle

Keven Newsome

2nd Edition

ISBN-13: 978-0-9989596-4-1

© 2017 Keven Newsome
All Rights Reserved

KevenNewsome.com

PRESS EPIC

To Winter.
My ink and paper daughter.
And to all the fans who love her.

Agent Greg Erickson ended the phone call and focused on his partner sitting across the table from him in their Cherithville field office. "There's not much time. That was Summer. They're coming for Kaci now. Winter and Ayden just discovered that Claire is an impostor and asked Summer to watch Kaci. So they've revealed Kaci's identity too. Summer is going to wait five minutes and then make the phone call to Xaphan's people like she's supposed to."

Agent Golbeck narrowed his eyes. "You mean to set a trap?"

Erickson nodded as he picked up his phone again. "Make the calls. We need five-point surveillance on the apartment, two to a point. Three points in the front and two in the back. You and I will be inside with Kaci."

As Erickson phoned Kaci and rushed out the door, Golbeck followed close behind, making the other calls.

Erickson and Golbeck crouched in the darkness, flak jackets tight over their chests, as Kaci waited in the bathroom of the apartment. The call had just come in from one of the points outside. Claire approached on the sidewalk.

Erickson keyed his radio and whispered, "Wait until she's in the center and then all positions close in." A quick succession of acknowledgments followed. He glanced at his partner who held his gun pointed to the ceiling. Golbeck nodded back and shifted on his feet.

The silence thickened. A bead of sweat trickled down Erickson's brow. Despite the years of field work and hours of training, his heart still pounded as if he were a rookie. He took a deep breath to center his focus.

The amber street light streaming in through the sliding glass door snuffed out. The apartment plunged into a total darkness penetrated only by the ambient light of the kitchen appliances.

Screams outside.

A single gunshot.

Shouts.

More screams.

A demonic roar pierced the air. Something crashed into the sliding glass door and thumped to the ground. Just enough light permeated the room for Erickson to see the long smear leading to a crumpled heap on the balcony.

Silence returned. Then footsteps outside.

Erickson trained his gun on the door. Golbeck did the same.

Then a thick darkness fell upon them like ash floating through the air. It swirled around the room like sand caught in a violent wind, nipping at Erickson's skin, sucking the oxygen from his lungs. The door opened with a slow creak and Erickson fired through the dense blackness toward the sound.

Something slammed against his head, knocking him to the

ground. Another demonic screech sliced through the air, pressing against his eardrums. Erickson pressed his hands against his head, but it couldn't stop the gouging sound nor the sound of his own screaming.

Golbeck fired right beside him again. With another loud thump, the shots stopped. Something slammed against the wall. Against the ceiling. Then Golbeck's twisted body fell on top of Erickson. Warm blood trickled onto Erickson's face. He shoved at the body to roll it away, but it wouldn't move.

The darkness faded. The light from the street returned. Someone near the door turned on the lights. Erickson blinked against the sudden brightness, wiped the blood and sweat from his eyes, and tried to focus.

Claire loomed over him, one foot on Golbeck's body which still lay on top of Erickson. Her eyes glowed red and she smiled so maliciously that Erickson's blood ran cold. Claire glanced over her shoulder to the door and Erickson followed her gaze.

Two more stood there. A man in a silver and black mask and a young woman with long white hair covering her wet naked body.

Claire's gaze zeroed in on the bathroom door down the hall where Kaci hid. She stepped toward the door as the other two descended on Erickson.

Erickson awoke lying on a cold stone floor. Blue light flooded the room from a moonlit night beyond a small barred window high in the wall. A stainless-steel toilet sat in a dark corner. He pushed himself up and peered around. A smooth door was the only way in or out of the tiny room. No handle. No window. Only a small rectangle cut out at the bottom.

He scrambled across the floor and lay down to peek through, but only pitch darkness could be seen.

Then the whispers started.

He huddled in the corner, head on his knees and fists clenched. Every muscle in his body strained. Sunlight from the high window illuminated the room with sharp shadows.

Whispers…

"Leave me alone," he moaned and shook his head, the thick hair on his face dragging against his dingy pants. How long had it been since he last shaved? How many days?

Whispers… Invisible fingers on his skin.

"Just leave me alone," he moaned again. The whispers and fingers never left. Always there.

He heard scraping on the floor, the tell-tale sound of food. He crawled across the floor but stopped halfway when he saw a delicate hand beneath the door instead of the usual bread and meat.

The hand turned over, palm up and fingers laid back. Erickson waited in the middle of the room, not sure what to do.

The hand withdrew and then the food slid in. He crawled toward the food again, but the plate slid back out and the hand returned.

Erickson clenched his teeth and reached out to it, just barely touching the tip of one finger. The hand immediately withdrew, and the food returned to stay.

The next day it was the same. Then the next. After several days of touching the hand, suddenly the hand could be no longer satisfied with a mere brush. Not even touching it gently in the center of the palm would earn his food.

"What do you want?" Erickson asked when he withdrew his hand for the third time. The hand simply closed gently and then reopened.

He slowly put his hand into the other and closed it. The cold and clammy fingers squeezed fondly and then released.

Now he received the food.

Time became a blur. Endless repetitions of daylight and dark. The hand always returning, every few days demanding a little more of his touch to earn his food. Now it took nearly a minute of holding and caressing as if they were in a relationship.

A day finally came when the door opened. The woman he had seen at Kaci's apartment entered. Her long white hair still draped wet over her naked body. Erickson backed far into the corner as she approached. She knelt in front of him, his plate of food in one hand and her other outstretched.

He knew what she wanted. He reached out, took her hand, and they stared into each other's eyes. Even in the dim light, her eyes shone like jewels, almost as if they glowed ever so slightly. It was impossible to guess her age. The firmness of her eyes and confidence on her face suggested a maturity in years beyond even Erickson. Yet the softness of her skin and delicateness of her body implied that of a woman in her early twenties. After a minute or two, she smiled, set the plate down, and walked out.

For several days she came in to hold his hand. Sometimes she held both hands. Sometimes she held one and gently brushed his cheek with a finger. But she never spoke. Erickson even began to enjoy his moments with the woman...a bright spot in his otherwise miserable existence.

Then a day came when the woman did not open the door. Instead, the man in a silver and black mask came in...the killer from the Tishbe University shooting. The Eater, he called himself, according to FBI files. Erickson scrambled backward across the floor until he cowered in a corner. The Eater grabbed Erickson's arm and hoisted him to his feet, jamming a syringe needle into his neck.

Within moments, the world spun. Erickson's head lolled on his shoulders as the man dragged him out of the cell. Emotions bubbled to the surface. Anger. Hate. Lust. He smiled thinking about the naked woman with the long white hair. His blood boiled with rage at the man who took him away from her.

As the emotions reached a breaking point, Erickson's vision speckled. Moments of time bled into one another. He only remembered flashes of stone-lined halls, a brightly lit room, a stainless-steel table. Something held his arms at his sides. A man in a white coat walked around him...blurred...like a ghost.

Erickson's arm burned. He screamed. The man dug something into it. The pain echoed distantly, detached. Yet it seared his brain like a parasite chewing deep into his skull.

The next thing he knew he lay on the floor of his cell, lifting his head from the musty concrete. The drug still lingered in his system, but if he concentrated he could focus. The door opened again, and he scrambled back into the shadowy corner.

The woman entered. She knelt in front of him with a sympathetic frown. She grabbed his arm and inspected it. For the first time, Erickson saw the one-inch cut, neatly sutured, in the middle of his forearm.

The woman brushed his face as if to apologize. The lingering effects of the drug sent a surge of lust through Erickson. He wanted her. He needed her. He grabbed her face and kissed her as passionately and as deeply as he could. She merely chuckled a delicate laugh and returned the kiss.

She let him do anything and everything he wanted.

This new affair with the young woman, always naked and never speaking, became the normality of his days. The woman would enter with his plate of food, but before he ate he would satisfy his lust with her. Memories of before his time in the cell faded away to a dream-like haze. His love for the woman could not be rivaled by anything in his former life. Still, she never uttered a word…only gave him food, coy smiles, and satisfaction.

The more she came the more he craved her until he awoke each morning screaming at the door for her to visit. Beating on the door. Weeping. Pleading. Then she would finally arrive and her presence rivaled life itself.

She was his life. Without her, his existence was meaningless. Without her, he had no soul.

A day came when she did not return. Erickson heard a commotion outside his cell. Shouts. Gunshots. He stood in the middle of the cell watching the door, wondering if his love was all right. Smoke seeped into the room from the cracks around the door. His heart pounded. He rushed forward. The door slowly opened.

It was not her. Instead, a little girl stood before him, golden brown hair splayed over her shoulders. Thick smoke roiled through the hall behind her.

He stopped and backed up.

The little girl frowned and stepped inside. "You need to escape."

"What have you done with her? Where is she?"

The girl shook her head as she eased closer. "They have tainted you. But I will free your mind." She reached up to him, seeming to grow in size briefly, to touch his forehead.

His mind cleared. For the first time, he could count the days of his internal clock, realizing he had been there for months. He mentally relived all that the woman had done to him, and his stomach flipped with repulsion. He turned aside and vomited as if to expel the ball of tar the woman had inserted in place of his soul.

"It will get better," the girl said. "There is only one person who can take the darkness away completely."

"Who?" he asked as he straightened and wiped his mouth.

"You already know. You just have to admit it to yourself."

He clenched his teeth and glanced beyond the girl. Smoke billowed now. Dim orange light flickered. Fire. "What do I do now?" he asked.

"Escape," she said. "And then get to work. They still need your help."

The Lord utters His voice before His army;
surely His camp is very great,
for strong is he who carries out His word.
The day of the Lord is indeed great and
very awesome,
and who can endure it?
Joel 4:11 (NAS)

1

Present Day

Winter Maessen waited behind the wheel of her parked car, engine still running, at 8:25 in the morning, in front of a salon in Cherithville. She glanced at the doors and then checked the clock...five minutes until her appointment. A flicker of panic coursed through her and she whimpered. Staring at herself in the visor-mirror, Winter grabbed a lock of her hair and glared at the two inches of golden brown roots.

"I can do this...It's only hair..." She bit her lip and whimpered again. Could she do this?

Winter reached for the ignition and violently twisted the key to turn off the engine. She jumped out of the car and rushed up to the doors of the salon before she could give the matter any more thought or talk herself out of it.

A brass bell jangled as she entered, and both of the hairdressers at work on customers gazed her way. The two early morning customers, both over sixty, briefly became quiet before resuming their conversation with each other. Five other chairs sat empty, waiting for other hairdressers to arrive for work later in the day.

"Sign the list, sweetie, and we'll be right with you."

Winter found the clipboard on the counter. She scanned down the list of crossed-out names from the day before and scribbled her own at the bottom. Then she sat and fidgeted with her hands, the ends of her hair, and her phone, all to avoid thinking about what would soon happen. Finally, one of the elderly customers finished and crossed the room to the counter to pay. When the lady had left, the hairdresser, a young woman not much older than Winter, smiled at her.

"Good morning," she said to Winter.

Winter smiled back. "Good morning."

"My name is Jessica. You ready?"

"Not really."

Jessica laughed at her and waved Winter forward. "It'll be fine, I promise." As she herded Winter to the chair, she continued to chatter. "So what are you doing this beautiful Thursday morning?"

"My friend's getting married this evening."

"Oh, so this is a wedding do? I'm glad you told me. I'll make sure it looks extra great and you won't have to worry about it." Winter eased into the chair and Jessica pulled gently at the sides of Winter's hair. "So what are we doing today? Looks like it's time to color, but do you want to get anything cut?"

Winter shook her head. "Not really. Maybe just trimmed. I'm really here for the color."

"Black?"

"Not this time. I want you to match my roots. I want my original color back." Winter's stomach fluttered.

"Simple enough. Are you sure about this? It's a pretty big change."

Winter nodded. "It's been black for almost seven years. I'm ready to be me again."

Jessica smiled. "Then let's get started."

An hour later, after having her hair washed, colored, trimmed, and finally styled, Winter stared at herself in the mirror, trying not to cry. The raven locks were gone, replaced by soft golden-brown curls that wrapped around her face and beneath her chin. Without black hair, her skin appeared darker than before. And beneath the golden brown, her blue eyes suddenly gleamed back with the barest hint of hazel.

A worried look settled on Jessica's face. "What's wrong? You don't like it?"

"No, it's not that. I just forgot how much I look like my mom." Winter rubbed her eyes and smiled at Jessica. "It's good. It's perfect. Thank you."

With a satisfied smile, Jessica unfastened the smock.

Winter left the salon and drove directly back to her new apartment just outside of town. The duplex lay tucked in a small, sleepy neighborhood, with plenty of trees around and a forest just to the back. Three other identical duplexes finished out that end of the street, most housing young families or newlyweds. How Kaci's dad managed to find one with both apartments in a single duplex available, Winter didn't know. But Chris did most of the work and came through with the perfect new home for Winter, Ayden, Kaci, and Peter, where they could live next to each other and figure out what to do next after last spring's near-miss. Even though Kaci and Peter had graduated, school remained a priority for Ayden. Winter couldn't care less and fully expected to have to leave school if an opportunity to stop Xaphan presented itself.

Winter sighed with relief when she found the graveled parking area empty. Of course, she knew it should be. Peter and Kaci were already in Grady, no doubt beside themselves as time ticked ever closer to the wedding. Ayden was there too, since her parents lived not far from Grady. Winter didn't know where Summer and Davis were at the moment, but she knew they wouldn't be showing up here. Summer was probably already with Kaci, like a good bridesmaid should be. And wherever Summer went, Davis wouldn't be far away. Only Graham made her nervous and sent her heart fluttering. He had asked Winter to come pick him up in Cherithville, and she expected him to arrive any minute now.

She parked and rushed inside to her new bedroom. After checking around to make sure nothing had been disturbed, she took another long look at herself in the mirror. Golden brown hair, a red and orange shirt, and blue jeans. She barely recognized herself.

Crunching gravel outside jolted her attention away from her looks. She grabbed the overnight bag she brought with her when she came down the day before, pulled the bridesmaid dress from her closet, and rushed to the front door.

Graham crossed from his car toward the door when she opened it. He stopped and stared at her, and it took a moment for recognition to appear in his eyes.

"Whoa," he said. "Winter? Is that really you?"

Winter scrutinized the ground. "Yeah."

"Wow. I mean…you look amazing. Have you always looked like that?"

She lifted her head and glared at him. "Actually, I have, thank you."

"I didn't mean…"

Winter shoved past him, feigning insult because she did know what he meant. She opened the back door of her car, tossed in her bag, and hung the dress. "Are you coming?"

As Graham put his things into Winter's car, Winter ran back to the apartment to make sure she hadn't forgotten anything. At the last minute, on an impulse she didn't understand, she ran into the kitchen and pulled two empty large soda bottles from the trash. Then she locked the apartment door and ran back to the car.

"What are those for?"

"I don't know," Winter said. She tossed the bottles into the trunk.

Graham studied her with a half-smile from over the roof. He sat in the car at the same time she did and didn't ask any questions. She cranked the car and then noticed something else she needed by the side of the building. A brick. *A brick?* Her stomach fluttered, not understanding what she was doing or why the nudges demanded these random items. But she jumped out to retrieve it anyway.

"Be right back."

After lugging the brick to her trunk, she settled back behind the wheel.

Graham watched her with open amusement now. "Should I ask?"

"Wouldn't do any good. I'm not sure what I'm doing myself. Just following a little nudge."

"Right…"

Winter stared at him. "If you're done patronizing me, we need to go."

"By all means then."

But more nudges came. As they barreled down the highway, Winter slammed the brakes and pulled onto the shoulder, not even sure why she needed to stop. She waited until there were no vehicles passing, then hopped out and ran a few feet into the grass just beyond the shoulder. There she found a three-foot length of small chain. She threw it in the trunk with the rest of the stuff and sat back in the car. Graham just shook his head but made no further comments.

About halfway to Grady, they passed a large reservoir on the right of the highway. The water called to her, pulling her as if the nudges all led there.

"Sorry," she said as she took the next exit. "Just one last thing, I promise."

Graham chuckled. "Whatever."

She followed the road for several miles, before making the first of several turns. Eventually, they found the far side of the massive body of water. The trees peeled back and the road crossed a long dam. To the left, the dam dropped far away in a sheer precipice. To the right, the peaceful reservoir glistened in the sunlight. The shores showcased large houses straight out of the pages of a fancy magazine.

Winter slowed and parked halfway across the dam. She studied the water, wondering why this place…why now. Somehow, she knew exactly what to do with the random items in her trunk, but what was the point? She didn't understand, but her nudges demanded the task be done. She pressed the button to pop her trunk and opened her door.

"Help me," she snapped at Graham as she climbed out.

"That's not very nice."

Winter huffed and leaned back in. "Will you help me? Please?" She flashed her teeth at him and then strode to the back of her car without waiting for a response.

After twisting the caps off the bottles to let them air out, she grabbed the chain and stared at it.

A moment later, Graham was at her side. "What are we doing?"

"Attaching these bottles to the block with this chain."

"Why?"

Winter shrugged, her face flushing. "I don't know." She picked up each bottle, shook them through the fresh air vigorously, and then screwed the caps back on tight.

Graham took the chain, wrapping it around the bottle in experimentation. "I'm not sure how this is going to work."

"What if we did this?" Winter took each bottle and shoved it through one of the holes in the cinder block."

"Brilliant. Then we just wrapped the chain like this…" Graham began wrapping the block. "…so that they don't come out." He looped the ends of the chain around itself into a knot.

They stepped back and studied the contraption as it sat in the trunk.

"Now what?" he asked.

Winter reached in and grabbed it. Graham took the other end and helped her hoist it out. "Into the water," said Winter.

"What?"

"Throw it."

They eased to the edge of the dam, took a couple of momentum swings, and then sent the chain-wrapped bottle-block combo into the reservoir. It bobbed once and then slowly began to sink.

"Is that it?" Graham asked.

Winter took a deep breath, internally searching for more nudges. "That's it. Let's go."

Winter clapped the dust off her hands and sprinted back around her car. As they sped off back toward the interstate she checked the time. With any luck, they'd still arrive in Grady right on time.

"Um," she said a few miles down the road. "Don't tell anyone about this."

Graham leaned back against the headrest and laughed.

Winter jutted out her jaw, turned up the radio, and ignored him.

2

After an awkward eternity of riding with Graham, they finally arrived in Grady. Winter took them straight to the church, where the parking lot was already filling.

"Kaci's going to kill me," Winter said.

"Relax," said Graham. "We're still a couple of hours early. We've got plenty of time. Most of these people probably aren't even guests."

Winter glared at him as she put the vehicle in park. She ground her teeth and climbed out without speaking another word. After retrieving her dress, she draped it over her arm and ran to the back building, not really caring what Graham was doing behind her.

As she ran through the door into the dining area, a group of people she didn't recognize stopped talking and turned to her. At first, Winter wasn't sure if they were looking at her. If they were, then the weird cautious looks she had grown used to over the years were missing. Several of the guys actually smiled.

"Kaci?" Winter asked.

"Down the hall," said a woman. "Last room on the left."

Winter nodded and jogged away. She hesitated just before

entering the room, butterflies pinging the inside of her abdomen. After a deep breath, she went in.

The other bridesmaids were already there. One that Winter didn't recognize sat by the wall in a cushioned chair. Young, with short, light brown hair, the girl held a phone in front of her face, not paying attention to anyone else. Summer, the only other bridesmaid, stood beside Kaci. Kaci had her back to the door, sitting in a cushioned chair herself. She sat in front of a mirror and looked up at Winter through the reflection as Winter walked up behind her. Everyone in the room stopped talking to watch Winter cross the room.

Kaci spun in the chair, golden curls swinging. Her dress shimmered like pearl and her makeup sparkled with glitter. She watched Winter with wide eyes as her jaw lowered. "Winter?"

Winter gazed at the floor, self-conscious of her golden-brown hair that swung next to her face.

"Wow," said Kaci. "It's…you look…wow. I never knew. But why?"

Winter shrugged as she came to Kaci's side. "Time to stop hiding, I guess."

Kaci turned back to the mirror and resumed makeup application at the skilled hands of Summer. "Well, it looks great. But you're still late. Where have you been?"

"I went back to Cherithville last night. Graham had to work late and needed a ride this morning."

"Why did he need a ride?"

"I don't know. He said something about the company car and…I don't know. He really didn't make it clear."

Kaci smirked. "You know he didn't really need a ride, don't you?"

Heat crept into Winter's cheeks and she averted eyes.

"Never mind that." Kaci stood and turned to the other bridesmaid that Winter didn't recognize. "This is Rachel, Peter's sister."

Winter smiled at her. "I didn't know Peter had a sister."

"Figures," said Rachel without looking up from her phone.

Kaci glanced up at the clock on the wall. "Not long now."

"Are you ready?" asked Winter.

Kaci grinned at her. "Absolutely."

Winter waited in line behind Summer and Rachel, all three of them wearing identical dresses of shimmering periwinkle. She shuffled the small bouquet of white tulips from hand to hand, trying to find the least awkward way of holding them. Somewhere behind them, Kaci hid around a corner so no one could catch a glimpse of her through the door as the bridesmaids entered the chapel. If she ran, no one would know. Winter firmed her jaw and trained forward, resisting the urge to turn around and search for Kaci.

The music began, soft piano phrases moving with emotional purpose, followed shortly by the baritone voice of the cello. As the cello sang out the melody, Summer stepped through the doors. She took long, slow strides to the gentle rhythm of the song.

Winter nibbled her lip and put a hand up to check her hair, maybe to make sure it was still the right color, and then immediately regretted letting go of her perfect grip on the bouquet. As she fidgeted with the flowers again, Winter lifted up onto her toes to peer beyond Rachel's shoulder. It wasn't a huge crowd in the chapel, maybe only thirty people, but all heads faced their direction. All eyes swept repeatedly from the bridesmaids to beyond, obviously trying to catch a glance of the hidden bride. Near the front of the chapel, Winter spotted her dad. Steve smiled at her when they made eye contact and he winked. She fell back onto her heels again to hide behind Rachel, only to have Rachel step out into the aisle and leave her exposed to everyone. At least she had found a new passable grip on the flowers.

Winter took a deep breath. She could hear the swishing of Kaci's dress as she moved into position behind her. Rachel reached the halfway point of the chapel and Winter stepped out, trying not to turn her head from side to side to glare at everyone staring at her and trying not to believe the only reason they stared was her new hair. Winter pushed the thoughts aside and focused on stepping properly and not tripping in those stupid heels. She fixed her eyes on the altar, where Summer took her place at the far end as Rachel arrived at the steps.

Opposite the girls stood Peter and his groomsmen. Peter's dad stood directly next to Peter in the best-man position, a slightly taller and grayer version of Peter. After Peter's dad stood Graham and then Davis. They all watched Winter, except for Peter who already craned for his bride. After a quick glance at each of the watching men, Winter locked eyes with Graham and found herself unable to look away. Only when she recognized the stretching of her cheeks into a wide smile did she blush and gaze at the ground, rushing the final few feet to take her place in the maid-of-honor position.

The piano and cello slowed, then paused. The tune changed, not the traditional bridal march, but more lively and emotive than the previous tune. The crowd stood. All heads not already watching for Kaci turned to the back. Peter stepped forward a little so he could get a clearer view of the aisle. Winter cast from Peter to Graham and found Graham watching her again. He grinned and swiveled toward the back of the chapel with everyone else.

Kaci appeared. Her shimmering white dress draped in smooth lines down her body, shoulderless but long-sleeved. Tightly against her chest, she held a larger, more colorful version of the tulip bouquet that Winter held. Her curled hair twisted up in the back, with ringlets caressing her cheeks. Small jewels glimmered from her hair and a pearly ribbon choker wrapped her neck.

Kaci's dad, Chris, walked alongside her, arm in arm. His tense red face couldn't stop the tears he tried to hold back. He stared straight ahead, not really focusing on anyone or anything, with his chin high.

Kaci reserved her eyes and smile for only one person. Peter watched her approach with an identical smile and unashamed tears on his face. Winter bit her lip and pushed back the stinging at the corner of her own eyes.

When Kaci and Chris reached the steps, Peter descended. Chris took Kaci and Peter by the hand and bowed his head, saying a prayer that only the three of them could hear. Then he squeezed Kaci's hand and passed it to Peter's. He kissed Kaci on the cheek and led them up the steps, taking up his place at the head of the wedding party to officiate the ceremony.

As the couple turned to face one another, Winter caught Graham watching her again. This time, she didn't mind. She smiled at him...a real smile, letting a tear escape from her eye. She swiped it away and turned her attention back to Peter and Kaci.

3

Four Years Ago

As Winter climbed the steps of the bus, easily the oldest person there besides the driver, a hush fell. Elementary kids stared, wide-eyed and pale-faced at the black-clad, black-haired senior. Winter didn't give them a second glance as she eased toward the back seat. The further back she walked, the older the students. Junior high kids whispered to each other, panic spreading almost like a plague through their ranks. The high-schoolers wouldn't even look at her. At some point, the very back seat had been vacated. Winter took it and sat, not really caring what any of those kids thought of her and just wanting to get her last year of high school over with.

At the school, it was much the same. Winter avoided direct contact with anyone, and everyone obliged willingly. In what little bit of eye contact with her fellow seniors she didn't manage to avoid, she found pity rather than fear. She took that pity and absorbed it into her own, allowing it to strengthen her resolve to just go through the motions.

It continued throughout the first few days. Occasionally, she would pass by Stacy in the hall, standing and staring at Winter with desperation on her face. Winter tried to summon some sort of feeling for Stacy, fondness or pity, but the numbness inside of her was complete now…her shell solidified. She gladly accepted this about herself, knowing she couldn't possibly connect with her friend on a level Stacy deserved.

Winter at least spared time enough to recognize the fact that it was just her and Stacy now. She supposed high school required inevitable tragedy, especially a school as large as this one. But she and Stacy had been at the epicenter of most of it.

She paused at this last thought and glanced back at Stacy. Stacy had turned away, rubbing her eyes with the heel of her hand, and then she rushed off to class. Winter sighed. No one else in the entire school understood the depth of what the two of them had to endure. She could see on Stacy's face that her friend felt just as alone as Winter. But Stacy didn't have a numbness to shelter beneath.

Winter resumed her walk to class. Maybe she'd speak to Stacy tomorrow.

As the week progressed, the other students on the bus slowly realized Winter had not come to steal their souls. They stopped staring as she walked to the back of the bus, carrying on as they were before Winter had been picked up. But they always left the back seat vacant. It was the same in the classroom. Winter faded into the pattern, no longer noticeable, and more of an afterthought or a glitch in society, something to be sighed over and ignored because nothing could be done about her. No one considered her a threat to the well-being of the whole.

She was simply the resident freak.

Winter preferred this new dynamic. It gave her the solitude to deal with her own thoughts on her own terms, and it gave her the space to concentrate on doing her best school work so she could graduate with some measure of satisfaction.

Stacy never left her side, but stayed too far away to speak to and yet close enough that Winter knew Stacy lurked on purpose. Every time Winter saw her she wanted to go speak, but could never figure out the right words to say to Stacy's continuously broken-hearted face. It was easier to remain silent.

On the last day of the first week, as Winter placed books in her locker before going to her bus after school, she had not given Stacy any thought for hours. She slammed her locker door and spun, colliding with Stacy, who had her face to the floor, rushing past.

Shock crossed Stacy's face. "Sorry."

"No, it's my fault," said Winter, managing a faint smile. "Where are you going so fast?"

Stacy stared at her for a moment as if Winter should know. "To my car."

A flush crept up Winter's neck. "Oh yeah. Right." She nodded toward the exit behind Stacy. "I'm headed to the bus." Winter sighed and moved to step around Stacy.

"Um, you don't have to," Stacy said to Winter's back.

Winter paused and turned around.

Stacy looked to the floor and pushed her hair behind her shoulder. "I mean…you could ride with me. I don't mind." Her eyes flicked back to Winter.

Winter glanced toward the buses and then to Stacy. "Are you sure? I don't want to impose or anything."

Stacy shook her head eagerly. "No, it's fine. Really."

Winter nodded, still wishing she could feel something… excitement, gratitude, anything…and followed Stacy silently the other way, out into the parking lot, and to Stacy's car. Neither of them spoke. The awkwardness filled the car. As Stacy entered the line of vehicles trying to exit the school, Winter decided to break it.

"So, what have you been up to?"

Stacy shrugged. "Not much really. I've just sort of…been doing my own thing."

Winter knew what that meant. She also already knew that Stacy had been struggling just as much as Winter had. "Yeah, me too.

Maybe we should hang out more, you know…so that we don't…" Her thought path derailed.

"I know. I'd like that, actually. I haven't had many people to hang out with. We could ride together every day if you want. I mean, it beats riding the bus. You don't live that far from me. I could pick you up in the mornings and bring you home. You know, like I did some last year."

"It would be nice to give up the bus, but I don't want you to go out of your way for me."

"I don't mind. We're friends, right?" The question hung in the air, more genuine than rhetorical, as if Stacy wasn't sure anymore.

"Of course," Winter said. "But I thought you had your church friends."

Stacy shrugged. "They're not perfect. Recent…um…events have sort of made them want to keep their distance from me. But I don't really go to church for them anyway."

"Sounds like a great bunch of friends."

"It's not really as bad as it sounds. The whole point is so that imperfect people can get closer to God. That includes them…so I don't mind, I guess."

"Doesn't sound like it."

Stacy frowned. "You should see for yourself. We're having a sort of party for back to school."

"I don't do church."

"It's not church. It's at someone's house. Why don't you come?" Stacy gave her a desperate pleading blink. That's when Winter understood that if she didn't go Stacy might not actually have any friends there at all.

"I'll think about it."

Stacy nodded, wide-eyed. "Okay."

"I'll tell you tomorrow.

"Okay."

Winter smiled a little. "When you pick me up."

Stacy relaxed with a sigh and grinned at her. "Okay."

4

Present Day

Winter curled up in her black papasan chair in the corner of the living room of her new apartment. She wiggled a little, sinking deeper into the perfect spot that she had grown to love since she first bought the chair for college three years ago. As she grabbed the remote to search for a new channel to watch, she laid her head on the edge of the chair.

"See if Hunt Commandos is on," said Ayden, stretched out on the couch.

"You don't actually like that show, do you?"

"It reminds me of some of my uncles."

Winter shook her head. "What about Paranormal Truth?"

"Totally fake. And it'll give me nightmares."

Winter abandoned the chair and tossed the remote to her. "Find what you want. I'm going to get something to eat."

As she walked to the kitchen just opposite the living room, Winter's phone chirped. She checked the text message and grinned.

"Kaci and Peter are back. They'll be here in just a few minutes."

Ayden sat up and turned off the TV. "About time. I wonder if she's knocked up yet."

As Winter passed by Ayden to get to the door, she punched Ayden in the shoulder.

The two apartment doors of the duplex faced each other across a concrete pad. Winter sat in a lawn chair in the alcove and faced the street to wait for Peter and Kaci.

Within five minutes, Kaci's car topped the hill, Peter behind the wheel. Winter couldn't suppress the grin on her face when she saw Kaci peering at her with a grin of her own. As they pulled in beside Winter's car, Winter rushed to Kaci's side. Kaci jumped out and flung her arms around Winter and they squeezed tightly.

"How were the mountains?" asked Winter.

"Beautiful," said Kaci. "I wish we could have stayed longer."

Peter closed his door and ambled back to the trunk. "Our cabin overlooked a small mountain creek and there was absolutely no one around us within five miles."

Winter narrowed her eyes and winked at Kaci. "Sounds perfect."

Kaci blushed and glanced away, but it wasn't a happy blush.

"Was everything okay?" Winter looked at Peter.

Peter firmed his lips. "Everything is fine. We had a great time."

Winter gazed back at Kaci. "You know I'll find out," she said softly.

"I'll talk to you later, okay?"

Winter nodded. "Okay." As Kaci scurried to open the apartment door, Winter joined Peter at the back of the car. "Can I help?"

Peter flashed her a smile and handed her a bag. "Sure."

Peter began his new job at the Family Fitness Center later that week. He'd be working late nights, closing the center after the evening crowd left and then finishing the rounds before the cleaning crew took over. Winter waited patiently all week and watched through the blinds for him to finally leave that Thursday night. As soon as his car turned the corner, Winter made straight for Kaci's door and knocked.

Kaci answered, eyes wide and red.

"You've been crying again," said Winter.

Kaci wiped her face. "I'm fine."

"No, you're not. I can hear you two through the walls. I hear the yelling and I hear the screaming. And it's all coming from you. So I want to know why." Winter pushed past her and planted herself in Kaci's armchair.

Kaci grabbed a box of tissues from the shelf and sat on the couch across from Winter. She took a tissue out and blew her nose, staring at the carpet. "The honeymoon didn't exactly go according to plan."

"They usually don't."

"No, you don't understand. The first time we…" Kaci bit her lip. "Yeah?"

"All those memories came back. All I could think about was…" Kaci covered her face with both hands.

Winter waited. She let the silence fill the emptiness.

"I tried," Kaci continued. "I really did. I hid in the bathroom until I stopped crying, but I think he knew. He tried to give me space, but it was our honeymoon, you know? It wasn't fair to him. But by the end of the week…I just couldn't anymore. Now, anytime I even think he wants to touch me all I can see is that night, and I just get so angry that I start screaming."

Winter nodded. "I get it."

Kaci crossed her arms and stared at the wall, tears flowing down her crimson cheeks and her chin quivering. "I can't be the wife he needs me to be. I just can't. It was a mistake getting married."

"Don't say that. You love each other, and you'll work this out. Peter knows it'll take you some time, so give him a little credit."

"But what I am supposed to do? I don't even want him to look at me, how can I be intimate with him?"

"I think maybe you should go see someone…a therapist."

Kaci furrowed her brows. "Do you think it would help?"

"If you want to give your marriage the best shot possible, I think it's the best thing." Winter crossed the room and sat next to Kaci on the couch, wrapping her arms around her. Kaci leaned against her and sobbed. "This isn't your fault and it isn't Peter's fault. You'll figure it out, I promise."

5

Winter hated leaving Kaci behind when classes began. Winter and Ayden carefully wove their schedules so that Kaci would never be alone. Graham installed state-of-the-art security measures at his own expense. Despite knowing they had done all they could, Winter still didn't feel good about it.

What made her feel better about leaving for classes was what waited beneath the trees as she stepped out of her apartment. The unmistakable outline and tail swishing of a huge horse lurked in the shadows across the street. The rider, also cloaked in deep shadows, turned in her direction. Winter blinked and the figure disappeared.

She stared after it for several seconds, remembering the angelic horsemen that had come to her aid at the trainyard and wondering which one of the four now patrolled around the apartment. Could it be the same one that had spoken to her on the road in Romania? When the horseman didn't show himself again, Winter checked to make sure she had locked the door behind her and walked to her car.

The commute to campus took a little longer than last year because their duplex lay more isolated than the previous apartment complex. Winter still hadn't decided if she thought it a good thing or a bad thing. On the one hand, being isolated meant less interaction with people that might spread the word about them. But on the other, if Xaphan located them it'd be easier for him to approach.

Winter found an empty parking spot in the commuter lot not far from the Union. She checked the time on her phone and decided to swing through the Union to grab something quick to eat on the way to class. She hated these early morning classes, but it was unavoidable in order to keep her and Ayden as separated as possible.

After grabbing a pastry and a mug of coffee, Winter sat on the steps of the Union facing the Meadow. Other students shuffled past like new-born zombies. The freshmen were easy to spot, wide-eyed, walking just a little too fast in one direction before changing and running in another, dressed as if they had been awake for hours. Maybe they had. But they'd learn soon enough that it only required five minutes or less to wake up and make it to an eight o'clock class.

Winter smirked as a freshman boy tripped over the same crack that she had her first year. At least he didn't plant his face into the ground like she did, but he still goggled around red-faced at the upperclassmen who just chuckled, shook their heads, and went about their business. The boy fled toward the education building, face glued to the sidewalk for any more surprises, and almost crashed into a group of girls headed to the Union.

Winter took another bite of her pastry and dug in her backpack for her schedule. Five of her six classes were all in the religion department: Hebrew 2, History of the Church, Biblical Worldview 2, Biblical Interpretation, and Cultic Studies. Her last class, logic, would be in the Psychology building. But that class was on Tuesday and Thursday afternoons. Today, she had the Hebrew and history classes back to back, then she had to swap with Ayden for several hours before coming back late in the afternoon for an evening section of Biblical Worldview. Such were her Mondays, Wednesdays, and Fridays. Tuesdays and Thursdays were practically identical, except she only had one early class before swapping and returning for two afternoon classes. Why did Ayden get to sleep in every day?

Winter grunted and stood to amble toward class.

"Hey!" Summer called to her, jogging down the Union steps from behind.

Winter slowed for her to catch up. "Hey."

"Do you have morning classes too?"

"Every single day."

"Me too!" Summer bounced a little.

Winter rolled her eyes. Summer didn't seem phased by the early hours. Her perfect makeup and hair suggested she began construction on her appearance long before the sun rose.

"Listen, I heard something strange over the weekend in my dorm. I wanted to see if you knew anything about it."

"What?" asked Winter.

"Well, a bunch of us were in the lobby talking, and it turns out that one of the girls on my floor was shot in the Meadow second year," said Summer.

Winter's eyes widened. "And she's okay?"

Summer nodded. "She's fine now. She took last year off but decided to come back this year. Anyway, some of the girls started asking her about it. I thought maybe they were being insensitive, but the girl didn't mind. She actually seemed excited to talk. She said she didn't know what was happening until she turned and the killer was right there beside her. Next thing she knew, she was on the ground and she knew she was dying. But then this little girl showed up out of nowhere, put her hands on her, and healed her. She stayed on the ground, still hurting and weak, but she said she watched the little girl walk all through the Meadow, stopping and touching people."

"Wow." Winter stopped and faced Summer directly. "Are you serious?"

"You told me once you had seen a little girl in visions or something. Do you think it's the same one?" Summer asked.

Winter shrugged. "Maybe. But I didn't think she was…you know…*real*."

"Well, she was certainly real to the girl in my dorm. Maybe others. I think I'll ask around and see if anyone else saw her that day."

"Yeah," said Winter. "Let me know, too. I'd like to talk with them."

"Sure. Hey, since we both have early mornings, how about we meet up for breakfast?" Summer asked. "I feel like we didn't get to spend enough time together last year."

"Maybe," said Winter. "But I'm not promising I'll make it on time every day."

Summer pivoted to face the other direction. "Well, try to make it tomorrow, okay?"

"Yeah, sure."

Summer smiled. "My class is this way. I'll see you later."

"Later." Winter watched her for a moment as Summer took the first five steps in a jog, swinging her carefully crafted blond hair the way only she could. Could the little girl be really *real*? Could she be the reason more people didn't die that day? Winter sighed and turned.

A wall of dark black hair stood just in front of her, and Winter nearly slammed into it. She held her breath and took a step back. The warhorse, easily the size of a Clydesdale, paused and blocked the path. Winter let her eyes drift up the black muscular flanks to the black-armored legs of the rider and up to his helmeted head. A sword, wider than Winter's leg and longer than she was tall, hung at the rider's side. He slowly pivoted to look down at her, gleaming white eyes set in an indistinguishable shadowy face.

Another groggy student slumped past her, vanishing through the horseman as if it were nothing more than a hologram.

"What do you want?" Winter asked the horseman.

The rider gazed up behind her. He swiveled his head to scan one end of the Meadow to the other. Then the horse began moving again. Winter watched him walk toward the Ancient, pausing every few strides to scan the Meadow. Similar movement between two buildings at the opposite end of the Meadow caught her eye. Another rider, wearing blood-red armor on a dark bay horse. He scanned the area too and then disappeared again between the buildings.

No one else could see them. But then again...there weren't many people left in the Meadow anyway. First the little girl and now horsemen? Could they be connected? She'd seen three of the four from last year already that day, so where was the fourth horseman? Winter tore her eyes from the black horseman and ran the rest of the way to the religion department.

6

Four Years Ago

A car horn yelped. Winter's stomach fluttered and she walked outside to Stacy's car waiting by the curb. As Winter climbed in, she carefully tried not to look Stacy in the eyes.

"Are you sure this won't be too late? My dad wants me home by eleven," Winter said.

"I promise," said Stacy. "It should be over by nine o'clock or so. I think you'll enjoy yourself, but if you decide you want to leave just tell me and we'll go."

Winter nodded and faced straight ahead as Stacy drove.

When they arrived, Stacy parked on the side of the street behind several cars. A few other teenagers had also just arrived and were walking up to the door in a group. Winter glanced up the quaint street, then studied the smallish house nestled behind a few ornamental trees and wondered if anyone here would recognize her. Most of them were probably from her school, but some might be from other schools in the city. She might actually have a chance to make a new first impression on some of them. Stacy grinned and climbed out. Winter took a deep breath and followed.

As they neared the front door the loud beat of music pulsed through the windows...not the standard pop music, but similar, with Christian words. The quiet and uneventful entrance Winter hoped for shattered as Stacy led her inside. Everyone turned to stare at them, even the people Winter didn't recognize. Winter was used to it, really, but the way they stared went far beyond the standard fear and loathing she usually saw.

She glanced at Stacy. Stacy shook her head and leaned toward her to talk above the music. "It's okay. They just weren't expecting you, that's all."

Winter sidled along the wall to the nearest corner and stood there until everyone went back to whatever they were doing. Stacy followed, constantly straightening her skirt.

As Winter watched, she didn't really see much of a party happening. She leaned over to Stacy and asked, "Is this what passes for a party with Christians?"

"What do you mean?"

"They're just standing around talking and eating snacks."

"What did you expect?"

Winter shrugged. "I don't know, dancing maybe? Do Christians dance or is it a sin or something? Please tell me Christians know how to have more fun than this."

"Sure we do. Daniel will probably start some games soon."

Winter felt the blood in her veins chill. "Daniel's here?"

"Why wouldn't he be? He's the youth minister. This is his house."

Winter folded her arms and shrank deeper into the corner, but she didn't say anything. The desperate look on Stacy's face kept her quiet.

The minutes ticked by and nothing changed with the party dynamics. Nothing at all. The promised games hadn't begun and Winter hadn't even spotted Daniel. The most notable thing to Winter was the total lack of people attempting to have anything to do with her or Stacy.

"Is it always like this?" Winter asked.

"Like what?"

"You mean you don't notice?"

Stacy furrowed her brow. "I'm not sure I know what you're talking about."

Winter glanced around at the people and then back at Stacy. "Do they always treat you like this, or is it just because of me?"

Stacy's face sagged and she gazed at the floor. "Yeah. I guess it's always like this...at least lately. I don't know. They used to all be my friends when I first started coming. But..." She looked up and grinned. "Like I said, I don't come here for the people anyway."

"It's because of me, Claire, and Alison, isn't it?"

"No...not really. Maybe a little. Most of them grew up in church and everything, but I didn't. I never understood how Christians could be so secluded in the people they hang out with. So I never bothered to act like that. I wouldn't give up my friends. Guess they noticed and put me back on the outside."

Winter narrowed her eyes and leaned closer to Stacy. "Then why did you ask me to come? Was it just so you could finally have a friend to talk to here?"

"No." Stacy cringed. "Maybe." She cast away again and then clenched her eyes. "Everyone's gone, Winter. Everyone but you."

Winter sighed. "I know."

"I just...I don't know...I just want a friend to join me in the things I care about."

"But why do you even care about this? Why would you try to force me to hang out with people who don't like you either?"

At that moment, Daniel emerged from the other room and placed an armful of board games on the coffee table. Then he immediately glanced up at them with a big smile plastered across his face. Winter wanted to hide, seeing that smile as a condescending accusation, recognizing it as a reflection of Ryan's. She glared at

Stacy, but Stacy had suddenly lit up with excitement, lifting onto her toes as Daniel crossed the room toward them.

"Can we go?" asked Winter.

Stacy gaped at her. "Um. Sure, just a minute, okay?"

Daniel was nearly there. "I'll meet you at the car," said Winter and she turned to flee toward the door before Daniel could speak.

Outside, the music still boomed from the windows, but the soft beat echoed almost peacefully under the open sky. No one on the street paid attention to the party going on at the youth minister's house, but a few gave her a couple of second looks, knowing she didn't belong with the usual church-kid crowd. Winter leaned against Stacy's car and watched the front door. After a few minutes, Stacy emerged, brushing the hair over her shoulder and trying to suppress a grin.

As Stacy rounded the front of the car to the driver's side Winter shook her head. "He's a little old for you, isn't he?"

Stacy paused, one foot in the car. "It's not like that."

Winter smiled. "That's not what it looked like."

Stacy averted her eyes and blushed, and then dropped into the car without arguing.

7

Present Day

The first week proved to be the roughest. But by the second week of school, everyone locked into the new routine. Without even a whisper of Xaphan, the newfound relaxation intoxicated Winter. For the first time in a while, she enjoyed her classes, able to immerse herself in the subject without having the nagging sensation that she needed to be elsewhere. The early mornings came easier and Winter looked forward to her daily breakfast rendezvous with Summer. Winter and Ayden found the overlap between classes more than enough time for the trek back and forth from campus, allowing the daily switch of Kaci duty to be much simpler than they expected.

Peter seemed to enjoy his new job working evenings at the Family Fitness Center, which also helped. Since he could stay with Kaci himself during the day, Ayden and Winter had little to do until the evenings. Graham's security measures included wireless alarms in both apartments and an exterior camera system that any of them could review from any mobile device. He had also placed miniature cameras at the end of the street and behind the house.

Everything went as smooth as they could hope for. In a way, it put Winter a little on edge, knowing that eventually Xaphan would show up. But she tried to enjoy the ease of everything that year as much as she could. Before she knew it, the air began to cool and October was upon them.

As Winter collapsed onto the couch one Friday, having just traded off with Ayden, Kaci knocked on the door and came in. She curled up in Winter's papasan, wide-eyed and lips pursed.

Winter sat up from where she lay stretched out on the couch.

"Am I bothering you?" Kaci asked.

"No," said Winter. "I'm just tired. I'm fine. How are things? Better?"

Kaci slipped her hair behind one ear and nodded. "Much. Thank you. I just wasn't ready like I thought I was. Thank God Peter's so patient with me. Honestly, I don't know why he wanted to marry me in the first place."

"I wish you'd stop doing that."

"Doing what?"

"Putting yourself down so much. You're more than worth it. How's therapy?"

Kaci shrugged. "We've made good progress already. It's a lot of my own emotional baggage, but they are things I have to own and choose to overcome. I can't let those things steal my future from me…not anymore. Peter deserves me to be the best wife I can be. The therapist is really helping me learn how to build new emotional meaning in my relationship and to take control of my anxiety and my thoughts, by focusing on the future instead of the past."

"Fancy," said Winter.

Kaci chuckled. "I think I've still got a long way to go, but at least I can…you know…*be there* for my husband without having a breakdown."

Winter smiled. "That's really great to hear. But as much as I'm pleased your sex life is beginning to work out for you and everything, that's not exactly why you came over, is it?"

"Can't I just want to come spend some time with you?"

Winter furrowed her brow. "No. Spill it."

Kaci blushed and stared at the floor. "I'm late."

Winter sat forward on the couch. "Do you mean you're…"

Kaci shrugged. "Maybe. I haven't taken a test yet."

Winter glanced at the still closed door. "Does Peter know?"

"I didn't want to say anything yet. I need your help. Since you've all forbidden me to be alone, I need you to go to the drugstore with me. We can go after Peter leaves for work."

Winter checked the clock. "He leaves in a couple of hours, right?"

"Yeah."

"Well, if we go right now you'll have time to take the test and maybe tell him before he leaves."

Kaci shook her head furiously. "No. I want to make sure the time is right."

"Do you think he'd mind if we go anyway? Suddenly, there's something I want to do before it gets dark." Winter shook her head a little as a nudge pounded inside. Same as before the wedding. What crazy thing would it require now?

Kaci hesitated. "I don't think so. I'll go let him know."

As Kaci left, Winter found her keys and wallet and stood outside the door waiting for Kaci to join her. After a few minutes, Kaci emerged with a smile on her face. Winter drove them toward town intending on going to the nearest drugstore, but as she passed a hardware store the nudge berated her and she turned in.

"What are you doing?"

"I've got to get something. I'll be right back." Winter slung off her seatbelt and left the car running, jumping out before Kaci could question her further.

As she rushed in, she ignored the friendly greeter at the checkout counter and scanned the aisle signs for anything that jumped out at her. Something did…rope.

She found the aisle, passing by coils of chain of different link thicknesses until she came to an impressive variety of rope. Different materials, different strand configurations, different thicknesses, different lengths. Winter had no idea what she was even doing there, much less how to select rope she didn't know she needed.

Instinctively, following the nudge at the back wall of her skull, she passed over all the synthetic ropes and settled on those made of natural fibers. From there it was easy—fifty feet, quarter inch. She snatched it off the shelf and went to the checkout.

"Is this all?" the man asked.

Winter smiled and nodded, but then panic coursed through her. She searched all around the immediate area, scanning the end-caps and displays for the thing she needed. Then she found it and stepped over to a display just a few feet away, snatching up a pair of heavy duty wire-cutters. "This is all," she said as she placed the wire cutters on the counter.

The man furrowed his brow but rang her up.

Back in the car, Winter tossed the rope and the wire cutters into the back seat.

"What's that for?" Kaci asked.

Heat filled Winter's cheeks. "I don't know."

"You don't know?"

"Yup. Now, the drugstore, right? Got to find out if you're knocked up or not." Winter stole a glance at Kaci and found her tight-lipped and blushing. Perfect. Winter hoped that'd shut her up.

As they parked at the drugstore, Kaci stared at her fearfully.

Winter rolled her eyes. "You get your own test."

Kaci sighed and opened the door. As she watched Kaci enter the store, Winter felt the nudge again. She followed Kaci in, scanning the drugstore for what she was supposed to do next. Nothing caught her eye and she was about to go back to the car when she saw the helium tank behind the counter.

Her heart fluttered, the nudge vibrated, and she advanced upon the attendant, pointing to the tank. "Do you do balloons?"

"Yes we do," the lady said.

"Good. I need one."

"Just one?"

"Fifteen." *Fifteen?* Winter firmed her face and scowled at the lady like she meant to say that number.

"Any particular color?"

"No. Just whatever."

The lady nodded and began filling balloons, tying each with a length of ribbon and securing the ribbons in a bundle.

"What are you doing?" Kaci asked behind her.

Winter jumped a little and spun. "Um…not sure."

"It looks like you're getting balloons."

"I am. Got what you need?"

Kaci nodded. "I got two just in case."

The lady handed Winter the bundle of balloons, a weight tied to the ends of the ribbons. "Anything else?"

Winter shook her head and followed Kaci to check out. After they returned to the car, Winter struggled to shove all the balloons into the back seat. As they drove, several of them wandered into the front and they had to keep swatting them away.

"What exactly are these for?" Kaci asked.

"I don't know yet. But I think we need to make one more slight detour."

"Where?"

"I'm not sure, but I'll know when we get there." She glanced at Kaci and found the same bemused look Graham had given her.

It didn't take long before Winter knew what to do next. As they reached the outskirts of town, Winter felt the nudge pull her toward a gated entrance to a cattle field. She left the car running as she climbed out, opened the back door, and carefully pulled all her random things out. Kneeling on the ground, she carefully untied the weight from the balloons. Then she ran the ends of the ribbon through the coil of rope and tied them tightly. The wire cutters she just left on the ground. Those were for later. Apparently. Whatever.

Kaci watched her in silence, half-turned in the seat. Winter ignored her, though she could feel Kaci staring. After securing the rope to the balloons, she crossed over to the fence and held them high in the air. The time wasn't right yet, but it neared...she could feel it. The moments slipping by, converging on just the right second...The nudge knew what to do. It waited. Just a little longer.

Now. She released them into the air, the winds carrying them forward faster than they rose upward, the weight of the rope almost too much for the balloons. As they passed over the field they rose high enough to clear the trees and eventually disappeared from sight.

"That was weird," said Kaci as Winter sat back in.

"I know."

"Care to explain?"

"I can't. Just trust me, I guess."

They rode in silence the rest of the way back to the apartments. Peter had already gone and Ayden had not yet come home from her evening class. Kaci took her little plastic bag with the tests straight to the bathroom in Winter's apartment. She emerged after only a few minutes.

"How long?" Winter asked.

"Two minutes."

Winter started a timer and they both sat on the couch to watch the digital number slowly count down. Two minutes had no right taking so long. When the minutes were finally up Winter blinked expectantly at Kaci.

Kaci shook her head. "I can't. Please. You go look."

"Are you sure?"

Kaci nodded.

Winter handed Kaci the timer and scurried into the bathroom. The test waited gently on the counter and Winter saw the result immediately.

What she didn't expect was the wave of pain and heartache that plunged through her soul. She clenched her eyes and took a deep breath to compose herself. Some things she just wasn't ready to talk to Kaci about yet.

She eased back into the room, the turmoil inside easily masking any tells that might be found on her face.

Kaci watched her, eyes wide. "Well?"

Winter smiled and nodded. "You're pregnant."

Two weeks later Winter sat in class, scanning through her textbook as the professor lectured about Justin Martyr's role in the early church. As she stared at the pages, her hearing tunneled and the voice of the professor faded away. Other than the nudges, she had not yet experienced this kind of sensation since returning to school. She lifted her head slowly and panned the room, waiting for the rest of the information to present itself and wondering what kind of action she might be required to perform. Her heart throbbed as the adrenaline coursed through her. What she used to call a premonition, she now recognized as the whispering of spiritual beings unseen…or a spiritual being. Now the whispers began to click future moments into place like the falling of dominoes. Little things, but still nothing of significance.

Then she heard a horse snort. She turned to peer out the window and found one of the horsemen standing outside. Only the lower portion of the dark bay horse and the gleaming red armored leg of the rider could be seen, but she knew she had been summoned. Or at least she took it as such. For some reason, whenever she looked at the horsemen she found a gap in the information poured into her mind by the whispers as if they existed beyond what the foreknowledge allowed her.

She took a deep breath and quietly gathered her things. As she stood, the professor paused his droning and gazed at her.

"I'm sorry," she said. "Something came up. May I leave?"

"Of course," said the professor. "I hope everything is okay."

"Me too." Winter shouldered her backpack and hurried to the door at the front of the class, the weight of everyone's eyes on the back of her neck. Once in the hall, she picked up speed, trying not to run, but sensing an urgency to get outside as quickly as possible.

Only a few students and professors free of class traveled through the Meadow. Movement to the right made her turn, and Winter saw the crimson horseman emerge from between two buildings, eying her with his sword drawn. He pointed with his sword and Winter followed with her eyes, finding two other horsemen positioned strategically around the perimeter of the Meadow—the black and chestnut horsemen, the first wearing gleaming black armor and the second one gold. Only the white rider was missing.

What are they waiting for?

Suddenly another nudge struck her, different than the premonition from the classroom and more related to what she felt with the balloons and rope just the other day and the soda bottles the day of the wedding. Now in the midst of the whispers of her premonition, she recognized the nudges as something even more other-worldly than the whispers, as if another layer opened up beyond the angelic whispers to a purer divine knowledge. If she concentrated, she could even hear the faint rumbling that sometimes filled her ears. In a way, these nudges resonated within her similar to the time she had prophesied to Kaci...the prophecy about the baby Kaci now carried inside of her. Whatever the source of the nudges, what they asked of her far outweighed the whispers.

She bent down to the landscaping outside the building and

selected three stones bigger than her palm, but small enough she could still clench one-handed. She jogged to the Ancient and carefully placed them among the gnarled roots.

She turned and ran. All the horsemen watched as if she broke ranks from what they obviously expected of her. The whispers of the premonition filled her mind, converging on the administration building next to the student union. All the horses faced that direction, though the riders still watched her run. Something at the administration building demanded her attention. But not yet. The nudges required her presence in the English building next.

She passed by the administration building and the student union and sprinted up the stone steps of the English building. Inside she could hear the murmur of professors within the classrooms, at least those who had left their doors open or cracked. Everything proceeded in an ordinary and mundane routine. She scanned every inch of the wide hall, the off-white walls, the wooden floors, but nothing drew her attention until she gazed upon the entrance to the stairwell.

The slow taps of horse hooves told her one of the horsemen had followed her inside. She glanced back to find the golden rider turning his chestnut steed to guard the entrance. Winter took a deep breath and crossed as fast as she dared toward the stairwell.

Just before reaching the stairs, the last door on the right stood open. The light gleamed in the office, but there was no one inside, most likely because the professor who inhabited it currently droned in a classroom nearby. Winter stepped in quickly, a nudge telling her to grab something from the desk. She knew exactly where to find it…on the left side beneath a few loose papers. She lifted the papers gently and found the small pack of sticky putty. Winter shoved it into her pocket, then fled to the stairwell.

Inside, she gazed up as the stairs stretched heavenly to the fifth floor. She had never been to that floor of this building, but for some reason the nudge told her to climb to the top. She ascended as quickly as her trembling legs could take her. Her mind kept wandering to the administration building, knowing that some danger waited there, knowing that she would face it soon. The whispers berated and pulled her, conflicting with her current divine mission. Winter knew that whatever happened at the administration building, it wasn't something she was meant to prevent. That thought sent fear through her chest, fear that the unknown might be worse than anything she could imagine.

As she neared the fifth floor landing, she wiped the sweat from her forehead, pausing only a moment before pushing the door open. Of all the things she might have expected on this floor, she did not expect the silence. The dull and unpolished wooden floor wore a thick layer of dust, broken only by a few footprints, themselves covered in dust but not as much. She flicked the nearest light switch; some of the lights came on, but many of the fixtures either didn't work or had too many missing bulbs.

Winter inched down the abandoned hall, peering into the rooms. Some were small and divided into other rooms, obviously meant to be office space. Larger rooms had the feel of potential classrooms. Every room had the same thick layer of dust. Some rooms contained old desks and filing cabinets, storage boxes, and other random office or classroom accessories easily forty to fifty years old.

A nudge told her to enter one of these storage spaces and to go to an old office desk of pitted and splintered wood. In one of the drawers, she found a screwdriver and she shoved this in her pocket with the sticky putty.

Winter returned to the hall and looked around for the correct door. It was there somewhere…but hidden. Inside another door. With that revelation, she jogged further down the hall, past several classrooms and office spaces, and found what appeared to be the largest, most complex office arrangement on the entire floor. Behind the first door was an empty room that probably once served as a secretary's office. Off to one side, a hall led to three more offices and a restroom, each with their own closed door. Winter moved down to the last room, knowing already she'd find the largest of the offices. Inside, the office had a single plate window that gazed out upon the service road that passed behind the building. In front of the window stood an old, but nice-looking desk, and to one side of the room a closet door hung ajar.

The nudge came again, filling her mind with what she needed to do, pouring in an urgency to do it quickly and return to the Meadow to face what would come next. She ran to the desk and flung open the middle drawer. An abandoned assortment of old pens and pencils rolled forward, but in the tray to one side waited a small metal ring of keys. One she recognized as a handcuff key. Could this have been some kind of security office once? Winter slid the handcuff key off and then ran to the closet. She felt along the carpeted floor to the back-right corner and tugged at it until the corner came up. She placed the key under the carpet and shoved the corner back down.

Then she turned to examine the closet door. It had a large aluminum vent in its lower half, framed on both sides, but held in place on the inside by four screws. Winter took out the screwdriver and removed all four screws. The vent stayed in place, snapped together somehow with its other half. She tugged at it until the inside half came apart. Where the screws had been, she placed a small piece of sticky putty and pressed the vent frame firmly against the door so it would hold. For good measure she moved to the other side of the door and pried the outer frame off, placing sticky putty behind it too. After completing the modifications, she shoved the screws into her back pocket and scrutinized the vent. It didn't appear she had done a thing to it, unless you looked close enough to notice the screw heads missing from the inside. She tested the door with a couple of slams, but the vent stayed in place. Perfect.

The urgency crashed upon her again, the whispers louder, the nudges agreeing now. She had to get to the Meadow quickly. Winter ran out of the offices and back down the hall. She tossed the screwdriver into the room she'd found it in without breaking stride, and then descended the steps two at a time, jumping the last three at each landing. Back on the first floor, she ran into the office and returned the pack of sticky putty.

The horseman waited in the middle of the hall by the entrance now, watching her with impatience, the horse tamping the wooden floor loudly and dancing as a war horse might before charging into battle. She ran right past him and into the open air, rushing down the steps and into the Meadow. She didn't know where to go or what to do, but she knew something was about to happen. She planted herself in the middle of the Meadow and turned to face the administration building.

9

Four Years Ago

After the disaster with Stacy the weekend before, Winter refused Stacy's request to join in with Wednesday youth group the next week. Stacy continued to try every week, until suddenly in mid-October she gave up. Winter shrugged it off as a victory.

Instead, she stayed in her room, eating frozen pizza and streaming movies online. Her dad didn't seem to mind, maybe because he was too busy to really notice. Summer was over and autumn floated through the air, so work had totally consumed his life. He spent so much time on projects, at least on the outside of the buildings, trying to get them all done before the winter weather hit. He wasn't even home yet.

The doorbell rang downstairs. Winter paused the movie and set down her pizza. She slipped into her flip-flops and shuffled to answer. The bell rang a second time just as she peered through the peep-hole. Shannon, Madam Morial's daughter, stood outside, her dark hair hanging in pigtails on either side of her face.

Winter opened the door. "Hey. What's going on?"

Shannon shrugged. "I just wanted to come talk."

"Yeah, sure. Come on in." Winter moved back into the living room as Shannon closed the door and followed. "Want some pizza?" Winter asked.

"No thanks."

"Well, I do. We can talk in my room…I'm eating up there."

Back in her room, Winter took up her plate and found a comfortable spot on the bed, leaning against the headboard with her legs crossed. Shannon sat in the chair in the corner. Winter took a big bite as she watched Shannon fidget with her hands.

"Well, this is a little awkward," Winter said. "What's up?"

"I just wanted to know if you wanted to come hang out with us this Saturday. We're sort of having a thing at my house."

Winter raised an eyebrow. "Why are you inviting me?"

"You were Claire's friend and so were we. We all miss her. I just thought…"

Winter tossed the pizza back to her plate, her stomach lurching within. "Listen, thanks and all, but no thanks. I'd rather just stay here."

"Alone?"

"Yes. Alone. I seem to do better that way. You don't want to be my friend anyway. Something bad always happens."

Shannon studied her hands. "Well, if that's the way you want it. But the invitation stays open if you change your mind."

"I won't. But thanks."

"Michael will be disappointed."

Winter cut her eyes to Shannon, who now stared at her. "Why would I care about that?"

Shannon shrugged. "You tell me."

"He didn't even bother to call me all summer."

"He tried at first but you wouldn't answer. Guess he gave up."

Winter folded her arms. "He could have come over."

"Maybe. But how would your dad have felt about that?" Shannon paused. "Listen, I know we're not exactly the kind of friends you probably envisioned yourself having, and I know you don't care much for our beliefs, but I think if you give yourself a chance we could become a family to you."

"What does that even mean?"

"It means you'll have people who care for you unconditionally, who won't judge you, and who you can depend on to be there for you when you need them. Everyone needs people in their lives like that and I have a feeling you're missing it."

"Why are you doing this?"

"Because believe it or not, we're nice people. We know you've been through a lot and that you don't have very many people to rely on. We just thought it'd be nice to reach out to you."

Winter shook her head. "I gave another friend a chance like this recently, and it didn't work out. Why should I give you a chance?"

"Maybe we're different. You've hung out with us before, you tell me? Are we like other people you've been around?"

Winter shrugged.

Shannon sighed and stood. "Just think about it, okay?" She placed a piece of paper on Winter's bed. "My phone number. Give me a call. I'll come pick you up if I have to."

Winter stared at the small piece of paper with Shannon's phone number scribbled on it. As she reached out and grabbed it, Winter heard her bedroom door open.

"Shannon, wait," Winter said.

Shannon turned, one hand still on the doorknob.

"Okay."

"Okay?" Shannon asked.

"Okay, I'll come. Just this once."

Shannon smiled. "Great. I'll come pick you up Saturday around four. Is that okay?"

Winter nodded. "That'll be fine."

10

Present Day

Winter scrutinized the building, knowing it was too late to raise the warning and too dangerous to rush forward herself. She wasn't supposed to anyway. It would happen, any second, and she could do nothing about it. The nudges had vanished and the whispers returned to consume her attention. They told her to wait, just a heartbeat longer. She pivoted to either side and found the horsemen lining up beside her, facing the same direction. She didn't know what they intended to do, but she really didn't care. At this point she suspected *they* were her supernatural bodyguards…perhaps they always were. Maybe they whispered to her through the spiritual world. They stared at the building and waited, so Winter turned back and continued to do the same.

A heartbeat passed and a figure floated up out of the roof and glared down at them. A woman, thin and ageless, with long blond hair that draped over her naked body. Her pale skin and hair glistened with tiny sparkles of water.

"Who is that?" Winter asked softly, mostly to herself.

"Mavka," answered the black horseman immediately to her left in a deep booming voice. "A demon of the old world who calls herself the Wretch in this form."

The Wretch lifted into the air and floated toward them, staring straight at Winter. The horsemen closed in tightly, drawing their swords. Winter stepped back as the Wretch reached ground level and floated forward to within just a few feet. The demon stopped as the two horsemen on either side of Winter extended their swords in her direction.

The pale, ageless girl tilted her head and studied Winter, not bothering to acknowledge the horsemen. "I didn't realize there would be two," she cooed in a sing-song voice.

Winter bit her lip and clenched her fists, wishing Ayden was at her side.

"No matter." The Wretch glanced up at the horsemen, and then back to gaze deep into Winter's eyes. "I will kill you both. Later." She turned to hover away. Both bone and organs gleamed through the sickly pale skin on her back. The Wretch floated a few feet and then disappeared completely.

Another heartbeat passed and the first explosion came like a clap of thunder, heard but not seen. A rumbling sent tremors through the ground, punctuated by other thunderclaps. The windows of the building burst out, quickly followed by mortar and brick blasted into the Meadow. Winter tensed and stood her ground. The horses danced next to her, ready for battle. Dust swirled in little eddies, the ground shook violently, and the administration building crumbled in on itself. It fell mostly straight down, as if a giant hand compressed it into the dirt, pulverizing the building materials into gray dust.

A thick cloud billowed into the Meadow, engulfing the screaming students fleeing from the scene, and slamming into Winter like a sandblaster. She braced herself and tucked her chin with one hand covering her mouth and nose. She waited for the rumbling to stop…waited for the signal to engage.

Finally, silence filled the air, save for the pattering of dust and debris upon the ground. The screaming had stopped as if everyone had collectively taken a breath of shock and a moment to stare at the devastation. Then, as quickly as the silence had descended, it disappeared again, replaced by renewed screams and shouts from those remaining in the Meadow and from the fire alarms that issued from all the other buildings at once.

Winter knew the campus security would arrive soon to take charge and usher everyone away from the scene until rescue workers could begin their work. But at the moment, no one would venture toward the rubble to help those who were trapped. No one but her.

Time to begin.

Winter closed her eyes and took as deep a breath as she could through the dust, trying to slow the pounding of her heart and clear her mind. When she opened her eyes the world had changed around her. She saw the physical realm in dull and muted colors, now with a new layer of reality overlaying the things she could normally see. A swirling mist-like substance clung close to her and around the horsemen, at times taking almost human-like shape. As she glanced upon the horsemen, they shone with a vividness beyond worldly description, as if she had never truly seen anything so beautiful in all her life.

She turned her focus back to the clouded pile of rubble that so recently held the form of the administration building. There, lives had been lost, lives waited to be saved, and lives faded away. She could feel the presence of every one of them, all fifty-four, as if powerful magnets pulled her. The white mist launched forward, splitting into pieces and standing like monuments over every living, dying, or dead body. Twenty-two alive and not in any immediate danger, trapped but safe. Thirteen dead and beyond help. Nineteen hung in the balance. These Winter concentrated on, and the angelic spirits that hovered above them pulsed brightly like strobe lights.

Winter felt a real human presence step up beside her. She

glimpsed over at Ayden standing there, staring at the debris, face pale and trembling.

"I had a feeling you might need me. I came as quickly as I could," Ayden said.

"What about Kaci?"

"Peter is home. She'll be okay for a little while."

Winter nodded and turned to study the angelic mists. "Can you see them?"

Ayden shook her head, so Winter put a hand on her shoulder. "What about now?"

Ayden's sharp gasp told Winter the answer.

"Those that are flashing...those are the ones we go to first."

Ayden nodded.

Winter clenched her teeth and ran to the edge of the debris. She had to slow down to climb, but rushed as quickly as she could to the first marker behind a partially standing wall. The mixture of wood, brick, and mortar tore at her fingertips, but she persisted in clenching and shifting whatever she could grab hold of. After shifting nearly two feet worth of debris, she grunted in frustration as she wrenched another splintered piece of wood out of the way. Beneath it she found an arm. Reenergized, Winter began clearing forward trying to find the person. The person's chest still moved and that gave Winter a glimmer of hope, but their clothes were saturated with blood. Finally, she uncovered the head of a male student, chalky white from the dust. It was all she could do for now.

As Winter rushed to the next marker, she became vaguely aware that several other people had joined in the rescue efforts; many were campus security. Winter grabbed the arm of an officer as she passed him and pointed.

"Here! Dig here."

The officer nodded and went to work.

Across the rubble Winter made eye contact with Ayden. "Show them!" she shouted. Ayden nodded and began directing the rescue workers, at least those who paid her any attention.

Winter turned a circle, trying to decide what marker needed her attention next. A familiar gleam of polished cherry wood stood askew not far from her, and beside it pulsed ever brightly a swirling column of white mist. Winter ran to what she knew to be the president's splintered desk, circling it to find the easiest way to dig. On the back side, she found a bloodied hand reaching out. Winter grabbed it and it squeezed back.

As she frantically shifted debris and bricks, without a word Graham appeared beside her to help. One particular wooden beam required them to shift a good deal of debris in either direction until they could both wrest it from its place. They followed the arm deeper until they found a shoulder, then cleared outward toward the head. One final piece of shelving, and Dr. Streffield's face blinked back at them through the thick layer of chalky dust.

"Winter…" he croaked.

"It's okay, we'll get you out."

"No…my other hand."

"Don't worry about it right now," said Graham. "Let's just keep you alive."

"Too late for me."

"No it's not," said Winter.

Dr. Streffield tugged with his trapped arm, struggling to pull it free. "Help me."

Winter nodded and they shifted the debris to free his other arm. She didn't realize she was crying until she wiped her face and felt the chalky mud spread across her cheek.

Finally, his arm broke free. He pulled it, elbow bent, across his torso, where it lay with fist clenched. Then he took his other hand and grabbed Winter's, moving her hand to his fist. "I deserve this."

Winter shook her head. "No you don't."

"Use this. I don't know why, but this is for you to save someone else." He slipped a small cylindrical object into her hand. "A little girl told me to give it to you…just a few minutes ago. She said to hold it and not to let go until it was in your hands."

"A little girl, huh?" She gave him a warm smile and squeezed his hand.

He returned the smile and nodded. He closed his eyes and stopped breathing.

Winter sat back and covered her face with her hands. Graham put an arm around her and pulled her tight. After a few moments staring at Dr. Streffield's lifeless body, she pulled her hand away from her face and inspected the object he had put into it…nothing more than a small, unmarked flashdrive.

11

As the sirens advanced upon the campus, Winter rose to gaze down upon the body of President Streffield. Graham stood with her simultaneously, keeping his arm tight around her shoulders. She pivoted to survey the chaos. So many people had returned to help dig through the rubble for the survivors…almost too many. Yet it filled Winter with the hope this war could be won after all. Would the little girl make her appearance today to help again? Would she reveal herself to Winter this time?

Amongst the rescuers, the onlookers, and the injured, the girl could not be found.

Then the whispers returned, unsatisfied and urgent. Winter's heart sank, knowing this wasn't the event that demanded her to stand up and leave class in the first place. This wasn't the reason the horseman required her attention. The explosion, the deaths, the chaos, served as something else, auxiliary, a portion of her responsibilities that day, but not the primary emergency. The dread that gnawed in the pit of her stomach still craved to be fed. More was coming. Winter scanned the dust-clouded field for anything else.

That's when she noticed the horsemen had disappeared. And then she understood.

"Kaci."

"What?" asked Graham.

Winter grabbed his hand and clambered through the debris. "We have to get to Kaci," she said over her shoulder. "This was a diversion. They knew I'd be here so they made sure I'd stay. And they knew that something this big would draw Ayden away."

"But Peter is with her, isn't he?"

"Yeah, he's there. But what if they want him too? Ayden and I are both here, what's to stop them?" She grabbed Ayden's arm and tugged. "We have to go. Now!"

Ayden searched Winter's face and then scanned the unfolding chaos, her forehead wrinkled.

"We've done all we're supposed to do. Kaci's in trouble," Winter said.

Ayden nodded, and Winter rushed to the edge of the debris and slid down to ground level. As she ran to the Union parking lot, she pulled out her cellphone. She jumped in the car, dialed Peter, and slammed the phone to her ear. Graham and Ayden jumped in just moments after her, and Winter reversed the car before Ayden had finished closing the door. The phone rang twice before Peter picked up, by which time Winter had already fishtailed through the parking lot.

"Peter?"

"*Yeah?*"

"They're coming."

Silence on the other end for a moment. "*Got it.*" Peter hung up.

Winter tossed her cell into Graham's lap. "Hold on."

As Winter sped down the street, emergency vehicles and police flew the other direction, lights and sirens screaming, unconcerned about the speeding BMW going the other way. She allowed the whispers to guide her movements, projecting the paths of every other vehicle on the road so precisely that Winter easily passed and dodged each one.

In mere minutes, Winter slammed the brakes and drifted the car sideways to turn onto the street for her apartment. Everything appeared to still be in place, and only a few curious elderly neighbors peeked through their windows to spy the crazy driver squealing down their road. She slid to a halt in front of their apartment, taking a moment to breathe and study what waited in front of her. Everything looked normal, except Kaci and Peter's door stood cracked open.

"Well?" asked Ayden.

Winter clenched her jaw and opened her door, placing one foot on the ground, prepared to jump back into the car if needed. She strained her ears, but couldn't hear anything, so she reached back into the car and turned it off.

"Kaci?" she called to the apartment.

After a few moments of silence, a muffled cry echoed through the trees behind the apartment, followed by a desperate shout from Kaci. "Winter!"

The whispers poured into Winter's head like hourglass sand. In her mind she could see everything, the terrain, every tree, every gully, between the apartment and the road a quarter mile away. There the assailants had a car running, and a dark demonic presence lurked. She could see Kaci being dragged in that direction by two men and a third pointing a gun at her from behind. She could see Peter, some two hundred yards away, unconscious, being dragged by three more men to a deep gully where they intended to dump him and shoot him in the head.

After only a heartbeat of assimilating the knowledge, the whispers cut off the feed of information and prodded her to move. Winter spun to Ayden and Graham, both now standing beside her, Graham with a pistol in his hand.

"Follow me," she commanded and darted around the side of the apartment to the back. She scanned the tree line briefly in stride, reviewing the details in her mind, calculating speeds and trajectories. Finally, she paused for the others to catch up and pointed. "You two…go that way. Run. You'll intercept the ones with Peter before they have a chance to kill him. You don't have much time. Go!"

Graham blinked at her, but Ayden nodded and dashed past him. Graham scrunched his face, raised the gun to his shoulder, and ran after Ayden.

Winter turned her focus to Kaci, knowing she had no line of interception and the head start of the kidnappers was nearly too large to overcome. But Winter also now had a technical map of every detail of the forest embedded in her mind. If she had to, she could run it with her eyes closed. She lowered her head, bent forward, and took off as fast as her legs would allow. Her mind raced to feed her body the necessary information…holes in the ground, branches to dodge, the perfect line between trees. The ground sloped down several yards in, a muddy slew at the bottom. As she descended, she lept forward, landing perfectly on the right combination of roots, leaves, and sticks to keep from slowing down in the soft ground. At the bottom, she planted her right foot on a large tree root and launched into the air to land perfectly on a solid outcropping of clay no bigger than the size of the end of her foot. She didn't need anything bigger, and immediately scrambled up the embankment back onto level ground.

Winter was gaining, the calculation of her speed versus their speed told her that much. But she also knew that unless something changed, they'd be at the car when she caught them, where an unknown demon waited. She tried to push her body for more speed, but none would come.

Thirty seconds. The trees thinned ahead, an empty line in the canopy that told her the road, the car, and the demon waited on the other side. After passing two more trees, she saw movement ahead, men dragging a now gagged but frantic Kaci.

Twenty seconds. Gunshots rang out through the forest to her

right. Graham and Ayden had reached Peter, but she didn't know who had fired. The shots had drawn the attention of the assailants in front of her. They paused and looked in that direction...just what she needed to give her the extra few moments to catch them. But they also saw her coming.

Ten seconds. The men dragging Kaci yanked at her more violently, toward the car just beyond the underbrush. Kaci finally saw Winter rushing toward them. She kicked and pulled with renewed ferocity and the men slowed, one of them dropping her. He struck Kaci with his fist, but Kaci never stopped.

The third man in the back, the one with the gun, stood his ground and sighted Winter in. He grinned and squeezed the trigger.

Winter didn't flinch. For the briefest of moments the world shifted around her, pulling her out of time, opening the window to the spiritual realm. White mist swirled around her, puncturing a path like the prow of a ship through hellish black creatures in front of her. Beyond, a massive, hulking black mass waited where the car should be.

A flash of fire from the end of the gun preceded the small gray object traveling slowly through the space between her and the man. An arm materialized out of the white mist and slapped it. The bullet changed course. Another shot. Another arm, redirecting the bullet away.

The world shifted back as she reached the man, having crossed the space in a fraction of the time humanly possible. He whimpered, eyes filling with terror.

Winter grabbed the gun, twisted his arm, pulled him off balance, and shoved his face into the ground. As she planted her knee into the back of his head, she whirled the gun around to point toward the underbrush. The other two had already dragged Kaci through it to the road. Winter took a deep breath, letting the whispers guide her hand, feed her the visual knowledge she needed to see through the bushes like x-ray. She fired once, then shifted the gun slightly and fired immediately a second time, hitting both men in the leg. They fell to the ground, howling and cursing.

A moment later Kaci came crashing back toward her, yanking off the gag. "Winter!"

Still holding down the first man, Winter pointed back toward the apartment. "Go! I'll catch up with you."

Kaci didn't hesitate. She passed Winter, red-faced and hyperventilating, and had soon disappeared into the forest.

Winter stood and pointed the gun at the man's head.

He rolled over slowly, blood streaming from his nose, eyes wide, and hands up defensively. "What are you?"

"You tell him what happened here," Winter said. "You tell him *exactly* what happened."

The man backed away on the ground for several feet, then twisted to run through the underbrush toward the car.

"Peter," Winter whispered as she spun in the direction of the others. She held the gun to the side of her face and ran again. It wasn't long until she found Graham running through the trees toward her. She slowed to catch her breath as he approached.

"Are you okay? I heard shots," he said.

Winter nodded. "I'm fine. Peter?"

"I fired a warning shot over their heads when we got close. They dropped him and ran."

"Is he okay?"

"He was hit over the head pretty hard…might have a concussion. But he's awake. Ayden's helping him back to the apartment. What about Kaci?"

"She's fine. She should be back now."

Graham nodded. "Where'd you get the gun?"

"I took it from the man shooting at me," Winter said.

Graham raised an eyebrow. "You…took it…"

She rubbed a hand through her hair and grimaced. "He tried to shoot me."

"So you…grounded him?"

Winter twirled the gun in her palm to point the barrel down and the handle toward Graham. She shoved it into his chest. "Shut up."

12

Four Years Ago

Shannon picked her up five minutes after four that Saturday. Winter wasn't sure how to dress, so she just wore the most comfortable pair of black jeans she owned and one of her favorite black and purple tee-shirts. Winter relaxed as she noticed that Shannon wasn't dressed much differently.

"So, where are we going?" Winter asked as she sat down and buckled up.

"My place this time. I insisted. I've told Michael no more drugs, so if he wants to hang out with us he's going to do it according to my rules. He'd never smoke pot in front of Mom, she hates the stuff…although, I'm pretty sure she did her fair share when she was our age."

Winter smiled. A small disappointment tickled her insides that she wouldn't get another chance at marijuana, but she could ignore it easily enough.

Winter remembered Shannon's house when they finally arrived, though she had only previously seen it at night when she came here with Claire. She wondered how many people were actually going to be here and if it would be as awkward as the last time she came. But she saw only a couple of cars in the driveway.

"Doesn't look like a very big party."

Shannon glanced over at her. "I never said it was a party."

"Not a party?"

"No. We just wanted to have you over."

Winter wrinkled her forehead as she followed Shannon through the garage to the door. The door they entered brought them directly into the kitchen. There didn't seem to be anyone home, except for soft conversation coming from a television in the other room.

"Want anything to drink?" Shannon asked.

"Sure, I guess."

"Soda?" Shannon crossed to the refrigerator and pulled it open. Winter nodded and Shannon extracted a canned soda and handed it to her.

"You said at my house you were having a thing," Winter said.

"Yeah, my mom's cooking. That's usually a big deal, because normally it's just junk food or frozen dinners around here."

"So, you invited me over just to have dinner with your family?"

Shannon smiled. "Is that all right?" Shannon passed Winter to go into the next room.

Winter followed her, a little slowly at first, still skeptical of a deeper, ulterior motive, and feeling a little tricked into coming. In the living room, Shannon took a seat next to Michael on the couch. Michael gazed up at Winter and smiled.

"Hey," he said.

"Hey," said Winter as she crossed to the nearest chair and sat on the edge of the seat.

"It's good to see you," said Michael.

Winter gave him a warm smile. "Thanks."

Michael turned to Shannon. "I thought you said Mom was cooking."

Shannon shrugged. "She said she was."

"Then why does the kitchen look like it hasn't been touched in a month? And where is she anyway?"

"Maybe she went to town to get groceries or something."

Michael snorted. "Well, I brought over some movies. Want to start one?"

"I don't care," said Shannon. "Winter?"

Winter shook her head slightly. "Doesn't really matter. Whatever you two want."

"What did you bring?" asked Shannon.

As Shannon approached the entertainment center to peruse the movies Michael had stacked there, Winter took a deep breath and sat back into the chair fully. She scanned the room, soaking in the details. Her eyes fell upon the wall of happy family photos, Michael, Shannon, and both parents at different ages through the years. She knew they were just photos, posed by a photographer to capture a certain mood and the happiness wasn't exactly real…but it looked real. And real or not, she didn't have any photos like them of her family. Maybe one or two with just her mom, like the cherished photo she carried in the locket around her neck, but nothing even close with her dad.

"What's that?" Michael asked.

Winter turned to him and he pointed to her neck. Winter hadn't realized she'd been fidgeting with her locket.

"Um, nothing," she said and shoved it under her shirt.

"This one," said Shannon as she put the disk into the player.

"Which one did you pick?"

Shannon plopped down beside him. "It's a surprise."

As the movie played, Winter slipped off her shoes and pulled her legs into the chair, trying to release the tension in her muscles. By the time Shannon and Michael's mom came home, half-way through the movie, Winter had almost forgotten how miserable she had dedicated herself to be. Shannon had picked the perfect train-wreck comedy and several times Winter had to cover her mouth to keep from laughing louder than the other two.

"Couldn't wait, huh?" asked Madam Morial as she walked through the door.

"I thought you were cooking." Michael paused the movie and stood.

"Who's got time for that? I picked up chicken. Come…let me say thanks and we'll eat."

"Thanks? You bless the food?" asked Winter.

Madam Morial smiled. "Do you think Christians are the only ones thankful for what they eat?"

Everyone closed their eyes, and Winter followed.

Madam Morial began. "Blessed be the Sun who brings life to our planet. Blessed be the Earth…"

Winter cracked open one eye and watched the others skeptically. Why was Stacy so afraid of these people? What was so wrong with them? Were they really any different than Stacy's youth group?

"Blessed be our family and friends," Madam Morial concluded. "Blessed be."

"Blessed be," echoed Shannon and Michael.

"Winter, you first." Madam Morial smiled at her and handed her a paper plate.

13

Present Day

Peter lay on the couch as Kaci pressed an ice pack against his head. His eyes were open and he seemed to be feeling okay, but Kaci insisted he stay still for a while longer.

Winter paced the room. Ayden watched her from a nearby chair. Graham stood against the wall with his arms crossed.

"They can't stay here," said Graham.

Winter nodded and chewed at her lip.

"They know where they live. They'll come back with more people. You know that."

Winter nodded again.

"We have to move."

Winter stopped and glared at him. "Would you please shut up and let me think?"

Graham narrowed his eyes and firmed his lips as Winter resumed her pacing.

"We could go to my parents' house," said Kaci.

"And put them in danger? No," said Winter.

"I knew this would happen," mumbled Ayden.

Winter turned to her and pointed. "You can shut up too. You're not helping."

"Well, I don't want to move again. I can't just leave in the middle of a semester," snapped Ayden. "It's pointless, anyway. They'll find us wherever we go."

"I know. If not here then the next place. They'll always find us," said Winter.

"But if we don't move now, that day is today. We have to move quickly," said Graham.

Something shifted outside and Winter stopped to gaze out of the window. The white horseman stared back at her from beyond the road and nodded to her.

"I can't come with them," Winter said.

"What are you talking about?" asked Graham.

Everything clicked into place in Winter's mind and her heart beat faster. She turned to Graham. "Can you keep them safe?"

"Of course I can. I may not have whatever it is you two have, but I'm capable enough as long as I get to choose the place."

"And if you need to keep them moving?"

Graham nodded. "We'll be ready to relocate in an instant, no matter where we are. The first sign of trouble and we're gone."

"Winter, I'm not sure I understand what you're planning," said Kaci.

Winter ignored her and spun to Ayden. "They know you're connected with me, so once I'm gone they'll think you're the one protecting them. So stay here, keep up appearances, and don't do anything stupid."

"I'm the bait?"

"You're the decoy. Besides, we can't leave Summer and Davis alone. Xaphan knows they're connected too. If they're exposed, he'll use them to get to me."

"But I thought you were supposed to protect me," said Kaci.

"What you're saying…"

"It's what we're supposed to do. For the past three years it was my job to protect you, but now things are beyond that. Xaphan has to be stopped and now that's my job."

"What do you mean it's your job?" asked Kaci.

"I don't know." Winter pointed out the window. "I've been seeing horsemen…these, sort of angel warriors. They follow me around. Last spring one of them said the army was being prepared for me to command." She peeked back out the window to the horseman and let her arm drop. "I have to lead the battle, that's what he meant. That's why you…" She turned back to Ayden. "…have the gift too. You're my replacement. Protecting Kaci will be your responsibility when this is over. Right now I'm supposed to stop Xaphan at any cost. His next attack might be far worse than this; there's no end to what he'll do to get Kaci. And there's no sense in just waiting for him to come to us, constantly looking over our shoulders. But if I get to him first…"

"He'll kill you," said Graham.

Winter shrugged. "Maybe he will, but not before the job is done."

"Let me come with you," said Graham. "There's no way you're doing something like this alone. You need a partner. Everyone needs backup."

"Weren't you listening? Kaci has to stay safe. One of us has to be with her, and that's you."

"What about school, Winter?" Kaci whispered.

"I'll just…I'll have to drop out, I suppose."

Kaci stood. "Winter, I don't think this is the answer. I mean, there's got to be another…"

Winter held her hand out to quiet Kaci. "There is no other way. This is why I'm here. Don't rob me of my purpose."

Everyone stared at her and the silence grew.

"When?" croaked Peter.

"Right now."

They all continued to stare, and she widened her eyes for emphasis.

Graham straightened himself from the wall and clapped his hands. "Right now. Let's get started. I'll call a buddy of mine who owes me a favor. He has a hunting cabin about ninety miles away. I'll tell him I just need a few days to get away. It's secluded and big enough for us, so it's perfect."

"And still close enough for me to get there quickly," said Winter.

"Closer than I'd like, though," said Graham. "We'll be safe enough there until we can figure out the next move."

For the next half hour they shoved clothes, both dirty and clean, into bags and deposited them into the back seat of Kaci's car. They packed food and anything else they could grab and anything important enough or sentimental enough not to leave behind. Everyone helped, packing Kaci's car and some of Graham's with anything Peter and Kaci could possibly need. Peter's car would stay behind as part of the decoy.

After hugging all three of them, Winter stood back. "Keep me updated on everything. Just a short text every once in a while. But never tell me your location. Don't tell any of us, not even if we ask. Not even your parents, Kaci."

"But what if you succeed and we are safe? How will we know?" asked Kaci.

Winter surveyed everyone. "Only me or Ayden can call you back in, but only if we talk to you by voice and only with a code word. If we've been captured they may try to force us to get your location or to call you back. The same for if I need to come to you. If you don't hear the code word, run."

"What is it?"

Winter thought for a moment. "Moriah has fallen. That's the code. If we don't say it, then it's not safe. Either don't come home or give us a fake location. Got it?"

Everyone nodded.

"Now go," said Winter.

As Winter watched the two vehicles drive away, a hollowness inside whispered she might never see them again. She wiped the tears from her eyes and went inside.

Winter couldn't sleep that night. She lay upon the couch of Kaci and Peter's apartment, wondering if the attackers would come back to finish the job that night, wondering if they had been sufficiently scared away, and wondering what the next attack might look like when blowing up the administration building, killing or injuring dozens of innocent people, could serve as a mere distraction to get to Kaci. She wondered if Kaci and Peter had made it to the cabin safely. Guilt gnawed at her lower abdomen because she hadn't been the one to go with them, but she knew the right decision had been made. Kaci and Peter were safe for now. They would stay safe so long as Winter didn't fail in the next task given to her.

The constant manipulating of what-ifs gave Winter a headache as she clenched her eyes, trying to will her mind to shut down and let sleep fall upon her. The hours ticked by. Against her better judgment, she kept checking the clock by the television. Eventually exhaustion claimed the rights to her consciousness, and the last time she remembered seeing the clock was three fifty-one.

She fell into sleep consciously. As she lay still, she felt her mind rocking against reality, tipping ever so close to the edge of sleep. With each rock toward the ledge, the static in her ears pulsed. Finally, she allowed herself to fall over, down a tunnel of stars, into an existence without her body, an existence totally of her mind. Yet she still had awareness, fully functioning as a thinking being.

Winter landed in the Meadow, but it wasn't the Meadow as it should be. Directly ahead of her lay the remains of the administration building, the bodies of the dead laid out in front in a neat row. Beside that, the Union smoldered as a pile of ruble, dust still swirling in the air as if it had only happened recently. Winter turned slowly and found every building along the perimeter of the Meadow nothing more than a pile of debris. The Ancient lay on its side, dried and withered. Where the Olamel bell tower should have been, smoke and flames licked the sky. Winter followed the smoke upward, discovering the sky amber instead of blue, the world aged uniformly in sepia tones. Winter narrowed her eyes, willing her vision to zoom telescopically so she could see beyond the Meadow, beyond the campus, beyond Cherithville. Everything…the whole world was nothing more than a ruinous heap.

"It's more than you know," said a little girl's voice.

Winter spun to see the same little girl she had seen over and over, now standing just beyond reach. "Who are you?"

"That's not important."

"Why not?"

The girl frowned. "Please. Focus on what is at stake. This hasn't happened yet. It's all up to you. His plans go beyond this place to the entirety of the world, but it's your choices that will determine whether or not he succeeds. No matter what happens, you can't let her or the baby die."

"I'm leaving to find Xaphan and stop him. What else am I supposed to do?" Winter asked, kneeling on the ground to face the girl eye to eye.

"You already know. "

Winter's heart sank. There was something familiar about the little girl's eyes…something she hadn't noticed before. "Who are you?"

"You have to finish this. And in the end, you will have to finish it alone."

The girl smiled at her, a soft, sympathetic smile, and then faded away.

"Who are you?" Winter shouted.

As the girl disappeared, so did the Meadow, so did Winter's reality, so did her lucid dreaming. She didn't remember anything else until she awoke late the next morning with the words still ringing in her ears.

You will have to finish this alone.

14

Winter sat up and panned the empty apartment. The early morning light washed everything in twilight. She moved her hand to her thigh and felt the flashdrive in her pocket, knowing she had to get someplace safe before she could even open it.

Trying to be as quiet as possible, she eased open the door and went across the breezeway to her own apartment. Ayden lay on the couch and glanced up at her. Dark circles ringed her eyes and her wild hair betrayed she'd had just as restless a night as Winter. Maybe dreams too.

Winter went straight to her bedroom and pulled out a duffel bag. She shoved in as much of her most comfortable, black clothing as she could, leaving behind anything that had significant color, knowing the more she could do under a cloak of stealth, the more time she could purchase for everyone else. She almost regretted letting her hair go back to its natural color, but grabbed her black stocking cap to help cover the golden-brown locks. Winter stood in the middle of her room, scanning everything, grabbing as many little items she might need. Small nudges told her she needed a few random things from other rooms. With a full duffel hanging from her shoulder, she moved to the laundry room and rummaged around until she found a roll of duct tape. Then she entered the kitchen and grabbed her laptop, shoving it into her computer backpack. Winter paused by the pantry cabinet, and then grabbed some granola bars and crammed them beside the computer. She heard movement behind her as Ayden came into the kitchen.

"You're going now?" she asked.

Winter hesitated, then faced her. "I have to…I can't wait. He could come back any day."

"I know."

"Once he realizes I'm going after him, he'll focus on me and leave everyone else alone."

"I'm not so sure about that." Ayden straightened, as if prodded. "I need to give you something." She rushed over to the drawer beside the refrigerator and dug through it until she came out with a utility click-lighter. "Take this."

Winter slowly reached out and grabbed it. "Why?"

"I don't know, but make sure you have it with you when you…when you…" Ayden clenched the sides of her head with her hands. "Argh…it's not clear! There's a house…trees…a cliff. Just make sure you have it then."

"I'll keep it with me at all times." Winter shoved the lighter into her back pocket. "Keep a close eye on Summer and Davis."

Ayden nodded. "I promise."

"I know their part in this story is not over with yet. He'll come after them too, eventually. We'll need everyone by the end."

"And how does the story end, Winter?"

"The way it's supposed to end. The only way it can." She wiped away the sudden tear that fell from her eye and pushed past Ayden. "I've got to go. If things get out of hand, call me. Remember the code word."

Without looking back, Winter rushed out the front door and

eased it closed. She glanced around at the early morning darkness, searching for the horsemen, but didn't see any. A wet chill clung to the air and the beginnings of a fog crept in from the trees. She departed quickly as she drove her car down the road, out of the neighborhood, and headed north on the highway, not really knowing where she needed to go.

The computer backpack sat on the passenger seat. Winter glanced at it and knew that the first thing she needed to do was find someplace safe and random so she could examine that flashdrive. She suspected the information she needed to find Xaphan would be on it.

Soon after the sun burned off the lingering fog, an exit sign loomed ahead for the town of Dempsey. Winter had heard of it, though she had never been there. The interstate ran right through the heart of the town, a town slightly smaller than Cherithville. At the end of the off-ramp, Winter craned her neck toward both directions and spotted a coffee shop.

"Perfect."

The coffee shop teemed busier than she would have liked, but after parking she quickly found a table in a corner where she could pull out her laptop in privacy. As the computer booted up, she went to the barista to purchase a mocha. Just before she plugged in the flashdrive she deactivated the Wi-Fi, just in case the drive activated something that could bring Xaphan to her.

The flashdrive snapped into place. The computer worked to recognize the device. Then a window popped up with the contents.

The drive contained only one folder, named with random numbers and symbols. She clicked on it. A single text file waited inside, also named with numbers and symbols. She clicked on it, and it opened in her word processor.

The compatibility wasn't completely right. Some of the characters in the document translated to weird symbols, but Winter could still work most of it out. Transcriptions. Specifically, it looked like electronically generated phone transcriptions. As Winter scanned through the contents, it became clear that Dr. Streffield had been running some kind of transcription program on his phone in order to secretly record all the black-mailing Xaphan had been doing to him.

Winter read about the threats to Streffield's family. She read about his agreeing to set off the fire alarms on campus a year and a half ago in order to cause a big enough distraction for the Eater to find Sandy. She read about Streffield backing out when Xaphan demanded to have Winter expelled last year, just before Claire showed up at the apartment. She read conversations with the FBI about taking Streffield's family into protective custody.

Winter sat back and covered her mouth. She had no idea he had been fighting so hard. What else had been going on that she didn't know about? Who else had a story to tell?

The people Streffield spoke with weren't always clear. She easily recognized Streffield's voice in the transcript, and she could tell a difference between the FBI and someone working for Xaphan. But whether Streffield spoke directly to Xaphan or someone else was unclear.

After nearly two hours of reading, she finally found something useful. Winter sat up and peered closer. A face to face meeting arranged with Streffield just two weeks ago.

"You've got to be kidding," Winter said out loud. A nearby coffee patron glanced at her.

The meeting had happened in Dempsey. She was already in the right place. And she spotted a name. Cain Golia.

Winter yanked out the flashdrive and shoved her computer into the backpack. Now she only needed to wait until nightfall before she could find the right people who might have the right additional information.

15

Four Years Ago

Winter thought long and hard about her past two experiences. She knew that deep down Stacy meant well and didn't blame her for what happened at the youth party. But seeing Daniel again filled Winter with a kind of guilt she didn't want to face. She couldn't face. He didn't blame her for Ryan's death, but when he smiled at her...she only saw Ryan's smile. He might not blame her, but she blamed herself enough for the both of them.

Then there were the other teens in Stacy's youth group, the ones who judged her with a variety of accusatory assumptions. She knew what they thought of her, what everyone really thought of her...that the cursed freak kills everyone who gets close to her. A few looks contained pity, but Winter hated that even more.

But at Shannon's it felt natural, it felt peaceful, it felt like she belonged. It had been the same last year when she had hung out with them and Claire. It came from Michael when he had waited with her by the river last spring, his arm around her, pulling her close like she was the most precious thing in the world.

As Winter sat in her room late the next Friday night, thinking of these things and not really paying much attention to the syndicated sitcom on television, her phone rang on the bed beside her. She eyed the caller ID and saw Stacy's name. Winter picked up the phone and considered it, at war with herself about whether or not to answer. She wanted to stay connected with Stacy, wanted to keep that friendship alive, but if Stacy insisted on bringing her to more things like last time...

Winter shook her head and touched the ignore button. Maybe she'd call Stacy back later. Instead, she forced her mind to stop wandering and to focus on the program she watched. But the guilt of ignoring Stacy wouldn't go away. Stacy didn't deserve to be ignored. Maybe she could convince Stacy to hang out alone. Could she even convince Stacy to hang out with Winter's other friends?

Did she actually have other friends?

As if in tune to Winter's internal conflict, her phone rang again. This time the call came from Shannon. Winter stared at the caller ID like she had before. Could this actually be the new start she wanted? Did these people really care for her?

If given the option, Winter knew she would choose Shannon over Stacy, though it had nothing to do with Stacy. Somehow Stacy represented an entire group of people who hated the idea of Winter's values and couldn't give Winter the kind of chance she needed to prove herself. Stacy wasn't like that at all, of course...the crass judgmentalism affected Stacy just as much. But hanging out with Stacy meant subjecting herself to the same continuous devaluation.

On the other hand, Shannon, her family, and friends...they were all different. Maybe Winter didn't care for their beliefs, but they didn't care about Winter's lack of belief either. They liked her exactly for being *her*.

Winter touched the answer button and put the phone to her ear. "Hey."

"Hey," replied Michael's voice. *"I was about to hang up."*

"Yeah, couldn't find my phone," she lied.

"Oh. Sorry to call you with Shannon's phone, but you wouldn't answer my calls this summer."

Heat crept into Winter's cheeks and she didn't know what to say.

"Winter?"

"I'm here."

"I just wanted to tell you how nice it was to see you again last week. It was a lot of fun. My family really enjoyed having you here."

"Thank you. I don't get out much."

"I know," said Michael. *"That's why I called. Shannon was the one who organized the whole family thing…she can be sentimental that way, and I guess she thought you'd like that better than other options. But I thought I'd invite you to something a little different."*

"Like what?"

"Some friends are getting together to go out to the state park. It's fall and, well, the equinox is this weekend. That's when we usually hit the forest and have some fun."

Winter twisted her lips. "There's not going to be anything magic-y is there?"

"No, not really. I mean, in our minds there's something special about connecting with nature on the equinox, but we're not actually doing anything magic-y. Just come and enjoy. We'll do a nature hike and then hang out at the park for a while."

"I don't know…"

"And it'll be a little more your speed…not like hanging out with parents or anything. I'll have some friends, Shannon's bringing hers. We'll all be able to be ourselves."

"Michael…listen, thanks but…"

"Is this about the kiss? I don't want anything to be awkward between us. It was a nice kiss, but it was just that. You were upset, I was upset, and it happened. But we can forget about it. Okay?"

Winter's nostrils flared and she curled her lip. "Fine. Can I let you know later?"

Micheal hesitated. *"Yeah, I guess so."* The flatness in his voice betrayed his disappointment.

"Thanks," said Winter, heat spreading down her arms and up her neck. "I've got to go."

"Sure. Well, bye then."

"Bye."

Winter tossed the phone back onto her bed and stared at her TV. Did she really want to go with them again? Yes. What held her back? Nothing, she admitted to herself. Maybe if she eased into it…maybe if she kept herself guarded…maybe if she stayed with Shannon…maybe it would turn out exactly like she hoped. Then maybe she could help Stacy too. But why did she get so angry? Why did the thought of being next to Michael in the forest infuriate her? Those questions she wouldn't allow herself to think about. The more she avoided them, the angrier she became.

It *was* a nice kiss.

16

Present Day

Finding the right contacts in Dempsey turned out to be far more difficult than Winter expected. For the next week and a half, she stayed out most nights, hitting the kinds of places she and Michael used to frequent, in the hopes of running into some Wiccans or other occultists that might have the information she needed. But Dempsey's darker side did not stir nearly as actively or populous as Trenton Hills.

She stayed out most of the night each night and slept in her car until nearly noon. She even found a campground with a public shower house where she could clean up. In the afternoons she stationed herself at the mall, hoping to run into the right kind of people in the pre-Halloween crowds.

Just a few days before Halloween, she waited in the food court, sinking into people's thoughts as she had done in the past, but not finding much. However, she took it as a good sign that God had activated that ability. She also checked in a few department stores, but only came across stay-at-home moms and retirees. After lunch, the high-school dropouts, unemployed twenty-somethings, and the night shift workers arrived. Winter wandered toward her favorite store, and the favorite of many other Goths, Razor's Edge.

The front part of the store showed off a collection of nerd culture and random fan items that only smaller sub-cultures of teens and young adults might care about. In the back they kept the darker, more adult type merchandise. Winter checked the jewelry racks, reminiscing about all the earrings and t-shirts she used to purchase at Razor's Edge.

Within just a few moments of stepping into the store, a tall skinny man with buzzed hair, gauges in his ears, and tattoos coloring his arms approached. "Need any help?" he asked.

Winter made eye contact with him and swirled into his memories, the color draining from the store into a meld of shapes that morphed into another room…another place. For a brief moment she could see through his eyes, smoking a joint, staring at a TV, watching…a chick flick? Was he crying?

She tore herself back to reality and flicked her gaze to his name tag. Mark. "No, thanks. I just want to…" she paused and bit her lip. "Actually, I'm supposed to meet someone here. I don't suppose you've seen him?"

The corners of his mouth tugged downward and his eyebrows lifted. "I don't know. What's his name?"

"Cain."

If he recognized the name, he didn't show it. He just shook his head. "Sorry."

"That's okay," she said. "I'll just look around until he comes."

Winter wandered around the store for about a half hour. Mark mostly ignored her, going about his normal work but checking on her from the corner of his eye. Winter found some purple and black striped socks she liked and thought about purchasing them just to appease Mark. She took them from the shelf and continued to shop…eventually picking up a t-shirt too.

A steady stream of shoppers came into the store, but never more than one or two at a time. Winter tried to position herself to make eye contact with each of them, delving for a few seconds into their memories for clues about Cain.

She found nothing significant until a natural blond came in wearing black and pink, more punk than Goth. As the girl browsed through earrings, Winter eased to the opposite side of the gondola. When the girl glanced at her, Winter made eye contact.

The colors of the room swirled away again as Winter fell into the girl's memories. She landed in a dark room, sitting around a table. Others sat at the table too, but the girl stared alone into the center of a pentagram drawn on the tabletop. Candles flickered at each point of the star. A bowl of dark liquid sat in the center.

The memories drew away and Winter returned to the Razor's Edge as the girl broke eye contact. It wasn't much…but it was a lead.

Winter immediately went to check out. The guy smirked at her. "Not showing, huh?"

"Yeah, well, forget him. I can't wait all day."

"Maybe you're just waiting for the wrong guy," he said with a twinkle in his eyes as he scanned her items.

Winter glared at him. "Are you flirting with me?"

His eyes widened and he stammered. "I…I…no. Sorry. That'll be $22.60."

Winter handed him her card and cast over her shoulder for the girl. She was walking out. Winter tapped her foot and turned to take her card back. She snatched her bag and rushed out after the girl.

As she caught up to her, Winter reached out and touched her on the shoulder. "Excuse me," Winter said. "I wondered if you could help me."

The girl spun and locked eyes, and Winter instantly swirled into her memories again. She saw a group of people dressed in black. A bonfire. A bald man with a red goatee. "It'll be over soon, Chessa," said the man.

"What?" the girl asked.

Winter pulled away from the vision. Chessa crossed her arms, furrowed her brow, and narrowed her eyes.

"I'm looking for someone," Winter said. "Maybe you know him. Cain Golia."

Chessa's face blanched and she turned her face to the floor. "Sorry. Never heard of him." She pivoted to leave.

Winter grabbed her shoulder again. "Your name is Chessa."

Chessa spun back, flushing in her cheeks. "How do you know my name?"

"I just do," Winter said. "Just like I know that you were pledging to Skotos. I know you know Cain, so please, help me."

Chessa's eyes widened. For a moment, Winter thought she might turn and run. Instead, Chessa lowered her arms. "Are you...Winter?"

Winter nodded. "You've heard of me, then."

"Just whispers. I don't think I should be talking to you."

Winter shifted all her weight to one leg and held her palms open at her sides, as best she could while still clinging to her bag. "I'm not here to hurt you or anything. I just need to know where Cain is."

"Why should I help you?"

"Because you haven't finished pledging yet, have you?" asked Winter. "You backed out. They didn't like that, did they? Every day you look over your shoulder in fear, thinking they'll come back for you. If you help me, you won't have to worry about them any longer."

"How do you..."

"Because I don't see the hate in you. I don't see the brokenness. You were pledging, but something unexpected happened, didn't it? The pledging stopped for some reason or it went too far, so you ran. Am I right?"

Chessa nodded. "A little over a year ago I was just starting. I had gone through all the introductory stuff and gotten to know some of the members. They took me in like family. Cain was setting up my final induction ceremony, but he wouldn't tell me what was going to happen…"

"Trust me, be glad he didn't."

"Then they all just disappeared. One moment everything was great, I had purpose and meaning, and then nothing. I had to move on, and the more I moved on the more I realized that Skotos wanted too much from me. I'm sorry, but if you want to find Cain I can't help you. I haven't seen him for a long time. I've actually given up on the Wiccan stuff."

"Good for you. You're very lucky. I've heard about what they do to inductees. They would have enslaved you for the rest of your life."

Chessa pursed her lips.

"I still need to find him," Winter said. "So think. Is there anything you can tell me? A meeting place or something?"

Chessa's eyes went to the ceiling as she considered it. "We met at houses mostly, and a few times in a forest. But I went back to all of those places when they disappeared. Nothing."

"Anything else?"

"Maybe," Chessa said. "My induction ceremony was supposed to be behind this old abandoned power plant."

"Where is it?"

"On the outskirts of town. Listen, why are you doing this?"

"You seem like a nice person, Chessa. These Skotos people are not. They lie and manipulate to get what they want, and they trick good innocent people into becoming monsters like them. They're not really Wiccans. They're probably more related to Satanists. We're talking murder, rape, human sacrifice…"

Chessa's face paled. "I almost…"

"But you didn't. You got away. As bad as they are, they were working for someone worse. You heard stories about me, right?"

Chessa nodded. "Just that you were the enemy and that you had an unnatural power."

"I'm a prophetess of God…yes, *that* God," Winter said at Chessa's furrowed brow. "The power I get comes from him. And I'm not just trying to stop Skotos, I'm trying to stop the evil they've been working for. If I succeed, you won't ever have to worry about them coming back for you, because trust me…if I don't stop them, they will and they won't let you go again. So please, whatever you can do to help…Not just for my sake, but for your own."

Chessa nodded. "Okay. But I've told you all I know, what else can I do?"

"Directions to Cain's house or wherever you used to meet him the most. And directions to the power plant. If I need anything else I'll be in touch."

17

After writing down all the information Chessa would give, Winter left the mall and drove through town. First, she wanted to locate the place where Cain used to live. Chessa didn't know if he still did, but Winter suspected not. When she drove slowly by, she found an overweight father mowing the yard while two kids played on the porch. Winter kept driving. She went to the next house on Chessa's list. Then the next. Each occupied by new residents. By late afternoon she had checked off all of Chessa's locations except the abandoned power plant. It was a random place to have a ceremony, so Winter's hopes weren't high enough to expect anything.

Knowing she'd be out much of the night again, Winter showered at the campground and parked beneath an isolated shade tree for a nap. She reclined her seat and rolled down her windows, letting the cool autumn air and the sounds of children playing roll in. She knew she'd need all her strength to face Skotos. What exactly *was* she going to do if she actually found them? She only knew she needed to extract information about Xaphan. This from a group of people he had tried to exterminate, who at one point had been trying to murder Winter.

A little extra time to rest and clear her head seemed like a good idea.

As she relaxed and her body numbed, she dreamed again. Nothing about the future and no message telling her exactly what to do next. But she remembered…she relived…

She stood in the train yard facing Claire, whose glowing red eyes covered Winter in a hatred more dense than cold blood. The shadows swirled around Claire, clawing at the air and reaching out toward Winter. Then Claire flung out her arms toward Winter and shadows jetted forward, splashing around Winter like water upon rocks. The angelic white light came next, flowing from behind Winter, to surround her and beat back the demons.

Claire swelled into a giant monster filled with thousands of demons writhing as skin. It stepped forward, reaching out toward Winter, but the angelic light returned, gushing like the breaking of a dam to pierce the monster, growing within it, and fracturing the demonic crust from the inside out. The shadows dispersed like fleeting fog.

Lying on the ground was Sophie. Sophie tried to escape with her, but the demons wouldn't let her go. They reclaimed her while she screamed.

Winter awoke. The lowering sun approached sunset. Most of the children had left. Significantly cooler air wafted through the window and she pulled her coat a little tighter, raised her windows, and turned the ignition.

Where was Sophie now? The question nagged her more than wondering where Xaphan might be. Perhaps the two things were connected. Maybe that was it…the thing she needed to do next. She had to find Sophie. Maybe finding Cain would lead her there. Maybe she'd find them together. That thought clicked inside of her and Winter's heart pounded.

She pulled back onto the road and headed back toward town to get some food. By the time she had finished eating, darkness had nearly fallen and she began the drive to the outskirts of town to find the abandoned power plant. The gate lay sideways upon the ground, matching Chessa's description. The old building beyond, covered with rusted metal and broken windows, truly did look abandoned.

Yet Winter had a strong gut instinct that inside she would find the answers she needed. Maybe people. Maybe just a clue. But she knew she had found the right place and followed the right trail.

Winter eased her car as close to the decrepit building as she could before parking and getting out. Darkness watched her from the broken windows. She checked the nearest door and found it locked tight. Despite the dents and scratches on the old metal door, the knob and lock looked brand new. She studied them, knowing that the door would unlock and she could just walk in if needed. But if people were here...

Winter knocked, the rapping of her knuckles dull in the cold air. She waited a few minutes and knocked again. If no one came to the door after fifteen minutes, she would just walk in. Finally, after knocking three times over the course of ten minutes, Winter balled her fist and beat on the door as hard as she could for at least thirty seconds.

After that, it didn't take long for results. She felt the flicker of her premonition several seconds beforehand, but let it slide and waited patiently as a black-clad man slipped around the corner of the building with a gun trained on her. Winter calmly turned toward him and raised her hands.

"What do you want?" he growled as he eased closer.

"To talk, that's all," she said.

"How did you find us?"

"Do you know who I am?"

The man's eyes narrowed. "Yes. Why should I not shoot you right now?"

"Because you know it wouldn't be that easy," she said. "I'm not here to start any problems. I just want to talk."

"And if *we* don't want to talk?"

"That's up to you, I suppose. But I know that he's hunting you. I know you can't hide forever. I can help. I want to stop him, and if I do you'll all be free."

The man pursed his lips and his gun drooped. "Are you armed?"

Winter shook her head. "You know it wouldn't matter anyway. Just give me ten minutes."

The man stepped backward. "Wait here."

As he disappeared around the corner, Winter faced the door and waited. After a few more minutes, the locks on the door scraped within. The door cracked. A bald man with a red goatee stood in the gap, muscular arms crossed, a gun held casually in his hand.

"You've got ten minutes," he said and then stepped out of the way.

Winter followed and entered into the remnants of an office, with halls to either side leading to additional offices. With a bright light on above, Winter checked the windows and found crude metal boxes covering each for the illusion of a dark interior. She scanned the room, counting the number of people — six. Pallets lay on the floor between the desks. Piles of trash littered the tops of the desks and floors, most being the remnants of fast-food meals. An airy hum drifted through the air. Winter followed the sound past machinery and giant conduits until she found a small window with an AC unit. She hoped it could produce heat for the downcast inhabitants on the freezing floor.

An internal magnet pulsed inside of her. She followed it until her gaze passed through a set of double doors at the back of the room. The next room opened into a large space full of dusty capacitors and power transformers. Beyond this equipment stood another door, plain and easily overlooked. Here the magnetic pulse rested.

Sophie was there. Winter could feel her presence. This power plant, this room, this task…it almost felt as if she had done these things before, and Winter knew that strange feeling meant she had followed the exact course of actions she needed to. She was supposed to find Skotos because she was supposed to find Sophie. Winter took a deep breath, remembering exactly what her last encounter with Sophie and the Acolyte had been like, and prepared to confront her again to get the information she needed.

"What do you want?" asked the bald man.

"Are you Cain?"

The man nodded.

"I need to find Xaphan. I'm going to stop him once and for all this time."

"We don't know where he is. Unless you've forgotten, we're trying to stay away from him."

Winter shook her head and nodded back toward Sophie's door. "I need to talk to her. She knows."

The man frowned. "There's no one else here."

"Sophie is here. She is beyond that door." Winter allowed the magnetism to reach through the door and touch Sophie. "I can feel her. She's broken. Frightened. Culsu has left her."

"How do you know all of that?"

Winter turned back to Cain. "I'm not here to do anything to any of you." She panned the others. "I know what you are. I know the kinds of things you have done. I know the oaths you have taken. But I can tell most of you want out. You've left the other clans of Skotos and now you're here, hoping that Xaphan won't find you. I am not here to hurt you or turn you over to the police. All I want is to talk to Sophie so I can find out how to reach Xaphan. Once I find him, this will all be over." She faced Cain again. "I'm trying to ask nicely."

Cain glared. "What if we don't want your help?"

Winter shook her head. "How bad must it be? You've had to leave your homes…probably leave your families, if they haven't been killed. I'm not sure any of you fully realized what kind of person Xaphan was, no matter how evil your oaths to Skotos. How many clans has he wiped out?" Winter waved her arms. "Look at yourselves. Look what he's done to you."

Everyone watched her with wide, frightened eyes. Winter saw regret on more than one face. How many really realized the extent of their oaths before they pledged? How many were tricked into this like

Chessa almost was? How many threatened and blackmailed into compliance like Sophie? How many given empty promises of revenge like Alison? How many abducted and forced into servitude and indoctrination? How many others in the country were hiding from Xaphan and trying to get out just like these? Winter wanted to hate them, to think of them like hell-born animals. But in reality, they were all broken and hurting human beings...like she used to be.

"When this is over," Winter said to them, "you can go back to a normal life. You can be free. You can be forgiven. Trust me. I was once heading down the same path that led you here. I didn't think I could come back from it. But I did. There is a way. There's nothing so tainted that you can't be forgiven." She turned back to Cain. "Just give me ten minutes with her."

Cain stared at her for several tense seconds and then nodded slowly. "Ten minutes."

Four Years Ago

Winter did go with Michael, Shannon, and their friends to hang out at the state park. Though she went with the intention of giving Michael the cold shoulder, by the end of the day she found herself walking the trails and laughing with him, while Shannon and most of the others walked ahead. It didn't feel intimate or date-ish, only like she had finally discovered a new best friend.

Over the next month, Shannon brought Winter to her house twice more for movies and dinner. Michael always came, and Winter gravitated more toward him than anyone else. As flippant as Shannon seemed about Winter spending more time with her brother than her, Winter suspected Shannon pushed Winter and Michael together on purpose. Still…Winter didn't mind.

At the end of October, Michael himself extended the invitation for Winter to return to their Samhain ceremony that year. Michael picked her up from home as the sun set. Her dad waved at her as she left, but said nothing really. He no longer seemed to care what Winter did. Winter thought he secretly counted the days until she graduated so he could finally be rid of her and things could return to the way it used to be before she messed it all up.

As Winter climbed into the car, Michael reached over and squeezed her hand, giving her a warm smile.

"You ready?"

"Oh, yeah," Winter said. "I definitely need a change of scenery."

"That bad?"

Winter shrugged. "Let's just say my dad's not the only one that will be happy when this year is over. I won't exactly be missed."

He frowned. "It depends."

Winter flashed her eyes at him and then gazed away as a blush crept up her cheeks.

He drove the now familiar route through town to the outskirts where his parents' house sat behind trees away from the road. In the spacious backyard, another large bonfire had been built but had not yet been lit. They were early for the party.

Winter stared at the wood piled high, just visible around the edge of the house from where she sat rooted in the car.

Michael sighed. "I promised, didn't I?"

"Yeah, but I know everyone wants me to stay."

Michael shook his head. "I don't think anyone is expecting you to stay for the Samhain ceremony this year. I know how tough it was last year. We'll leave, I promise. Maybe we'll go to my place…" A hint of suggestiveness tinted his voice…

Winter's heart pounded and she blushed again. But she didn't refuse. Instead, she opened the door.

Shannon met them at the corner of the house and hugged Winter. "How are you?" Her sympathetic smile made Winter grimace.

"I'm just fine," Winter said through clenched teeth.

Shannon frowned and nodded, her eyes tightening before she turned away to lead them around the house. "You should know that there will be a special remembrance for…" She trailed off and glanced over her shoulder.

"I wasn't planning on staying."

"Just let me know when," said Michael.

Both Winter and Shannon nodded at him.

As the sun fell behind the horizon, more people arrived. Madam Morial and Shannon arrayed the refreshments on a table as Michael and his dad ignited the fire. Winter watched Michael work, sitting in the furthest chair she could find from everyone, with her arms folded across her chest.

She wasn't sure what the uncertain flutter of emotions meant, like wrestling with a butterfly that refused to land. There were moments she wanted to draw in her knees and cry, and moments where she just wanted to scream at everyone who looked at her with that condescending *pity*. Part of her wanted to get away from here, to go home and hug her dad. Another part wanted to let Michael take her back to his apartment and...Winter felt her cheeks redden at the thought. With the thought came the guilt...guilt about Ryan. That made her want to cry again. The butterfly just wouldn't land.

She realized Michael watched her now with something like the same pity she found on everyone else's face. She ground her teeth to keep from screaming. His mouth tightened and he scurried into the house. When he came back out, he carried two bottles in his hand. He pulled a chair next to her and handed her one.

"Have a beer," he said.

She took the open bottle and smiled. "Contributing to the delinquency of minors again?"

"Not my first time." He winked and took a long drink. "Maybe it'll take the edge off."

"That obvious, huh?" Winter copied him with a swig of her own.

Michael shrugged. "We can go do something else if you want. Maybe a movie?"

Winter considered it. It would certainly be good to not have to face things right now. But she knew she couldn't avoid those feelings forever. She took a deep breath. "I think I'll stay just a little longer. I can manage that at least."

Michael nodded. "Well, if you're going to stay, you can't just sit here and stew. Come on. Let me introduce you to a few people."

Winter took a swallow, wishing the alcohol would hurry up. She smiled at him, stood, and bobbed her now half-empty bottle. "Is there more?"

"Plenty."

Michael led her around the yard to the various small groups, introducing Winter to so many people she couldn't possibly remember all their names. Men and women of all ages had gathered that night for the Samhain ceremony, and for the first time she actually felt like she had found her real family. These people didn't pretend to be something they were expected to be by others, but were comfortable in who they were. Many of them had a dark, haunting look in their eyes that reminded Winter of the hollow iciness she felt inside her own chest. These people understood her and what she'd been through better than anyone else in the world. They knew her in a way no one else could begin to know.

After swinging back inside for more beers, they spent the next half hour with Shannon and her friends Melissa, Katherine, and Mary.

Winter remembered seeing Katherine and Michael together last year and wondered why they broke up. Did it have anything to do with Winter? Or the kiss? Whatever it was, the two of them seemed to have maintained a civil relationship, and Katherine didn't balk at Winter and Michael being together.

Were they actually *together*?

Before Winter realized it, Michael had left her, and the four other girls assimilated her into the group. Winter cast around for Michael, finding him just outside on the patio talking to a couple of guys his age. Winter thought she recognized one of them, but couldn't quite place his name. Michael saw her watching and flashed a smile. Then he glanced at the fire and stepped toward her.

Winter felt a hand on her arm. "The bonfire's about to start," said Shannon.

Winter bit her lip and turned to Michael as he approached. "You ready to go then?" he asked.

Winter took a deep breath, grateful that the beer had helped her relax, and smiled. "Actually. I think I'll stay."

19

Present Day

Winter took a deep breath and followed Cain to the back room, where he stepped aside at the door. She hesitated only a moment before grabbing the handle firmly and entering. Windowless darkness inside hid everything, so she ran her hand against the wall until she found a light switch.

The moment the lights came on, sudden movement erupted from behind a desk. A frightened and dirtied face, squinting against the light, peaked up over at Winter.

Sophie's cheeks had sunken in so skeletally that Winter hardly recognized her. Her matted hair looked as if she hadn't brushed it in months, and her pale skin blotched with the sudden movement, as if she hadn't tried to do any kind of exercise or even seen the light in days.

The door slammed behind Winter. The lock clicked.

"What do you want?" Sophie croaked.

Winter eased over to the desk and passed around the side until she came into view of Sophie's tattered pallet of ragged blankets.

"Are you living here?" Winter asked.

Sophie pushed herself up until she sat back on her ankles. Winter knelt in front of her, suddenly feeling a great surge of pity.

"More of a prisoner than anything else," said Sophie. "They won't let me leave. But I don't mind. It's the only place *he* hasn't found me."

"Let me help you."

"You can't help me. It's too late. Even if I did want to trust your god, Culsu will never let me go."

Winter shook her head. "That's not true."

The circles around Sophie's eyes darkened into a deep crimson and tears rolled down her cheeks. "But it is. I've made my choices."

"You can change."

"Not me. Never me. It'll always find me, and I can't take it anymore."

"What if I could stop him? What if I could set you free? Would you help me?"

"Me? What kind of help can I be?" She held out her gaunt arms to the side. "Can't you see me?"

"I just need to know where he is."

Sophie tilted her head and studied Winter for a long time, letting her few silent tears trace lines on her dirty face. Then she slowly nodded. "If you can get rid of him and *it*, I'll tell you. I'll tell you everything."

Winter sighed. "Good. Because that's why I'm here. I'm going after him to end all of this."

Sophie sat quietly for a long time and Winter thought maybe she wouldn't answer. Finally, Sophie's lips parted and she spoke carefully and precisely. "If he catches you..."

"I know. And I don't care. There's nothing he can do to me that I haven't already thought of. I have to do this. It's the only way any of us can be free."

Sophie blinked at her and wiped her face. "Can you really stop him?"

Winter shook her head. "Not me...not by myself at least."

"But it can be done?"

"Yes. It can be done. It will be done. So please...talk to me. Tell me everything."

Sophie's mouth hung open and her lips twitched as if she wanted to say things that wouldn't quite come out. Finally, she glanced away and started talking. "My brother was the first."

"Your brother?" Winter asked.

"Logan. You met him once."

A face flashed in Winter's mind, accented with her supernaturally perfect memory. A young man stared at her over a hedge at a CLC party two years ago...then again from the side of a building just before the shooting began.

"He was looking for Sandy," said Winter. "You both were. I had no idea he was your brother. I saw things in his memory...horrible things..."

Sophie nodded. "He was the first. He had always been pushed away in high school. So he got involved in some darker stuff. At first it was Wiccan stuff...then full-blown Satanism. Finally, he found Skotos."

"What about you?"

"I was going to Tishbe, and for whatever reason they were planning something there. I didn't know about Xaphan then, only that they were trying to get as many of Skotos on campus as possible. Most of the time they weren't even students. They just wandered around posing as students. A few enrolled to audit some classes second semester. They wanted to cause distractions for some reason. They were looking for Sandy even then, but they wanted to make sure no one knew what was going on."

Winter nodded. "I remember them. A few stood up in one of my classes. But what about you?"

"My brother told them I was going to school here and would be living on campus. They wanted a legitimate student that could help. At first I didn't want to...I just wanted to be normal, you know? But Logan warned me that they wouldn't be happy if I refused. I refused anyway. That's when they kidnapped my grandmother." Sophie's chin quivered.

"When I first came here, you had a boyfriend."

Sophie nodded. Sadness tugged at the corners of her eyes. "Jason. We were high school sweethearts, you know? We had a plan. We were going to go to college together, get good jobs, get married, start a family. But I was angry all the time. I couldn't help it. Skotos kept asking me to do things I didn't want to do. Jason confronted me about it and I told him everything. He looked so disgusted with me..."

"You could have walked away from Skotos," said Winter.

"And let them kill my gran? I did everything I could to keep that from happening."

"I'm sorry. I saw what they did in Logan's eyes."

Sophie turned away and wiped her face. "I didn't even get to say goodbye. After you faced Xaphan in the bell tower first year, they wanted me to kill you. I told them no." She faced Winter again. "They killed her because of me! Because of you! What else could I do? They would have tracked down every person I loved and killed them too...including Jason. My gran didn't do anything!"

"Why didn't you try to kill me after?"

Sophie shook her head. "My orders changed. I was supposed to watch you and start looking for Sandy myself. They said that even if I didn't find Sandy on my own, you might lead me to her. Logan came to stay with me for a while to help. If we found anything, we were supposed to contact the Eater. We didn't dare disobey the Eater. He was more demon than human...an old demon called Moloch."

"The first Sandy. The freshman?"

"Logan got it wrong. He had to report back to Skotos. They

flogged him for that. You know flogging, right? They do like the ancient Romans used to. He almost died."

Winter pursed her lips. "But you kept going. They gave you an office and everything. A front to keep digging."

Sophie nodded. "It was all I could do. I never found anything, really. Not until Summer came. She slipped the note under my office door, telling me it might be Ayden. I didn't know they had gotten to Summer too. I immediately contacted my brother and he notified the Eater. We rendezvoused with him behind the administration building. He told us there would be a signal...a distraction or something...and that he would go find her. We were to hang back and watch in case something went wrong. We didn't find out Ayden was the wrong one until much later. In fact, it wasn't until the next school year when Summer turned in another report. We had been digging for information on Ayden all summer."

"So you knew that soon?"

"Practically all of last year. I kept working. Summer kept working. No one suspected it was actually Kaci. When we weren't getting results, that's when Xaphan summoned the Acolyte." Sophie stared at the floor.

"How did it find you?"

"I was called in...to meet with Skotos leadership. I had only been taking orders from them, I wasn't really one of them. But they wanted to make me one of them. They tied me up...they did these *horrible* things to me..." Sophie covered her face. "It makes me sick just to think about it. I feel so..."

"I understand." Winter's throat tightened at the thought of what they did to her. She reached out and lightly touched Sophie's arm.

"They told me they would stop if I would just call out to this spirit," Sophie continued, speaking into her palms. "So I did. I wanted it to stop so badly. That's when Culsu came. I don't think they were expecting what happened next. It possessed me...like I was trapped in my own body. I could sense some of its thoughts. It had already been talking with Xaphan, and Xaphan wanted Skotos destroyed. The moment it possessed me, I…the Acolyte…just broke free and started killing them. A few got away, so Xaphan told me…the Acolyte…to hunt all the rest down." She looked up, her eyes glistening, her face red and twisted with horror. "I remember killing my own brother. Do you have any idea what that feels like? I remember it all, Winter. I was there. I could see my hands tearing people apart." Her chin trembled. "I could feel the blood on my skin. And I couldn't stop. Culsu controlled everything in me."

"I'm so sorry," said Winter, voice cracking. She grabbed Sophie's hand.

"Then you showed up when I killed Shannon."

"It wasn't you. Never think it was you." Winter squeezed.

Sophie eyed her for a moment, sniffed, and pulled her hand away. She took a deep breath and wiped her face dry. "When the Acolyte killed Shannon, Culsu recognized you. She laughed in my head and I could feel her excitement. She wanted to learn more about you for some reason…and then to kill you slowly. Culsu wanted you for some kind of twisted science experiment. So she pulled people from your past and made you see them instead of me. Then Xaphan found out and took it as an opportunity to use you to find the real Sandy. I tried to warn you…but you wouldn't listen."

"How did you do that? How did you get away from it? How did you get away now?"

"Get away?" asked Sophie. "I never get away. Sometimes it leaves me for long periods of time, but I think it's always watching. Even now I'm probably not safe. After the train yard Xaphan was so angry. Culsu left me and I ran. I found Cain and he's been hiding me ever since. They're like Logan and me…they wanted out. So when Xaphan started purging all of the Skotos clans…when I, I mean the Acolyte, started killing them…they all fled and hid. If Xaphan ever found us…"

"He won't find you because I'm going to find him first. Culsu has been dragging you all over the place, and I bet you know where Xaphan lives. Tell me. Please."

Sophie took a deep breath and nodded slowly. "West of Mordensfield. There's a road called Water Bridge. Go south until you find his compound. It should be obvious when you see it."

Winter bobbed her head and gave Sophie a soft smile. "Thank you. I'll come back for you. Don't give up, please."

As Winter stood, Sophie held a shaking hand out to her. "Winter, there's something else."

"What?"

"What he wants to do…what he's planning…it's bigger than you can imagine."

"What do you mean?"

Sophie pursed her lips. "You can't just stop him. You have to stop everything. If you don't, millions of people will die."

Winter's heart froze. "Millions?"

"Kaci is just the beginning. He thinks he has the right to be the forerunner of the Antichrist. He thinks killing Kaci and stopping the prophecy will prove himself worthy. After that…"

"After that what?" asked Winter, more forcefully than she meant. "What's he planning, Sophie?"

"To make an offering to the Antichrist."

Winter shook her head. "What does that mean? You said millions?"

Sophie nodded, but as she opened her mouth to explain, screams erupted from the other rooms.

20

The screaming grew louder. Crashes. Bumps. The building shook. Gunshots rang out.

Winter stood and glared at the locked door. Waiting.

Sophie wept behind her. "No! It's here! It found me!"

Winter cast a glance over her shoulder and extended a hand back toward Sophie. "Don't worry. It's going to be okay."

"How can you say that? You can't stop it, Winter! I told you, it's not human!"

Winter took a deep breath and ignored her warning. She squared her feet toward the closed door and the growing sounds beyond. After only a minute, one final gunshot signaled the end of the chaos. Silence fell.

Click. The door unlocked. Winter squeezed her fists. The door gently swung inward.

Only a wall of blackness filled the door as if all light had been sucked away beyond the threshold. At first Winter thought it just darkness, that the lights had been turned out. Then the darkness moved forward into the room like a giant column. It glided gently, purposefully, not heeding Winter's presence but focused on reaching Sophie.

Sophie screamed the desperate scream of the dying.

"No!" Winter shouted at the darkness. "You can't have her!"

The darkness paused only briefly and then continued to move forward. Inch by inch. Winter put one foot behind her to brace herself and then extended both arms to press against the darkness. It collided with her hands like a solid wall. The darkness slowed momentarily and she thought she might actually be able to hold it back, but then her feet began to slide backward. Winter twisted, trying to find a grip with her shoes, but the weight of the darkness could not be stopped.

From somewhere deep inside the darkness laughter echoed. The laughter scraped across her skin, heat rushed to her face. She ground her teeth and growled as fury inflamed her muscles. At the point of contact with her hands and the wall, a white glow blazed. The laughter in the darkness turned to rage, and the darkness paused again.

Then in the space of a heartbeat the column scattered, filling the room like exploding powder. No more wall. No more solid mass. The darkness engulfed the entire room and the light above could not shine through it.

As Sophie's screams reached a new feverish height, Winter heard her thrashing on the floor.

Winter's heart pounded. She pushed forward through the darkness toward the door, hoping to escape before having to face the Acolyte again. It took her a moment of fumbling before she found the opening, but even as she ran into the next room the darkness fell away like ash. The lights were indeed out in the room as she had suspected, but a little ambient light filtered through small, dingy windows so that she could make out enough shapes to navigate. The second room stared at her pitch black from beyond an open door ahead. As she entered the dark room, she glanced around for the exit, but couldn't see anything.

She fell to the floor and started groping for a place to hide. Her hand landed on a bloody dismembered arm, and she almost screamed. Claire entered the room, stopping two steps in. Winter scrambled behind an old work table.

"Winter!" shouted the voice of Claire. "Why are you hiding? I know you're here. We have much to talk about since we last spoke. You are a curious puzzle. I'd like to know more about what you are."

Winter could hear Claire moving through the room, positioning herself strategically so Winter couldn't get past.

"Show yourself!"

Winter squinted in the darkness around her for anything, any clue or item she could use to get past Claire, but found nothing.

"It doesn't matter how much power you bring against me, I will destroy you this time," the Acolyte said. "I've been waiting for you. I knew you would come again. Does it help you to know Sophie's in here with me? Screaming to get out? She feels the pain, you know. Anytime something happens to me, Sophie is the conduit for all that pain. This is why you will fail. Your compassion is your weakness. You wouldn't want to hurt her, would you? I shall enjoy ripping your skin off, and not even the entire horde of Heaven can stop me!" After a moment of silence, Claire's voice said softly, "There you are."

Winter's time was up. She clenched her eyes and prayed. Then without knowing why, she stood, eyes still clenched, and started walking...straight toward the voice of the Acolyte.

"What is this? Another trick?" asked the Acolyte with a hint of uncertainty. "What are you doing?"

Winter bit her lip and screwed her eyes tighter, but didn't dare slow down. Then she heard the Acolyte scuffling as it backed away from her.

"Where are they?" it shouted. "Show them! I will not be tricked!"

Winter kept walking. More scuffling. Panting. A crash.

The Acolyte roared. Winter could make out bright flashes against her closed eyelids. A nudge in the back of her mind told her to turn left, so she did.

"NO! I won't let you escape me! Not this time!" More shouting. Cursing. More flashes.

Winter kept walking. She took ten more steps, reached out with her left hand, and found a doorknob.

"NO!" the Acolyte screamed from right behind her, close enough for Winter to feel the vibrations from her voice. "You're mine! You're mine!"

Winter lifted her right foot to step out of the door, the cool air of freedom wafting against her face. Then she stopped. The nudge in the back of her mind told her that if she wanted she could do something else. Her choice this time. Winter smiled at the idea and put her foot back down. She spun to face the Acolyte and opened her eyes.

She saw through the room as clearly as if the lights were on. Claire stood in front of her within arm's length, red eyes wide and face contorted with rage and hate. Its shadow-enshrouded arms pummeled at Winter, but each strike recoiled in a brilliant white flash. A moment after Winter opened her eyes, Claire looked into them and nearly fell backward.

Winter smiled. "We'll meet again," she said. "But I want you to remember this moment right now the next time you think your power could ever be stronger than the power God pours into me."

Winter balled her fist, drew it back, and aimed for Claire's face. As her arm flew through the air, white mist enshrouded it, becoming a bright hammer cocooning her fist. When the hammer connected with Claire's face, Winter felt nothing. But the power and force lifted Claire into the air, flinging her across the entire room to slam into the far wall.

"Sorry, Sophie," Winter whispered as she spun and sprinted out.

21

Four Years Ago

Michael called her two days later just to chat. Then two days after that. By the end of the week, he finally asked her out…one on one. Winter quickly agreed to dinner and a movie, something simple and fun but commitment-free. She still wasn't sure she wanted a relationship, but it was nice to have someone treat her as worthwhile rather than as a mistake or a nuisance.

They ate dinner at a pizzeria, chatting the whole time over the electronic noise of arcade games in the background. Winter relaxed, enjoying the conversation that never seemed to have any awkward pauses. The movie afterward was surprisingly romantic for an action movie, and Winter tensed every time Michael's arm brushed against hers on the armrest between them. At the end of the movie, they filed out with the rest of the crowd, and he held the door for her to climb into his car. But instead of taking her home, he drove to his apartment complex.

"Your place?" she asked. "I thought I said…"

"Relax. I just want to show you something."

Winter smirked. "I bet you do."

Michael rolled his eyes and climbed out, rounding the front of the car to open the door for her. Her face flushed as she got out and then followed him down the walk to his apartment.

"Make yourself comfortable," he said as he stood to one side of the open door.

Winter chuckled. "Yeah...okay." She shrugged off her coat and tossed it over the back of the couch before plopping down on the end seat. She crossed her legs and folded her arms, tiny butterflies swarming in her stomach.

Michael came back in, a little red-faced and staring at the floor. Beneath his arm he clutched several large flat books. As he approached, she sat forward, eying the books as he laid them gently on the coffee table.

"What are these?" she asked.

He avoided her eyes. "Just look. I don't show many people, so..."

Winter grinned at his blushing face and reached for the first book, flipping open the cover.

The first page showed the last thing she expected and her breath caught in her chest. Gently shaded charcoal blended in dark and light shades, creating a perfect scene of a cliff overlooking the ocean. The attention to detail, despite the lack of color, bore an almost photographic quality.

"This is..." She inhaled deeply. "Amazing." She flipped the page. The next one was an old man sitting on a wooden porch and smoking a pipe, each wrinkle in the man's wizened face painstakingly rendered. The next, a forest, dark and boding. The next, a 3D abstract that looked like the paper had been sliced and curled upon itself in four places. The next, a young gypsy girl dancing in the moonlight.

She blinked up at Michael, mouth open. "Did you...did you do these?"

He flopped next to her and nodded. "It's been a hobby since I was young."

Winter gazed at the stack of books with a new sense of wonder. "Are all of these…"

"Yup. These are just the ones that I'm most proud of…the ones that are most recent. I've got a whole closet full."

Winter shook her head as she reached for another book, slowly flipping through the pages of exquisitely detailed drawings. "These should be in a museum or something, really…"

"No. Not really my style. I do these as a creative release, you know? It's therapeutic."

"Do you just come up with the ideas yourself?"

He shrugged. "Sometimes. But some of the more detailed ones I drew from photographs."

"Wow," she whispered as she thumbed through the next book. "I just don't have any words."

"I'm glad you like them."

"They really are amazing." She leaned back on the couch and turned to face him. "Is this why you wanted me to come over here?"

He shrugged. "Kind of."

Winter eyed him suspiciously. "What do you mean, 'kind of?'"

"Whenever I get inspired by something, I like to draw it immediately. I'm afraid if I don't I'll forget or lose the inspiration or something."

"And?"

He blushed. "And…when I picked you up this evening…well, I was inspired."

Winter felt the heat creep into her cheeks. "Inspired? What…to draw me?"

"Well, yeah. Is that okay?"

Winter shook her head. "I've seen that movie. If you think…"

He held up his hands. "No, no!" He chuckled. "Nothing like that. I promise. Just a quick sketch as you are. That's all. Then I'll take you home."

Winter studied him, measuring his intentions, but she couldn't deny the genuineness behind his eyes. And it felt nice to have inspired someone. She'd never done that before. "Just a sketch?"

Michael nodded.

"Okay. What do you want me to do?"

"Wait right here." He jumped up and ran back to the bedroom. After a minute or two he returned, a fresh sketch pad and pencil in hand and a joint in his mouth.

"Do you have to get high to do this?" Winter asked.

Michael shrugged. "It helps the creativity flow. This is a lovely. It has angel dust in it."

"You mean PCP? Sounds intense."

He leaned in close to her with a grin. "Same high, but with an amazing kick." He handed it to her. "Try it."

Winter simpered and took the joint from him. "What do you want me to do now?" she asked as she gently inhaled.

He sat on the coffee table opposite her. "Just look at me."

"Look at you?"

His pencil scratched the surface. "In the eyes."

Winter locked eyes with him whenever he wasn't looking at the paper. With each glance up, her heart fluttered a little faster. With each second, the pit of her stomach turned more into mush. She felt exposed and vulnerable, her soul at the mercy of his attentive gaze and his busy pencil. Or maybe that was just the weed and the angel dust.

They passed the lovely back and forth, and with each hit Winter relaxed a little more. The colors in the room danced for her as Michael's bright blue eyes shone like lights. Eventually her apprehensions disappeared and she actually wished he would draw her like in that movie she once saw. She lifted her hand and unbuttoned a couple of her top buttons, exposing a little of her bra, imagining herself as the actress. Michael grinned and she laughed.

Still his pencil scratched, more feverishly by the moment. Each time he glanced up, she saw more desire on his face, more longing, and more eagerness. She couldn't tell if it was for the drawing or for her. Either way she didn't care. In that moment Winter finally felt important to someone again, and she didn't want to give it up anytime soon.

22

Present Day

The cursed town radiated more rot and despair than it had two years ago, with even more abandoned storefronts than before. Winter saw only a handful of destitute individuals wandering around. Where the bank she had visited once stood, an adult video store flashed a neon sign. With no traffic and no reason to slow down, Winter reached the other side of town after only a few minutes. She didn't come to mourn Mordensfield. Her spiritual magnetic sense of direction drew her elsewhere...just beyond the outskirts of town, validating Sophie's directions.

By late afternoon Winter had finally found the road Sophie had told her about, and it didn't take long to find Xaphan's compound. An ominous security gate with razor wire on top barred the way. A prison-like fence, twelve feet tall and crowned with even more razor wire, stretched in both directions.

She drove on for nearly a mile, searching for a place to stash her car. A road intersected to the right, and she turned, sure that this road also followed the perimeter of Xaphan's compound. The trees obscured her view to the interior, but she found what must have once been a place where a road connected before the compound had been built. The pavement widened at the shoulder and straw-covered gravel led up a slope into the trees. She could see the fence gleaming beneath her headlights. No gate. No guards. It was the perfect place to leave her car...maybe the perfect place to enter.

She parked in the shadows, beneath a clump of pines, and pulled her stocking cap tight against her head. From the trunk, she retrieved the utility belt that she had been given after FBI training with Agent Erickson. She no longer had the gun, but she had the expandable baton, a knife, and a flashlight on the belt. More importantly, it held the pair of heavy duty wire cutters she had purchased at the hardware store. She slung a small duffel bag over her shoulder in case she found something worth taking. Finally, she shoved the click lighter from Ayden into her back pocket.

After double-checking behind her, peering into the distance to make sure no vehicles approached, she eased toward the fence. Then she went to work cutting the chain link, starting at the bottom, and snipping her way through each strand. The thick wire required more force than Winter expected, but she gripped tighter and took her time. After making a two-foot incision in the fence, she grasped the bottom two corners and folded them back along the fence to give herself a small triangular opening free from the jagged edges of the wire. After tossing in her belt and duffel bag, she lay on her back and shimmied through.

She fastened her belt, slung the bag over her shoulder, and took out a small flashlight. Moving toward what she gauged to be the center of the compound, she found a cliff face about a quarter of a mile in. She frowned at it, not wanting to chance such a climb in the dark, and then peered in both directions for an easier path. The slope descended slightly to the left, so she followed the cliff for another quarter mile until she finally found a grade gentle enough she could climb without fear of tumbling to her death.

Once on top, the land evened out nicely, though the tree cover thickened. Winter had to pick her way through the dense evergreens, hoping she was actually going in the right direction even though something in the back of her mind steered her like a compass. After half an hour, she saw lights ahead, and despite the fact that the dense vegetation might make crossing the terrain almost impossible, she turned out her flashlight. She eased forward, trusting in the outlines and silhouettes of the trees to guide her forward without injury. Twenty feet from the point where the tree line ended, Winter could finally see the compound ahead.

Instead of the strict military installation she expected, she discovered a mansion at least a hundred years old, or what had been built to look that way. The stone building had large double-sized windows on the first floor, with the windows on each of the next three floors getting progressively smaller until they were nothing more than slits in the uppermost gable. A rounded turret-like structure, with a pointed roof, stood at the leftmost corner of the house. With the half-dozen gables and at least as many chimneys protruding from unseen locations on the roof, the whole mansion had a distinct castle-like quality. Why anyone would build such a work of art in the middle of nowhere didn't make any sense to Winter. Still, she knew more of the mansion lay hidden than could be seen.

Winter inspected the darkened sky above the mansion, eerily untouched by any of the lights below. She thought she could almost see dark swirls in the blackness...the demons that had engulfed her last year at the train-yard. For now, they remained mostly invisible to her, but she sensed them waiting and watching.

Probably for the best, she thought as she took a deep calming breath and analyzed the grounds further for an unseen approach path.

Other structures surrounded the mansion. The circle drive before the front doors wrapped around a fountain with a statue of a mythical faun, currently dry and covered in dead leaves. Closer to her and left of the mansion stood what she thought might be a garage. A covered walkway stretched between the garage and a side door.

So far, Winter had seen no signs of life. Lights glowed inside, randomly on each floor, but she saw no change in the fifteen minutes or so she watched. None went out and no more came on. Winter wondered if anyone were home at all.

Looking back at the garage, she determined that she could keep inside the trees and get behind the building. She crouched down and labored through thick brush. Leaves and branches rustled and cracked no matter how carefully she stepped. At the corner of the garage, she peered around to the shadowy side of the house, wondering how in the world she would get in and what she would do when she did.

Then she spotted the one thing that could ruin this whole plan…a camera just above the side door beneath the walkway joining the garage. Winter eased back into the shadows of the trees.

Would there be *any* way in without being caught? Probably not. She cast her gaze into the darkness of the trees, thinking briefly of secret tunnels and even sewer drains, but neither would be any better than the door right in front of her. But the camera…

She lowered herself to the ground to think, and her knee struck large rocks, sending a shiver of pain through her leg. She brushed the rocks aside and massaged her knee, staring at the camera. Her hand hesitated over one of the larger rocks, nearly too big for her to grasp with one hand.

Winter tilted her head in thought, staring at the camera, a small nudge in her mind…the round lens, the rectangular body, the spindle arm that held it to the wall. Maybe if she could…She took up the rock and stood, easing forward just far enough to be comfortable with the distance, and hurled the rock at the camera. It fell short, rolling across the ground and striking the door with a loud boom. Winter crouched, holding her breath, and waited. Then she picked up another, lighter rock, and threw it. Another miss, but closer. The third rock fit the palm of her hand perfectly. She rolled it with one hand, eyes closed, muttering a prayer. This time she planted her feet properly, envisioning the rock and the camera and what she wanted to happen. Without opening her eyes, she hurled it as hard as possible at the image formed in her mind.

A moment later, she heard a metallic clink and a soft thump. She opened her eyes. The camera now pointed off toward the back of the house, perpendicular to the door. She smiled and made the wide arc to the door, certain that once she touched the knob, she would find it unlocked.

23

As she eased the door closed behind her, she held her breath and listened while staring down the short narrow hall in front of her. A couple of doors were on either side of the hall, but she instinctively crept toward a third door waiting at the end. She pressed her ear against the door, straining to hear beyond the pounding of her heart, but heard nothing. She couldn't believe this place would be empty…there had to be someone here. If she took her time, maybe she could avoid them altogether.

Slowly, she twisted the knob and cracked the door to peer through. The dark room beyond had just enough residual light from appliances for Winter to recognize it as a kitchen. She eased in, crossed to the next door, and repeated the process. So far, so good…but what next? Where was she supposed to go? Should she skulk through the entire house like this until she stumbled upon…upon what? What was she even doing here?

In a moment of panic, Winter realized she couldn't possibly find the information about the plans Sophie mentioned without knowing exactly where to go. Xaphan would never be so foolish as to leave that kind of information out in the open. It had to be hidden somewhere. But where? Winter leaned against the kitchen counter and bit her lip, trying to rationalize the madness of storming Xaphan's compound. Not only would the information be hidden, but it was probably in the exact place where Xaphan spent most of his time, too. He wouldn't walk openly through the house, from bedroom to office like a normal person…no, he was too paranoid and careful for something like that. And if his compound were searched by authorities, he'd want to make sure none of his information could be found. She needed to look for something so secretive that not even the police could find it.

Winter rolled her eyes to herself. *As if this couldn't get any more difficult. This is a big house. It could be anywhere.*

With that thought, another realization came. Or was it a nudge? Definitely a nudge. He'd want to have a safe room and maybe even an escape route. An escape route meant bottom floor. She smiled. A bottom floor safe room narrowed the search considerably, and it meant a way out if she needed it…a way that probably wasn't as highly monitored as the rest of the house. But where? And if she *did* find Xaphan, would she actually stop him?

Winter eased back to the kitchen entrance and cracked the door open, waiting for the next nudge…the next premonition. Wall sconces dimly lit the dining area beyond, shining on a perfectly polished cherry table large enough to have a dozen plush chairs all around. Winter wondered if this perfect picture of sophistication was all just part of the show, meant to give a false impression of what really happened at that house. For that matter, Winter wondered then if the house wasn't co-occupied by someone else who actually lived and held parties here as a way of masking Xaphan's presence.

A cased wall opening to the right led to a sitting room, carpeted and complete with several wingback chairs, a tall fireplace, and an ornate mantel wearing a golden clock. Winter almost laughed at the parody of it all. In her mind's eye, she imagined the sitting room led away toward the foyer and that if she held straight through the dining room she would come to a great room near the center of the house, where she would find that same foyer to her right.

Double doors that swung inward easily on their hinges revealed exactly that. The great room stretched at least fifty feet across. A lavish crystal chandelier dangled over the middle of the great room, perfectly centered over a thick rug that covered at least a third of the hardwood floor between her and the far wall. Three doors were in the far wall, and turning to look down the wall where she stood, she found two more. A glass wall lined the back of the room, passing beneath the floating staircase. All was dark beyond the glass wall, and Winter suspected it led to some sort of open-air gallery. A wide banistered staircase demanded the center of attention, rising to a second-floor balcony, and then splitting into two staircases and doubling back on itself, continuing to the third floor. The upper staircases floated across the expanse without support like the second half of the bottom staircase, but an oval-shaped wall encased the bottom half for support. Extravagant artworks decorated this wall, each piece with its own accent light.

Winter took a deep breath. *Nudge.* Someone like Xaphan wouldn't want to skulk in the shadows in a place like this…he had too much pride for that. He would most certainly want to gloat over hiding his secrets in plain sight.

She peered again at the central staircase, this time focusing on the support wall that showcased the artwork. Crooking her head to listen one more time for movement in the house, she glided across the floor and beneath the staircase as quickly as she could. Now standing beside the support wall, Winter saw that the inside of the encasing could certainly hold something as big as a room, not just a few support beams.

Nudge. She ran her hand along the wall and over the paintings, paying special attention to the frames. Each painting hung professionally secured to the wall, not just stuck on a nail. She found no seams, but one painting in particular loomed large enough a grown man could step through. She paused in front of it, sliding her hand over the frame, massaging it for any anomalies. It was so well crafted, so intricately carved, that there could be any number of seams and she'd never find one. Near the top right, she pressed another of the decorative leaves like she had done all over the frame, but this one gave a little, like it sat upon a stiff spring. She pressed it harder and felt, rather than heard, a soft click. The leaf popped out a little and she grabbed it and tugged. It came out upon a spindle where she could rotate it if needed. She felt beneath the leaf and found a small keyhole.

Frowning, she lowered her hand. Now what? Remembering all her past experience with locks, she set her teeth and reached back up, tapping the keyhole hard as if she had the key at the tip of her finger. Then she rotated her finger as if turning the key... the lock turned with it, a full quarter, and clicked. An invisible seam at the edge of the painting popped loose and the painting swung backward a little on hidden hinges. As she lowered her hand, the locking mechanism fell back into its first position. She stepped over the two feet of wall beneath the painting, reached up and pressed the leaf cover back in place over the lock, and eased the hidden door closed with a soft click.

Winter smirked. Using Xaphan's own arrogance lightened her tension considerably.

Inside the hidden room, Winter found another ornate set of stairs almost as fancy as the ones above, but not nearly as wide. More wall sconces illuminated the path down, less like entering a secret dungeon and more like discovering a back area of a library. At the bottom, a long hall widened to at least ten feet. Several doors connected to the hall, but by now her premonition had fully activated, feeding her moments and possibilities as a continuous stream. She eyed the one door she needed...the last door on the left. She'd find her information there.

To her surprise, the door had no lock. Maybe it was another act of arrogance, as if to say no one could possibly discover the lair beneath the mansion. Winter entered without hesitation, flipped on the light to the windowless dark room, and peeked around. Shelves lined the walls immediately to the left and right, full of books…thick books, with writing on the spines in a variety of languages. Winter had never seen books as old as some of these, not even in the unused back areas of the Tishbe library.

In contrast to the ancient library, flat paneled monitors and a variety of futuristic devices Winter had never seen before covered the back wall. A command center desk sat beneath the monitors and a single leather office chair could turn and roll from the command center to the polished desk in the middle of the room. The tidy executive desk displayed only minimal office supplies, and two wingback chairs waited in front of it.

Winter eased around the desk, searching for file drawers, and found some beneath the command center. Each set of file drawers had a different label, most with random words she didn't understand…codes of some sort. The third one on the right bore the label "Sandy." She immediately reached for it and drew it halfway open when a ping in her mind redirected her attention to the drawer next to it. "Project R6." The urgency that coursed through her demanded this drawer be opened first.

Winter glanced up again at the cracked door, holding her breath, and listened. Satisfied she was still alone, she eased open the drawer and began pulling out files. The first folder, labeled "Distribution Points," contained a collection of maps. Winter spread them out upon the command center surface and quickly perused each, mumbling to herself as she tried to work the puzzle.

Each map had a single point in the middle, with concentric circles drawn around it. Within each circle were numbers, increasing exponentially as the circles grew. At the bottom right of each map she discovered another number, larger than all the others, labeled,

"Estimated Casualties."

Winter sucked in her breath and held it, glancing back up at the door, thinking she had heard a thud down the hall. After listening for a few tense seconds, she went back to the documents.

With the maps, she found a small bound document that turned out to be some kind of scientific paper. Winter tried to scan the first page, but the terminology flew so far over her head she couldn't make sense of anything. At the top of the first page she found a summary sentence that read, "Trial report of long-term and short-term exposure to super-concentrated *Nymphaea Caerulea* infused *Phencyclidine*, genetically edited with CRISPR into *Enterovirus D68 (EV-D68)* administered in aerosol form upon chimpanzees (*P. Troglodytes*)."

"What in the…" she whispered. She thumbed through a couple of pages of it, but still couldn't make any sense of it.

Another, separate document, just two pages long, stapled and shoved into the larger study, had the header "Experiment WAM." She skimmed a little bit of the tiny print. It was obviously a document about a human trial of the drug named in the larger document, but in liquid form on someone simply named Subject WAM. Her skin became clammy as she realized she already knew some of the details. Then with a jolt as if she had been popped by static electricity, Winter recognized WAM as her own initials.

It only took a moment for the initial shock and the clamminess to dissipate, but as it did hot anger filled the void. She remembered, if only as remembering a dream, that moment making out with Peter that almost ruined everything. She remembered vividly the aftermath and the confusion of not knowing why she had done such a thing.

Winter opened her duffel bag so she could shove the documents safely in. Then she went back to the drawer to look for more.

A faint shadow filled the room as if all lights dimmed at once. The hairs rose on Winter's arms.

"Do you really think you could come into my house and peruse my things without me knowing?"

The cold, seething voice washed over her like an icy wave. She straightened, heart pounding, and turned.

"Xaphan…" she breathed.

Xaphan blocked the door, arms crossed and eyes narrowed.

24

Four Years Ago

Stacy plopped down in front of Winter at lunch the Monday after Winter had gone out with Michael. She wrinkled her forehead and her lips paled from pursing so hard.

"Something on your mind?" Winter asked.

Stacy stared at her lunch tray and pursed her lips even harder.

"Look, my class is leaving soon, so if you want to talk…"

"I'm having some friends over this weekend. Want to come?"

Winter shook her head. "I can't. I've got plans."

Stacy leaned toward her as if she had expected Winter's answer and already had a planned response. "Why is it you're willing to hang out with Claire's old friends, but you won't give my friends a chance?"

Winter frowned. "Claire's friends happen to be my friends too."

"Yeah, but why? What makes them so much better? And I want an honest answer for once."

"They understand me and they don't judge me," Winter said.

"Are you saying my friends are judgmental? Of all the

hypocritical…"

"Drop it, Stacy," Winter sneered.

"Is it because my friends were Ryan's friends too? Because of Daniel?"

"I said drop it!"

"You can't run away from life, Winter! You're making a mistake!"

Winter pounded her fist on the table. "I'm not running away from things! You just don't get it, do you? Your friends are not my type, okay?"

Stacy shook her head, but still wouldn't look Winter directly in the eyes. "I know my friends aren't perfect…"

"Aren't perfect? They hate me…and you too, by the way."

"No, they don't." Stacy glared at her. "They don't hate either of us. We're just different, and they're not sure how to process that. But that doesn't make them bad people."

"You asked me to give them a chance and I did. They failed spectacularly."

"Maybe if you just give them some time…"

"Time to what? Learn to tolerate me? How much time have you given them?"

"It doesn't matter!"

"I don't want to just be tolerated!" Winter shouted.

Stacy's eyes widened and she took a deep breath before speaking. "Your new friends are the ones who got Claire involved in drugs and witchcraft, the very same witchcraft that drove Alison crazy. Have you forgotten that? Or have you forgiven your new friends for the role they played in the crash? Nobody's perfect…not even your new friends."

"At least they're better than yours," Winter said through clenched teeth.

Stacy shook her head. "You don't get it, do you? It's not really about them."

"Then what is it?"

"It's all real, Winter. What people keep telling you about God...it's real. Maybe some of these friends of mine don't really believe that, maybe they really are jerks. But that doesn't change the fact that God isn't. And I go to church because that's the only place I can go to get *real* truth."

"He may be real for you, but I don't want it."

"So you want that other stuff? The magic?"

"Why do you always have to get involved? Why do you always have to fix things? Maybe I just don't want your way...maybe I don't want your God. Maybe it's time you started accepting me for who I am instead of trying to change me into another Christian clone."

"Winter..."

"I don't want your religion and I don't want your God. For the record I don't want witchcraft either, but at least these friends accept me for who I am and aren't trying to change me."

"But I'm your friend, too. I just want to help."

"Really? When was the last time your help didn't have anything to do with you or your God? When was the last time you actually made an effort to care about something I care about? You're selfish and judgmental just like the rest of the Christians, and the only reason you call yourself my friend is so you can convert me."

"That's not what I'm doing! I'm just trying to help you! Everyone believes something. And the more you're around something, the more it influences you...the more you change."

"Well, maybe this is the better of the two options."

"Is it? When has this witchcraft stuff ever done anything good for you? What have you lost because of it?"

Winter slammed her hands on the table. "Shut up!"

Stacy stared at her, tight-lipped. "You know I'm right."

"No! You're wrong! God did those things to me!" Fire spread through Winter's cheeks.

"It's so easy for you to take credit for the good things and blame God for the bad. Maybe it's time you gave credit to God for the good and blamed yourself for screwing everything else up."

Winter jumped up and leaned over the table toward her, trembling throughout her entire body.

Stacy shook her head, her face softening. "You don't have to do this. You don't have to *be* this."

"How would you know?" Winter seethed.

"Because I've seen the truth."

Winter grunted so forcefully it escaped like a growl. She snatched her backpack from the floor, left her tray on the table, and stomped away.

25

Present Day

Winter couldn't help staring into the dark void of Xaphan's eyes...eyes not quite human, eyes more monster and death than anything natural found on the earth. She held up her hands in reflex. Her mind raced, the nudges so strong and so fast that she couldn't fully process the actual moments, much less the upcoming moments.

This was it. She should stop him now...put an end to everything like she had planned. But the nudges told her otherwise. The information she had found was more important. Stopping Xaphan was meant to happen later. For now, the nudges told her to escape.

All the heat leached out of the air, replaced by the familiar sensation of evil she had come to associate with Xaphan, and now fully realized as the presence of demons swirling around her, clawing at her as if to rip the flesh from her bones.

She opened her mouth to speak, to get information from him, to do anything to give the nudges more time to sort out the cacophony and the overload that berated her mind, to give her a clear path of what to do next. Somewhere behind Xaphan, she heard the faint cries of guards, the rushing of feet, some sort of alarm, but more than that she could feel the surge of all the evil at Xaphan's disposal rushing to join in the slaughter of the Prophetess.

Still the nudges streamed into her head, faster, stronger, thicker, pulsing with her heartbeat. She realized she didn't have to understand it…she just had to surrender to it.

"Wait…" she managed to croak at Xaphan. Just a little more time, a little more data, a little less of her own hero complex.

"No more waiting," he sneered. He reached to his back waist in a blur of muscle movement too fast to be human. When his hand came back into view, it gripped the black metal of a gun.

Something clicked inside Winter, like the sudden onset of lock tumblers releasing into their open positions. With that click, time screeched to a crawl as it had done only twice before, the night she pulled Kaci from in front of the train, and the day of the campus bombing when she saved Kaci from being kidnapped. Now time did not stand still to save Kaci, it stood still for survival, for escaping the hellish hole Winter had climbed into.

Inching forward, making seconds out of milliseconds, Xaphan slowly, predictably raised the gun. As he did, the white mist Winter had come to expect in these moments outside of time materialized…the servants of the nudges, the substance to the whispers, swirling around her and creating a pocket of light amidst the inky claws visible now to Winter and lashing out for her soul. The white swirl spun faster, stronger, feeding her time, feeding her knowledge, feeding her infinity…all still too much to contain, stretching her skin like an over-inflated balloon.

Winter gave in. She stopped trying to grasp and understand what she had to do next and simply watched as the white swirl swelled faster, stronger, louder, deeper, thicker. It drowned out the snarls of the demons, eclipsing the darkness like a spotlight, unimpeded by the breach in time, defying infinity with its speed.

The gun leveled at Winter, and a cosmic explosion blasted

through the room. The white swirl burst out in all directions, knocking back the demons, tossing them through space and time. Winter no longer heard the whispers, no longer felt the constant feed of foreknowledge, but also no longer heard the demonic snarls. The void of sound pressed against her ears, and silence filled the room as Winter and Xaphan faced each other spiritually alone in the room.

Time restored. Xaphan's face twisted with confusion and a flash of fear passed behind his eyes. In that moment, the gun wavered. In that moment, Winter acted.

In one quick motion, she snatched the duffel bag from the desk and slung it at him. As he flinched away, Winter vaulted over the desk, grabbed his wrist with her right hand, spun against his body, and shoved her left elbow into his face.

Xaphan's grip on the gun loosened, but he didn't drop it. Winter couldn't let up. She had faced Xaphan physically once before, and once he regained composure she would have no chance.

Pulling his gun hand forward, she continued the twisting momentum and kept him off balance until they had spun, trading places, with his back now inside the room and Winter facing the hall. Another tug forward on his gun arm brought him leaning almost on her back, and then an immediate release of his arm, a shoulder into his chest, sent him stumbling back a step. He tried to bring the gun around, but Winter had already connected her foot to his chin in a sidekick that sent him sprawling backward onto his own desk.

With that, she snatched up the duffel bag and grabbed the door, knowing that for the first time it would lock when she needed rather than unlocking. It clicked a heartbeat before Xaphan slammed against it. He hurled curses at her through the door and beat at the doorknob, but the lock held. When bullets punctured the door, Winter ran, following what little she deciphered from the nudges, deep into Xaphan's underground complex.

The hall teed a few yards further in and she immediately turned right, pushing herself to run faster. She passed several more long halls in both directions. How big was this place?

The sounds of pursuit grew louder. Shots echoed from behind. The main hall turned and she found herself facing a door with an electronic keypad. Without thinking, her fingers flew over the numbers, the light on the pad blinked green, and she rushed out. She made to run again and banged her foot on the first step of a set of carpeted stairs. As she fell forward, she twisted to make sure the door had closed behind her, landing on the click lighter in her back pocket.

Winter jerked out the lighter and stood. Then she ignited it and shoved the flaming tip into the carpet of the stairs. "Come on, come on," she muttered as the gentle flame licked the synthetic fibers. The strands began to smoke and melt, and as the top layer peeled away a small flicker of self-sustaining flame appeared.

Winter pocketed the lighter and glanced back at the door. The thumping footsteps were close. Leaving the growing flame behind, she lept up the stairs three at a time. She estimated climbing maybe a floor and a half before finding a landing and another door with an electronic keypad. As her fingers flew over the numbers, she heard the door below her open, shouts, and the snarling of dogs. She glanced back, surprised to find half the stairs blazing with an angry fire. The guards hesitated, and the dogs shied away. One guard spotted her and leveled his gun. As Winter slung the door open, bullets ricocheted off the frame.

She didn't slow down, despite the surprise of crashing into thick foliage. She had done it…escaped through Xaphan's secret tunnel she wasn't even sure existed when she first arrived.

Glancing back at the mansion, she found that the tunnel had exited more to the back than she needed, so she adjusted her angle toward where she hoped her car would be. Bare branches scrapped at her face as she barely dodged trees that lept out at her in the darkness. After nearly tripping, she had to keep her running feet high off the ground to avoid entanglements in brambles or roots. The odd silence behind her gave her hope that perhaps she had finally managed to put some distance between her and the guards. She slowed to make sure, turning to peer back into the forest. Orange flickering light glowed where the mansion should be.

A voice moaned through the still night air, pressing in on her head. Winter brought her hands up to cover her ears. Then the voice formed a word, unnaturally loud, yet a whisper in her mind. "Winter…"

Winter's heart thumped and the sweat on her back and arms ran cold.

"Are you leaving already, Winter?" It was the voice of the Wretch. Despite having only encountered the demon once before, she couldn't mistake the sweet cooing. Images of the pale wet skin and long white hair covering the naked demon flashed behind Winter's clenched eyes. She shook her head clear and turned to run again.

Moments later, she burst through the edge of the trees and skidded to a halt at the precipice of a cliff. She eased to the ledge and peered over, the bottom more than fifty feet below. A low fog rolled across the land below, almost up to the bottom of the cliff. Through the trees ahead, she spotted headlights approaching and knew the road was near. If she had run in the direction she thought she had, that meant she had found this same cliff coming in and her car shouldn't be far away.

She had to get down now.

A screech behind her made her turn, and her heart sank. The glowing figure of a beautiful woman with long, flowing hair glided through the forest. Outlying shadows deepened with finger-like tendrils creeping toward Winter. Further away in both directions, Winter heard the baying of dogs, which meant the guards still pursued despite the fire and had now split to cut off her escape. Even if she thought she could make it to a gentler descent before the guards and dogs cut her off, the demonic tendrils already surrounded her on either side. She could stand her ground like she did at the train yard, but the documents in her bag were far too important to risk another confrontation.

Winter looked back at the cliff, and then turned a complete circle, looking for anything, any inspiration, any way to escape. The only way out was down...Could she make that high of a jump? She shook her head, staring at the tops of the trees nearly eye level with her. She might survive, but she would never walk away.

A cluster of colors glimmered in the faint moonlight from a branch just a few feet away, like strangely shaped and colored fruit. The back of her mind pinged and she took two quick steps over.

Balloons. Old, deflated balloons. Winter inhaled sharply as she studied them, and then grabbed them with both hands, pulling to find the ribbons. She traced the ribbons down to the bottom and found her rope, exactly as she had tied it months ago.

Winter slipped two fingers into the loop of ribbon and yanked as hard as she could, the ribbon digging into her skin, until it popped and dropped the rope onto the ground. She snatched it up and pulled an end free. Then she wrapped it around the nearest tree, securing it with a quick square knot she hoped would hold.

The sound of the pursuers continued to grow louder, dogs snarling, and shouts as the men followed the edge of the cliff from both directions. The Wretch and shadow tendrils that accompanied it had disappeared, which frightened Winter even more. For all she knew, the demon waited for her at the bottom of the cliff, but she didn't dare look. Instead she clenched her teeth and leaned backward into the rope, and began walking down the cliff face as fast as she dared.

The noise of pursuit in either direction convened at the cliff's edge just above her...now twenty feet away. Shadowy heads peer over, and then a gun shot.

Winter almost let go of the rope, sliding several feet before burning her hands to stop. The rope quivered as a guard climbed down after her and creaked beneath the strain of two bodies. Winter descended recklessly fast. Then her ankles reached for nothing but air. She kicked for more rope, but she had reached the end, still several feet from the ground.

The man above her came fast. Winter wrapped the rope around her left hand and reached for her back pocket with the other for the lighter. Concentrating, she clicked it and set it against the rope just above her hand. It only took a moment for the dry fibers to catch flame, and as they did Winter let go and plunged the last few feet to the ground. She landed hard, falling onto her back. She squinted back up against the sudden brightness of the engulfed rope. The man scrambled for the top as the fire raced upward.

Winter didn't wait to see if the man would make it back up or not. She spun on her knees, found her feet, and jetted into the fog toward the fence.

Why had the Wretch disappeared? Why had Xaphan not pursued her himself? The anxiety of those questions kept the adrenaline pumping, even as she found the fence and quickly located her car and the breach she had cut. Every shadow and every small noise, even though the sounds of pursuit never left the cliff, kept her jumping, expecting Xaphan or the Wretch to materialize.

She sprinted to the car, jumped in and locked the doors. She slammed her hand against the back seat and floorboards just to be sure nothing hid in the darkness. Still, she saw no sign or sound of Xaphan, the Wretch, or any further pursuit from the human guards.

As her car roared to life and she barreled down the road, the rush of adrenaline ebbed away, replaced by the reality of what she had just done…and the sinking dread of what Xaphan might do in return. The only consolation was knowing exactly where she needed to go next. Only one person in the world could help her understand what the medical jargon in the folder meant.

Stacy.

26

Winter headed back the way she came in, toward the interstate on the far side of Mordensfield. Only when she neared the on-ramp did she stop to punch in the address to Stacy's apartment at the University of Williams Ferry…easily a six-hour drive. Once back on the road and pointed in the right direction, she settled the car down to a manageable speed and pulled out her cell.

"*Hello?*" came Stacy's voice thick with sleep.

"Stacy. It's Winter."

A brief pause, and Stacy came back sounding much more alert. "*Are you okay? Do you need help?*"

"I'm fine for now. But I've done something…there could be trouble. I'll explain later. I need you to help me with something."

"*When?*"

"As soon as I get to you. I'm on my way now. I'll be there by morning."

"*What's it about?*"

"Some medical stuff I don't understand. Listen, don't tell anyone I'm coming, ok? There may be people after me right now and I certainly can't go back to my place."

"*Winter…what did you do?*"

Winter wrinkled her nose. "Kind of a long story. I'll tell you when I get there. I just wanted to let you know I was on the way."

"*Should I stay up and wait on you?*"

Winter smiled. "No. Sorry I woke you. I'll see you soon."

"*Yeah. Be careful.*"

"I will." Winter hung up. Then she carefully dialed Graham. "Hey, it's me."

"*It's two in the morning.*"

"Yeah, I know. Listen, I did something pretty serious tonight."

"*What did you do?*"

"Long story. I'm headed away for a while. Can't tell you where. But I need you to check on everyone and let them know to be extra careful, in case Xaphan comes looking for me."

"*That bad, huh?*"

"Very bad. Just be careful. Make sure Ayden knows to keep an extra eye on Summer and Davis. And call my dad for me, will you?"

"*You want me to do this now?*"

"Please. It can't wait."

Graham sighed. "*Why do you have to be so much trouble?*"

"Story of my life…"

"*I'm joking, you know. I'll start calling right away. How long will you be gone?*"

"I don't know. I'll give you updates when I can. If I'm right, I've just made a huge step toward stopping Xaphan."

"*Good. The sooner this is over, the better.*"

"It'll be over soon. I promise." Winter bit her lip, half wishing she hadn't said that and half recognizing she spoke the truth…one way or another. "I'll talk to you soon."

"*Ok,*" said Graham. "*Be careful.*"

"I will."

She hung up and put her concentration on the road. So much

residual adrenaline remained in Winter's body that she didn't think she would ever sleep again. But after another fifteen minutes of monotonous darkness and the metronome-like way the road lines passed, Winter's eyelids began to drop and she could feel the energy draining from her body. Despite the frigid weather outside, she switched her AC from heat to cold and pointed the vents to her face. With loud Christmas music blaring all around, it became a little easier to resist sleep.

Near dawn, Williams Ferry came into sight as an orange glow in the sky ten minutes before she arrived. She checked her rear-view mirror again, found nothing but twilight behind her on the road, and sighed. The GPS led her off the interstate, turning left toward the University of Williams Ferry. Despite the bright street lights lining the road at regular intervals and the safety lights that stood nearby at every house and apartment, a stillness hung over everything…as if the world held its breath in anticipation of what would soon happen. In a wave of paranoia, Winter ignored her mirror and spun in her seat to see if anyone followed. Still nobody.

By the time she arrived on campus, enough sunlight filled the cloudless sky to see every building clearly. She gave Stacy another call. Stacy grunted at her and said she'd meet her outside and then hung up. Winter wondered if she should call Ayden and Summer too…maybe just to make sure they were okay…but resisted with the fear that Xaphan might be able to track her exact location. Graham said he'd handle that, anyway.

Winter drove to the far side of campus, just beyond the official school boundaries, to a large apartment complex. Stacy stood on the sidewalk near the apartment stairs, in fuzzy slippers, a blue robe, and a ponytail. Winter parked, snatched up her duffel, and walked quickly to her.

Stacy smiled and met her halfway. "Hey!" They hugged each other tight.

"Hey," said Winter.

Stacy turned to lead her toward the stairs. "I hope you're not planning on getting started right away. I'm not awake enough for that. You kept me up most of the night."

"Yeah…sorry. I'm not awake enough either. Maybe after a nap."

"Take my bed. I'll doze on the couch. By the time you wake up, my roommate will be away at work and we can talk about whatever you want." Stacy opened the apartment door. "Welcome home."

Winter didn't wake until lunchtime. After showering, she found Stacy sitting on the couch, watching TV and eating.

"Don't you have class?" Winter asked.

"It's Saturday."

"Oh."

"There's food in the kitchen. Help yourself."

"Thanks."

As Winter made a sandwich, Stacy came over to sit at the table. "So what kind of trouble are you in, anyway?"

"Hold on," Winter said as she put her sandwich on the table and jogged to her duffel in Stacy's room. She retrieved Xaphan's folder and came back. "Remember the Satanic priest I told you about?"

"Of course," Stacy said. "Not exactly something I'd forget…especially finding out my friend from high school is a prophet."

"Prophetess. Anyway, things have gotten pretty bad. I know I need to stop him, and soon. I tracked down where he lived…"

Stacy gulped. "You what?"

"And I broke in. I found this folder and escaped, but not before burning down his house."

"You burned down his house?"

Winter flashed a sheepish grin. "Yeah…"

"So *big* trouble then. Do you think he'd come here looking for you?"

Winter shook her head. "I don't know. I think he has the resources to find me wherever I go. But I'm not sure he knows about you."

"Well," said Stacy. "You can stay here as long as you need to."

"Thanks. That means a lot. I'm not sure I have any other place to go. If I go anywhere, even my dad's, he'll find me and I'll be putting others in danger. If nothing else, I need to keep his attention off of everyone and on me. I promise, if I even think he's found me here, I'll disappear overnight."

"Maybe it won't come to that. You wanted my help with something?"

Winter slid the folder in front of her. "I need to know what this means."

As Winter ate, Stacy took the folder of maps and flipped through them with a frown. Then she pulled out the spiral bound document and stared a long time at the first page. She slid out the separate stapled document and seemed to read it all the way through. Putting it aside with the maps, she went back to the spiral bound document and began slowly going through each page.

As the minutes ticked by, Winter fought not to bounce in her chair. The adrenaline returned and she could barely keep from shouting at Stacy. Finally she gave into an impatient, "Well?"

Stacy took a deep breath but didn't answer. She thumbed through the final pages and leaned back away from the document, then ran her hand through her hair, sighed, and rubbed the bridge of her nose.

"Well?" Winter asked again.

"There's a lot there that's over my head. I'm just a pre-med student, after all."

"But you understand some of it?"

She nodded. "Enough, I think."

"What is it?"

Stacy leaned forward. "Everything in the folder, the two reports and the maps, are all part of the same study. It all has to do with something called Project R6." She opened the spiral document and pointed to the title.

Winter read it again. *Trial report of long-term and short-term exposure to super-concentrated Nymphaea Caerulea infused Phencyclidine, genetically edited with CRISPR into Enterovirus D68 (EV-D68) administered in aerosol form upon chimpanzees (P. Troglodytes).* While Winter read, Stacy fiddled with her phone.

"Phencyclidine is a drug called PCP. You've heard of it?" Stacy asked.

Winter nodded. "I've heard of it."

"Highly addictive and very dangerous. It's a hallucinogen. This…" She pointed to *Nymphaea Caerulea.* "…is this." Stacy held her phone out to Winter, a search window open. "The Blue Lotus plant. Also a hallucinogen and a sedative. Both affect the brain in different ways. I can't imagine what these two ingredients might produce when combined with each other, but it isn't good. It could cause brain damage or a stroke. That's what this study was about, long-term and short-term exposure to a super-concentrated mixture of this stuff. From what I gathered, short-term exposure produced extreme hallucinations and sometimes paranoia, followed by a sudden onset of unconsciousness. Long-term exposure found that the hallucinations and paranoia grew stronger, more intense, and lasted for a longer period of time. The unconsciousness did the same thing, until it got to the point where the chimp just didn't wake up."

"It died?"

Stacy nodded. "It looks like they were looking for a lethal dosage."

"What's all this mean?" Winter pointed to the last half of the title. "Enterovirus. I've heard of that."

"That's what's so disturbing. Enterovirus is one of the most contagious viruses around. Everyone gets them occasionally, and they're not really a big deal. Usually it's spread through fluid contact. But what they've done here is genetically edit the virus with this...*poison*. I don't know how, like I said, this is way beyond premed stuff. But if they made it work then they've engineered a virus as contagious as enterovirus, but with the lethal effects of these combined drugs."

"Seriously? And it says aerosol...so that means it spreads through the air, right?"

"Looks like it."

Winter's blood ran cold. "So the maps..."

"Distribution points," Stacy said. "Estimated casualties. It doesn't look like the virus can self-replicate, so Xaphan is planning on releasing this stuff in every major city across the world. His estimated casualties? About a third of the worldwide population. And if this virus is as deadly as it appears, is as easily contracted as enterovirus, and really is airborne, there's nothing to prevent it from killing everyone who comes in contact with it."

"*The answer could change the world...or end it...*" Winter mumbled.

"What?"

Winter shook her head. "Nothing. Just something one of my old professors said to me before he died." She took a deep breath. "What about that?"

Stacy frowned at the smaller stapled document. "You know what that is, don't you?"

Winter had a sinking feeling she did. And with that sinking came the blurred memories of her stolen moment with Peter last year. "They did drug me last year, didn't they?"

Stacy nodded. "They exposed you, in liquid form it seems, and not as potent. But the same virus none-the-less. I assume it was that incident with Peter you told me about. That's the, uh, report of the results. He used you and Peter for a human trial."

Winter shook her head, indignation rising up. She didn't want to see it or admit it, but she knew it was true. The horror of what she did…

"What I don't understand," said Stacy, "is why he would create something like this and not use an existing bio-weapon."

"I remember what it felt like," said Winter. "This drug made me want to do things I would never have considered doing. Could you imagine a whole city under this kind of influence?"

"It would be chaos."

Winter nodded. "He wants to drive the people to anarchy so they destroy themselves. Anyone who survived would die anyway from the drug."

"That's sick," said Stacy.

"But just the kind of thing Xaphan would enjoy."

Stacy shook her head and looked back down at the paper. "There's one more thing. This name…" Stacy pointed to the name *Valeska Makino, MD, PhD,* a name featured prominently beneath the title of the report.

"What about him? He did the research, right?"

"*She* wrote the report, which means she was in charge of the research. She could have had who knows how many people working with her."

"So?"

"So…I've heard the name, and if I'm right…" Stacy tapped at her phone again and then nodded. "I'm right. She's an internationally known geneticist and she's the new president of Tishbe University." She held the search results out for Winter to see.

"What?" Winter shook her head. "I…I…How?"

"She was approved this week, it seems. Unanimously." Stacy pointed to the maps. "And Tishbe University is listed as a distribution point."

Winter worked her mouth, but couldn't find anything to say. Suddenly, the hopelessness of everything crashed on her like the waves of the rising tide. She took a long, deep breath and asked, "What do I do?"

Stacy shook her head. "I was about to ask you the same thing. What do you *think* you should do?"

Winter trembled. She had never felt more frightened in her entire life. "Oh, nothing much I guess. Just, you know…save the world." She gave Stacy an insecure little laugh, and then…

Head. Table.

27

Four Years Ago

It was her eighteenth birthday. Michael had been planning the celebration for months, ever since their first official date when he sketched Winter in his apartment. He bought tickets to a Bleed Like Me concert, a group that Winter often listened to but had never seen. The last time the band came to in Trenton Hills three years ago, her dad wouldn't let her go with her friends.

As far as Winter knew, it would be just her and Michael that night. Her dad still wouldn't go for a concert with a punk-metal Goth band, especially since she'd probably be out most of the night, so she just told him she wanted to spend her birthday night out with some friends and would be staying over at Shannon's house. He had heard her mention Shannon enough times that he simply shrugged and went about his business.

Winter wore her favorite black peasant top, a red plaid skirt that went halfway to her knees, black tights, and knee-high black boots with three-inch heels. She might get cold, even with her black trench coat, but if Michael had to keep her warm, so what? Winter made sure to don all her piercings and took extra time to make her pale makeup and black eyeshadow perfect. She stared at the final result in the mirror, her raven hair perfectly framing her face.

On the bed lay a small duffel bag with a change of clothes and some pajamas. As she zipped it up she smiled. Tonight would be a perfect night.

When Michael arrived to pick her up, Winter double-checked to make sure her dad wasn't paying much attention.

"I'm gone," she said as she came down the stairs, slipping into her coat and sliding her black stocking cap onto her head.

He glanced up briefly from watching TV and nodded.

Winter bit her lip and rushed out the door, checking over her shoulder to see if he watched to make sure she actually left with Shannon. He didn't. She pulled the door closed and jogged down the sidewalk to Michael's waiting car.

"Ready?" he asked as she jumped in and tossed her duffel bag into the back seat.

Her heart fluttered and she blushed. If Michael could see the things she'd been thinking about him… "Let's go."

He grinned as he pulled away.

The Trenton Hills Arena teemed with black-clad teenagers as if someone had kicked a giant Goth anthill. Michael circled the area three times before finding an available place in a parking garage four blocks away. As they walked down the long sidewalk back to the crowds, Michael grabbed her hand and wouldn't let go. She leaned closer to him so their shoulders touched. She didn't even mind that the heels of her knee-high boots rubbed her foot raw.

At almost two hours early, the line already stretched long enough to wrap partly around the building. They joined the queue, and sat on the terrace wall beside the sidewalk.

Winter bumped her shoulder against him, looked up, and smiled.

"What?" he asked, grinning.

"Nothing." She blushed. Part of her just wanted to skip the

concert already…

When the doors finally opened an hour later, the line moved fairly quickly into the arena. Michael pulled her through the crowd in order to get down as close as possible to the stage. There, they sat and talked while the arena slowly filled with other concert goers.

The opening act came on ten minutes before the hour, followed by another act, and then Bleed Like Me finally took the stage. Michael grabbed her hand again and dragged her away from their seats to the mosh pit, where other teens and twenty-somethings gathered to dance at the foot of the stage.

The music raged. The bodies bobbed in time. Winter just let herself sink into the driving drums and screaming guitar. She drank in the lyrics, singing the ones she knew, humming the tune of the ones she didn't. The thumping of the beat rattled inside of her, vibrating her organs and competing to be the new heartbeat of her life. Michael handed her a joint and she eagerly inhaled, recognizing the extra bitterness of PCP laced inside of it. She handed it back but he motioned for her to pass it on to the guy next to her, so she did.

The slight buzz from the weed helped engross her into the music, so detached from reality that she didn't even notice Michael had disappeared until he reappeared at her elbow with two cups of beer in his hand. He urged her away from the impassioned crowd for a short break.

Reluctantly, she let him lead her away, taking a beer from his hand and drinking deeply to cloy her thirst. He led her out of the main arena into the outside hall where the music didn't thump quite as loud. She leaned against the wall, almost finishing the beer in another long draft.

With one hand on the wall and the other holding his own beer, he leaned over her, grinning. "It's good to see you completely loosened up."

Winter laughed. "I guess I needed to really unplug. It's been such a long time since I've felt free enough to let myself go." She bit her lower lip and shot him a smoldering look to help him pick up the double meaning.

He shook his head. "You're going to be trouble tonight, aren't you?"

She nodded and grabbed the back of his neck with her free hand to pull him down for a long, deep kiss. When she finally let him go, she finished off her beer and handed him the cup.

"I've had enough of the concert," she said.

"Are you sure?"

She stepped toward him and ran a finger down his cheek. "Yes. Let's go back to your place for a while." She simpered with big eyes and leaned close, taunting him with her lips.

"For how long?" he whispered.

"All night."

"Are you sure you want to sleep over?"

She nodded. "I'm eighteen now. I can do whatever I want. And I don't plan on sleeping." Finally, she placed her mouth so gently on his and pressed her body against him so intentionally, he could in no way mistake her meaning.

After meeting with Stacy's roommate, a Jamaican girl named Jina, and discussing the situation, Winter called Graham to give him an update.

"How long are you going to stay?" he asked.

"I don't know," Winter said. "At least until I can figure out what to do next."

"You could come here. I...We would be glad to have you."

"No. I don't want to give away your safe house. That's probably the last place I should go, just in case."

"Do you trust Stacy?"

"With my life."

"And her roommate?"

"I don't know. But she's not even from the country. They've been roommates since freshman year. It's unlikely she's hiding anything."

"Regardless, just be careful what you say around her. If they got to Summer, then they could have gotten to her in the hopes you might show up one day."

"Yeah. Maybe. I'll be careful, I promise. Are you sure everything is okay with Summer? Davis and Ayden?"

"Summer and Davis have officially set a date."

"Really? Why didn't she tell me?"

"You haven't exactly been very accessible."

A pang of guilt rippled through her abdomen. "I know."

"Davis is walking at the end of this term. I understand he's been offered a job there in Cherithville with a company that has another office near New Port. Summer graduates in the spring, so I think their plans are to move back to Summer's hometown and get married over the summer."

"Sounds nice."

"I also get the impression that Ayden is a little lonely."

Another pang of guilt.

"But otherwise everything has been fine for them. They've just been going to school like normal. Since Kaci's parents came and cleared out Kaci and Peter's apartment, Ayden has been spending a lot of time with Summer. I think she stays in Summer's room most nights."

"Probably not a bad idea."

"Listen, do you want me to get the rest of your things and take it all to Trenton Hills? With you gone, Kaci moved out, and Ayden crashing with Summer, there's no sense keeping an empty apartment."

"Maybe. Talk to Ayden again and see what she thinks. But, you're right. It's unlikely I'll be coming back. Not now."

Graham became quiet for a moment. "Are you sure you don't want my help?"

"I'm sure. I have to do this alone."

"No, you don't."

Winter sighed. "If I need you, I'll call. Promise."

"You'd better."

Winter agreed to stay with Stacy, at least until Winter's birthday. Every day she studied the contents of the folder, hoping to get a better handle on what to do next. She slept on the couch and pitched in as much as she could, since she wasn't much help with the bills. While Stacy and Jina crammed for finals, Winter took it upon herself to keep the apartment clean and to cook most evenings.

Despite Winter's fears, Xaphan didn't seem to be retaliating immediately. A part of her felt relieved. Another part of her took it for an even worse sign than if he'd struck out immediately. She checked in with Graham every day, just in case. By the end of the second week their phone calls lasted an hour or more, with less than five minutes consisting of updates.

As December passed and Winter still didn't know what to do next, she longed to go home and decided to do so immediately after her birthday. Stacy planned a fun birthday celebration…something Winter had not had in a long time. Dinner and a movie turned into a late game night. Despite not going to bed until well after midnight, Winter was glad she delayed and thankful for the days she had to reconnect with Stacy.

The morning after her birthday, Winter began the long drive back to Trenton Hills to do the rest of her waiting in the comfort of her old bedroom. As she parked that evening next to her dad's truck, she sighed, feeling that maybe here she could relax, clear her head, and make a plan. Steve helped her bring her things in and, to her surprise, had dinner waiting.

Christmas morning, Winter awoke early and let her dad sleep in. She took the flowers out of the fridge and headed toward the cemetery during the cold dawn, taking the extra alone time and stillness of the cemetery as an opportunity to do some deep thinking. As she walked toward her mom's grave, the clouds broke and a cold wind whipped through the cemetery. Winter tugged at her hat and tucked her chin. When she reached the tombstone, she leaned forward to slide the roses into the vase and then stood back to reread the words inscribed on the marble and stare at her mother's picture.

The quiet did help. She still didn't know exactly what to do next, but at least she felt good about being home for a little while. Eventually Xaphan would resurface, and when he did she would be ready. It could take months or it could happen right...

Thunder washed over her. Clouds roiled across the sky from all directions at once, colliding together directly above her. The ground shook and Winter nearly lost her balance. A tree sapling shot out of the ground just in front of her mother's tombstone. It climbed ever higher, growing and sprouting as if on fast-forward. Winter scrambled backward as the branches flung out toward her. In just a few moments it towered over lonely monuments, and Winter recognized it...a tree she knew more than any other. The Ancient.

The Ancient twisted gently at the trunk, flinging its branches to either side like a rattle drum. Everything held its breath, waiting to see what the Ancient might decree when it finally stopped its dance, the gentle swishing of the leaves as the branches pulled through the air now the only sound. Above the tree, the clouds changed shade-by-shade from gray to red, as if directed by an invisible light source shining up from beneath the tree. As the clouds changed, so did the atmospheric filter through which Winter viewed the world, plunging all colors into sepia and drawing sharp contrast lines with each shadow.

Suddenly the Ancient stopped. Silence filled the cemetery like an instantaneous onset of deafness. Winter turned to scan the area for any sign, anything that might help her understand. Was it Xaphan? Here? Was it a warning?

As she completed the circle and turned back to the Ancient, Davis and Summer sat on the ground, back to back at the base of the tree. They looked up at her, pleading with their eyes. Winter tried to cry out to them, but her voice could not penetrate the thick silence. She tried to run to them, but her feet clung to the ground as if her shoes had grown roots.

Then the ground shook again, more violently than before, an earthquake that made everything vibrate and bend like something out of a surreal children's book. A crack opened in the ground on the far side of the cemetery. It shot toward the Ancient, toward Davis and Summer, like the earth itself unzipped.

Before Winter could react, before she fully understood what happened, the earth swallowed Davis, Summer, and the Ancient.

Winter blinked. And in the space of the blink, the cemetery returned to normal. Nothing had changed.

Winter spun to dash back to her car, her heart pounding in her chest. The vision could mean only one thing…As she sped out of the cemetery, she called her dad.

"Hey," he answered. "I didn't realize you were gone."

"Dad, listen. Something's wrong."

"What do you mean?"

"I have to get back to Tishbe immediately. Davis and Summer are in trouble. I'm sorry."

"What's going on?"

"I'm not sure. But I'll explain more when I find out. I need you to get my things, please. I'll swing by as I'm headed out. Just shove it all into my duffel," Winter said.

"Is it that bad?"

Winter took a deep breath. "I think so."

"I'll meet you at the curb then."

He hung up and Winter concentrated on getting home as quickly as possible. As she turned the last corner, Steve waited by the road, duffel bag in hand. She pulled up beside him and popped her trunk. As he put the bag in, she climbed out.

"I'm sorry to ruin Christmas."

"Hey, after what you've told me, I'm just glad I got to spend a little time with you."

She hugged him tight. "I love you."

"I love you, too." He held out a storage container toward her. "Pizza. For the road. Sorry I had to microwave it. I know it's not as good that way, but you didn't give me much time."

Winter grinned as she took it and climbed back into her running car. "Thanks, Dad."

"Be careful."

"You know me…" Winter gave him one last smile, slammed her door shut, and sped off.

29

Winter drove as fast as she dared and reached Cherithville by three that afternoon. On the way, she tried calling Ayden, Summer, and Davis, but no one answered. She made a slight detour before heading to campus and went by the apartment looking for Ayden. Even though Ayden's car was missing, Winter unlocked the door and burst in.

"Ayden?" No answer. She checked Ayden's room and found that most of her clothes were gone. The apartment appeared to have not been lived in for weeks.

Winter swore and ran back out to her car. Something wasn't right. She sped toward campus and tried calling Summer and Davis again, but still no answer.

The campus was deserted except for a few random cars belonging to people staying through the holidays. She parked in the closest spot she could find near the Meadow and dashed for the Ancient. As she stood before the tree, trying to recreate her cemetery vision, she pivoted to scan every building adjacent to the Meadow for any clue or sign of Davis and Summer…anything to tell her what

Xaphan might be doing. Everything looked normal. No one even glanced in her direction. The only thing out of the ordinary was the machinery parked by the debris from the collapsed administration building.

A gentle breeze rocked the Ancient, twisting it in a miniature replication of her vision. The cold air bit against Winter's face. Like a magnet she slowly angled left, following an imaginary line that traced where the crack in the earth opened up in her vision. As she faced the English building, the color drained from the world until only the English building retained its hues. She bolted forward, across the sidewalk, and up the steps. Just inside the doors, a sign stood to one side that said, "Administrative Offices. Fifth floor."

That's when she remembered the name on the file...the new President of the university and a cohort of Xaphan's plan. That meant Davis and Summer might be up there. With her.

Winter sprinted past the sign and turned out of the foyer onto the long hall. There she saw a lady with glasses and a power suit walking toward her as if to exit. Winter skidded to a halt, heart pounding. The lady stopped too, and they both stared at each other in silence.

Winter knew immediately that she faced the new president, Dr. Makino. She had seen the woman before...that ageless face, that long hair. Though the person in front of her appeared thoroughly human with slightly different features, Winter clearly recognized the demon within. What Winter couldn't tell was just how much humanity of the woman who used to be Dr. Makino had not been consumed.

"Mavka..." Winter said, her voice echoing across the wooden hall floor.

The woman smiled. "Good to see you again." She spun to exit out of a side door instead.

Winter clenched her teeth and jetted toward her. The pounding of her feet reverberated from the walls. Just before Winter reached her, Dr. Makino glanced over her shoulder. An invisible hand slammed into Winter and she flew through the air to be pinned against the wall. Winter growled as the full spiritual power of God fell upon her. In a bright flash, the unseen force released her and Dr. Makino stumbled backward.

Winter slid to the floor, planted her feet, and clenched her fists. "I won't let you escape."

Dr. Makino did the same, and her flesh rippled as the human exterior peeled away to reveal the chosen form of the demon Mavka, long wet hair draped over her naked body. Mavka lowered her chin and glared at Winter with her solid white eyes. "You cannot stop me and save your friends at the same time," she cooed.

"Try me," Winter hissed.

"The bomb has a timer on it, and you don't know how much is left. Are you willing to risk it?"

"I have enough time for this."

"Are you sure?" Mavka smiled and raised an eyebrow. Then she backed away. "They could have mere seconds. If you waste your time on me, you'll kill them and yourself. As for me? This woman's body may die, but I'll be perfectly fine."

"You're lying!"

"Then by all means," Mavka shouted, "stop me!" She spun and glided away, hovering just above the ground, as fast as if she were running, laughing the whole time.

Winter swore under her breath and turned for the nearest stairs at the center of the building. She ran up, taking the steps two at a time. At the landing of the top floor, she paused to catch her breath, trying to listen for voices in the hall. Only silence greeted her. What if Mavka told her the truth? With a twinge of panic, Winter searched the wall for a fire alarm. She found one, just across the hall from where she stood at the top of the stair, and took a giant step forward, reached out, and pulled the switch.

The clanging of bells filled the hall, pressing in on her eardrums. Winter glanced to either side, waiting for a nudge in the right direction, but none came. She walked toward the side of the building where Mavka had been below, hoping that maybe Mavka had come from there. She moved quickly, forcing herself to remain calm enough to notice any clues that might point to Davis and Summer. She let her mind clear and took deep breaths to concentrate on her internal spiritual compass. The more she calmed, the more she could feel Davis and Summer like a magnetic presence deeper in the building.

She slowed to let the compass draw her in the right direction without accidentally missing something. As she reached the middle of the wing, she came to the largest complex of offices on the whole floor. That's when she realized she had been here before. Not in a premonition...but literally, physically. Winter knew now exactly where to go and exactly where to find Davis and Summer.

A little in and to the left, a hallway led to three offices and a restroom. Winter jogged to the last office and eased through the cracked door, looking carefully for attached explosives. Now inside Dr. Makino's office, what Winter believed to be an old security office, Winter moved across the room to the closet. Summer and Davis were locked inside. The door handle had been sheared off from this side. Whispers told her it was a red herring to get her to pry the door open in a hasty attempt to rescue her friends, which would set off the bomb that sat just on the inside of the door with them. She pulled her hands away from the door and knelt instead.

"Summer, Davis...It's me," she shouted to cut through the fire alarm.

Muffled panic came from within.

"I'm going to get you out, but I need your help. First, whatever you do, do *not* try to open the door."

More panicked muffles. Winter shook her head.

"Listen, just try to calm down. We need to communicate. Grunt once if you understand, twice if you can't hear me good enough."

One grunt from each of them.

"Good," said Winter. "Do not open the door. There's a bomb attached to it."

One grunt.

"You're probably handcuffed. In the back-right corner, just beneath the carpet, you'll find a key. Get it and release yourself. Tell me when you're done."

Summer cried now, still muffled. Winter heard shuffling inside. Several minutes ticked by. Then finally, Summer's crying erupted with full voice and Davis yelled out, "Done. How do we get out of here?"

Winter's heart pounded. "I need you to feel gently around the vent in the door and make sure there are no wires or anything touching it or attached to it."

A moment later, Davis said, "Nothing. I think it's higher up either around the top of the door or the handle."

"Good." Winter sighed. "Grab the edge of the vent and pull. It should open up." Winter did the same thing on her side. The sticky putty she had put there months ago in place of the screws stretched and popped. As she set her half to the side, Davis did the same and urged Summer through. Summer scrambled out, red-faced and makeup-streaked. By the time Davis crawled out, firefighters entered.

"Is everyone okay?" asked the first man.

Winter shook her head as she helped Summer and Davis to their feet. "I think there's a bomb on the back of this door."

The man's eyes widened, and he began speaking quickly into his radio.

Winter urged Summer and Davis past the firefighters and into the hall. A few asked if they were okay or needed help. Winter shook her head and kept them moving. By the time they reached the stairs, the firefighters were in full bomb-mode and were urging them out of the building.

Finally outside, more sirens wailed in the distance. Winter kept them moving quickly until they reached the car, before anyone thought to stop them.

As Summer and Davis sat huddled in the back seat, Winter turned to them. "I'm sorry," she said. "But there's no going back now." She put the car into gear and floored it away from campus.

30

Four Years Ago

Christmas morning, Winter awoke still elated over the night of her birthday. She couldn't believe she'd gotten away with it and couldn't wait to see Michael again. If she could arrange it she might try to go out with him that very night, and if she could get away with it again maybe stay over. He had called her every evening after her dad had gone to bed since, but they hadn't had a chance to get back together. Deep inside her chest she ached to see him again, and it nearly drove her crazy.

But it was Christmas morning, and Winter had an obligation to at least give her dad a little of her time. She dressed and went downstairs. For the first time in a long time she found her dad smiling at the stove as he made pancakes.

"Good morning!" he said.

Winter flopped down at the table. "Is something wrong?"

He shook his head. "No. But it's Christmas, isn't it? We can be happy for one day, right?"

Winter forced a smile onto her face. Deep down she didn't want to be there at all...she wanted to be with Michael again. "Sure. I guess. You know, you really don't have to cook."

He laughed. "Don't worry. There's a pizza in the freezer for lunch. I'm just doing breakfast, I promise."

Winter grunted and stood to get a soda out of the fridge. As she opened the refrigerator door, her stomach clenched. A package of roses lay on the bottom shelf.

"Dad? Why are there roses here?" she asked, even though she already knew the answer.

The smile on his face drooped a little. "I thought it would be nice. We took roses last year...maybe we could make it a yearly thing."

Part of Winter wanted to curse at him and punch him in the face. The other part wanted to hug and thank him. She settled for grunting again, grabbed her soda, and then went back to the table.

He eyed her sideways as she sat, then smiled broadly again as he delivered her a plate full of pancakes and an envelope. "Merry Christmas," he said.

Inside the envelope she found a simple gift card and gave her dad a genuine smile this time...small but real. "Thank you."

He sat beside her with his own plate and they ate in relative silence.

Most of the morning they sat around watching Christmas movies on TV. Winter broke away for about an hour to talk with Michael on the phone in her bedroom. She tried to convince him to sneak over that night, but he refused.

After lunch, Winter opened the refrigerator and stared at the roses. She did want to visit her mother's grave again, and maybe this was as good of a time as any. Two years in a row. Maybe it really should become a yearly thing. She pulled the roses out and cradled them in her arms. When she turned, Steve stood at the entrance to the kitchen, keys in hand.

They had no need to say anything. Winter didn't want to say anything. She wanted to exist and let the melancholy of the moment have its way with her. Steve drove to the cemetery and parked. As she opened the door he said, "I'll be visiting my parents."

Winter nodded and walked away.

It felt odd how easily she could remember the path through the headstones to the one that would always tear a hole through her heart. She didn't have to think about it much, only let her feet carry her there. When she first caught a clear view of her mom's headstone, Winter paused and chewed the inside of her cheek. She cast her face to the ground and eased forward until she could see the shadow of the headstone upon the ground. Then she knelt on the cold earth and slowly raised her face to stare into the eyes of her mom in the lacquered photo on the granite surface.

She released her heart to ache. The corners of her eyes stung, but she didn't think she would actually cry this time. She had cried enough last year. Still, a tear fell and rolled down her cheek. Winter studied the rest of the headstone, something she hadn't really done before. The picture of her mom was just below her mom's name written in cursive. Beneath the picture, also etched into the stone, was the Bible verse John 16:22, *"So you have sorrow now, but I will see you again; then you will rejoice, and no one can rob you of that joy."*

She grimaced.

To one side of the headstone stood the small statuette of an angel. To the other, an empty stone vase. Shouldn't the stems of the old roses still be there? Winter shrugged off the thought and placed the new roses in. Then she returned her hands to her lap and stared again at her mom's picture.

What should she do now? How long should she stay?

She glanced around for her dad, but couldn't find him. However, off to her left about fifty yards away she did see someone she recognized. Daniel. He stood before a grave, and Winter knew exactly whose. Suddenly she remembered her prom night with Ryan, and for the first time felt a little guilty about her night with Michael. What would Ryan have thought of her now?

More so than the memory of losing her mom, the thought of Ryan's disapproval, of his sweet voice, stabbed her through the heart so hard she couldn't help but burst into tears.

"Mom, I'm so confused," she whimpered as she turned back to face the picture. "Did I do the right thing? Michael makes me happy, and isn't that good? Why do I still miss Ryan so much? Why can't I just get over him?"

She clenched her eyes and lowered her chin toward her chest. Thinking of Ryan not only made her heart ache, it made her feel polluted inside, as if she had betrayed him on the most intimate levels with Michael. But what was she supposed to do? She couldn't just live alone the rest of her life and not try to move on…

She peeked over at Daniel, who had left the gravestone and already wandered half-way back to his car. She watched him walk the rest of the way before turning back to the picture of her mom.

"What should I do? I can't stop thinking about Ryan, but I don't want to stop seeing Michael. I don't think I *can* stop seeing Michael." She sniffed, not fully realizing she had teared up again. "I think I could love Michael. Doesn't he deserve the same chance I gave Ryan? Maybe this is the way it's supposed to be, right?" She squinted back to the ground. "I really wish I could talk to you now. I miss you so much…" As the tears came freely this time, her voice trailed off. She let the tears flow, feeling a little foolish for doing so. She should be getting over this by now, right? She should be stronger than this.

Winter ground her teeth and closed the door to her heart until the tears subsided. Then she rubbed both eyes dry with the heels of her gloved hands. After taking one last look at her mom's picture, she stood to return to her dad's truck. He already waited for her inside.

31

Present Day

As Summer whimpered in the back seat and Davis comforted her, Winter called Graham.

"Yes?" he answered.

"It's Winter. Listen, there was an incident on campus. I'm bringing Summer and Davis to the cabin."

"What kind of incident?"

"Xaphan got to them. They're okay now, but they can't stay here anymore," Winter said. "I'm bringing them to you."

Silence on the other end. "Are you sure?"

"Yes. Moriah has fallen. I need to get them to you now."

"What about Ayden?"

"I don't know. I've been trying to call all afternoon but she's not answering," said Winter.

"I'll see what I can find out. Do you know how to get here?"

"Text it to me," said Winter as she glanced at Summer and Davis in the rear-view mirror. "How far out is it, anyway?"

"About an hour and a half from Cherithville."

Winter nodded to herself. "See you soon then."

On the outskirts of Cherithville, Winter found a small gas station to stop for fuel and put the cabin's location into her GPS. Davis moved to the front seat while Summer continued to rest in the back.

"I guess this means we can't go back?" Davis asked as they started again.

Winter nodded. "Most likely. I'm sorry. This is all my fault. I shouldn't have gotten you involved."

Davis sighed. "We were always involved. I suppose we should have eventually expected something like this. Any news from Ayden?"

"Not yet. Graham is going to try. Do you think Summer knows anything? Wasn't Ayden staying with Summer some?"

"Most school nights since you left. But I haven't seen her in a couple of weeks. You don't think something bad has happened, do you?"

Winter shrugged. "I would think Xaphan would want us to know. So no news must be good news, right? How did they get you anyway?"

"I don't know," said Davis. "Summer and I had gone out to dinner. I remember leaving the restaurant and parking at Summer's dorm. That's it until I woke up in the closet."

Winter checked on Summer through the mirror. "We'll figure this out, Davis. I promise."

He pursed his lips and nodded.

They arrived at the cabin, which was more of a 1970s era house built in the middle of the woods. It was shortly before five that afternoon and the sun had already reached the horizon, painting it in deep orange. As soon as they drove up and parked beside Kaci's and

Graham's cars, the front door opened and Kaci, Peter, and Graham all stepped out onto the porch.

Summer still slept, but stirred as soon as Winter turned off the car. Davis helped Summer out and Kaci came toward her, belly already larger than Winter expected. Kaci caught Summer up as best she could in a hug. Summer leaned against her and cried.

The other four gathered on the porch.

"Do you have anything?" Graham asked.

Davis shook his head. "We didn't go back. As soon as Winter rescued us, she put us in the car and came here."

"We'll get your stuff as soon as we can," said Winter as she studied Graham.

Graham nodded and his eyes tightened. "If I need to, I'll drive down myself."

"In the meantime," said Peter, "there a general store not far from here. Davis, let me show you around." Peter gave Winter a meaningful raise of his eyebrows and led Davis into the house.

Kaci had taken Summer to a couple of chairs on the porch and they were talking quietly.

Graham motioned with his head for Winter to follow him around the house to the back patio where they could see the sunset more brilliantly. "While you were on the way, Peter and Kaci made plans to talk with them, away from you, just to gauge where they are."

"Do you think they blame me?" Winter asked.

"I'm sure it's not like that. We all knew what we were facing when we each decided to help you. But in a way, none of this would have happened if you hadn't come into their lives."

"That's not true. It would have happened anyway. God sent me here to help."

Graham nodded. "I know. We all know on some level we would all be caught up in what Xaphan is doing, with or without you. But when things go wrong it's easy to forget."

"What about you?" Winter asked.

Graham shrugged. "I knew getting into private security as a profession there might be a few scary moments." He laughed. "Granted, I didn't expect this. But I'm good."

"You're good?"

"Yes. I'm good. If Peter and Kaci weren't in trouble, then I'd never have met you." He stared at her, face blank.

Winter didn't know what to say or how to respond. What did he mean by that? What did she want him to mean? Kaci had hinted at Graham's feelings for her before, but did he still feel that way? Did *she*?

"Well, I'm glad you're here to help," she said and turned away, gazing out into the forest behind the cabin. "What is this place, anyway?"

"A hunting cabin. It belongs to a buddy of mine from police academy. It sits in the middle of five hundred acres, most of it wooded."

"And he just let you stay?"

Graham shrugged. "He owed me a favor. Besides, he lives about a thousand miles away and doesn't use it very often. It's family land so he hangs on to it, but he only comes back during his vacation times. Otherwise he rents it out during the hunting season." He pointed toward a grove of trees. "There's a lake behind those trees. Maybe I'll take you out in the canoe and show you a little more of this place."

"I don't know," said Winter. "I'm not much of a country girl."

He laughed. "Come on. You'll love it."

"Maybe later."

At that moment, Peter walked around the house. He motioned with his head for them to return, and stood waiting at the corner of the house.

"They're shaken up, but they're okay," he told them. "A little rest and time, and they'll be fine."

Winter nodded. "I have a good idea why this happened, and there may be more to come. I need to talk to everyone about it."

"That serious?"

"I don't think it could be any more so."

"Whatever it is," said Graham, "can it wait until morning? Everyone's tired and overwhelmed, especially Davis and Summer. I'm not sure they can handle what you have to say tonight."

Graham and Peter watched her for a moment, both sets of eyes tightened.

Winter finally nodded. "First thing in the morning." She crossed her arms and led the way back to the front of the house, where Kaci waited for them. Summer and Davis had already gone inside.

Kaci smiled at Winter as they approached, and as soon as Winter reached the landing, Kaci embraced her tightly against her baby-belly as the guys went in.

"I've missed you," said Kaci.

"Ditto," said Winter. "How have you been?"

"Everything's been great. My parents drop by every once in a while, and the pregnancy seems to be just fine…at least according to my mom. As long as she felt good about things, we decided not to involve any outside doctors yet. We didn't want to take any chances with *him* still out there."

"I'm sorry it's taking so long. I really wanted you to be free by now."

Kaci shook her head. "Don't apologize. This has been a long battle, practically my whole life, and I don't expect it to end in just a few short months."

"Yeah, but still. You need to be free from all of this."

"I am free," Kaci said, her eyes wide. "He can't hurt me, I hope you know that. God has a plan and it doesn't matter what happens, he's going to make sure that plan takes place. There wouldn't be a prophecy about my baby for nothing."

"I know," said Winter. "I just wish it could be over sooner." She glanced down at Kaci's stomach. "So how much longer do you have?"

Kaci laughed. "I'm only four months along. I'm due about mid-May."

"Are you going to have it here?"

"I don't know where I'll have it," she said with a frightened grimace. "My parents plan to rendezvous with us close to the due date. If need be, my mom can do the delivery I suppose."

"Kaci, you don't need to avoid the hospital altogether. It isn't safe."

Kaci looked to the floor. "I know, I just..." She sighed. "I just don't want him to..."

"I know," said Winter. "He won't get his hands on the baby. I promise. I'll be there. We'll all be there. Nothing will happen. Just make sure you have a safe plan to have this baby. I don't want you to be in the back of the car or anything. You deserve better."

Kaci nodded. "I'll talk to Peter and my mom about it. Maybe we can figure something out."

"If nothing else," said Winter, "leave the state. Go as far away as you can. I know he's followed you all over the country, but he can't follow you that far that quickly."

"Maybe," said Kaci. "We'll talk about it."

They both turned to join Graham and Peter inside. Graham waited for her by the door, and closed it as she entered. Inside on the couch, both Davis and Summer were on the phone. Peter sat nearby, worry on his face.

"What's going on?" Winter asked. "What have you not told me?"

Graham took a deep breath. "I've been trying to contact Ayden since you first told me she was missing. I even tried to pull a GPS signal from her phone. There's been nothing. She hasn't answered or called back."

"Do you think she's in trouble?" Winter asked, surprised at the panic in her voice.

"I don't know. I'll keep trying." He turned to Davis and Summer.

"They're talking to friends of theirs on campus. I think they're using some kind of family emergency as a story. Their friends are going to get the stuff together. Peter and I are going to drive down after dark and get as much as we can."

Winter snatched out her phone and dialed Ayden. As it rang unanswered against her ear, Graham shook his head.

The pit of Winter's stomach sank and she put the unanswered phone away. Graham was right. The rest of the bad news could wait until morning.

Winter called everyone into the den of the lodge immediately after they all awoke and had either breakfast or coffee. As they sat, Winter pulled a chair from the dining table and positioned herself where she could easily see everyone.

"You all need to know exactly what's going on," Winter said. "At the end of October, I tracked down Xaphan's mansion. I managed to get in without being seen and I located his office in an underground bunker."

"Was he there?" asked Graham.

Winter nodded. "We had an incident with one another as I was getting away. And…well, I burned down his house."

"You what?" asked Peter.

"It was an accident…I think. I don't know, it just happened so fast. I lit the fire, but I didn't think it would get out of hand. I thought they'd try to put it out and forget me. Instead they kept after me and let the house burn." Winter faced Davis and Summer. "What happened to you and Summer is because of me. Not just now, but when Xaphan tried to use Summer last year. He knows the names of all my friends." She cast around at everyone. "And now it's obvious that he's going to use anyone he can to get to me…maybe even our families."

"What are we supposed to do then?" asked Summer.

"First, we wait here until we hear from Ayden. I refuse to think she's in trouble. If something had happened to her, I think I would have heard about it by now. Xaphan's not going to do something to draw me out or try to kill me without making sure I know. Which means she's disappeared for a good reason and on her own terms. I hope. Maybe she found out something or maybe they're after her…I don't know. But right now Ayden's out there in the trenches and we're on the sidelines."

"What about our families?" asked Davis.

Winter shook her head. "I don't know. There's no easy solution. They're in danger, but I'm not sure how much is safe to tell them. If we warn them, they may go to the police, and we already know that Xaphan can influence the police and FBI. If Xaphan is blackmailing anyone, like he did Summer and Dr. Streffield, then we risk tipping him off that we're on to him. On the other hand, he may take them or hurt them…but not without using that to draw me out. I don't know what to do. So it may be best to do nothing and just wait."

Uncomfortable silence filled the room. Winter scrambled for something positive to say, but couldn't think of anything.

"What happens when we hear from Ayden? Or when we get more information on Xaphan?" asked Graham.

Winter flashed big eyes at him, thanking him for the help. "Then I go. I find Xaphan again and I stop this. I probably should have tried harder to stop him when I had him in front of me. But I knew I had to get this information out safely. Now that it is, the only thing left is him."

She took out the folder and passed around the contents as she explained everything about the virus, the test trials, the distribution points, and the estimated casualties.

"He's not going to let me keep this information for much longer," Winter said. "That's why as soon as we get a lead, I have to face him."

"You can't do that alone," said Graham, handing the folder back to her.

"I have to," said Winter. "I can't risk anyone else getting hurt. This needs to end." Winter stared at him and firmed her lips. Just then her phone rang. She stood and pulled it out of her pocket. When she glanced at the ID, her heart fluttered. "It's Ayden."

32

"Ayden!" she shouted as she put the phone to her ear. "Where are you?"

"I'm headed back to Cherithville," Ayden said in a hurry. *"As fast as I can. Everything's fine but we need to talk."*

"What's going on? Are you all right? What happened to you? You've been gone for weeks! I needed you yesterday!"

"I found Erickson," said Ayden

"Agent Erickson?"

"Do you know any others? Listen, we have to talk to you and it can't wait."

"Okay," Winter said. "Get on the interstate and drive north. Find a place about forty-five minutes north of Cherithville and text me the exit number. I'll meet you there."

"We're on the interstate now and almost to Cherithville. It'll be about an hour."

"Perfect," said Winter. "I'll meet you there."

Winter lowered her phone and surveyed everyone. They all stared at her with wide eyes. "I've got to go meet Ayden. She found Erickson. I'm not sure what's going on."

"We heard," said Graham. "I'll come with you."

Winter studied him, noting the softness in his eyes and the gentleness in his voice. Then she glanced at Davis and Summer, sitting close to one another, Davis's arm around her and Summer's face still pale with fear. She looked at Peter and Kaci, Kaci leaning forward a little, one hand on her pregnant belly and Peter rubbing her back as they both watched Winter.

She turned back to Graham. "No. Someone has to stay here with them."

"But…" Graham began.

Winter stepped toward the table for her keys. "No. I'm sorry, but I have to go alone."

Graham looked around the room as she had done and then nodded to her.

"Listen, everyone," Winter said. "I shouldn't be gone more than a few hours. Get some rest and we'll figure this out when I get back."

She paused at the door, keys jangling in her hand, to toss a worried glance back at Graham. He nodded again in reassurance and she bolted out of the door.

As Winter drove her black BMW down the long, winding gravel road through the forest from the cabin, she checked her phone for messages. She had no doubt she could find Ayden, but didn't want to miss anything, especially if something happened over the next hour.

She turned left out of the drive and accelerated quickly, letting her instincts lead her through a small community with the general store, to a larger highway, through a town about the size of Cherithville, and finally to the interstate. She took the ramp toward Cherithville. After half an hour on the interstate, Ayden sent her a text with the exit number. It took Winter another ten minutes to reach it, pushing her car a little past the speed limit.

Ayden's car waited on the side of a gas station away from the main thoroughfare of traffic. As Winter pulled into the empty spot beside Ayden's car, she spotted Ayden standing near the back corner of the building. Beside her crouched a man she barely recognized. He wore a dirty hoodie. His unshaven facial hair protruded a little from the hood pulled over his head. If Winter didn't know better, she'd have mistaken him for homeless. Maybe he was.

Winter eased out and cautiously approached. Ayden frowned at her, cutting her eyes to the man and then back to Winter. Once Winter came within a few feet, the man pulled back his hood.

"Erickson?" Winter asked. "Is that really you?"

He nodded and stood. "We have to talk fast. Xaphan is on his way. Now."

"What do you mean he's on his way?" asked Winter. "Does he know where we are?"

Ayden stepped in. "What he means is that something is chasing him. That's where we've been. When I found him, he was hiding in an abandoned building. It wasn't long before this demon showed up. We ran. I knew I couldn't leave Erickson and I didn't want that demon to find you or Kaci. That's why I haven't contacted anyone."

"What kind of demon?" Winter asked.

"A woman. Naked with long hair covering her body and water dripping from her. You could see straight through her back."

Winter's stomach fluttered. "That's Mavka. The Wretch."

"You know her?" Erickson asked.

"I've run into her a couple of times. Tell me where you've been." Winter crossed her arms. "You and all your friends just disappeared. The FBI has disavowed you and your entire operation. You left us with no resources, no protection, and no answers. Explain."

Erickson glanced around nervously and then scratched his unshaven face. "When you contacted Summer about Claire being an impostor and about Kaci's identity, Summer contacted us as we planned. We decided to let Summer proceed with what she was expected to do and we would work it as a trap. But Claire..." He took a deep breath. "She wasn't human. I've never seen anything like it. We couldn't see. This living darkness surrounded us and people started screaming. That's when I ran. I'm ashamed to say it, but I ran. I tried to call in for backup, but officers showed up to arrest me. So I ran again."

"How do you explain that?" Winter asked. "Why would your own people try to arrest you?"

Erickson shrugged. "My only guess is that Xaphan has people in the department. Maybe he was trying to find Kaci that way too. And when the information came out, everything happened at once. His people in the bureau manipulated the case files and the personnel files, getting rid of all of the evidence from within. Since I survived the attack, they probably manipulated evidence to have me silenced another way. I knew Xaphan was dangerous, I just didn't realize just how dangerous he had become. Is Kaci safe?"

Winter nodded. "She's fine. We're protecting her."

"Take me to her then."

Winter instinctively took a step back. "I'm not sure that's a good idea."

"Why not? I've been helping to protect her since she was a child. Do you think I'd turn on her now?"

"I don't know," Winter said. "But you've been missing for a long time. How do we know you've told us the whole truth? How do we know *any* of it is true? For all we know you could have been captured."

Erickson stepped toward her and Winter backed away again. Erickson held up his hands in a gesture of servility and backed against the wall. "Look, I've always been on your side. You can trust me like you always have. Let me help."

Winter tightened her eyes at Ayden. "Can I talk to you? Alone?"

Erickson grunted and turned away. He propped himself against the building near the back corner, and Winter and Ayden walked the opposite direction out of his hearing.

"I don't know about this, Ayden," Winter said. "Something isn't quite right. He's not telling us everything."

"I know," said Ayden. "I'm not sure what it is. It's just out of reach. But this demon, Mavka, has this horrible obsession with him. Worse than that is when Erickson sees her, it's like he goes into this trance. I practically have to drag him to safety."

"She hasn't attacked you?"

Ayden shook her head. "I don't get it. It's like a game to her. We get away for a few days, but she always finds us."

"You said you had a dream and that's how you found him?"

Ayden nodded.

"Tell me about it. Everything."

Ayden closed her eyes for a moment, took a deep breath, and then reopened them. "I was walking through this big house. The walls were on fire. Things were crumbling all around me. I saw something huddled in the far corner. I thought someone was hurt, so I went over there to help. It was Erickson. When he saw me he was terrified. He grabbed me and said, 'One, two, three, Sunshine.' Then he shoved me down and ran away."

Winter shook her head. "That's not a very encouraging dream. How did you find him from that?"

"What he said. I remember seeing this abandoned motel on the outskirts of Cherithville. The Sunshine Inn. He was in room 123…hiding more like it. He seemed very surprised to see me. It looked like he hadn't had a shower in days."

Winter bit her lip and glanced back at Erickson. He stared at the ground with his hands in his pockets. "Did you recognize the burning house?" Winter asked as she turned back.

"No," said Ayden.

"Do you remember any details about it?"

"I walked around this large staircase in the middle of a room. I remember seeing all kinds of fancy paintings going up in flames."

Winter blinked. "That's what I thought. Xaphan's house. You saw it burning down. I was there."

"You were there?"

"I burned it. And I stole some information from him."

Ayden frowned. "If I saw him in Xaphan's house hiding in the corner, do you think he's been with Xaphan this whole time? Maybe he escaped during the fire?"

"Maybe." Winter glanced back at Erickson still leaning against the gas station wall. "Very likely, actually."

"So with his reaction to Mavka, do you think there was brainwashing? Torture?"

"I don't know," said Winter. "But that's not the right question."

"Then what is?"

Winter furrowed her brow. "Why would you have a dream showing you how to find him if we didn't need him for something? My gut tells me he's still a part of this somehow."

"Good or bad?" asked Ayden.

"I don't know."

"So what do we do?"

"Keep him away from Kaci, to start," said Winter. "We need to know more. We need to know if he's really telling us the truth."

"But we can't just let him go, can we?"

"No, we can't. We'll have to stay separated. And I'm afraid you'll have to take responsibility for him."

Ayden frowned but didn't object. "What do I do with him?"

Winter's eyes widened with the onset of a new idea. "The plans I took from Xaphan's house...some serious apocalyptic stuff. I have a list of locations where Xaphan is planning on releasing a genetically modified virus. Are you up to checking those out and maybe doing something about them?"

Ayden narrowed her eyes. "Sounds very dangerous."

"It is. But it'll keep Xaphan's attention away from us and our families, give you a chance to find out the truth about Erickson and if we can trust him, and we'll be tearing apart Xaphan's plans. All at the same time. It might mess up school, though."

"Forget school," Ayden said. "What about you?"

Winter sighed. "For now, I guess I'm sidelined. I'll be with Peter and Kaci to protect them just in case."

Ayden stared at her with a frown.

"I'll email you the details and locations," Winter said.

Ayden glanced at Erickson. Facing back to Winter, she said, "Okay. I'll do it."

33

Four Years Ago

After Winter's birthday night with Michael, her dad no longer pressed much over how late she stayed out…if she even came home at all. All of the fight seemed to have disappeared from him. Maybe he really did look forward to her graduation, when she could finally leave and begin her own life. Maybe he really did want her out of the house so he could resume his. Winter didn't care anymore, so long as he left her alone and let her do whatever she wanted. She was eighteen now…what could he do to her?

Over the next few months, Winter practically moved in with Michael on the weekends, lying to her dad and telling him that she hung out with Shannon instead. If it wasn't for school, and a little tinge of guilt, she would have moved out completely. It would only be a few more months anyway and she'd have no more qualms about doing so. With each passing weekend, it became harder and harder to pack up her clothes and go home on Sunday evenings. But if she didn't come home, or if she slowly started leaving more of her clothes at Michael's place, her dad might begin to suspect something. Despite her fierce determination for complete independence, she wasn't ready to deal with that yet…not until she could truly move out guilt-free.

Michael took to sharing his space with her as if he'd done it before. Winter suspected he had, but she never asked. She reveled in her time alone with him, away from prying eyes, away from judgmental opinions. Just her and Michael…together.

Still, it didn't feel the same as with Ryan. With Ryan she had a deeper warmth that filled her heart completely. They'd had no pretenses and no expectations between them. If she had to define the relationship, it would have been simply love.

With Michael it was different. He filled her with infatuation, passion, and danger. Rather than a warmth in her heart, she felt electricity throughout her entire body. She thought maybe one day she could love him like she loved Ryan, but she didn't care if she felt that way yet or not. Being with Michael was too much fun.

The first Friday of April, Michael waited for her at the curb of her house as the bus dropped her off. When she stepped onto the ground and spotted him, Winter peered around nervously before scurrying to him.

"What are you doing here? What if my dad comes home early?"

Michael shrugged. "So? He can't do anything, you know. If he finds out, then you just come stay with me."

"You know why I'm still staying here," Winter said.

"I know. But the weekends are mine, right?"

Winter grinned and blushed. "I'll go get my things."

Michael returned the grin. "Maybe I'll help you."

"Maybe I want you to."

She grabbed his hand and led him into the house and to her room, trying to not giggle as she did so. Once in her room, she locked the door and turned on him, pressing into him and kissing deeply for several minutes.

"What if your father comes home now?" Michael asked as Winter tore off his shirt.

Winter laughed and rubbed a hand over the skull tattoo on his chest. "Then you'll just have to jump out of the window."

Steve didn't come home. Winter and Michael left at nearly five, and he still had not come home from work.

"So what do you want to do tonight?" Michael asked as he drove out of the neighborhood.

Winter bit her lip. "I have an idea. But you'll probably think it's dumb."

"I doubt that."

"I want to get a tattoo. I was thinking about yours, and I think I'd like one too."

Michael glanced at her and then back to the road. He shrugged. "You mean you don't have one yet?"

Winter laughed. "You know I don't. I never had the courage to get my dad's permission. But I don't need it now, do I?"

Michael shook his head. "I think we've established that you're old enough to do whatever you like."

"So, where do we go? How much does it cost?"

"That depends on what you want."

"Nothing big," Winter said. "Maybe a rose. A purple rose."

"A purple rose?"

"Yeah. That's what I want."

"Okay. Well, I know a guy," said Michael. "He did mine and he'll give us a good deal. Something like that shouldn't be more than sixty or seventy bucks."

Winter nodded. "I think I have that much."

Michael chuckled. "It's on me."

"Are you sure?"

"Your first tattoo?" he said. "Of course I'm sure. We'll just drop your stuff off first."

"No," Winter said. "Let's go straight there while I still have the nerve. I've already been nauseated most of the day just anticipating this weekend. If you don't take me there, I think I might throw up thinking about it."

Michael laughed again. "Don't worry. It's really not that bad. Maybe you should eat something first."

Winter shook her head. "Not much of an appetite right now. Let's just go do it."

He nodded. "Okay. We'll go straight there."

Michael drove to the other side of Trenton Hills, on the outskirts where a shopping neighborhood lay hidden beneath carefully avoided trees. He drove past the major strip malls and retailers, past an actual mall that Winter had never been to, and finally found an older shopping center with a few outcast and start-up businesses. The first two storefronts had been taken over by a fitness center, and a Tae-Kwon-Do dojo sat right next door.

Next to the dojo hung an orange and black sign that read *Rabbit Room Ink*. Beyond that were a thrift store and a cellphone repair shop.

Michael parked and gazed at her with a bemused smile. The nausea had sunk to the pit of her stomach at full force, and she shivered as the cold sweat leaked from her clammy skin.

"Are you okay? Are you sure you want to do this?"

Winter nodded. "I'm fine," she croaked. "Just give me a second."

She pointed the air vents directly to her face and adjusted the air to blow cold, despite the chill already outside. She closed her eyes and took deep breaths, letting her mind drift away from needles and blood and pain...

"We can do this another time," Michael said. "Maybe we should go back to my place and let you lie down."

"No," she insisted. "I'm fine." She turned to him, the nausea abating a little. "I want to do this. I'll be fine."

As if to prove her point, Winter took off her seatbelt and opened the door. Michael turned off the car and followed.

The outside fresh air, and just the act of moving, helped to settle her nerves. She didn't know why she felt so anxious...especially after performing most of her piercings herself without numbing anything. But she supposed it could have been some lingering guilt of everything she had been doing behind her dad's back...and of what Ryan might have thought, too.

She put all of those things out of her mind, flashed a smile at Michael, and walked to his side. He grabbed her hand and led her in.

A receptionist desk waited between the lobby and the back area, where a break in a low wall separated the nooks of the tattoo artists at work. Beside the desk stood a shelf stacked with binders full of samples of artwork. Detailed artwork hung framed over every wall in the lobby, showcasing the talents of the tattoo artists employed there.

A man with a sharp goatee and slick black hair peeked up at them from behind the desk and smiled. "Do you have an appointment?"

"No," said Michael. "I'm a friend of Thumper. Is he here?"

"Yeah, he's with someone at the moment. I'll go let him know you're here. Your name?"

"Michael Morial."

The man left and Winter wandered around the empty lobby, studying the artwork and trying to settle her stomach further.

"You know, you should look through these books and make sure you know what you want."

Winter nodded and crossed over to the shelf.

"Are you sure you want to do this? I mean, normally we'd need to make an appointment and come back, just to make sure you don't change your mind. These things don't come off, you know."

"I know," said Winter. "I've been thinking about it for a while now." She found a book with hearts in it flipped through it. "This," she said as she pointed to a small simple red rose bloom with a short stem and a few leaves. The entire bloom was no bigger than a quarter and the stem twisted down another two inches. "This is perfect. But purple."

At that moment, two college girls came from the back, followed by a large man who looked at Michael and grinned. He wiped his bald head with a towel, flexing his tattoo-covered biceps.

"Hey, Mike," he said and stuck his hand out.

Michael grabbed it. "Thumper. This is my girlfriend, Winter," he said as he motioned toward her.

Winter stepped forward, her eyes wide.

"Winter, huh?" Thumper said, extending his hand. "I'm Thumper. Nice to meet you."

"Hi," Winter mumbled.

"She wants a tattoo. We don't have an appointment, but I thought maybe if you weren't busy..."

Thumper shrugged. "Just giving a consultation. I might could work it in if it's not too complicated. Got a little time before my next appointment."

Winter turned back to the shelf and grabbed the book. She showed him the rose. "This. But purple."

Thumper reviewed it for a moment and then glimpsed back at her. "Shoulder? Hip? Ankle?"

"Hip," Winter said.

"Left or right?"

"Left."

Thumper nodded. "Shouldn't take more than an hour or so. I think I can work you in. But you need to be sure. Tattoos are permanent."

"I...I know," Winter said, stumbling over herself trying to get her justification out. "I've been thinking about it for a while now, and I'm definitely certain. This is what I want."

"She's a little nervous," Michael said.

"Nervous I can handle, so long as she's certain. You eighteen?"

"Yes," said Winter. "And I'm certain."

Thumper glanced at Michael and shrugged. "Not usually how I do things, but I'll make an exception if you're both sure about it."

"I want to do it," Winter said, almost pleading.

"Okay, then." Thumper turned to the man behind the counter. "Greg, give them the papers and send them back."

After filling out the paperwork and having her ID photocopied, Winter followed Greg through the gap in the low wall, past four nooks that looked like a mix between salon booths and torture chambers. One nook had a man sitting in the black chair, arm propped on the armrest and a woman tattoo artist buzzing over his arm with a long metal thing.

Winter's heart fluttered and her stomach lurched again. She bit her bottom lip and turned away.

Thumper waited in the last nook. He had the rose picture propped up on his workstation, and busied himself with his own long silver torture device. The black chair loomed in front of him. Winter half expected to see medieval restraints.

"Have a seat," said Thumper.

Winter eased into the chair and Michael took a chair off to the side to watch.

"Now, I'm going to lower you flat."

The chair reclined. Winter took a deep breath and stared at the ceiling.

"I need you to raise your shirt a little, undo your pants and slide them down, front and back, just enough to expose where the tattoo is going. Then turn a little on your side."

Winter nodded and followed his instructions. The cool air made goose bumps on her hip and exposed abdomen. She flashed a smile at Michael to reassure him.

Thumper took a temporary outline of the rose and laid it on her hip. He placed the head of the rose just at the top of her hip bone, with the curling stem falling toward the back of her hip.

"Lean up and take a look. Let's make sure it's where you want it."

Winter nodded. "That's fine. I like it."

He dabbed the paper with a sponge and peeled it off, leaving the outline on her skin. "Check once more."

Winter looked again and nodded.

"Last chance," said Thumper as he picked up his silver instrument.

Winter clenched her eyes and concentrated on the music playing in the parlor. "Do it."

For the first half hour, he worked on the stem and leaves, on a more fleshy part of her hip. Winter clenched her teeth the entire time, her stomach roiling, but controllable. The waves of pain raked deeper than she had expected, but not quite as much as when she had done all her piercings.

After finishing the stem, he changed out his inks and began on the rose bloom. As soon as the needle hit her hip bone with an excruciating flash of pain, her stomach lost control. She lurched forward. Thumper swore and pulled away.

"Are you okay" asked Michael.

Winter covered her mouth. "I'm going to be sick."

"Grab the can," said Thumper.

Michael slid the small trash can to Winter just in time. Everything in her stomach came up in a rush.

"Maybe we should take a break," said Thumper.

"No," said Winter, wiping her mouth with the paper towel Michael handed her. "I'm sorry. I'm fine now. Keep going."

She clenched her eyes again and braced herself as the needle resumed work on her hip. Her stomach still lurched and her skin grew clammy again, but without anything left inside of her at least the dry heaving was easier to control.

34

Present Day

"Are you okay?" asked Graham one morning three weeks later, while Winter leaned forward with her head in her hands as a cooking show droned in the background.

"I need to be doing something," she said. "I should be out there with Ayden."

"Any more word from them?"

Winter shook her head. "Not for two weeks...not since that last text about finding one of the distribution points."

"No news is good, right?" asked Graham. "We can assume they're making progress."

"I suppose. But I still feel useless. I'm tired of pacing. I'm tired of wandering around outside." She clicked off the TV and tossed the remote onto the couch. "I'm tired of these three stupid channels." Graham opened his mouth to speak, but Winter cut him off. "If you offer to take me to the lake one more time..."

"I've got to make a grocery run. Why don't you come?"

Winter hopped up. "Are you sure?"

He shrugged. "I think it would be fine. Most anyone that would be looking for you would still be looking for your black hair. Just wear some of Kaci's old clothes, instead of your regular Goth wardrobe, and I don't think you'll be recognized quickly."

"Getting out would be awesome. But not exactly what I'm talking about." She glanced out of the window to where Kaci sat on the porch by herself. "I just can't stand being on the sidelines, you know? It's supposed to be me out there chasing Xaphan and saving the world, not Ayden. She won't even tell me what they're doing, only that they've been in some pretty intense battles and some pretty awesome things have happened to help. I mean…I don't even know what these distribution places look like!"

"If things are happening this way, that's how they should be happening. Right?"

"I know," said Winter. "I just feel pointless."

"You'll have more to do, don't worry. Right now, just concentrate on spending time with Kaci. In the long run, protecting the baby may do more to save the world than destroying Xaphan's super-virus."

"You're right, of course. You're always right."

"Not always," Graham said. "You know, Kaci's been dealing with this stir-craziness for a lot longer than you."

Winter sighed and moved to the door. "Yeah, I know. Maybe I'll pass on the grocery run today. I'll go next time."

Graham followed her out, jingling keys. "Suit yourself."

Winter plopped into the chair next to Kaci as Graham drove off. "Are you okay?" she asked Kaci.

Kaci gave her a wry smile and patted her belly. "As good as I can be, I guess. Have you heard from Ayden?"

Winter shook her head. "Not in a while."

"She and Erickson must make a good team," said Kaci.

"Maybe," Winter said gazing into the trees. "I'm sorry this is taking so long."

"It's not your fault. This has been going on all my life, remember?"

"Yeah, but I promised I'd put an end to it."

"You will," said Kaci. "Just not now."

Winter crossed her arms. "Have I ever told you how much I hate waiting?"

Kaci laughed. "Actually…yes."

The weeks slogged by, with no more updates from Ayden except the occasional text or quick phone call. Ayden and Erickson made good progress with Winter's list. Ayden couldn't give her many details, but they had been as far away as Paris already, able to destroy at least four of Xaphan's distribution points. Winter couldn't help but feel a little jealous with each update, but she would get over it by seeking out Kaci…or Graham.

After refusing that first invitation to get supplies, Winter never missed a chance to get out of the cabin and go to town with Graham. She told herself a change of scenery would help rid her of boredom, but after the sixth week since Ayden and Erickson went out, Winter discovered she enjoyed going just to get some one-on-one time with Graham.

It was during one of these supply runs in the first week of April that Peter called her. "Don't panic," were the first words out of his mouth.

"What's wrong?" Winter asked, sitting forward in the car. Graham swung his head to glance at her.

"It's probably nothing," said Peter. "Kaci passed out so I took her to the emergency room."

"She passed out?" Winter shouted.

"But she's awake now. They're running some tests."

Winter glared at Graham. "Hospital. Now."

Graham took the next turn and sped up.

"We'll be there in a minute," Winter said and hung up.

Ten minutes later, Graham pulled up to the curb as close as he could to the emergency room entrance and Winter jumped out. As he went to park, she burst into the emergency room and cast around frantically. A nurse behind the check-in booth peeked up at her and frowned. Winter rushed toward her.

"I need to find Kaci Strong. She's here somewhere. She's pregnant."

"What's your name?" asked the nurse.

"Winter Maessen."

The nurse nodded. "I'll go ask them if it's okay for you to come back."

Winter scowled at her. "You do that."

When the nurse had left, Winter paced around the waiting room, ignoring the stares of the few patients waiting to be seen. One young boy sat beside his mother, the boy gingerly cradling his arm beneath an ice pack. In the far corner, an elderly woman huddled beneath a blanket, coughing. Winter clenched her teeth and looked away, suddenly reminded once again how much she hated hospitals. Graham came in and sat in the chair closest to her, watching her with a furrowed brow.

The door opened to the back and the nurse stepped out. "Winter, you can follow me."

Winter glanced at Graham. He held up his hands. "I'm good. I'll wait here."

Winter nodded and the nurse led her into the back and around a couple of corners to an exam room. Inside, Kaci sat upright on the bed, pale but smiling. Peter sat next to her on a stool, holding Kaci's hand.

"Hey!" said Kaci as enthusiastically as she could.

"Hey, yourself. What's going on?"

"She's severely anemic," said Peter.

"I thought you had vitamins for that," said Winter.

"I do. But I guess they weren't enough," said Kaci.

"So you're okay?"

Kaci nodded. "I'm fine. I just got really dizzy…"

"You passed out," said Peter.

Kaci rolled her eyes. "I'm fine."

"They want to keep her overnight," said Peter. "Just to be safe. They weren't too happy that she hasn't been seeing a doctor."

The door opened up and a technician came in with a cart holding a machine with a large screen at the top.

"How are we doing?" the technician asked.

"Better," said Kaci.

Winter moved to stand beside Peter. Then she spotted a chair and sat.

"We're just going to do a quick ultrasound to make sure everything is fine with the baby," said the tech.

Kaci lay back. The technician helped Kaci cover herself mostly with the sheets, and pulled the hospital gown up enough to expose her stretched-out belly.

The technician squirted some jelly onto Kaci's belly and then sat onto a stool. She turned to the machine and pressed a few buttons, then grabbed the probe and twisted back to Kaci.

"Have you had one of these yet?"

Kaci shook her head. "Not yet."

"So you haven't seen the baby yet?" the technician grinned.

Kaci bit her bottom lip, eyes wide.

Winter leaned forward, watching the screen of the machine.

"Well," said the tech. "You're in for a treat." She placed the wand on Kaci's belly and moved it around in the jelly. Then she tilted it and slid it as she watched the screen. "Let's see," she said and then she tapped the machine with one hand and the screen froze. "This, is your baby's face."

Winter glanced at Kaci and Peter and found them both crying. A lump formed in Winter's throat as she looked back to the machine. The tech moved the probe around some more, took more screenshots, and made notations on the screen.

"Looks like everything is fine from what I see, but I'll take all of this to the doctor. She'll be in to see you a little later. And I'll print you out a copy of your baby's face before I go. I've just got one more thing to look at." She moved the wand around and stopped, taking another screenshot. "So do you want to know?"

"Know what?" asked Peter.

"The sex."

Winter shot her eyes at them again as Peter and Kaci studied each other silently. Then Kaci nodded and they turned back to the tech.

"Yes," said Kaci.

The tech grinned and moved the cursor around on the screen, circling a particular set of lines. "You," she said, "are having a boy."

35

When the ultrasound tech left, it wasn't long before the doctor came in. Winter excused herself and left the room. She found Graham in the waiting room.

"Is everything okay?" he asked.

Winter nodded. "She's fine. They're going to keep her overnight."

"And you're staying, of course."

"Of course."

Graham stood. "Then I should finish the supply run and get back to the cabin. Let me know if you need anything."

"Thank you," she said. As Graham walked toward the exit, Winter crossed her arms and watched him, feeling like a small piece of her left with him. After he disappeared, she intended to go back to Kaci's room, but instead she kept walking deeper through the corridors of the hospital. She needed to walk…to clear her head. Seeing the baby on the ultrasound…A boy?

Winter glanced over her shoulder toward Kaci's room before she turned the first hallway corner. How could it be a boy? It didn't make sense. She had been seeing a little girl, and she was so sure...

When Winter turned the corner, the little girl waited for her at the end of the hall by a set of closed double doors. Two nurses came through the door and walked by the girl as if she didn't exist. The little girl reached out to Winter and crooked her finger. Winter's heart pounded, because now she thought she knew who the girl was. If she wasn't Kaci's, then there could really only be one other possibility.

The girl spun and passed through the closed doors like a ghost. Winter bit her lip and hurried to follow. Beyond the doors, Winter saw the girl turn a corner. She followed the girl through the hospital corridors, always just out of sight, always turning the next corner. Winter wanted to run, but running might draw attention to herself and she also knew it wouldn't do any good. So she continued as best she could, knowing the girl would wait long enough for Winter to see the next turn before disappearing. The girl led Winter through the hospital, possibly through places Winter shouldn't have been going, until they came to a wing that seemed to be mostly unused. Winter didn't know hospitals had unused areas, but before she realized it she turned a corner and found herself alone with the little girl.

The girl glanced up at her and entered an empty patient room at the end of the hall. Winter sprinted down the corridor and went in.

The little girl stood at the foot of the empty hospital bed. Her long dark hair draped over her shoulders in gentle waves. She wore a light green dress that brought out the light freckles speckling her rosy cheeks. She didn't move or speak, but just watched Winter with sky blue eyes.

"Who are you?" Winter said, trembling, afraid she already knew the answer.

"A little girl never loved. Never held. Eternally in the arms of God."

Winter's hand dropped to her abdomen, suddenly feeling an emptiness she had not felt in four years. "But how?"

The girl frowned. "It doesn't matter how. I am here now like this because you've needed me."

Winter took a small step forward. "You've been helping me?"

The little girl nodded.

Winter broke. Tears erupted that should have been shed years ago. She fell to her knees and ogled the girl directly in the eyes. "I am so sorry…I wish I could have…"

"What is done is done," the girl broke in. "What has been done was meant to be done and cannot be undone. There's nothing you can do to change it, and you shouldn't anyway. Your past has led you here. Without your past you could not face the future. And what you do here today and in the near future is what you were always meant to do. I have seen it and soon you will see it too. It will happen, has always happened, and is even happening now."

Winter rubbed her eyes with the heels of her hands. "What am I supposed to do with that?"

"Be encouraged. You may not understand why or how, but things are as they should be. Keep going. You're almost there."

"Is that the only reason you came? To tell me to keep going? After everything that's happened, all the times you've refused to talk to me, you're doing this now? What else is there? Why are you really speaking to me?"

"You have to save Kaci and the child. You have to do whatever it takes. Don't…" The little girl paused and a shadow of uncertainty crossed her face. "Don't leave her. Ever. Every moment from now until Xaphan is defeated, stay at her side."

Winter nodded. "Okay. I'll try."

"And you need to tell Graham how you feel. Tell him before it's too late. I know you. I know your thoughts. I know you will keep your feelings bottled inside and you'll miss something good right in front of you. You need to let your heart love again, even if it's for a short time."

"How do you know?"

"Because I'm a part of you. Tell him."

"And what if he doesn't feel the same?"

The little girl laughed. "He does. You're just too stubborn to admit it to yourself."

"I don't know if I can."

"You will. You've already done it. You just don't know it yet."

At that moment a strong sense of déjà vu washed over Winter. She saw the intervening moments with a clarity so intense that she knew what each of the next seconds would bring. She knew the little girl was right. She knew she loved Graham and knew that she would call and tell him just like the girl had said.

She also knew that the girl would disappear.

"Don't go," Winter whispered. "I don't even know your name."

The girl gave her a soft smile, almost sympathetic. "Yes you do."

"But I'll never see you again…"

"You will. I promise. Just not here."

Winter's heart sagged as the girl backed away. "I need you," she sobbed as she fought the impulse to rush over and hug the girl tightly.

The girl shook her head. "Not anymore. You're almost ready now. Go. Tell him."

The premonition vanished and a moment later so did the girl. It was as if the lack of her presence left a vacuum in the fabric of existence that held the girl's shape for a heartbeat. And then the vacuum invaded Winter's heart.

She slumped back against the wall, laid one hand against her abdomen and her head against her knees. Then she cried.

Four Years Ago

The bell rang. Winter waited until the rest of the class had exited into the hall before slowly leaving herself. Butterflies pounded inside of her. She tried not to make eye contact with anyone, and hoped Stacy had assumed she'd taken the bus today. Since their last fight, Winter and Stacy had assumed an unspoken agreement not to intrude on each other's social life. Winter never spoke about her Wiccan friends and Stacy no longer talked about church. They needed each other still, and they both knew it. But to Winter's disappointment, Stacy waited for her at the lockers, a big grin on her face.

"You're riding with me today," she announced.

Winter shook her head.

"Come on," said Stacy. "It's the first warm day we've had all year. I know we'll have another cold snap before April is over, but please!" She jumped up and down. "I want to put the top down on my car, put my sunglasses on, and crank the music up! Then maybe we can work on our senior projects together."

"I can't," Winter said. "I've got to stay after school."

"What? Why?"

Winter shrugged. "Just some makeup work. I'll ride with you tomorrow, I promise."

Stacy frowned. "Fine. But I'm letting the top down with or without you."

Winter gave her a smile. "Have fun."

As Stacy left for the parking lot, Winter busied herself at the locker in case Stacy glanced back. Then Winter relocated to the front entrance of the school and waited long enough to make sure most of the students had gone. With the coast clear, she shouldered her bag and started the long walk home. Despite it being warmer than usual, the wind still held a cold bite. Winter wondered if Stacy actually did let the top down in her convertible, and if she did how long she left it that way before giving up.

The four-mile walk home would take her a couple of hours, but she needed to go by the drug store...secretly. About half-way between school and home she found the corner drug store and went in. She circled inside three times to make sure there wasn't anyone there who might recognize her, then she found the aisle she had come to browse and stood staring at the pregnancy tests.

Winter bit her lip. How could this have happened? Maybe it was just a fluke. Maybe it was stress. There were a hundred reasons she could be late.

Two weeks late.

Winter swore under her breath and reached down to snatch up a pack of tests. She held it to her side as she slinked to the counter. The older lady didn't blink at all when Winter presented the test. She simply rang it up, bagged it, and accepted the cash Winter offered.

Back outside in the warm sun and chilly wind, Winter adjusted her cap and then shoved the pack of tests into the inside pocket of her black trench coat. She pulled the coat tight and resumed her long walk home.

An empty house greeted her. Her dad had been working late,

especially since the first of the year. Winter thought maybe he wanted to do everything he could to avoid her, or maybe he suspected more of what she did on the weekend than she realized. Today, she really didn't care. She wanted as much privacy as she could get.

She went upstairs and locked her bedroom door, took off her coat, and put on some pajamas, being careful not to aggravate her still sensitive new tattoo. Then she sat on her bed and held the box of two pregnancy tests in her hands. She read the entire box twice, her heart pounding in her chest, then tore the end open and dumped the entire contents out onto the bedspread.

Two silver-wrapped rectangles lay there with a folded set of instructions. Winter picked up the instructions, opened them, and found the side in English. Then just like she had done the box, she read the entire thing twice.

Her heart still pounded. Her stomach fluttered. She knew that rereading everything was really just stalling the inevitable. So she took a deep breath, grabbed one of the rectangles and went into her bathroom. She opened the test and let it rest on the counter, studying it and referring back to the instructions just to make sure she knew exactly what to do. Then with another deep breath, she took the test toward the toilet to take it.

Afterward, she laid it back on the counter as instructed and then retreated to sit on the bed for the required three minutes. She stared at the clock beside her bed, crumpling the instructions in her hand and biting her lip.

Waiting that first minute felt like eternity. The second minute took even longer. Winter suspected she started watching the clock halfway through the first minute. Should she give it an extra thirty seconds? She tossed the instructions aside, crossed her legs in front of her and grabbed her ankles. She could probably turn on the TV and pass the time more quickly, but would it really help?

When the third minute appeared, her heart drummed even faster, beating so hard she could hear it throbbing in her ears. She chewed the inside of her cheek and her vision speckled ever so slightly with the anticipation. The third minute completed, but she wasn't sure how much of the first minute had already passed when she started watching. So she counted slowly. She figured if she counted slowly to thirty, that might be enough time to complete three full minutes. What if the test was positive? What would she do? What would her dad think? What would Michael think? What would Stacy think? What would her mom think? What would Ryan think?

She counted so slowly that the clock changed before she had even reached twenty. The sudden change of the number made her jump a little.

This was it. She couldn't put it off any longer. Winter gazed into the bathroom to the little white stick sitting on the counter. The truth waited for her...no avoiding it. She just had to get this over with and then figure out what to do.

Winter took a deep breath, eased off the bed and crept toward the test. She watched herself in the mirror, avoiding the little result window on the stick, until she stood right in front of the test. She clenched her eyes tight. "Please God, just this once," she mumbled. Then she opened her eyes and looked down. Positive.

Winter collapsed onto the floor and wept.

37

Winter checked in on Kaci and found her smiling and watching TV while an IV of fluids dripped into her arm.

"Are you okay?" Kaci asked her.

Winter nodded, though her stomach still twisted in knots. "I'm fine. Where's Peter?"

"He went to get something to eat."

Winter plopped on the edge of the bed. "Do you ever wish things could have been different? Like maybe you had a normal life? Your real parents raising you?"

Kaci turned off the TV. "I miss my real parents every day. I was young when they were killed, but it still hurts."

Winter faced her, twisting to put one knee onto the bed. "That didn't answer my question."

"Do I wish things had been different? Yes and no. It would have been great to have lived a normal life and to not have had all the crazy things happen to me. But they did. And those things have brought me here and now. Those things helped me become the person I am today. If anything had been different, then I'd be a different person. I don't want to be a different person, I want to be me. So yes, it would have been nice. But no, I wouldn't change anything. I wouldn't have met Peter, I wouldn't have this wonderful child growing inside of me. And I wouldn't have met you...my best friend. Don't ask me to give any of that up just for the sake of an easier life."

Winter stared at her own clenched hands. "I'm not sure I could say the same. Am I a monster for saying that?"

"No," said Kaci. "You're not a monster. You've lost so much. I don't blame you. But who would you be today if not for what you went through? You would be someone else. And you wouldn't be here with me now."

"And the people you lost?"

"I know you've lost a lot of people. But none of that was your fault."

Winter put her face in her hands and broke down again.

Kaci grabbed Winter's knee and squeezed.

"Remember the baby I told you about?" Winter sobbed.

"Of course I do. I haven't told anyone."

"I was going to name her Rebecca."

Kaci squeezed again, handed her a nearby box of tissues, and let her cry.

After a few moments Winter choked the tears back, wiped her eyes, and lifted her head. "I'm glad you found your happiness," Winter said. "I really am."

Kaci smiled. "You'll find yours too. Who knows? Maybe you already have."

Winter chuckled. "You mean Graham? Everyone keeps telling me that. I just don't know."

"What is it you're unsure about?"

Winter shrugged. "I don't know if it's worth the trouble. Maybe I like him..." She shot a sideways grin at Kaci. "...a little. But I don't want him to get hurt, you know? I've had two serious relationships in my life…only really loved one of them, but almost started a family with the other. And both of them…" Winter chewed the inside of her cheek to keep from crying again.

"There's no reason to think something like that would happen again."

Winter tilted her head. "Isn't there? Everyone I've ever been close to has had horrible things happen to them. Everyone. Well, maybe not Stacy. At least she escaped the curse."

"You're not cursed."

"I know." Winter sighed and eyed the tissue in her hand. "But sometimes it's hard not to think that way. Maybe I just need something to eat. And a nap."

"You look tired."

"I haven't really been sleeping. Too much in my head."

Kaci nodded. "And now that you've talked out some of it, it's time to crash." She pointed to the side of the room. "There's a chair. It'll recline pretty far. Go take a nap. I think I might too. It's been a long morning."

Winter stared at the chair and took a deep breath. "Just a short one, maybe."

"It'll be fine," said Kaci. "Nothing's going to happen here. You'll feel better once you've had some rest. I'll text Peter and tell him to bring you a snack for when you wake up."

"Okay." Winter stood, stretched, and collapsed into the chair. "But tell him to wake me when he gets here."

Kaci laughed and shook her head, and Winter knew that Kaci wouldn't. But Winter didn't have the strength to argue. The weariness had sunk so deep into her muscles that Winter thought she might pass out any moment. So she closed her eyes and fell asleep almost instantly, even with Rebecca still on her mind.

Winter awoke a couple hours later when the nurse came in to begin preparing Kaci to transfer to a regular room for the night. After getting the new room number, Winter excused herself and walked outside into the cool, fresh April air, surprised to find the sun over halfway down to the horizon.

Winter pulled out her cellphone and clenched it as she walked around the building to the main entrance. She hesitated before going in, wanting to find a private place to make the phone call. As the sun set, a chill blew through the air so she entered. The main entrance opened into a large general lobby, with a small fountain to one side and chairs positioned in small groups near the windows. At the back of the lobby stood an information desk. The main hall passed by the desk to the right, where Winter could see three elevators.

Winter cast around for an empty corner, pleased to see only a couple of people taking advantage of the spacious lobby. She crossed to the far corner, stood against the wall, and called Graham.

"Hey," she said when he answered. "It's me."

"How's Kaci?"

"She's okay. They did some blood work and everything. It was only anemia, but they want to keep her overnight to make sure and to get her iron levels up."

"The baby?"

"He's fine."

"It's a boy?"

Winter grinned. "Maybe I shouldn't have told you that. I'm not sure if they want anyone to know or not."

"Don't worry. I'll keep it to myself. Do I need to come get you or are you staying overnight?"

"I'm going to stay," Winter said. "I'm not comfortable leaving her and Peter alone here."

"I understand," said Graham. *"If there's anything I can do, just let me know."*

Winter sighed as she thought about Rebecca's words to her.

Should she tell Graham how she feels? Now that she'd had time to consider it, she no longer doubted he felt the same way. But could they ever have a normal relationship? No, Winter decided just then. Not with Xaphan still out there.

"I've been thinking," Winter said. "Things will never be normal until Xaphan is stopped. I'm the only one that can do that, but I'm stuck here. I need to find a way to trade places with Ayden."

"You want to go after him again?"

"I want to do what I have to do. I want to get it over with."

Graham was silent a moment. *"I'm not sure I trust Erickson no matter what Ayden has been saying. I'll come with you."*

Butterflies sprang to life in Winter's stomach. The idea both excited and frightened her. "I can't ask you to do that. You need to keep the others safe."

"Actually, I've been talking with Davis. He's pretty sharp about these things. I think between him, Ayden, and Peter, they'll have it well covered."

"You can't…"

"I'm not asking. You need me."

Winter chewed her lip. She did need him, but not that way. She wanted desperately to tell him how she felt, but she couldn't bear the thought of losing him. Saying it made it real. As long as she kept quiet it couldn't hurt as badly. But she *did* need him.

"Winter?" Graham asked into the silence.

"Sure, whatever," she said a little more cuttingly than she intended. "We'll talk about it some more in the morning." She hung up and leaned forward to bang her head against the window.

Winter found a chair close to her that mostly faced the wall so she could hide her face from anyone who might be watching. Then she clenched her eyes, leaned her head back, and let a few tears break free.

If Graham really did have feelings for her, it was because he didn't know much about her. The moment he did, the moment she dared to open herself up and spill her complete past, would be the moment she'd lose him. It would be the same story over and over again. People might change, but her history never would.

Brief moments of her life had brought her times when she felt loved. But it always came back to just her having to deal with things alone.

Always alone.

Even Kaci. Only Kaci knew most everything. Only Kaci knew about what happened between her and Michael. And about Rebecca. Kaci was different from everyone else. But Kaci had a new life with Peter and her own child. Soon would come a time when Winter would have to go her own way completely.

Davis and Summer drifted away from her too, and had been doing so for some time now. They were never really close enough to be confidants. Ayden never wanted to be a part of this to begin with, and would probably jump at the chance to resume her old life. And Graham...well, Graham was really only here for Peter's sake.

Winter pressed her fists against her cheeks. Four years. Four years with her new life and still nothing had changed. She would always be the unlovable freak...the outcast, the loner. She knew better, of course. Too many signs and dreams had shown her otherwise. But when your only companion is God, is it really the same thing?

Overcoming her loner complex would obviously take more than four short years.

Could Graham really be harboring feelings for her? Could she trust him with her past? Already she leaned on him naturally whenever she needed help. Was it so bad to think Rebecca could be right? Was it so horrid to be vulnerable with someone again?

A part of her heart wanted to be loved by another person. The way Davis loved Summer. The way Peter loved Kaci. Each time she had ever come close, something had gone horribly wrong. Did she dare let herself try again? Did she even want to?

Winter clenched her teeth and let the hardness of her heart take control of her weaker emotions. She had to get out of there, if even for a few minutes. She stood and rushed out of the lobby door. Maybe a short walk in the cool air would clear her head. Maybe some food. She found the sidewalk by the road and turned toward a cluster of fast-food restaurants.

Something orange flickered out of the corner of her eye. She spun toward it, but only saw the shadows against the hospital. Maybe the low sun just glinted off a window.

But what she thought she saw wasn't white like a glare, and it didn't flash quickly like a reflection. It flickered, angry and orange. Like fire. Winter stopped completely to study the hospital, staring past the ornamental trees to the front doors where she thought she had seen the flicker. She tried to imagine a form that matched what she briefly had seen. She *had* seen something. She knew it.

There. The orange flickered again from a window. Fire. Winter sprinted through the parking lot back to the hospital as quickly as she could, but as she neared the window the flicker disappeared.

Out of the corner of her eye came another flicker of orange. She lunged toward the next window, then the next…each one she could reach, but never finding anything. With every window she came to, the flicker of orange jumped to another, until finally Winter found herself running to the adjacent building, an outpatient clinic. When she found no other flicker of orange, she slowly panned back to face the hospital, squinting against the sun now glinting from the front entrance.

On the far side of the hospital in another adjacent building, the windows exploded with orange flame. Then the building next to it did the same thing. Like toppling dominoes, every window of every building burst with angry fire, crossing over to the hospital itself, back to where she stood. Cars exploded, tumbling through the air to crash in flaming heaps. When the building next to her blazed suddenly, the force of it knocked her to the ground.

Winter's heart drummed. Kaci. She bolted back to the hospital main entrance, and found the doors unpassable from the raging fire. No alarm blared, no hiss of sprinkler systems, nothing to stop the fires, and Winter couldn't get in. She sprinted away from the heat into the parking lot and pulled out her phone to call for help. The heat blazed against her back, and by the time she had the phone out sweat had matted her shirt to her skin.

She spun back to face the building, and she screamed. A man sat in front of her, bound to a chair, his skin black and charred. The tattered and burned clothes on his body were barely distinguishable from his flesh.

"Winter…" he croaked, a crackly airy voice that barely sounded human. He lifted his hand, snapping the ashen rope. Bone gleamed where muscle had been burned away, with the firelight all around them shimmering upon a film of congealed blood.

Winter stared into the man's face, not much more than a charred skull with remnants of bubbled flesh and cooked muscles. The eyes. The eyes were untouched, bright and clear as if fully alive. They pleaded with more strength than the voice could manage. And Winter realized she knew those eyes. The wordless scream rose from deep within her, filled the air and pressed against her ears without stopping, shaped into a word and transformed from fear to panic. "DAD!"

She scrunched her eyes from the gore and the fire. When she opened them again...everything was gone. Her dad, the burning buildings, everything. As her heart drummed against her rib cage, she spun around and saw only the everyday activity of a normal hospital. As it should be.

After a brief lull as she tried to process the vision, panic struck at her harder than before the fire. She lurched for her phone with both hands, so fast that she bobbled it and it fell to the pavement.

As she snatched up the phone, unable help the string of profanities that leaked out of her mouth. All she cared about at that moment was calling her dad.

Finally, she found his number and pressed the phone to her ear. She took a deep breath and clenched her teeth, but couldn't stop the shaking. He didn't answer. She hung up and checked the time. He should be off work by now. She dialed again; still no answer. She pulled the phone down and scowled at it, wondering if she could possibly call anyone else. Daniel, maybe? Then her phone rang.

"Dad?" she practically screamed into the receiver.

"*No.*" That slow methodical voice...

"Xaphan..." she breathed.

"*I'm going to get straight to the point with you. The fact that you broke into my house, burned it to the ground, stole my confidential documents, and now you've got friends trying to destroy my plans...those things are all incidental. You know who I want."*

"You'll never have her!"

"Then know that it is you who have raised the stakes, not me. Your actions have forced me to move faster than I intended. Therefore I must have her. No more waiting. Bring her to me, or the people you love the most will begin to die. You won't know when, or how, or how long their pain will last. But they will die and they will die painfully. You can't possibly save them all nor be everywhere at once. It's your choice. Burn down my house, and I'll burn down yours."

The phone clicked. Silence.

39

Four Years Ago

It was two in the morning in the middle of a school week before Michael dropped Winter home from what he promised would be a simple dinner and a movie. The smell of pot clung to her nostrils. Even though she refused to join in that night, she wondered about second-hand pot smoke and how it might affect the baby. At any rate, she prayed her dad would be in bed just in case the smell clung to her clothes. But he waited on the couch, awake, and staring at a blank television.

"Where have you been?" he asked. The calmness in his voice frightened her more than his presence. She felt a flush creep into her face.

"Out," said Winter.

He turned to her...not angry, but eyes weary and saddened. "Have you no more respect for me than that?"

Her fear melted into guilt and she shrugged. "I didn't think you cared."

"You don't think…" Steve stood and faced her. "You think I don't care for you?"

"You let me leave every weekend and never once ask where I've been. Why do you suddenly care what I do in the middle of the week?"

"Tell me," he said, voice soft and resolved.

"Tell you what?" Winter's heart thumped against her ribs. Did he know?

"Tell me what you think of me. Let it out. It's time we cleared the air with each other."

Sudden anger boiled up within her, a deep rage she had tried to suppress for so long. All the fury of the past four years had finally been allowed a target and given permissions to rampage freely.

"Why are you even waiting for me? Why are you even pretending? We both know what I am to you…a bitter reminder of Mom. You know, she may have cheated on you, but I doubt it's because you were such a great husband. If you treated her anything like you treat me, it's no wonder she went looking for someone else. But don't worry, I'll be graduating soon and you can finally be rid of me for good. In fact, I'll move out now if you want. I'm old enough. Then you won't even have to bother anymore." The long list of what she had been wanting to tell him failed beneath the lingering numbness in her mind and a residue of guilt. She stared at him with an open mouth, but nothing else came out.

Steve frowned. "Your mother and I did have problems. We both made mistakes, and in the end we had forgiven each other. You brought us back together in a way…making sure you could be happy and have a stable home after she got sick. I can't replace the years I was never there, but you've been with me now for over three years…I had hoped we could begin something new."

"That doesn't explain why you treat me like a mistake!"

"You're not a mistake! And I don't think of you like that. It's just, I don't know much about being a father…"

"You could have tried harder. All those years and you never wanted to be involved more than a couple of weekends during the summer and Christmas holidays? How do you explain that?"

"I'm sorry. I was selfish and frightened. The more time passed, the harder it was to work up the nerve to get involved. At first it was just me trying to avoid your mom, and then when she moved away and took you, before you started school… We both had started new lives, the distance was so far…" He turned away. "There's no excuse. I was wrong. Your mother was wrong. We should have worked harder to make sure you had two parents."

"Well, now it's too late." Winter spun for the stairs.

"It doesn't have to be," he said behind her.

She paused with one foot on the bottom step and glared over her shoulder. "Why haven't you asked about Claire?"

His face went blank. "Claire? Is something wrong with Claire?"

"She hasn't been over here in nearly a year, Dad."

"Were you not with her tonight? I thought…"

Winter shook her head and shouted, "Claire killed herself last spring!"

"What?" He took a step closer. "Why didn't you tell me?"

"I tried, okay!" She twisted to face him full-on and pointed at herself. "I tried! But you were too busy with work to listen to me! You're always too busy. And even if you're not, you still don't want to listen. You keep pawning me off on someone else, telling me to go talk to someone. And when I needed *you*, you weren't there for me. You've never been there for me!"

"Winter…"

Winter held up a hand to silence him. "It's too late. I've dealt on my own for this long. I don't need you anymore." She put her back to him and started up the stairs.

"Don't say that. What if something happened to me? What would you do?"

"It wouldn't make much difference," she mumbled.

As she reached the landing and walked down the hall, she thought she could hear him crying.

40

Present Day

The horror of the vision. The shock of Xaphan's threat. Winter collapsed onto the pavement while panic coursed through her from toe to head. She panned the parking lot with no idea what to do. Slow tears, jarred loose by the trembling in her muscles, crept down her cheeks.

She gazed back down at the phone clutched tightly in her hand and decided to call Graham again. His voice came through the phone after only two rings. *"Yes?"*

Winter bit her lip. "Graham...I need you."

"Winter? Is everything okay?"

"I need you, Graham, and before I think about the words coming out of my mouth...I think I'm falling in love with you, and if you even have a shred of the same in you..." Her voice choked. "I need your help right now, because I don't know what to do. I think something horrible is about to happen and I just can't..." She covered her mouth as her throat seized.

"I don't know what's happened, but I'm here. Whatever you need."

A sob bubbled to the surface. "I have to get home. I have to get to my dad. I had a vision and Xaphan called my phone...I think my dad's in trouble. But I can't leave Kaci here, and you've got Summer and Davis...Graham..." She inhaled quick and shallow. "I...don't...know..."

"Winter, just take some deep breaths and calm down. You're hyperventilating."

Winter held her breath as her chest spasmed and her body trembled.

"Just stay where you are. I'm coming to you right now. I'm already in the car."

Winter nodded, even though she knew he couldn't see her. "I can't do this...not my dad..."

"We'll figure this out together. You and me. Okay?"

"Okay," she croaked. "Thank you."

"I want you calm by the time I get there. Can you do that?"

Winter nodded again. "Yes."

"Don't let him get in your head. You're stronger than this."

"What about the others?"

"They will be fine on their own for a day."

Winter took a long, deep breath to still the rocking of her body.

"Winter?"

"I'm here." Her voice came stronger than before, and hearing the strength of it helped to calm her further.

"I'll be there soon. Be waiting for me."

"I'm in the parking lot near the front door."

"Good. Stay close. Go walk around and get your head back."

"Okay."

He hung up and she found the strength to stand and walk back into the lobby. Waiting seemed wrong, unnatural, as if she needed to run home that precise moment. Run home to hide from Xaphan, to hide from the world. She wanted to scream. She wanted to weep all night long. But Graham was right. She needed to clear her head. She needed to wait for him. She didn't have to be alone with this.

Her stomach rumbled. When did she last eat? As she came into the cafe, just the smell of it almost turned her stomach. Food was the last thing on her mind, but she couldn't keep her head clear in that state. She grabbed a cold sandwich from a cooler, some chips, a soda, and a candy bar. For good measure she grabbed a couple of granola bars. After paying, she took them all back outside and sat on the curb in the cool evening air. She opened the sandwich, found it mostly unappetizing, wrapped it back up and ate one of the granola bars. The soda helped more than anything, and by the time Graham arrived she had herself in a much clearer state of mind.

He had already screeched to a halt in front of her before she realized he was driving her car. As she stood, he jumped out, ran to her side, and wrapped his arms around her.

"Are you okay?" he asked as he squeezed.

Winter let his warmth sink in and let him embrace her as long as he wanted. Which turned out to be not long enough. "A little," she said. "You brought my car?"

He shrugged as he opened the passenger door. "I figured it was a better choice. Do you want to drive or shall I?"

Winter took a deep breath and rushed to the driver's side. "I will. I can get us there faster."

He nodded as he sat on the passenger side and Winter eased behind the wheel. In the back seat she saw two bulging backpacks. "What's with the packs?"

"We said I'd be going with you, right? So I started packing immediately after our first phone call, just in case. One for each of us."

"I'll try not to think about you going through my things," she said with a small grin.

He glanced at her, his face flushing.

Winter shook her head. "Forget it. I'm glad you did and I'm glad you're with me."

"What will we do when we get there?" Graham asked.

"I don't know. Get my dad out of there for one. And if Xaphan is stupid enough to show up, this ends tonight."

"How?"

Winter clenched her teeth. "However necessary."

"And if he's not there…"

"Then we find him. I'm tired of running and I'm tired of everyone else running. Hold on."

Winter took a deep breath and put the car into gear. She forced all her anxiety into the heaviness of her foot, and the car roared through the parking lot to the street.

It was a race to Trenton Hills now. And if Xaphan wanted a race, Winter would win.

41

Once on the interstate, Winter mumbled a quiet prayer and floored the car, letting the speedometer climb higher and higher. The sky faded into dark blues and eventually complete blackness, giving way to brilliant stars above and a rising three-quarter moon. Winter continued redialing her dad, with no result. Only one reason she could think of would prevent him from answering...and she refused to dwell on any such possibility. She *would* get there in time. Xaphan had not yet called to gloat...so there *must* be more time.

As she put her phone back down, Winter suddenly felt the unmistakable bend of time warping around her. Wisps of angelic mist floated alongside the car. Graham slumped in his seat. She glanced over and saw him asleep, wondering if it were some side-effect of the time-warp that she alone could endure. Only Ayden had experienced this kind of thing before, last year when they went to rescue Claire from the diner. To rescue the Acolyte, rather. But Ayden didn't really count as normal.

Winter squeezed the wheel, wanting to coax more speed out of her car. Instead she watched the mist and the scenery as it flew by.

She could see through the darkness, something that had only happened a few times in the past. The trees and brush beside the road didn't pass by in the normal way. One moment everything stood perfectly still and the next everything blurred until it solidified in another location. It was as if she teleported in quick intervals rather than driving. Yet if she watched the road itself, it flew by beneath her at an impossible speed. The cars on the road behaved exactly like the trees, seemingly motionless when she could see them and then disappearing with a blur.

Within a few minutes, Trenton Hills loomed in the distance beneath the hazy glow of the city lights. What should have taken her hours to drive had taken practically no time at all. At least that's how it felt. Winter had no idea what time it really was, or how fast she'd actually arrived.

As she approached the Trenton River bridge, time settled into its normal rhythm and the mist faded away. Graham jerked himself awake and gazed at her with large eyes.

"I'm sorry, I didn't mean to sleep so long. Are we here already?"

Winter nodded. "We took a shortcut."

"Shortcut?"

"I'll explain later."

As they crossed the tall bridge into the city, Winter unconsciously glanced to her left, toward the old bridge where so much had happened. She tried never to look at that bridge too long or think about it, but knowing what she might be facing had brought those haunting images back. She bit her lip and forced herself to look away and eye Graham again.

He watched her, but said nothing.

"What?" Winter asked.

"We don't know what we're going to face and it'll be best if we're together at all times."

"I wasn't planning on separating."

"I just want to make sure we're on the same page. Do you have your FBI gun still?"

"It's in the glove compartment. But I don't need it," Winter said.

Graham frowned and reached inside his coat to pull out his own nine millimeter. "Well, I hope you don't mind if I do." He popped out the magazine, gave it a quick look, and slammed it back. Then he racked the slide, checked the chamber, and held the gun pointed toward the floor as if he expected to have to pull it up and start firing any moment. "Besides," he said, "if we are chased out of here, I can cover you."

Winter nodded. "Whatever."

It must have been later than Winter realized. The shops stood empty and silent. Few vehicles drove through the streets. At traffic lights, if there were no other vehicles around, she eased through the red light instead of waiting for the green. It didn't take long for her to weave through the city proper and find the residential areas she knew so well.

"This is it," she said as they turned onto her street.

"Which one?"

"Fifth on the left."

"Anything look suspicious?" asked Graham.

"Not yet."

He nodded, and Winter slowed the car to a crawl, straining to see anything amiss across the shadowy street at her dad's house. She parked the car against the opposite curb and continued studying the dark house.

"His truck is there, so he's home. Why wouldn't he answer? Why aren't there any lights on?"

"Maybe he had his phone off," said Graham. "Or he's asleep."

Winter shook his head. "That's not like him."

"Try calling again."

Winter opened her door and stood beside the car, raising her phone to her ear. Graham exited and walked around the back of the car to stand at her side. After five rings, she finally heard the pause and soft click indicating someone had answered.

"Hello again, Winter," came that sneering voice she hated.

"Xaphan!" Winter took a step toward the house, eyes darting up and down the street. Graham grabbed her arm and pulled her back to the car with one hand and raised the pistol with the other, scanning the street in a more deadly way than Winter had. "What have you done with him?"

"Are you there? Are you home?"

"Where is he?!"

"Look closely and watch…"

Winter stared at her dad's house, heart drumming, skin growing cold, sweat forming on her forehead, muscles numbing. She scanned every window but could only see the icy reflection of the streetlights. Then an inside light illuminated in Winter's own bedroom. Steve was there in the window, mouth moving and frantically shaking his head at her.

"Dad!" she yelled.

With a boom that momentarily sucked the sound out of the air and then crashed into her like a brick wall, deafening her and searing her face…the house exploded.

42

Four Years Ago

Winter stomped through the hall of Trenton Hills High School the next day, still fuming at her dad and angry with herself. What was she going to do about the baby? If there was a baby. Maybe she took the test wrong. Maybe she wasn't...

In the meantime, she couldn't stop feeling weird about herself, as if her body demanded her attention. As if everyone stared at her. As if they knew. But how could they? No one here knew Michael and no one knew what they were doing.

Her heart beat rapidly and her abdomen fluttered. Could that be the baby? Shouldn't it be way too early to feel anything? The pit of her stomach also churned, threatening to throw up the few crackers she had choked down that morning. In between the bouts of nausea came waves of ravenous hunger. Then the mere thought of food almost made her double over in the hall. She was so sick of puking. Sick of her body not knowing whether to love food or hate it.

"Hey, Winter," Stacy said as Winter reached the lockers.

Winter didn't look up. "Hey."

Stacy stepped closer. "You look horrible. Is something wrong?"

Winter shook her head. "Just a little sick, that's all. I'm fine."

"Maybe you should go see the nurse."

"No. I'm fine. It's nothing." Winter turned to her, holding her books against her chest as if to conceal her secret.

"Your face is so pale."

"Stomach bug. I'm getting over it."

Stacy frowned but nodded. "You're not contagious or anything?"

"No. I'm fine."

"Well, if you need anything…"

"I know. I'll ask you. Can we just go now?"

Stacy's eyes widened. "Yeah, sure." She turned, and Winter fell into step beside her. "Are you ready for the English test?"

Winter swore. "Sorry," she said to Stacy. "I forgot to study."

"But you're good at that stuff. You'll probably be fine. I'll help you study over lunch."

"Yeah. Whatever."

"And then I want you to read over my senior poem."

"You're finished already?" Winter asked.

"Sort of. I'm still not happy with some of the rhymes." Just before they entered their math classroom, Stacy paused and faced her. "Are you sure you're okay? Is something going on?"

"I'm fine! Just leave it alone, Stacy."

Despite the acid in Winter's voice, Stacy's face softened. "You can talk to me, you know."

"What? About a stupid virus?"

"Not that. If there's something else…I mean, you're not acting like yourself."

"Maybe I didn't sleep well, did you think of that?"

Stacy sighed. "Okay. I give. Forget it."

As Stacy walked into the classroom, Winter frowned. She had been far too harsh with the only friend she had left at this school. She decided to keep playing off the grumpiness as lack of sleep and a virus. Maybe Stacy would just let it go.

By lunch, Stacy acted as if nothing had happened. But as Winter entered the lunch room, the smell of the cafeteria made her stomach flip again.

"You need to eat something," Stacy said as Winter left the line and took her books to the table. Winter put her head in her hands and took deep breaths to steady herself.

After a few minutes, Stacy sat next to her. "Look, you're not going to feel better until you eat."

"I promise, eating won't help."

"But you're going to make yourself even more sick. Here, I picked up an extra roll." She slid a small yeast roll on a napkin toward Winter.

Winter glanced at it and then up at the sincerity on Stacy's face. "If I eat it will you leave me alone?"

Stacy smiled. "I'll leave you alone. I promise. And then I'll call out the study guide to you." Stacy reached into her backpack and pulled out a typed piece of paper.

Winter pulled the roll closer and picked the top crust off of it. As Stacy called out questions, Winter chewed through her answers. Despite the flopping of her stomach, the roll didn't seem to be problematic. She picked it up and took a larger bite.

"Want me to get you something to drink?"

Winter shook her head as she finished off the roll. "I'll get something at the water fountain as we leave."

"Sure. Only five more questions. You haven't missed any yet, so I think you'll be okay on the test. Ready?"

Winter nodded. The movement of her head convinced her

stomach to betray her. It lurched so violently, she thought she would get sick right there on the table. Instead, she tensed herself and ran out of the cafeteria.

"Winter?" Stacy called.

Winter burst into the bathroom and found a vacant stall where she could empty her stomach.

Again.

As she knelt there on the bathroom floor, one hand holding her hair and the other pressed against her lower abdomen as if she could feel the baby growing, she began to cry.

Again.

43

Present Day

The roar of the inferno drowned all other sounds, but it couldn't drown out Winter's screams in her own ears...the blaze consuming her father and the screams consuming her heart.

An unseen force prevented her from rushing into the fire. She kicked against the ground, leaning with all her weight, trying to reach out to the house. She could save him; there was still time. She knew it...but despite expending all her adrenaline-laced energy, she couldn't move.

Her screams, the constant rumble of the fire, were not the only sounds. Another voice cried out to her from deep within a tunnel. It called her name. It held her back, gripping her arms like a vise...wrapping her tightly...pulling her away from her dad.

With one hand she stretched out toward the house as if she could grip the railings on the porch and pull herself free. With the other she clawed at whatever held her captive. The searing in her face crept into her eyes, and somewhere in the back of her mind she sensed the heat from the house slowly burning her face. She blinked against it, not sure if the blur of her vision came from the heat or her heart.

Still she couldn't get free. Still the screams. Still that distant voice called her name, louder now as if she approached the end of that tunnel. Something grabbed her face and turned her whole head away from the house.

Graham. Still there. Mouth moving, but she couldn't hear him over the torrent of shouts and screams and protests coming out of her own mouth. He wanted to take her away, but she couldn't go yet. She had to save her father.

"...in the car!" The only words she could make out from him, and then only while she took a breath and lurched back toward the house.

Suddenly her feet no longer touched the ground. She lay in Graham's arms as he carried her away. She stretched back toward the house a final time before the muscles in her arms fell limp and she pressed her face into his chest, away from the heat, and let reality have its way. The screams turned to weeping. The fight inside turned to trembles.

Somehow she landed in the car. She knew he must have carried her there and realized she could now move. And by the time the thought registered, the car already sped away.

"Where are you going? We can't leave him there!"

"We have to, Winter. I'm sorry."

She twisted in her seat, the house out of sight now. Black smoke billowed into the inky sky amidst an orange glow. "We have to do something. Please!"

"Think, Winter!" he shouted. "He knew you were there. He had your father's phone. He knew you were watching at that moment."

Winter turned to stare at him, not quite understanding.

Graham lowered his voice. "He must have been close...him and only God knows how many others. They could be following us right now. Think about it. The two of us in his hands are tickets to Kaci. We have to get as far away from here as possible."

Winter sat back and faced the road. "Where do we go?"

"I don't know. We just drive. We get a message to the others and we get as far away as we can."

Winter's mouth hung open, salty tears dripping at the corners. "But what about my dad?"

Graham pursed his lips. "I'm sorry. There's nothing we can do. I'm really sorry. If there was anything..."

"We can't just run away!"

"Winter!" Graham shouted. "That's *all* we can do! Don't you realize that? He'll murder everyone we know to get to Kaci, and he'll chase us down wherever we go. Maybe, just maybe, if we run fast enough and far enough he'll be so busy chasing us that he'll leave the rest of our families alone. We have to run."

"Turn around! I can stop him! I can do this!"

"Graham frowned at her. "No. You can't. Not like this."

Winter sat back and sagged in her seat as the weight of her heart pulled her toward the ground. Graham was right. If he could get to Davis and Summer, if he could get to her dad, then he could get to anyone. They had to lead him away before he killed again.

As Graham sped through the streets of her old neighborhood, heading in the direction of downtown and busier streets, the explosion replayed in her mind. The silhouette of her dad in the window. What must he have thought? What did they do to him? How long had he been sitting like that?

Why did she never tell him more often how much she loved him?

Winter sobbed. She couldn't see the road, and she didn't care to. She let Graham do whatever he thought he needed to do to get them away.

"I think someone's following us," he said, but Winter barely registered what that meant. The engine roared as he pressed the gas harder.

She didn't care anymore. All she could think about were the times she had been mean and ugly to her dad, all the times she had treated him like garbage. She wasn't even sure she'd ever properly apologized. Sure, she'd apologized some, but did she do it enough?

She should have said more. She should have talked to him more.

"I can't shake him. I think there's more than one."

Did he really understand how much she regretted the way she treated him during high school? Did he really understand how much she had changed?

"Winter! Are you listening to me? We're in trouble."

Winter blinked and pulled herself back to reality. "What?"

"We're being followed and I can't lose them. I think they mean to stop us or worse."

Winter spun in her seat and stared out the back window. A black SUV and a matching sedan lurched behind them beneath the street lights, less than a hundred yards away, side-by-side as they raced north on the four-lane highway.

"We can't let them catch us," Winter croaked.

Graham grunted. "I don't think they want us alive. Look around us. Do you see any other vehicles or any cops? This whole thing was a trap for you."

"What do we do?"

"I was hoping you might think of something," Graham said. "I can only keep this up so long. There may be more of them ahead."

"I don't know!" Winter shouted.

"What do you mean, you don't know?"

Winter leaned forward with both hands on the sides of her head. "I can't..." Tears fell from her eyes again. She heard herself wailing as if trapped in her own body and merely a bystander to her body's functions. He was right there at the window...She could have saved him...

From far away she felt a hand on her shoulder, shaking her. She heard a voice calling her name.

"Look at me!" the words broke through.

Winter fell back into her body and turned the head that wouldn't turn moments ago. Graham watched her with wide eyes, flicking his gaze back and forth from her, to the road, and to the mirror.

"You can have a breakdown all you want. But later. If you don't get us out of here, then we're dead too," he said.

Winter glanced wide-mouthed over her shoulder again. How could she do anything? She could barely put one coherent thought in front of another.

The two cars were right on their bumper, taking up both lanes. Graham had Winter's BMW in the middle of the road, jerking back and forth to keep them from trying to pass.

"Winter…now would be great," he said through clenched teeth.

Winter shook her head. "I…can't…" she whispered.

At that exact moment, the fronts of both cars slammed together. The side fenders crumpled as the two cars collapsed in upon each other, as if invisible battering rams had struck each car near the outer front tire. Then as they wrinkled in as far as physically possible, the cars stopped as if struck by an invisible wall. The speed and momentum carried the back ends of each up into the air.

Winter screamed. Graham cursed and shook the wheel as if he could coax more speed from the BMW.

Both vehicles landed on their roofs in a chaotic display of flying debris, some of which struck the back of Winter's car. The cars skidded behind them, the SUV bursting into flames, and eventually slowed down enough for Graham to put some distance between them.

Winter slowly turned back, almost as stunned as when her dad's house had exploded.

"What did you do?" Graham asked.

Winter shook her head minutely. "Nothing."

44

The sky glowed in the distance, the deep orange of a pending sunrise. Winter stared at it, arms crossed and numb inside. After escaping Trenton Hills, she never regained the emotional capacity to do anything or string rational thoughts together. She did listen to Graham on the phone as they left town, and spared a little thought to recognize his brilliance at taking care of everything that needed to be done.

He called Davis and Summer back at the cabin. He called Peter and Kaci still at the hospital. He called Ayden wherever she was with Erickson. He gave everyone the same warning: Xaphan was tracking them down. Everyone. Possibly even their families.

Winter listened in, but let him handle everything. He was good at handling things, much better than she. They made a good team. He never once mentioned her hasty, unfiltered confession of love she had made over the phone. Maybe he just wrote it off as emotional rawness.

After the lengthy conversation with Peter, where Graham tried to gently and quickly explain that Kaci needed to get away from the hospital as fast as possible, Graham put his phone down and offered her a smile. "So far everyone else is okay. They're all leaving immediately. Everyone is separating and going different directions. After a few days we'll return to the cabin and make sure it's secure before calling them back."

Winter nodded. "I don't know what to do anymore."

He reached over and squeezed her hand. "I don't expect you to. Not now…so don't worry about it. Just let me handle it for a few days."

As the sky turn light blued on the horizon, Graham found a small hotel. Winter simply waited in the car for him, still trying to get a better grip on her emotions, as he checked in. When he came to get her, he held her hand all the way to the room. Just inside, she stood and studied the one bed, not sure if she should object or not.

Graham seemed to read her thoughts. "It's just for a few hours so we can get some sleep. I'll take the floor. Maybe you should go shower."

As he returned to the car for their packs, Winter drifted through the room, her head thick and dazed. She showered out of habit and put on the same clothes instead of digging anything new out of her pack.

Graham already had a pillow and the extra blankets on the floor by the time she finished. The blackout curtains were drawn tight against the morning light, and only a faint glowing outline disturbed the darkness. Graham sat in a chair by the lamp, on the phone again. Winter didn't bother to listen. If Graham couldn't be trusted, then so be it. She only wanted to crawl into the bed, face the wall, and exist.

Graham's phone call only lasted another five minutes. Then she heard him take his turn in the shower. When he came out, he went back to his pallet and turned out the light.

In the darkness, the images of the house came quickly and vividly. Her imagination filled in the blanks…her dad's final seconds, his thoughts, what the hours might have been like for him leading up to that moment.

She cried again, trembling, silently, trying her best not to disturb Graham. But he began to move in such a way that Winter suspected he had heard her quiet weeping and had sat up to check on her.

She bit her lip. "Graham...I..." She broke again as she had in the car.

Graham came to her. He lay down beside her and took her into his arms. She lay her wet cheeks upon his shoulder and her curled fist upon his bare chest. As she cried against him, he simply stroked her back and head until she finally cried herself to a fitful sleep.

After only a few hours, Winter woke up to voices just before noon. The adrenaline pumped inside of her and she shot out of the bed, ready to bolt. But Graham stood by the door, shirt back on, as Davis, Summer, and Ayden walked in. Erickson stayed on the balcony with his hands in the pockets of his hoodie.

Summer took one blanch-faced look at Winter and then ran to join Winter on the bed, wrapping her arms around Winter's shoulders.

"I'm so sorry," Summer said, her voice trembling.

Winter just nodded and patted Summer's arm around her chest.

Davis sat on Winter's other side as Graham took Ayden back onto the balcony to talk.

"Is there anything we can do?" asked Davis.

Winter shook her head. "No. What are you doing here?"

"We insisted," said Davis. "After Graham told us what happened we had to come."

Ayden and Graham came back in after just a moment, both staring at Winter. Winter wasn't sure what Graham had told her but she suspected.

Ayden sat in the chair and gave Winter a grim look. She had changed. Ayden no longer had the face of someone trying to run away, rather her determined eyes said she had accepted and embraced her new life. "You rest. I've got things."

Winter tried to smile at her and only managed to nod her head. Then she eased herself back to the pillow and closed her eyes, though she didn't think she'd be able to sleep anymore. Still, it was better than facing her friends and actually talking.

Summer propped a pillow up against the headboard and sat beside her on the bed. Erickson finally came in, and he, Graham, Davis, and Ayden huddled close together in the lamplight and whispered. Winter tried to relax and recapture her sleep, but despite how tired her body and emotions, she simply could not. Instead she just listened to the quiet whispers and Summer's gentle breathing beside her, indicating that Summer had dozed off…they had probably been up all night too.

Winter had watched her mother die slowly. Whether she admitted it or not, on some level she had even prepared herself for her mother's inevitable death. She had time to build a granite shell that she could slam into place whenever she needed to protect her heart from the pending pain. It didn't always work, but it was always there.

But now…she didn't have time to prepare. She didn't have time to say her goodbyes. She didn't have time to rebuild her inner fortress. The fire and ice, the stabbing pain that made Winter think she might have been having a heart attack, all weighed on her with the weight of eight years of emotional neglect. All the pain she had hidden with her mom, Ryan, Claire, Michael, and now her dad…squeezed her numb.

She sat in it, like a child sits in a puddle of rainwater. She lay there, like a runner collapsed at the end of a race. She bled inside, like ink slowly filling a balloon.

She wanted to cry again, to wail and moan like the bleating of a dying lamb. But the depth of her anguish had fallen beyond trivial things like tears. In that moment, crying would have been progress in the right direction, but she had not yet finished her descent into emotional hell.

Still they whispered.

Still she slept.

And Winter lay alone in the room. Alone in the world.

45

Four Years Ago

As far as Winter could tell, she could possibly be as many as six weeks pregnant. The next day was Friday again. Michael would be expecting her to come over for the weekend, but she wasn't sure what to do. She knew she needed to tell him, but it frightened her how he might react.

The moment she arrived home that day she went straight to her bathroom to take the second test, just in case. Still positive. She sat on her bed trying to figure out what to do next. What if Michael didn't want to see her again? What if her dad kicked her out? What would she do? Where would she go?

With that last thought she took a deep shuddering breath and started to cry. She gazed through her tears to the phone by her bed, snatched it up, and dialed Stacy's number.

"Hello?"

"Stacy? It's me." She couldn't hold back the tremble in her voice.

"Winter, what's wrong?"

"I need to talk to you. Can you come over?"

"Let me ask my mom, but I think it'll be okay. Hold on."

Winter waited while Stacy left the phone. She grabbed a tissue and tried to compose herself. Was this the right thing to do? Would Stacy be able to help?

Stacy came back after only a few seconds. *"I'll be right over."*

"Thank you." Winter said, her voice much stronger now.

"Of course. See you in a few." Stacy hung up.

Winter checked herself in the mirror to make sure there weren't any tell-tale signs of crying, just in case her dad came home early. She hadn't worn any makeup that day, but her eyes were swollen red underneath. Still, it could be worse.

She went downstairs, grabbed a package of saltine crackers from the kitchen, and stood to watch out of the window by the door. If Stacy left her house immediately, it would only be about five or ten minutes before she arrived. Winter could have waited in her room or on the couch, but her nerves needed to see Stacy drive up and needed to stake-out her dad.

Just after ten minutes had passed, Stacy pulled up against the curb. When she reached the door, Winter opened it for her and Stacy stepped right in.

"What's going on?" she asked, reaching out to give Winter a hug. "Are you in trouble?"

"Maybe," Winter said, her voice wobbling. "Let's go to my room. Just in case my dad comes home."

"Sure, whatever you want."

Winter led the way back up the stairs to her bedroom and locked the door. They both sat cross-legged on her bed, and Winter stared at her hands.

Stacy reached out to grab them. "Whatever it is, you can tell me."

Winter opened her mouth, but instead of words she just started sobbing again.

"Winter…is it that bad?" A hint of panic tinted Stacy's voice now. "What's going on?"

Winter lifted her eyes to look at Stacy and tried to steady her voice. "I'm pregnant."

Stacy's eyes widened. "No! Are you sure?"

Winter nodded.

"But how…never mind. Who? Michael?"

Winter nodded again.

"Did you take a test?" Stacy asked.

Winter pointed toward the bathroom counter. "That's the second one."

Stacy went in and gaped at it for a full thirty seconds. "What are you going to do?" she asked as she returned to the bed.

Winter shrugged. "I don't know. That's why I called you. I don't know what to do. I wish it would just go away."

Stacy shook her head. "No. That's not an option, do you hear me? Whatever happens to you, you'll survive. But don't take it out on that poor baby."

Winter pursed her lips, but nodded. "So what do I do then?"

"Have you told anyone else?"

"No. Just you. Michael is expecting me this weekend. He needs to know, but I'm afraid he'll break up with me."

Stacy narrowed her eyes. "He's not as shallow as all that, is he? Winter, please tell me you didn't get *this* involved with someone who wouldn't consider having a real future with you, did you?"

"I don't know," said Winter. "We were just having fun, you know?"

"Do you love him?"

Winter shrugged again. "Maybe. I don't know. I'm so confused."

Stacy paused in thought for a moment. "Okay. Well, even though we're going to hope for the best, let's expect the worst. If you tell him and he breaks it off, so what? You'll still have this wonderful baby and you still have your dad."

"And what if he kicks me out?"

"Do you really think he'd do that to you? I think maybe you've been unfair to him, Winter. I think he loves you more than you give him credit for."

"But does he really want me to stay? I just don't know. I think he'd rather I move out. I think he's looking forward to it. Having a grandchild in the house…Stacy, it's just going to make things worse."

"Okay, so what? We're going to hope for the best, but expect the worst. If Michael breaks it off and your dad kicks you out, you'll need someplace to go. Doesn't Michael have a sister? What about her?"

"I don't know," said Winter. "We're not that close."

"But maybe she'll help you out. What about Michael's parents? Are they nice people?"

Winter nodded. "Nice enough."

"They might help too."

"What about you?" asked Winter.

"I'm going to med school out of state. You know I'd be there for you, no question about it." Stacy took a deep breath. "I'll tell you what…if everything, and I mean *everything*, falls apart here, then we'll make plans for you to come with me. We'll figure it out. Maybe we'll get an apartment together or something, I don't know. I can work in the afternoons…you can work at nights while I study and take care of the baby. We can make it work. So regardless, I want you to know that you'll have a place to go, okay?"

Winter nodded and reached out to hug Stacy. "Thank you."

Stacy squeezed. "That's what friends do for each other."

"I'm sorry I got into this," Winter croaked.

"We all make mistakes. But the mistake is done. It's in the past. Just concentrate on the future from here on out." Stacy pulled away. "God has something big planned for you, I know it."

Winter shook her head. "I doubt that."

"No, I think it's true. And I think you're going to find out what it is very soon now."

Winter narrowed her eyes at her. "Having a baby?"

Stacy flashed her a warm smile. "Maybe so."

Present Day

Winter woke up a couple hours later, still numb emotionally and physically. And now very hungry.

Graham was the only one there now. He sat patiently in the chair watching television. "How are you?"

Winter shrugged. "Not good."

"I wouldn't expect you to be."

Winter bit her lip to keep from crying again. She sat up. "Where's everyone?"

"Gone. Disappeared in different directions until I can check the cabin," he said. "I thought you needed some undisturbed time to rest, so they left quietly."

She swung her feet over the edge of the bed. "Do you think the cabin is safe?"

"I think so. There's no indication that he knows where it is. And we left a lot of supplies there. We need to pack that stuff up before we can relocate permanently, if that's even necessary. I'll have a better idea later. We'll give it a few weeks first. Don't worry."

Winter stared at the floor. "What if he goes for other family members? If he got to my dad…"

Graham glanced toward the window, peering through the crack in the curtains. "I know. I don't think anyone's family is safe."

"Is there anything we could do?"

"Probably not," he said. "If we tried to warn them, they would just freak out and go to the police. That would only make things worse. Kaci's parents are already running, according to Peter. But the rest…I just don't know what to do. Maybe this is so personal to Xaphan now, he won't reach beyond what would directly affect you or Kaci." He turned to look Winter in the eyes, his face grim.

"But it's only a matter of time," Winter said.

"Yes," said Graham.

"What about Erickson?"

Graham shook his head. "Ayden insists he's okay. They've been through a lot already in just a few months. I was surprised."

"Do you trust him?"

"I don't know. He helped take care of Kaci for years and Ayden trusts him now, with her life she says. I don't think he would do anything to hurt any of us. So as far as that's concerned…yes, I trust him."

"But…"

"But," said Graham leaning forward in the chair. "Do you think a worm knows that it's bait?"

"Do you think he was released on purpose to lead Xaphan to us?"

Graham shrugged. "I don't know. He doesn't have any devices on him that can be tracked. There's no one following him…I made sure of that."

"So where are they now?"

"Gone somewhere, like the others."

"You don't think it would be safe to take him to the cabin?" Winter asked.

"Maybe…"

"What do you mean maybe?"

Graham stood. "We'll be checking out the cabin before anyone else. We can make sure it's safe. And…we can get it ready. Think about it. If he really is bait, then they don't want us to know right? But if we know, then he becomes *our* bait. You want to find Xaphan?"

Winter nodded quickly.

"Then Erickson may bring him to us. We set the trap, call Ayden and Erickson in first and tell them Kaci is already there. Then when Xaphan arrives…"

"Are you sure it would work?"

"We need to end this soon and this may be our best chance."

Winter crossed her arms and rubbed herself. "I'm not even sure what's supposed to happen when I find him again. I don't think I could, you know…"

"Kill him?"

Winter nodded.

"You'll do the right thing, I'm certain of it."

Winter glanced up and met his eyes, and in that moment she made an impulse decision. She jumped off the bed and crossed over to him. She straddled him in the chair, grabbed his face with both hands, and kissed him deeply. He pulled her tight and kissed her back just as eagerly. After a minute or two, Winter pulled away and rested her forehead upon his, her eyes closed.

"We probably shouldn't," she whispered.

"I know."

"I think I want more of us…"

"…but the timing's not right."

She nodded. "When all of this is over, I'll be yours if you'll have me." She pulled back to gaze at him clearly. "But if you knew what I've done…"

He shook his head. "We all have things in our past we'd rather forget. When this is over…"

Winter leaned forward quickly to kiss him again. "I don't want to take the chance of missing this." She kissed him down the neck and reached to tug off his shirt.

He grabbed her wrists. "Not like this."

She sat up and tilted her head. "Why not?"

"Because I don't want you to regret it later. And I know you will."

She sighed and leaned her head against his shoulder. "This sucks."

He laughed. "We barely know each other, you know."

"I know. But it feels right."

"Then I promise you this. When all of this is over and everyone is safe, we'll be together. We'll get married."

"Mmm…and buy a house?"

He nodded. "White picket fence and all."

"I want a dog."

"You can have any kind of dog you like."

"And kids," Winter said. "Three kids."

"I was thinking more like five."

Winter laughed. "I don't think so." She closed her eyes and took another deep breath. "What else?"

"We'll travel. Europe, Asia, the Caribbean. Anywhere you want to go. We'll see the whole world. Eventually our three children will grow up and get married. One of them becomes a doctor, one of them a teacher. The third lives at home until he's twenty-five. We make him get a job at a supermarket and kick him out."

Winter laughed again. "Keep going."

"Our hair begins to turn gray. Our first grandchild arrives…a girl. They name her Winter Marie and she never leaves your side. Eventually more grandchildren arrive, each one just as awesome. We sit on the porch together…"

Winter didn't remember any more. She drifted off dreaming of the perfect life with Graham.

47

Winter and Graham stayed in the motel for the rest of the week. Graham continued to sleep on the floor to give Winter plenty of space, even though Winter tried to push the boundaries during the day. At the end of the first week they relocated and Graham made sure to get separate rooms. They spent most of their days wandering the city, holding hands, and practically dating. Winter let the flood of released emotion for Graham drown the heartache of losing her dad. But the pain stayed just below the surface. If she dwelt on it for too long, she broke down and Graham would take her someplace private and quiet.

One morning during the first week of May, after four weeks and four hotels, Graham sat at the table in the corner of his room talking on the phone like he did at some point every day. Checking his contacts for anything Xaphan might be doing. Checking in on the others. Winter sat on his bed, leaning against the headboard, watching TV with the volume low.

Finally he hung up and turned to her. "We're going back today," he announced.

Winter eyed him. "Do you think it's safe?"

"It's been quiet. The others haven't had any trouble. I think it's time we checked out the cabin. If nothing else, maybe we can retrieve all of our stuff."

"Did you tell the others?"

Graham nodded. "As soon as we know it's safe, we'll call Ayden and Erickson in. If nothing happens and Erickson is safe, we'll call the others. Everyone is just waiting on me."

Winter sidled to the edge of the bed and reached out for him. He stood to grab her hand and she pulled him down for a kiss. "If only..." she said.

"When all of this is over," he replied. He straightened and turned for the door. "I'll go check out."

Ten minutes later they were back in Winter's car heading toward the cabin. She let Graham drive again, not trusting herself to be able to concentrate. He took the wheel without even asking. Every time she thought of her dad, the hole opened up in her heart again. They drove all morning and most of the afternoon before they arrived late as the sun began to set and already mostly behind the trees.

A few miles before the road to the cabin, Graham slowed down and turned onto a small dirt road heading into the forest. When they were far enough in that no one could see them from the road, Graham stopped. He pulled out his phone and began tapping on it.

"What are you doing?" she asked.

"Before everyone came to the cabin, I set up several trap cameras. They're cellular-connected and upload photos to a cloud server. I checked them this morning, but I want to check again now. If anyone's been poking around, I'll know."

"Could they get through unnoticed?"

"It's possible, but unlikely. We're going to go in a back way just in case."

Winter nodded as he continued to work on his phone for several minutes. "Are you sure Kaci's safe?" she asked.

He nodded to her without looking up. "Probably safer than the rest of us. She and Peter have been using aliases...smart. I'm more worried about Ayden. But we'll know soon if Erickson's been compromised."

"Oh."

"Wait..." Graham said, pausing as he looked at his phone.

Winter leaned against his side. "Is something wrong."

Graham moved to another photo. "No...Tell me they didn't."

"What?" Winter snapped, craning to see. He showed her the photo. "That's Kaci's car!"

Graham moved to the next photo. "And Davis's."

"Is that all? What about the first one?"

He flicked back two photos. "I didn't recognize it." He showed it to her.

"Ayden..." Winter breathed and panic filled her body. "That means Erickson's there. If he's being tracked..."

Graham tossed his phone down and put the car into gear. "We have to get them out of there. Now."

"I'll corner Erickson," Winter said as Graham barreled through the back road. "We have to find out the truth from him. If he's behind getting Kaci in the open..."

Graham nodded. "I'll follow your lead."

Within a few minutes, they passed by the lake behind the cabin. Graham slammed the brakes in front of the house and skidded to a halt. Before the dust had settled, Winter jumped out of the car and ran to the cabin. She flung the door open and found everyone inside, TV on, as if nothing were wrong. Erickson sat at the table with Kaci and Peter, all of them in the middle of a laugh.

Ayden jumped to her feet from the couch upon Winter's violent entrance. "What's wrong?"

"What's everyone doing here?" Winter shouted. "You were all supposed to wait for the all clear!"

Peter stood. "Ayden called and said Graham told her it was

okay."

Graham pushed in behind Winter. "That's a lie!"

"She told us, too," said Davis, now standing. Summer grabbed his hand and rose to his side.

"He did tell me!" Ayden shouted back at Graham. "You said it was safe!"

"How did you even find this place?" asked Winter.

"I told them," said Kaci softly.

"I did not tell you that!" Graham had moved in front of Ayden.

"That's exactly what you said! You said you checked it and that it was safe!"

"I said I was *going* to check it!"

As Graham and Ayden continued to yell at each other and those still seated stood, Winter stared at Erickson. Erickson stared back at her, emotionless. One by one everyone but Graham and Ayden noticed the stare-down. As Peter and Kaci moved to a more neutral place away from Erickson, and Davis and Summer eased closer to Winter, Ayden suddenly clenched her mouth shut. Graham huffed and stepped to Peter's side. Silence filled the room, inflating like hot air.

With two giant steps, Winter crossed to within a few feet of Erickson. "How did you get free?" she asked through clenched teeth.

"What are you talking about?"

"Don't lie!" Winter shouted. "You didn't escape when Claire attacked. You were captured. Weren't you! *Tell—me—the—truth*!"

The color drained from Kaci's face. "Agent Erickson?"

Erickson took a deep breath and faced the floor.

"You lied to me?" asked Ayden leaning toward him with her fists clenched. "After all that we've done together?"

"Look," Erickson said. "You don't understand. It's not like that."

"I saw you in a burning house," said Ayden. "In a vision."

"I burned down the house," said Winter.

"Yes," said Erickson. "That's how I escaped."

"Or were set free," said Graham.

"Were you set free?" asked Peter.

"No...yes..." Erickson shook his head as if confused.

"Did Xaphan set you free?" asked Winter.

"No!" Erickson shouted as he stood and slammed his palms onto the table. "I escaped!"

"What happened before that?" Winter asked. "What did they do to you?"

"Nothing. They just kept me locked up."

"That's not true either," said Ayden. "You knew things. You told me things that happened on the outside while you were there. You knew about the explosion on campus before anyone told you!"

"You couldn't have known if you were locked up," said Winter. "They told you things. Why?"

"He's working for them," said Graham.

"No!" shouted Erickson.

"I trusted you!" shouted Ayden.

"No!" shouted Erickson.

"Then what?" asked Winter. "What did they do to you? What do you remember? Tell us!"

"They kept me in a room." He started to fidget, looking at the table and scratching his arm. "It's all fuzzy. They kept me drugged. I don't know."

"Think!" said Winter. "What do you remember? Impressions, dreams, anything. We have to know."

"There was another room. A table. They put me on it."

"Experiments?" asked Graham. "Brainwashing?"

"Did they want you to do anything?" asked Ayden.

"Did you lead them here?" asked Peter.

"No. They just strapped me down and sedated me. I don't remember anything else, I swear. It was just once. They kept me locked in a room otherwise." He still scratched his arm.

"Then how did you get out?" asked Graham.

"During the fire…I don't know. The door opened."

"Set free," said Ayden.

"It was all a setup," said Winter. "Even then."

"No!" Erickson shouted jerking his face back up at her. "A little girl let me out."

Winter's stomach fluttered. "A little girl?"

"Yes!"

"Are you sure?"

"Yes!" Erickson scratched his arm more violently.

"Why?"

"I don't know! She said I needed to help you!"

"What about the woman?" asked Ayden. "The one that's been following us?"

Erickson shook his head. "I don't know anything about her…"

"Liar!" Ayden shouted. "You knew her name! Why do you keep lying?"

"Why would you do this to me?" asked Kaci softly. "After everything?"

"Because I wanted you to trust me again. I wanted to help you like I've always been doing. I thought if I told you the truth…"

"Thought what?" asked Winter.

He snarled. "I thought *this* would happen. I was right." He scratched his arm again.

"What's that?" asked Ayden. "What are you doing?"

"I don't know. My arm itches. What of it?"

"I've seen you do that before," Ayden said. "You do it when you think I'm not looking."

Winter hurried across the room and snatched his arm, shoving the long sleeve up. "There's a red scar here. You said they took you to a table. What did they do?"

"I don't remember," Erickson said.

"Do you think they did something to his memory?" Winter asked Graham.

"Maybe. I don't know. He said something about drugs."

"What's that mark, then?" asked Ayden. "Did they implant something?"

Erickson reached over to scratch it, digging his nails into it and almost drawing blood. "There's something…"

"Something's definitely in his arm," said Winter.

"A tracker," said Graham.

"No…" said Erickson.

Ayden reached down to her boot and pulled out a knife. "Move," she said to Winter and shoved her out of the way.

Erickson jerked his arm away. Winter grabbed it by the elbow and pulled it toward the table. Graham and Peter grabbed him by the shoulders.

"Be still! We have to know," said Winter. "If you want us to trust you, we have to know what they did to you!"

Davis rushed over and pinned his wrist to the table. Summer and Kaci stood back, eyes wide.

Erickson tensed, but stopped fighting. His fist clenched tightly and he bared his teeth.

"Quick," Winter said to Ayden.

Ayden didn't bother being gentle. She jabbed the knife in just at the top of the red mark and dragged it through the skin. Erickson cried out and shook. Blood poured out of his arm. Then Ayden flicked the tip of the knife up and a small sliver of silver popped onto the table.

"What is it?" asked Winter. "Could it be a tracker of some kind?"

"Get a towel," Graham said to Summer. Summer rushed into the kitchen.

"Davis? What do you think?" asked Winter

Davis shook his head. "I don't know. Maybe. It's too small and a GPS chip needs a power source."

"What about RFID?" asked Graham. "It's bigger than the ones I've seen, but could it work?"

"Maybe," said Davis. "I don't know much about it."

Summer tossed Erickson the towel and he pressed it against the gash.

"You're the best we've got in the room, Davis," said Winter. "We need to know if they can find us from this. Think, is there any way possible?"

Davis closed his eyes. "It's not GPS, but it could be some kind of RFID or something similar."

"Those need external power, too," said Graham.

Davis nodded at him. "But one this size might be designed to draw a small amount of energy from heat."

"The itching," said Ayden.

"What would that do?" asked Winter. "Can they find us?"

"RFID contain stored information. Something this size could contain a lot of information, even some kind of computer virus or program. It would still need a connection or a way to communicate, and it would have to be close or strong to activate it with limited heat power."

"Like Wi-Fi?" asked Peter.

"Yes. That could work. When it encounters Wi-Fi it could activate a program or virus to hijack the signal and upload data."

"There's Wi-Fi here," said Graham.

"But could they find us?" asked Winter.

"It wouldn't be perfect. They'd only have a trail of connections, and only God knows what other kind of data. But if it were stationary for long enough, maybe. I suppose the virus could even jump into a phone or something with a GPS and send out a signal. I don't know. I'm just making this up here. I don't really know what this thing is."

Peter looked at Winter. "It doesn't matter what it is, we have to assume they can find us."

"We've been here all afternoon," said Ayden.

"Plenty of time," said Graham.

"Then they are coming," said Winter.

Summer squeaked.

"We have to go now," said Graham. "They could be here any minute."

"If they're not already here," said Ayden. "Listen."

Everyone stood still and quiet. The unmistakable thumping of a helicopter reverberated outside, coming closer by the moment. Then the squeak of brakes turned everyone's attention to the front door. Winter recovered first and rushed over, peaking through the nearest window.

"A van," she said. "There are men getting out with guns and flak vests. I can see the helicopter just over the trees circling."

"What do we do?" asked Ayden, coming to her side.

"We get Kaci out and then I'll…" Winter stopped. One of the men brought around a long black tube with an explosive sticking out of the end. "You've got to be kidding."

With a loud whoosh and a trail of smoke, the RPG flew through the air straight toward the front door.

Four Years Ago

Winter held the manila folder in her hand. She hesitated before entering her senior English class, knowing how much of her own vulnerability she had put into her Senior project. At the last moment, she had decided to write a poem like Stacy was doing. The rawness she poured into it after finding out about the pregnancy still clung to her heart. As other students pushed past her, she considered running back to her locker, hiding the poem, and telling her teacher she forgot the project at home.

"Winter?" Mr. Carey asked as he stood by the door taking up projects. "Is that your project?"

She nodded and handed it to him, then rushed to her desk. As she sat down, Mr. Carey closed the door and walked toward his desk with the projects in hand.

"Your assignments are on the board," Mr. Carey said. "Read the short story on page 220 and do the analysis questions at the end. It shouldn't take you more than half an hour. We will have discussion during the last half of class."

Winter turned to the story along with everyone else as Mr. Carey sat behind his desk and began reviewing the projects. Her abdomen cramped and she had trouble concentrating. All she could think about were the what-ifs of telling everyone about the pregnancy. Even though Stacy assured her things would be fine, she couldn't help the sense of dread that had settled permanently inside of her. She found herself re-reading the same page for the third time, so she took a deep breath and pushed away her anxiety so she could finish the assignment.

After about half an hour, most of the students had completed the assignment and talked quietly. Winter scrambled through the analysis questions, trying to at least put enough information down that she could adequately participate in the discussion.

"Winter," said Mr. Carey. "Would you come here for a moment?"

Winter glanced up, her heart fluttering. She stood and rushed to his side.

Mr. Carey had her project open in front of him. "This..." He shook his head. "This is brilliant."

"Thank you," she said softly.

"I'd like to share it with the class, if you don't mind."

"I don't know..."

"They'll read it anyway, you know. These projects are always published and copies go in the school library. The best two or three go into the city newspaper."

"I know," she said.

"This may be the best project I've seen so far. Can I read it to the class?"

"No." Winter bit her lip, chills rippling across her skin. "I'll do it."

"Are you sure?"

She nodded quickly and returned to her desk before she could change her mind. If she couldn't do this one simple thing, share this little poem with her class no matter how intimate, how could she face

Michael and her father about the baby? Her heart pounded, but she knew she needed to find the courage to do this. Like the pregnancy, everyone would find out anyway. Her only choices were to let them or reveal it on her terms.

Mr. Carey stood a couple of minutes later, her project in hand, and the rest of the class quieted and turned to face him.

"We'll have discussion in a moment...I hope you all enjoyed the story, it's one of my favorites. But before we proceed, I want to talk a little about your projects. I've looked through them all and some of them are quite impressive. Some need a little work. I'll be talking to each of you individually about getting these projects finalized for the library.

"There is one project that really stood out this morning, and I'd like to share it with you now. 'Remember Me,' by Winter Maessen. Winter's poem is quite moving and she's agreed to read it to you. Winter?"

Winter eased back out of her desk and to the front of the class with her head facing the floor. Mr. Carey handed the folder to her and stepped toward the wall. Winter opened it and scanned the poem she could almost recite from memory. Then she glanced up at her classmates, each of them watching her patiently. She took a deep breath and began.

"A single drop of salinated fear
Left a glistening track down my crimson cheek.
A growing darkness, a broken world,
Punched a cavern where my heart once beat.

As the fragile pieces returned to shape
With jagged cracks trembling in place,
A fateful night, a demon sworn
Crushed the vestiges feebly encased.

What would I give to lean on hope?
What would I trade for a friend to keep?
It seemed to be a timely companion,
If not for a watery leap.

A fractured world, a mutilated heart,
Facing life from the loneliest pit.
A smile so sweet did gently meet,
What have I left to give?

From the first breath to the dying night
Each moment a fight against the grand master life.
So begins the end, the end at the beginning.
We live to survive and survive only to die.

And now the pieces are in position, all the players in place
All schemes complete, seen and unseen.
For everybody knows that in order to win
Sometimes you must sacrifice your queen.

Who am I in this game?
Am I pawn? Am I grandmaster?
Am I a mother? Am I a daughter?
Am I a wife? Am I a mistress?

Maybe I'm just a picture on a wall, faded and forgotten by time.
Maybe I'm just a frame of a film, gone with a blink.
Maybe I'm just a verse of a song, caught in time and lost to the
    next beat.
Maybe I'm just a page in a book, gathering dust on my ink.

Will you remember me, admirer, when other colors are more
    vibrant?

Will you remember me, watcher, with more thrills on demand?
Will you remember me, listener, with a new tune beneath your
    feet?
Will you remember me, reader, with a new story in hand?

Thank you for admiring and for noticing at all.
Thank you for watching and seeing me true.
Thank you for listening and hearing my story.
Thank you for reading. Thank you."

As the class applauded softly, Winter handed the folder back to
her teacher and rushed back to her desk. She had never felt so naked
in her life.

49

Present Day

"GET DOWN!" Winter screamed. She spun, grabbed Ayden's arm and jumped.

The explosion shook the air, filling it with searing fire and flying debris. Around Winter and Ayden, a halo of white mist formed, deflecting most of the heat, but the shock of the impact still projected them through the air to thump into the opposite wall.

Winter slammed to the ground, dazed and half on top of Ayden. The shock wave rang in her ears, muting every sound and leaving only the rapid swishing of her heartbeat. She heard screaming...shouting...as if from a distance. Through the gaping hole in the front of the house the Wretch hovered, surveying them, as men rushed in. While two of them stood near the hole, guns trained in different directions at those fallen in the blast, two more rushed into the kitchen. Erickson stood up from where he had fallen, but he didn't go after the men; he stood transfixed, one arm outstretched toward the Wretch.

The men came back out, dragging Kaci. Kaci beat at them and

screamed. Winter tried to move, but her vision tilted. She teetered forward, almost crashing upon a splintered beam. Across the room, Peter found his feet, and one of the men struck him in the head with the butt of his gun. Peter collapsed back onto the floor.

Graham tried to stand too, but staggered and leaned against the wall, clutching his side. Was he injured? A sliver of horror pulled away, reserved for Graham alone, and in that brief moment Winter almost forgot about everyone else.

Kaci screamed again, sharper, piercing through Winter's hearing as the acoustic numbness subsided. Kaci's flailing feet vanished out of the gaping hole in the wall. Winter pushed through the nausea and vertigo, spreading her feet wide, and stood. She shook her head and tried to clear it, letting the spiritual power fill her and take control, hastening her recovery. She staggered toward the Wretch, but with one look from the demon Winter flew through the air, crashed into the wall, and tumbled hard onto the floor again. As the Wretch floated away, Winter could see the helicopter hovering just above the trees and the men shoving Kaci into the van.

Then Davis ran by and lept out of the opening after Kaci.

"Davis! No!" Winter shouted, the sound of her voice reverberating in her skull, her ears still not fully recovered.

Winter managed to get back on her feet, found her strength again, and stepped over Ayden moaning on the floor. As Winter passed through the breach, smoke and cinders burning her eyes, the sliding door of the van slammed. Davis careened toward it about fifty feet away.

Winter raced after them, sped along by the fury of the power now beginning to course through her skin, though her muscles still ached and her ears throbbed.

The last man behind Kaci spun around and aimed a handgun at Davis. The boom of the shot barely reached Winter's damaged ears, but Davis collapsing onto the ground sent icy slivers through her heart. He fell like a rag doll, as if all strength and momentum had suddenly vanished. He crumpled into a heap upon himself, arms twisted and face in the gravel.

"Davis!" she shouted again, a little more reaching her ears this time, the throbbing now coming from the helicopter as it whirled above.

The van tires spun. The vehicle pivoted and took off.

Winter fell to her knees beside Davis, grabbed his shoulder and rolled him over. "Davis!" His glazed, open eyes stared blankly into the sky. A dark red circle in his forehead leaked blood all over his face. "NO!" she screamed. "NOOO!"

She heard shouts from the house. Others emerged, running to her side. Ayden, still glossy-eyed and teetering. Graham, still clutching his side. Both disheveled and ashen-faced. Angry burns traced lines through Graham's arm.

"NO!" Winter kept screaming.

"Winter!" Ayden grabbed her by the face and turned her to look eye to eye. "Get Kaci! We'll take care of the rest!"

Winter rocked momentarily, gazing down at Davis's body. "I can do something...I can help..."

"Go!" Ayden screamed. "I'll do whatever needs to be done. You go save Kaci!"

Winter gazed at her for a heartbeat, back at Davis for another. Graham pressed the keys into her palm and Winter bolted for her car.

It only took a moment to spin the car around and point it to the main road. She caught a fleeting glimpse of Summer kneeling on the ground beside Davis before she floored the BMW. Rage took over. A pure fury, not human, poured into her from the divine. Every moment felt like slow motion. Every molecule stood out in perfect contrast to the molecules beside them, as if she could see the fiber of each created thing.

Her hearing returned, sharper than before, repaired, filled with the rumbling sound of Godly justice. Around her, she could see wisps of smoke, deftly preparing the path before her. One wisp in particular charged directly ahead, almost human-like, brandishing a sword...her premonition, her guardian, her standard-bearer. He led the way, taking her in the right direction, guiding her after the van with each turn through the country roads.

With one more turn, she spotted the van not far ahead, crossing a dam...sheer ravine to the left and deep reservoir on the right. Something familiar pinged her mind about that dam, but she didn't allow herself to think about it. All she did was pray for more speed from her car.

The van crossed the dam and disappeared around a turn. Then as Winter reached the dam, the helicopter returned, descending between Winter and the far end. It spun so that the side opening of it faced her.

In that opening protruded a giant machine gun in the hands of someone sighting her down. The road in front of her erupted in small plumes of dust. With loud raps, the bullets struck the front of her car.

The car sputtered. A tire exploded. The windshield shattered. Fire blazed through her left shoulder. Winter flung herself sideways onto the passenger seat. The speeding car twisted, overturned, flew through the air, crashed once upon the ground, and then landed upside down in the water.

50

The water rushed in fast through the gaping hole that used to be the windshield. Winter scrambled against her seatbelt that held her jammed into the car, but her left shoulder had fallen completely numb. She couldn't move her fingers or even bend her elbow. The water bubbled near her head now. She leaned toward the passenger seat for better air, still struggling across her body with her good arm to unlatch the seat belt.

With one final breath, the water claimed her and the car descended into darkness. The seatbelt wouldn't give, so she found the incline release and pushed the seat as flat as she could. Then she slithered backward, struggling to get free.

The shattered back window did not quite crumple in as far as the rest. The roof had folded around the roll bar in the front and left the back almost level, buckled only in a few places. Winter clawed forward toward the back window, barely able to make out the jagged edges of the glass in the depths of the murky water. Her lungs burned now, and her abdomen spasmed, but she finally pulled her legs free of the seatbelt.

Winter eased to the back window, dragging herself along with one arm as her left arm floated helplessly at her side. Beyond the shattered glass she could just make out the bottom of the lake a few feet away, approaching quickly. When the nose of the car hit, the vibrations pulsed through the water, and the car pivoted backward.

Winter scrambled through the broken back window, slicing her leg on the glass. With the car upside down, the trunk loomed above her, lowering quickly as the car's roof rolled onto the silt. She had barely enough space to pull herself through the muck. The moment she reached open water, the car rocked backward and sank down. The trunk hit the bottom of the lake, jamming a jagged piece of metal deep into her calf.

Winter screamed beneath the water, releasing what little oxygen was left in her lungs. She jerked at her leg, but the metal only tore deeper.

She peered through the murky water…and saw the Wretch sitting on the trunk, hair drifting in the water, watching her with a smile.

Winter could do nothing else. Her oxygen was gone. Her left arm still floated, numb and useless. Mavka held the car so tightly against the bottom that she couldn't get her leg free. Winter cast around desperately for an escape, and that's when she saw it.

Two empty soda bottles, full of air, chained inside a large cinder block. All within reach.

Winter snatched at the loose end of chain holding the bottles and dragged the whole thing closer. She pulled the cap off the first, bubbles glugging to the surface, and shoved her lips around the opening. She exhaled from her nose and breathed in deeply, keeping the bottle opening in her mouth. It wasn't great air and still held a tinge of carbon dioxide from the soda. But it had enough oxygen to clear her mind and relieve the burning. She waited as long as she could, eyes cut to the Wretch who stared back at her. She exhaled again through her nose and took another breath through her mouth.

She continued to breathe that way until the first bottle emptied.

By then she had strength enough to return to freeing her leg. She shoved against the trunk with her good arm, hoping to shift the car. She dug at the silt on either side of her leg as far as she could reach in an attempt to clear space enough to dislodge the metal. Then the Wretch slammed the car with her hands and Winter felt her leg snap. She cried out in pain despite herself, releasing some of the precious air in her lungs.

What could she do? Could she do anything? Was this it? Where was the power? Where was her guardian? Where was God? She clenched her eyes and attacked the second bottle, careful to allow as little air as possible to escape.

The second bottle went faster than the first. The pain from her shoulder and leg, and the loss of blood, had her heart pounding furiously. The more oxygen she gave her body, the more her body craved it. She tried to count in between breaths and give herself about a minute for each, but she knew she wasn't making it that long. Her lungs burned too badly and the oxygen was too sweet. Only a couple of minutes left. How long had it been? Had it even been five minutes yet? Help could never arrive in that little bit of time.

One breath left to take. Winter waited until she couldn't stand it any longer, until her vision speckled and her body shook. Then she let out the toxic air from her lungs and drained the last of the oxygen. The Wretch leaned forward with a toothy smile.

The fire in her lungs spread into her limbs, competing now with the sizzling still in her arm and the numb throbbing of her leg. She let herself go limp and tried to focus on other things, to think about the happy times and hold the involuntary convulsing at bay.

Graham. She could have loved him for a long time. If only things had been different…

Her body jerked no matter how hard she tried to stop it. The reflex to breathe in became unbearable. The Wretch floated off of the car and sat at her side. Winter clenched her eyes and stars speckled the backs of her eyelids.

Then two things happened at once. A light filled the water, so bright it pierced her closed eyes, yet she couldn't help but open them again. The beautiful Wretch transformed into demonic hideousness as she rocketed away. Then the pressure lifted from Winter's leg. She flipped sideways and almost released the vestiges of air clinging to her lungs. Cold water rushed past her as she left the bottom of the lake, pulled to the surface in a rush of bubbles, dragged upward by the metal hooking into her leg. A deep splash reached her ears, telling her the car had breached the surface. A moment later, she burst into the clear air right beside it and her leg popped free.

Winter gulped in the fresh air and tried to swim. Her heart hammered and she blinked away the water. Only one arm and one leg worked, the others limp and radiating pain, and she twisted to float on her back. The edge of the dam waited just to her left, the car bobbing against the concrete surface. Winter pulled with her good arm, trying to float toward the dam. Then there were hands on her arm. Winter glanced up at Ayden leaning over the dam, and she grabbed Ayden's outstretched hand. Winter screamed as Ayden clutched Winter's injured shoulder. Still Ayden pulled, leaning back to drag Winter over the concrete barrier as the floating car slowly sank a second time. Winter rolled over the top and crashed onto the road, screaming as the jolt sent more fire through her body from her shoulder and leg. She lay there and panted, concentrating on refilling her body with oxygen.

Ayden plopped beside her, eyes wide, full of fear and amazement. "It floated! I can't believe that worked!" Ayden said.

Winter tried to sit up, but her head lolled backward. She opened her eyes and her vision pulled away from the girl sitting beside her.

"Winter!" the girl said, voice echoing from a tunnel. "Winter! Stay with me!"

Then the lack of oxygen, exhaustion, and loss of blood overcame her and Winter fell into blackness.

51

Four Years Ago

The next day, Winter rode the bus back home and called Michael to let him know she didn't feel well and wanted to stay home that weekend. Despite his insistence that he come over and take care of her, she managed to convince him to stay away. Winter locked herself in her room and turned on her TV. When the phone rang, she ignored it, even though her dad would eventually pick up downstairs and call for her.

She suspected Michael was still trying to call. Stacy, too, most likely. Maybe Shannon, since Winter wouldn't let Michael come over. On the one hand she didn't want to be alone...but on the other she knew she couldn't face anyone just yet.

Winter placed a hand on her abdomen. She could do this. Could she do this? Have a baby? Become a mother?

Winter's stomach lurched again, but not from morning sickness this time. She trembled and wanted to break down and cry again. She couldn't do this. She couldn't handle it.

Steve came to check on her late in the afternoon. To allay any suspicions, Winter invited him in and stayed curled on the bed. She didn't have to fake looking sick. After all the puking and not eating, not to mention she desperately needed a shower, she was sure she looked as sick as she claimed.

Steve frowned at her and set a plate with a sandwich on her dresser. "If you need anything, just let me know," he said.

Winter nodded, but didn't say anything. He left her alone for the rest of the evening.

On Saturday morning, after cleaning herself up and getting a decent night's sleep, Winter felt a little better about herself and went downstairs. For once, she felt hungry enough to eat, and her stomach was cooperative enough to let her. She fixed herself four pieces of toast before it made a difference. Her dad busied himself about the house and out back, working on some carpentry side project for a friend.

An hour before lunch, Michael showed. She couldn't refuse to let him in, so she brought him into the living room as Steve watched from the kitchen. Steve had only met Michael once and Winter felt compelled to reintroduce them...even to come clean a little.

"Dad, you remember Michael, right?"

He nodded. "A little. He was trying to call all evening last night."

Winter stared at the floor. "Sorry. Michael is Shannon's brother."

"He is, is he?"

"We're..." she bit her lip. "We're dating."

Steve nodded. "I figured that out already. Now I understand why you go to Shannon's every weekend."

"Are you mad?" Winter shook her head at herself. Why did she care if he was mad or not? Why did she suddenly feel so guilty and caught?

He shook his head. "I'm not mad. You're eighteen and I know you don't want to stay with me more than you have to. I just hope you're making good choices."

"Of course," Winter said. "Don't worry."

Steve backed away. "I'll give you two some privacy then. If you need me I'll be out back."

Winter sat where she could see the back door, which meant the chair facing the kitchen rather than next to Michael on the couch. He watched her, confusion etched behind the dark circles of his eyes.

"What's going on?" he asked. "You don't look sick. Did I do something wrong?"

Winter shook her head and wrung her hands. "No. You didn't do anything. And I have been a little sick…"

"But that's not why you didn't want to come over yesterday, is it?"

Winter took a deep breath. "I'm sorry. I just needed some time to myself. To think."

"Tell me what's wrong. Maybe I can help." He leaned forward as if he wanted to grab her hands across the gap. She didn't offer them. "Let me help."

"I'm not sure you can."

"Let me try."

"You're not going to like it."

"You don't know that."

"I'm pregnant." She glanced up at him and held her breath. The words were out now. What would happen?

Silence. Michael stared at her for a long time, his face blanching and his jaw slowly falling open. He eased back into the couch and looked away.

"Say something," Winter said. Her heart drummed against her ribcage. Suddenly she regretted eating that toast…her stomach threatened to betray her again. "Michael?"

"Are you sure?" he whispered.

"Yes. I took two tests."

"And it's mine?"

"Of course it's yours. What kind of question is that?"

Michael frowned. "Are you going to keep it?"

"Yes. We can do this, Michael. There's no reason to be scared of it."

"We?"

Heat rose up into Winter's face. "Yes, we. I'm not asking to get married or anything, but we've got something good here between us."

"What do you want from me?"

"I don't know. Just keep being Michael. My Michael. Help me. You just said you would…no matter what the problem was. Well, this is the problem. We're both responsible. If you break up with me, fine…but don't take it out on this baby, okay?"

Michael leaned forward and put a hand over his face. "Yeah…um. Okay. Look, I just need to think."

"That's what I'm afraid of."

He put his hand down and locked eyes with her. The fear and frustration evident. "You know me. I'll do the right thing, right? I just have to clear my head."

Winter nodded and bit back the angry tirade boiling within. "Fine. Go clear your head. But I need you to help me figure this out."

He stood and nodded. "I'll…" He shuffled toward the door without looking at her. "I'll call you tomorrow."

Winter followed him, hoping he would turn and embrace her or kiss her or something. On the other hand, she wanted to punch him in the face. "Michael…"

He barely cast a look over her shoulder as he walked out. "Tomorrow." He pulled the door closed.

Winter stared daggers into the door, her knees trembling. She heard her dad come back in behind her.

"Did he leave already?" he said from the kitchen door.

"Yeah. I think he just left." Winter fled for the stairs.

52

Present Day

Winter had vague impressions of being in an ambulance. She remembered blurred faces bent over her. She remembered a siren far away. She remembered the flash of fluorescent lights overhead. And when she finally awoke completely, she lay in a darkened room with a curtain pulled mostly closed to block off the front half of the room.

Her left arm felt thick, her leg immobile. A tube of oxygen wrapped around her face to her nose. A drip of saline went into her right arm. When she gently pushed up enough to gaze around the room, Graham sat up straight in the corner chair by the window.

"You're awake," he said. "Good. They said once the pain meds wore off you probably would. How do you feel?"

"Like I was shot and almost drowned."

Graham narrowed his eyes at her. "You know, sometimes I can't tell when you're joking."

Winter eased back into the bed and stared at the ceiling. "It was a half joke. Can you lift me up?"

"Sure." He came to her side, leaned over and gave her a gentle kiss, and then pushed the button to raise the head of the bed. "I'll alert the nurse too," he said and pressed a second button.

"You were hurt."

He gave her a wry grin. "A scratch." He lifted his shirt to show her a wide bandage taped to his side.

"How long have I been out?"

"About six hours," he said.

Winter grimaced. "How bad is it?"

He pulled the chair over and sat. "Well, the bullet wound was a clean pass, but a big caliber. Nothing major hit, but it shattered part of your shoulder bone. They're going to talk to you about surgery."

"Great," she moaned. "And my leg?"

"A clean fracture just above the ankle. A few weeks in a boot and you'll be fine."

"We don't have a few weeks. I have to find Kaci."

Graham frowned. "Kaci's gone. And you're in no condition to go after her."

"Then Ayden…"

"If this happened to you, what do you think will happen to Ayden?"

Winter grunted and faced the wall.

"Davis?"

Graham sighed. "He's still alive, so that's something. His parents are on the way. Summer's too, I think. The doctors got Davis into surgery pretty quick and he made it through. But…"

"But it doesn't look good."

"He was shot in the head. His chances are very slim."

Winter turned back to him. "What about everyone else?"

"Summer won't leave Davis's side. She's fine. Erickson too. He's been on the phone since we got here trying to get any information about Kaci. Peter blames him. He's isolated himself, but he's here too. Somewhere. I don't think he knows what to do next."

Winter closed her eyes and a tear rolled down her cheek. "What do we do next?'"

Graham grabbed her hand and squeezed. "Maybe we do nothing, Winter. Maybe this is it. Maybe it's over."

Winter shook her head. "No. It can't be over. I have to save her."

"Do you? Maybe this is the way it was meant to be. Maybe you weren't supposed to save her."

"But…"

"But there's nothing you can do. We don't know where she is. You can't walk. The rest of us can't do it on our own. No matter how good Ayden is…she's not you. There's only one you. Without you, there's nothing we can do."

Winter studied him, her eyes wide and blurry. "I can't give up that easy. If you love me at all, you won't let me."

He frowned again and nodded. "I know you can't. I don't pretend to understand all the things you're capable of and I won't stop you. What can I do to help?"

"Just…just go get Ayden. Let me talk to her."

A nurse came in, smiling at them. "Look who's awake. How are you feeling?"

Graham stood.

"Please," Winter said to him.

Graham nodded and left.

"How's your pain? I can give you some more pain medicine if you need," said the nurse.

"I'm fine. I just need to check on my friend."

"Your friend?"

"He was shot."

"Oh. Him. There's nothing you can do," she said. "The best you can do is rest."

"I don't care," Winter said. "I need to see him. Please. Can I or can I not get up and walk around?"

The nurse frowned at her. "I'll speak to the doctor."

Winter sat alone for the next ten minutes, running over in her mind everything that had suddenly and drastically gone wrong. Her dad, Davis, Kaci. How many more would be lost before she ended this? Could Graham be right…was it over already? No. Xaphan would come after her next. It would never really be over. And what about the millions of people who might die from Xaphan's virus? Who would save them?

What about Kaci's baby? What about the prophecy?

Graham came back in, followed by Ayden.

Winter tried to push herself up more. "Ayden, we have to do something."

Ayden shook her head. "I don't think we can."

"You found me."

"That was different," Ayden said. "There was this overwhelming guidance to you. I couldn't help it. But that's gone now. I don't know where to start with Kaci."

"Then you have to get me out of here. Heal me or something."

Ayden's face fell with overwhelming tension. "I can't! I don't know how! If I did, don't you think I'd have done something about Davis already?"

"I didn't know how either, but I healed Kaci first year. Just put your hands on me and pray. That's what I did."

Ayden shook her head. "I can't!"

"Do it!"

"I'm not you!" Ayden backed against the wall and her voice softened. "I never asked for this. I never wanted this. I only did this because I had to and I've learned to accept it. What I've been doing with Erickson…that's different. It's action. It's in the moment. But what you're asking. I'm sorry, but I'm not like you."

"You mean you won't even try?" Winter asked.

"Even if I did, it wouldn't work."

Winter turned her face away from them. "Just leave."

53

At some point Winter must have fallen asleep in the quiet of her room and the ambient sound of the oxygen machine feeding to her nose. A sense of someone standing in the room woke her, and for a brief moment she thought she saw the little girl...Rebecca, her unborn daughter...watching her from the corner by the window.

The nurse must have been monitoring, because not long after Winter sat up she came in.

"Good," she said. "The doctor will be by in a minute to talk to you about surgery. How are you feeling?"

"Fine," she said, and then lay back down.

About ten minutes later, the doctor came in. He wore the standard long white coat, and his salt-and-pepper hair was cut short. The nurse raised the head of the bed, and the doctor sat on a stool next to Winter. As he explained the details of her injuries and the type of surgery they would have to do, Winter just nodded along. As he left, the nurse caught him and said something softly. Then the doctor turned back to Winter.

"You want to see your friend Davis?" he asked.

Winter fixed her eyes on his. "Yes. I just need to check on him and Summer. Before he…you know…"

The doctor nodded. "I understand. I don't see that it would be a problem. We'll get that arranged for you, okay?"

"Thank you," Winter said.

Not long after that a different nurse came in, wearing pink scrubs and pushing a wheelchair.

"Hi. I'm Robin. I'll take you to Critical Care. Just let me get your meds moved…" She carefully relocated the two bags and the pump from the stand by the bed to the hanger pole attached to the wheelchair. Then she removed the blood-pressure cuff from Winter's arm.

She helped Winter sit up, and with her uninjured foot firmly on the floor Winter swung into the chair. Robin lifted Winter's leg into the extended leg rest, adjusted the height, and placed a pillow under the elbow of Winter's injured shoulder.

"How's that?" Robin asked.

"It's good," Winter said with a grimace as she tried to readjust her ankle.

Robin wheeled her out into the bright hall, past the nurses' station, and to a patient elevator. They descended to the bottom floor, and before long they entered a long corridor filled with glass walls, behind which most had curtains drawn. They passed several darkened rooms before Robin slowed and eased into one.

Life support machines whirled and beeped. Summer slumped in a chair near the window, eyes closed. When she heard them enter, Summer sat up and stared. Her red, puffy eyes could barely open fully. Her disheveled hair stood out to one side. Smut still colored her cheeks.

"Can you give me a few minutes?" Winter asked Robin over her shoulder.

"Sure. Just buzz when you're ready."

Robin rolled her close to Davis and left. Summer just continued to stare.

Davis was unrecognizable. The sheet covered his entire body, and gauze wrapped around his head so thick little of his face could be seen. A large tube extended from his mouth and his chest rose and fell with regular intervals.

Winter couldn't take it. Her past hospital experiences aside, seeing her friend like this and knowing it was her fault...

She let her chin fall to her chest...and cried.

"Can't you do anything?" Summer whispered. "Please?"

Winter ignored her, not wanting to tell Summer the gut-wrenching reality. Just this once, she wished the premonition would shut up. Just this once, she wished the nudges were wrong.

"Winter? Please..."

Winter lifted her head and gazed at Summer through her prismed vision. "I'm sorry, I can't."

"Why not?"

"This is what was supposed to happen. Even if I tried, it wouldn't work."

Summer shook her head slowly. "But why?" Her voice creaked with the tracks of exhausted tears. "What did I do wrong?"

"You didn't do anything wrong...don't think like that. Sometimes bad things happen and they can't be explained."

"But I don't understand. Why doesn't God *do* something? Why did he let this happen at all?"

"I don't know, Summer. Maybe it's for something in the future. You just have to believe that everything's going to be all right."

"Be all right? How could it ever be all right?" Summer's chin trembled. "My heart...has been ripped out of my chest. I feel like I'm living my worst nightmare. It hurts like I'm having a heart attack, but for some reason I just won't die. Don't you dare tell me it'll be all right. You have no idea how I feel."

Winter straightened and wiped her eyes. "I love you, Summer, but don't you ever say I don't know how you feel. Of all the people in this freakin' place I'm the *only* one who knows exactly how you feel. You've had your heart ripped out once. It's happened to me five times. Five times! And Xaphan just killed my dad. I don't even have a body to cry over. At least Davis is still alive. It sucks, I know. But at least you still have him."

Summer looked away.

"I don't know how, I don't know when," Winter said with a softer tone. "But when I say it's going to be all right, you can believe me. I've lived it and I know. More than that, I can feel it."

"It *will* be all right," said Rebecca, suddenly standing in the corner by Davis's head. "He will live."

Summer jumped out of her seat. "Who is that?"

"You can see her?" Winter asked.

Summer nodded.

"What do you want?" Winter asked Rebecca.

"You have to save Kaci. You have to go now. Time is up. This has to end," Rebecca said.

"As you can probably see, I can't," said Winter.

"You will be able to in a moment."

"How?"

"How is not important," said Rebecca. "All that is important is why. You have to save Kaci and the baby. If you don't, millions of people will die."

At that moment, Ayden rushed in. "Winter, I have to talk to you." She paused when she saw Rebecca. "It's her…"

"What?" Winter asked.

"I know where Kaci is. I just had a vision. Graham went to go get Peter. We have to figure it out and go."

"What kind of vision?"

Ayden took a deep breath. "A round room."

Winter's eyes widened.

Graham ran in, closely followed by Peter. Both of them stopped short when they saw Rebecca.

"Who's that?" Graham asked.

"She's, um…I'll explain later," said Winter. "We have to find a way to get out of here."

"I will help," said Rebecca.

A nurse came in, with a stern look on her face. "Only two people are allowed at a time. Some of you will have to go."

Winter snarled at her and pointed to Davis. "Listen, we were all there when he got shot and he may not last much longer, so just give us ten minutes, please!"

The nurse narrowed her eyes. "Ten minutes. But keep it down!"

"Ayden had a vision?" asked Peter after the nurse left.

"A round room," said Ayden.

"The bell tower," said Rebecca. "Xaphan took her back to where it all began. She's there now."

"Then we have to get there," said Graham.

"But Cherithville is two hours away," said Summer.

Winter turned to Rebecca. "You said you could help."

Rebecca nodded. "But only you."

Silence filled the room, and after a moment Graham broke it. "No. I'm going too."

Winter shook her head. "You can't. I was always meant to finish this alone." She panned the room. "We all knew that."

"You won't be alone," said Rebecca. "We will do this together."

Graham reached out and grabbed Winter's hand. "I can't let you."

She smiled softly at him. "You have to. There was no one to save me when I needed it. So I'll be there to save her." Winter turned back to Rebecca. "What do I do?"

A white mist suddenly swirled around Winter and disappeared.

"Stand," said Rebecca. "Your clothes are here." She waved to a neatly folded stack of clothes sitting beside the wall next to Winter.

Winter slid her ankle out of the extended footrest and placed it on the floor. No pain. She flexed her shoulder and tried to roll it against the bandages. No pain.

"Help me," Winter said to Graham as she yanked the arm catheter out.

Winter slid the sleeve of her gown up and attacked the bandages on her arm and shoulder. Graham produced a pocket knife to help. With her arm freed and a pile of bandages on the floor, they did the same to her ankle.

After only a few moments, Winter stood out of the chair and Graham pushed it away.

She snatched up her underwear and black skinny jeans, and slid them in place beneath the gown. "You picked out my favorites," she said to Rebecca.

Rebecca gave her a sideways smile. "I know you. I want you to be comfortable."

Once her pants were on, she grabbed her favorite peasant top from the floor. "Turn around, Peter." Peter looked away. Winter yanked off the gown and slid the shirt on as quickly as she could, not caring that Graham still watched.

"Peter," she said.

Peter turned back to her, eyes to the floor.

She sat in the wheelchair to pull on her socks and black combat boots. "I'm going to save her. I promise. I'm going to save both of them. When I'm done, you'll be safe for good. Just promise me one thing."

"What?"

"Don't ever let them go."

Peter looked her in the eyes. His chin trembled and he wiped a tear from his cheek. "I won't."

"Summer," Winter said. "I don't know how it'll happen or how long it will take, but it *will* be all right. Davis is going to live. Just promise me you'll marry him and be happy."

Summer sobbed and nodded quickly.

"Ayden," Winter said. "I don't know how long this will take.

Keep them safe for me. And when it's all over, I hope you have the normal life you've wanted."

"I will," Ayden said, her voice tense.

When Winter finished tying her boots, she stood and faced Graham. "I'm not sure what to say to you."

"You're saying goodbye."

Winter reached behind her neck to clasp her locket into place. "Maybe. I don't know. I just wish we had more time. For what it's worth, I love you, and I think I could love you for the rest of my life."

"If that's true, then come back."

"I don't know if I can."

"Try."

Winter bit her lip.

"Promise me you'll try."

Winter nodded, leaned toward him, and kissed him as if for the last time. When she finally pulled away, she grabbed his hand and backed toward the corner where Rebecca waited. "I *will* try. I promise. Look for me."

"I'll never stop."

Winter finally let his hand drop. She took one last long look at all her friends watching her. Real friends. No matter what happened next, she would always have them.

"I'm ready," she said to Rebecca without turning.

Rebecca grabbed her hand from behind, and in a flash of brilliant white, the hospital disappeared.

54

Four Years Ago

Michael didn't call or come by the next day. Or the next. Winter tried to call him, but he wouldn't answer. She called Shannon, but Shannon hadn't seen him or talked to him in days.

She slogged through school that week, her abdomen constantly cramping and her chest aching. She didn't know if it was anxiety or the pregnancy, but she did know one thing…she had to get this settled with Michael. Whether he broke up with her or wanted to try to work things out, she no longer cared. She just couldn't handle not knowing any longer.

The next Friday, Winter went through her usual routine of lying to her dad about staying the weekend with Shannon. Michael wasn't at school to pick her up, so Winter convinced Stacy to drop her off at Michael's apartment. As the car idled at the curb, Winter studied the drawn apartment windows, stomach churning.

"Do you want me to go with you?" Stacy asked.

"No," Winter said without turning to her. "I have to do this by myself."

"Is there anything you want me to do?"

Winter took a deep breath. "Just…" she faced Stacy. "…stay by your phone."

Stacy nodded. "Text me either way. If things go bad, just walk out and I'll pick you up on the corner." She reached over and squeezed Winter's hand. "You can do this. It'll be okay either way, just remember that."

"I know," Winter said. "Thank you."

As Stacy drove away, Winter hefted her bag onto her shoulder and quickly walked up the sidewalk. She paused in front of the door and took a deep breath before testing the knob. Locked. She took out her key, unlocked the door, and eased in.

"Michael?" she called. No answer. Winter set her bag on the couch and slinked through the apartment, but he wasn't home. Then as she crept back into the living room, the outside door opened and he came in.

He stopped in the doorway and stared at her. He wore baggy jeans and a white tank top. His unshaven face and bloodshot eyes told Winter he'd probably been binging on drugs or alcohol again. But at the moment his eyes were bright and calculating.

"What are you doing here?" he asked, stepping all the way in and closing the door.

"We've had something good going on. I didn't want it to stop."

"I told you I'd call."

Winter crossed her arms. "I couldn't help but notice that you didn't. You can't just avoid me. That's not how this works."

Michael crossed into the kitchen toward the fridge. "I just need to clear my head, okay?"

Winter grunted. "All I want is for you to be honest with me. Tell me why you're so freaked out over this."

He pulled a beer from the fridge and popped the top. "We were having fun. I'm not ready to be the family type. A dad? Are you kidding? That's not me. I don't want that."

"Then you have to make a decision, because the baby and I are kind of a package deal now. If you don't want the baby, then you don't want me anymore. Is that what you're saying? Just be honest with me. Please. I can't take it."

"Fine!" he shouted. "I don't want the baby!"

"Then you don't want me!"

Michael slammed the beer down on the table and narrowed his eyes. "Why can't you just get rid of it? Get rid of the baby and we'll go back to the way it was."

Winter's hand went instinctively to her abdomen. "An abortion? I *want* this baby, Michael. I'm not going to kill just because it inconveniences you."

"So who's making the decision now? It's either the baby or me!"

"You can't do that! It's not fair!"

"It's the same thing!"

"No! It's completely different. If you don't want to be with me and the baby, fine. Walk away. But you're asking me to kill it?"

Michael collapsed into one of the dining chairs, put his head between his hands, and screamed. "Just shut up!"

Winter stepped back and bit her lip. "I want to be with you, Michael," she said more softly. "Do you want to be with me?"

He tilted his head to glare at her, his eyes flashing in a way that made Winter take another step backward.

"Michael?" she asked.

"I can't..." The words seemed to drag from his mouth.

"You can't? You can't be with me?"

"I can't..." He pressed his hands flat on the table. "I can't be a father."

"You don't have to be. I'll handle all the responsibility."

He shook his head. "I'd still have a child in the world. Don't you understand? I can't live knowing that I have a child somewhere. You have to get rid of it, please!" He picked up something and started fidgeting with it, but Winter kept her eyes locked with his.

"I'm not killing the baby."

He stood. "It's the only way we can be together."

Winter glanced to his hand and the object he had picked up. Scissors. She stepped back again. "Michael, you're not yourself. Just calm down. You've taken something that's got you worked up." Her voice trembled.

"I'm fine. You say you want to be with me, well, this is the only way, Winter."

Winter shook her head. "I'm sorry. I can't." She snatched up her backpack from the couch. "I should go."

Michael rushed to the door and blocked her way, pointing the scissors at her.

"What are you doing? Let me leave!" she screamed.

"I can't."

Winter trembled. "You're scaring me. Please, I won't go, just put the scissors down."

He stepped toward her.

"Michael!" she cried and backed away, almost tripping over herself. "What are you doing? Stop!"

"If you won't do it..." he whispered. His eyes clenched suddenly, and he whimpered as if in pain. He dropped the scissors and put both hands to his head.

"What's wrong with you?" she screamed. Winter looked down and reached into her pocket to draw out her phone. When she looked up, he was there, fist in her face.

Her nose cracked. She stumbled backward and fell. Her head spun and her eyes filled with stinging tears, blinding her. She tried to breathe, but only choking sounds came out. The shape of Michael hovered over her and she put her hands up to block him.

"Please," she croaked. "Don't..."

Then it felt like a sledgehammer hit her in the stomach. What air was left in her lungs vanished in a violent groan. Her knees jerked up into the fetal position and the next kick from Michael slammed into her knee, glancing off and landing against her chest. She held a hand out to stop the next kick, but beneath his full strength her wrist bent back. He leaned into it until something popped, her fingers went numb, and the foot pinned her hand against her neck.

"Mi..." she groaned.

The next kick slammed against her left side. A crack echoed through her chest and fire erupted beneath her arm.

Winter screamed and kicked at him through the pain, connecting with his knee. He stumbled backward. Winter rolled over and crawled past him for the door, leaving a smeared streak of the blood dripping from her face.

He knelt back at her side again. With one strong arm, he rolled her on top of her broken rib, and with the other he punched her stomach. She could only clench her body and endure. No screaming. No moving. No breathing. After several excruciating moments of continuous pounding into her abdomen, he backed away.

Paralyzed, Winter wanted to uncurl so she could crawl toward the door, but nothing in her body responded. What was happening? Why was he doing this? She opened her mouth for oxygen, and after a long painful inhale, she could only moan.

"You know," he said in a calm frightening voice. "If I let you go, you'll turn me in for this." She heard the scrape of the scissors being lifted from the floor.

"Please," she croaked.

Then he was back at her side. He kicked her once again and rolled her onto her back. She shrieked and clawed at him as he straddled her burning abdomen. He punched her in the jaw. Winter's head spun so fast that her arms fell limp. He raised the pair of scissors like a knife high over his head.

Through the hazy vision, she recognized his motion. Instinct and adrenaline kicked in. She raised both arms despite the numbness and caught his wrists, somehow with enough strength to stop him. Her weak arms couldn't hold him long. The tip of the scissors scratched down the upper side of her arm as he leaned forward to buckle her locked elbows. The more he leaned, the more he lifted from her abdomen. With a few inches of clearance, Winter brought both thighs up as fast as she could. He teetered forward, dropped the scissors, and reached out with both hands to stop himself from crashing into the door.

Winter did the only thing she had left to do. Summoning as much energy as she could from her aching body, riding a surge of survival adrenaline, she scrambled out from under him and crawled to the kitchen. As she pulled herself to her feet against the counter, Michael recovered by the door. As he rushed toward her with a growl, Winter pulled a knife from a drawer.

Michael halted feet from her.

"Leave me alone!" she bellowed, shaking the knife and teetering sideways.

"I can't let you leave." He stepped toward her, unafraid.

"Why are you doing this?" she cried as she backed away. "I thought you loved me…"

"I'm doing this because I love you."

Winter shook her head. "Just let me leave. Please."

He straightened as if prodded. "There's something about you…"

"Michael! What's wrong with you?"

He shook his head and then moved faster than she thought humanly possible. With one hand he knocked away the knife. With the other fist, still clenching the scissors, he punched her in the side where he had already broken a rib. She screamed and nearly collapsed, but then his first hand came back around and knocked her in the side of the face again, this time with the all the speed and strength of his entire body weight.

The collision spun her around. Her knees buckled. Her feet slipped in her own blood. Her forehead slammed against the counter, and Winter crumpled onto her back on the floor.

She could barely think or see. She couldn't move at all. Every muscle in her body burned. Every bone in her body felt broken. He knelt beside her head and brought the scissors up high again. This time her mental alertness and adrenaline-enhanced muscles failed. She couldn't stop him this time. Nothing in her body worked.

With a quick jerk, he brought the scissors down toward her chest, and then stopped halfway.

Michael trembled. His face turned red, jaw clenched, vein pulsing on his forehead. His muscles shook as if pressing against an invisible force preventing him from finishing his killing blow.

Winter's head cleared enough to notice something metallic beneath her right hand. She patted it once and recognized the knife. Without a second thought, she groped for the handle, squeezed it tight, and thrust it into Michael's abdomen.

Michael rocked backward. The scissors fell from his grip, almost landing on Winter's face.

She pulled out the knife and jabbed it in again. This time he fell away and landed on his back, clenching the bleeding wounds.

Winter ground her teeth and rolled to her hands and knees. She crawled to his side, still clutching the knife.

"Winter…" he whispered. "I'm sorry."

Something welled up inside of her that she couldn't control. A rage she had never felt before. Maybe it was the memory of Claire's dad. Maybe it was Ryan's death. Maybe it was Michael's betrayal.

Maybe it was the fact that she could already feel blood running down the inside of her thighs…

She lifted the knife high, and slammed it into his chest. She screamed and did it again. The screaming turned into weeping and she did it again. And again. And again.

When the life finally drained from Michael's eyes, Winter left the knife protruding from his chest and crawled through the pooling blood to find her phone.

55

Present Day

Winter opened her eyes as the cool night air kissed her checks. She stood alone in the Meadow, when moments ago she had just taken Rebecca's hand in the hospital. The Ancient swayed gently just in front of her. Winter panned slowly and found the campus deserted and most of the power out. But she could still see…the rumbling in her ears filled her eyes with inhuman clarity.

She squeezed her fists, for once not needing the premonition to tell her what to do next. Her entire life had been leading up to this moment…as if everything she had experienced had been hinting at this. She knew exactly what to do next and exactly where to go.

Winter spun back to the Ancient and took the last few steps to stand by the trunk beneath its long drooping arms. She knelt and picked up the three stones she had placed there months ago, slipping one into each back pocket and clenching the third in her right hand.

As she took a deep breath, she pivoted to face the break between the history building and the religion building. She started walking slowly at first, but a sense of urgency overwhelmed her and she began to jog. Before she left the Meadow, however, something told her to stop.

There was something she had to do.

Winter took exactly six steps into the grass to her right. Then she pulled her cellphone out of her front pocket and laid it on the ground.

As she straightened, she faced her original destination and ran. She passed through the space between the two buildings and after a moment exited into a wide clearing. Ornamental trees stood sentinel over a well-tended garden. A few larger trees watched it all like older chaperons. To the left waited the Chapel of Radiance, with the Olamel bell tower connected on its right.

Winter jogged to stand in front of the stone steps. She studied the double doors and her shoulders tensed. Beyond those doors waited the end of everything. What happened over the next few minutes would impact the future of the entire world.

Winter took the first step, climbing until she stood on the porch just in front of the doors. The rumbling in her ears grew louder. The clarity of her vision sharper. Winter could almost see through the door and into the inner sanctuary, though seeing couldn't truly describe the sensation. She felt the inner sanctuary with her eyes. Knew the impressions they made on the air and space around them. Could weigh the density of objects. Feel the temperature.

Two men waited on the floor near the front of the sanctuary. A third on the balcony to the right where the door to the Olamel tower stood. They were all armed and all expecting her. They would all three die that night.

The men were not the only ones inside. Winter felt the swirling of demons, writhing at the feet of the men, swarming in and out of the pews. A small army waited inside, and an even larger presence watched her from the dark sky above. Even though the men didn't know she was there yet, every demon stood ready and anxious.

Seeing all of this…feeling this…only made the rumble grow louder. Her skin tightened to the point she thought it might split.

Nothing inside or outside that room could stop her…she knew that just as certain as she knew that God would provide whatever power and resources she needed to get to Kaci.

The bells of Olamel rang out, tolling through campus and echoing back in hollow reflections. Midnight. Kaci had only moments left.

Winter didn't bother to reach out for the door handles and didn't care if the doors were locked. She simply stepped toward them and the doors exploded out of her way.

Black mist roiled together in miniature tornadoes and flew toward her sideways like torpedoes, invisible to the other humans. Winter took a step forward, brandishing the stone in her hand and launched it toward the man who first saw her and now swung his gun to aim. As the stone left her hand an angelic cloud collided with the oncoming demons, shattering the black mist to drift away like ash.

As the stone struck the first man between the eyes, sending him backward into the altar rail, the second man turned to face her. Winter fell to one knee, reached back for the second stone, still moving forward down the aisle, processing every movement as if in slow motion.

A shot rang out, the bullet flying wild over her head. She stood, stepped, twisted to her left to allow a second bullet to pass in front of her, stepped, leaned forward and let the second stone fly.

Step. She reached for the third stone. Step. The second stone struck the man in the throat. He dropped his gun and reached for his neck with both hands.

Another bell tolled.

Gunshot. A portion of a pew beside her exploded in fragments of wood as the third man on the balcony fired. Step. The first man recovered to swing his gun back. Step. Another pew exploded as the third man fired again. The second man snatched his gun back up from the ground.

Then the ash revived, swirling through the room with the white angelic cloud like a stripped windstorm. Winter could still see through it perfectly...feel through it.

She planted her feet and held both hands out to the first man, stone exposed toward him in the palm of her hand. He fired. The bullet struck the stone, shoving Winter backward and causing her to stumble. The third man on the balcony cried out as the ricocheted bullet struck him in the thigh. The other two glanced his way as he tumbled down the steps to the floor.

A third bell tolled.

Step. Step. Step. Winter crossed the remaining space. Sweep. Palm strike with the stone. The first man fell unconscious. The second sighted her down, trigger finger about to squeeze. Twist. Grab the gun arm. Elbow to the face. Turn. Leverage. The man landed on his back just in front of her. Palm strike to the face and he fell still.

At that moment the room blazed with a bright, white light. The angelic presence pulsed once in victory and the black ash fell from the air and disappeared.

She spun to the third man still on the ground, now scuttling away, arms up, leg bleeding profusely.

"No! Please!" he cried out.

Winter glared at him as the fourth bell tolled. She dropped the last stone at his feet, and stomped up the steps and through the door of the bell tower.

56

To the left waited those old wooden stairs. They wandered to the right, following the outside wall of the tower. Small candles sat on the steps, spread out—only one every four or five steps. They oozed lifeless blood that pooled at their base and coagulated into white scabs.

The first stair step groaned, but she didn't hesitate. She sprinted up the stairs two at a time, ignoring the feeble candles and their sycophantic blood. Slotted windows perforated the outer wall every few feet, beholding her with wide, startled eyes.

Darkness watched from beyond the candlelight...demons that knew her name and recognized her face. They whispered in fear, retreating from her to wait just beyond the bend. More than once she thought she recognized a shape in the shadows—a demon materializing to prove its bravery—only to flee at the merest flicker of Winter's gaze.

She passed a rough wooden door with an iron handle. It was not her destination, so she continued to run, ever upward, passing many doors the same as the first. The stairs dissolved into black eternity that would not be captured. Her feet fell light up the steps, her knees bent in a steady rhythm, and her heart pounded with a ferocity that could only come from Heaven. Each pounding footfall echoed in the empty stairwell, answered by moans from the wooden steps and the bells that continued to count down Kaci's final seconds.

She wanted to be there already—to defy time and go faster. But she must continue in this way. It was God's will. The timing must be perfect. Power pressed against her skin, eager to unleash. A light breeze drifted through a window, tinted in white, and she smiled knowing backup followed her just beyond the walls.

Finally, the endless line of candles stopped before a door just like all the others she had passed. Briefly she remembered a time when she had feared this door…when she had brushed the handle with the tips of her fingers and found it cold. Even now, the cold radiated from the door like heat from a furnace. She paused for one heartbeat and allowed her senses to feel beyond the door, giving her all that she needed to sense what was on the other side.

Xaphan was there, straining against a spiritual force stronger than Winter had ever felt. The Wretch cowered to one side away from the force contending with Xaphan. Others were in the room too, humans and demons, shocked and overwhelmed by an angelic squadron raging for Kaci's life.

And Kaci was there. Alive. Awake. Unharmed. Frightened.

The instinct to rush in took over. Every hair on Winter's body stood rigid. This was her ultimate destiny. Her calling. To save Kaci. And to save the child.

The heartbeat over, Winter lowered her chin and stepped forward. Again the door exploded before her, fragments of wood flying through the round room in every direction.

Kaci lay on an altar in the middle of the room. Xaphan stood with knife poised in the air to strike Kaci in the heart, the toll of the final bell still hanging in the air. A searing white light between the knife and Kaci kept it from falling as Xaphan struggled against the angelic force. Xaphan roared in frustration when Winter entered. He shifted his arm backward, twisted, and flung the knife into the air.

As the knife flew, what warmth was left in the room evaporated as the Wretch shrieked and recovered from where she cowered from the bright light.

The knife rotated one foot closer.

The walls shook. The floor shook. A bright light pressed in against the slotted windows of the room. An extra bell tolled with the vibration as the room filled with swirling white mist.

Winter stepped toward the knife, not bothering to move out of the way. The white mist gathered into a singular mass. The Wretch rushed toward her. The knife rotated closer. The white mist slammed into the Wretch. The knife rotated closer. The light shoved the Wretch toward a window. Winter took another step. She reached out and snatched the knife out of the air by the handle. The white mist pulsed and shoved the Wretch outside. Winter pulled her arm back and took a long step forward, launching the knife back at Xaphan. The white mist gathered and rocketed the Wretch toward the ground. The knife rotated through the air. Xaphan's eyes widened in fear. The Wretch shrieked as it fell. The knife struck Xaphan in the shoulder and he stumbled backward all the way to the wall.

Winter ran to Kaci's side and ripped the ropes away as if they were cobwebs. Kaci's panicked eyes darted once to Xaphan as he tried to recover, but Winter was already rushing her back to the door.

Now all Winter had to do was get Kaci out of the chapel before Xaphan could catch them. And once Kaci was safe she'd have to come back and finish the job.

"Come on," she whispered to Kaci as they stumbled down the steps.

"Winter!" Xaphan yelled from above.

"Faster," said Winter.

Kaci whimpered and doubled over. Winter glanced up the stairs, hearing Xaphan stumbling above.

"What's wrong?" Winter asked. "We have to go!"

Kaci shook her head and held her bulging abdomen. "The baby..."

Winter grimaced. "I'm not delivering that thing right now. You're just going to have to wait." She grabbed Kaci's arm and dragged her down another few steps, despite Kaci's protests. "We're almost there," she said as they reached the final landing. Sounds of Xaphan's pursuit had stopped and Winter wondered if he had succumbed to the blood loss.

She led Kaci back into the sanctuary, where two of the men still lay unconscious on the floor and the third sat slumped and bleeding next to a wall. He gazed up at them with a pale face filled with terror.

As they rounded the front pew and entered the center aisle, a shadow crossed before the gaping hole where the front doors used to stand.

Winter paused and hefted Kaci closer on her hip.

Then the Wretch stepped out of the shadows of the porch and into the chapel. Her long, white hair draped like a wet curtain over her naked body. Water seemed to ooze from her skin to drip on the floor. She stared at Winter with solid white eyes. "Did you think it would be that easy?"

57

Four Years Ago

Winter lay in the middle of the floor, just in front of the door, curled into a ball, her back to Michael's body, and cried softly. The pain wouldn't go away. It only increased. She cradled her phone in her hand a few inches from her head, the 911 operator insisting that she not hang up until help arrived.

She had told the operator everything. About the baby, about him wanting her to get rid of it, about the attack. Winter knew that all the sirens she heard quickly approaching weren't all from an ambulance.

Two officers came in with weapons drawn. They took one look around the room and split up, one coming to her and the other to Michael. Only after making sure there was no threat did they radio for the paramedics.

The two paramedics were gentle but quick. They helped her onto a stretcher and allowed her to stay curled in a ball until they reached the ambulance. Once inside, they eased her onto her back and began work checking her vitals and starting an IV. The ambulance left, siren screaming down the street.

"I'm pregnant," she whispered to the nearest medic, a woman old enough to be her mother.

The woman nodded and firmed her lips, but didn't say anything. She broke an ice pack and gently laid it across Winter's broken rib.

They arrived at the ER after only five minutes, and wheeled her through the hall to a private room. A nurse helped her change into a gown and gently cleaned the blood from Winter's face.

"I'm pregnant," she whispered to the nurse.

The nurse gave her the same firm look as the paramedic woman. "We have a doctor on the way to check the baby."

Winter bit her lip and nodded, then looked away.

The doctor finally arrived a few minutes later, and after a quick exam, he pulled over an ultrasound machine. A few minutes of rubbing the probe over her abdomen and he put it away. He picked up a chart, took a long look at Winter's nose and gently prodded her rib. Then he set the chart down and rolled over on the stool to sit next to her head.

"You have a fractured rib. It's not displaced, so there's not much we can do. We'll give you and your father some instructions on taking care of it."

"My father?" Winter asked.

He nodded. "He's on his way. You also have a broken nose. Also not displaced. We'll set it and you should be able to take the bandages off after a week or two. In a few minutes we'll get an x-ray of your arm. I don't see any kind of protrusions, so hopefully it's not too bad. We're going to run other tests to make sure there are no internal injuries, pump you with fluids and watch you for a few hours, but you should be able to go home this evening."

"And the baby?"

He broke eye contact and stared at his hands. "I'm afraid the baby's gone. The trauma was just too much."

The suddenness of Winter's tears made the doctor look back up.

"Are you sure? Can you check again? I don't want to lose it..."

He nodded. "I'm sorry."

Winter turned her head away, unable to face the doctor any longer. No matter how much Michael had beat her, no matter how much her body ached, none of it compared to the hollowness she now felt.

At that moment, someone came into the room, but she didn't bother to look up.

"What happened?" asked her dad.

The doctor stood. "Let's talk in the hall."

As they left, the nurse checked her rib again. "Would you like something for the pain?" she asked.

"No," Winter said. "I like the pain. It's distracting."

"In that case, a little sedative to help you relax and get some rest as well."

Winter grunted, but didn't refuse.

"What! Pregnant?" shouted Steve outside in the hall.

The low calm voice of the doctor continued, but Winter could only imagine what horrible things her dad thought about her right then.

The seconds ticked by. The nurse continued to work. The men continued to talk in low tones. The medicine buzzed in Winter's head. And then Steve came back in.

"Can you give us a minute of privacy?" he asked the nurse.

"Sure," she said and then left.

Steve came to the side where Winter faced and pulled a chair over.

"The police told me what happened at Michael's apartment. They also told me they found clothes and stuff belonging to you there. That's where you've been going on the weekends isn't it? How could you get into a relationship like that? He could have killed you!"

Winter clenched her eyes. The tears returned.

"The doctor said you were pregnant...you're lucky that's over. What would you have done with a baby?"

The disappointment dripped from his voice.

He let out a hiss of exasperation. "I've tried so hard to keep you happy and to stay out of your way. Maybe that was my mistake. Maybe I trusted you too much. That's always been my problem...I trust too much. I trusted your mother and I trusted you, and you both did the exact same thing to me."

"Dad..." she croaked.

"Pregnant, Winter? Pregnant? Do you have any idea how I feel right now?"

Winter sobbed silently.

"I can't go on like this. I can't live not knowing if I can trust my own daughter. If you have so little respect for me as this..."

"I'm sorry..."

"That's not good enough." He stood. At the door he paused and spoke to her back. "It's far too late for sorry. If this is the kind of life you want to live, then you're going to have to live it without me."

A few moments after he closed the door, the nurse returned. She heard Winter crying and said, "I'm giving you some pain medicine. You need it. The police want to talk to you again, and then after that we'll roll you down for x-rays. No need to get out of bed. By then the meds should kick in and you can rest." After a moment of silence, she said, "Do you need anything else?"

Winter held her breath to stay quiet. What did she need? She needed it to be over. Everything...just, over.

"Well, if you do, buzz."

Winter didn't notice dozing off. One moment she dwelt on her father's words and the emptiness inside of her, the loss of the baby, the loss of Michael...and then the next moment a detective was there asking questions about Michael. Then a technician took her to get x-rays. She fell asleep again during the x-rays and woke up back in the room. Soon afterward the nurse returned.

"Good news. Your wrist is just sprained. A soft brace for a few weeks is all you'll need."

Winter gave her a small nod. "Is he still here?"

"Your father? No. He left a while ago."

"Can I go?"

"I'm not sure you should. You're pretty bruised up. You should stay and rest as long as the doctor lets you."

Winter shook her head. "I want to go."

"Lay back and rest."

Winter fixed the nurse with a steady glare. "I want to go. You can't keep me here."

"We'll have to call your father…"

"No you don't. I'm eighteen, you don't have to tell him anything. So unless you want me to sue this hospital for telling him about the baby without my permission, you'll just let me leave!"

The nurse pursed her lips and left. She stayed gone for nearly half an hour, while Winter stared at the wall. She finally returned with the doctor.

"The nurse tells me you'd like to leave. I'd advise you to stay and rest a little while longer, overnight maybe. Let us make sure everything is okay."

Winter shook her head. "No. I'm ready to go now."

"Are you sure?"

"If you don't let me leave, I'll just walk out of here on my own. You can't stop me."

The doctor shook his head. "If that's what you want. Give us a few minutes. There are some papers for you to sign and some information we want you to have about treating your rib, your nose, your arm, and about what to expect after a miscarriage. I'll also give you a prescription for pain. Are you really sure about this?"

Winter nodded.

The doctor sighed and stood. "I'll have the nurse take out your IV and you can get dressed while we prepare your discharge papers."

They didn't finally discharge her until well after dark. An orderly rolled her to the exit and left her standing on the sidewalk, clutching a folder with the papers the doctor had promised, as a light rain fell upon the city.

She didn't know what to do now or where to go. It was all gone. She had nothing left. She truly was alone. She supposed it didn't matter where she went…she could start over if she wanted. No one would miss her. But what would be the point? She just needed it to be over…

Winter scanned the cityscape before her. From there she could see the new Trenton River bridge, its lights shimmering in the rain as a parade of vehicles crossed. Just beyond it, less illuminated, less grand, and far less traveled, lay the old bridge. Where Claire had jumped.

Winter took a step in that direction.

58

Present Day

"Kaci, get behind me," Winter said, pressing Kaci with her arm. As Kaci backed away Winter stepped forward. "Don't do this," she said to the Wretch. "You can't win."

The Wretch shook her head. "This is no forest. This is no train yard. You're in a controlled space that has been prepared for this moment." She spread her arms out. "How many times has my master tried to work out his plans only to have you interfere? So this time, he not only prepared for the sacrifice of Kaci and the child, he also prepared this place to be your doom. You will join her on the altar this night."

"I walked in easy enough. I plan to leave the same way."

"You were allowed in."

Winter clenched her hands against the tingling in her palms. Enough power raced through her to level the building. An army of angels had already fought by her side that night and another legion stood by waiting to help. Tonight Xaphan could never win.

But what if?

"You're lying. You don't have the power to stop me."

The Wretch smiled and opened her mouth. She released an ear-shattering shriek as if to rupture the crust of the earth. The room filled with thick shadows, blocking all light and sending the room into pitch blackness. The shadows rushed by like the winds of a typhoon, swirling around the Wretch, hissing and laughing.

Beyond that, Winter heard the rush of the angelic forces coming to her aid, like an avalanche falling upon a charred forest. They waited for her direction.

Behind Winter, Kaci whimpered. Winter took a step back toward her to narrow the distance between them. As the shadows rushed past, the room cleared, leaving a huge mass of fire and shadows standing to the right of the Wretch. The Acolyte.

As the Acolyte finished growing into its full height, it reached forward with both arms and shadows flew toward Winter like daggers. Winter reached out in the same manner and suddenly white swirled past her to meet the shadows.

Then the windows blew out. Darkness rolled back in, thick as oil. A man laughed, a deep cackle like a diesel engine. Winter spun around to find the Eater behind her, silver and black mask tilted to one side. The Wretch rose into the air to hover just over them.

Before Winter fully registered what happened, the gathering darkness wrapped itself around the angelic forces flying toward the Acolyte, ripping them away, encapsulating them in a black sphere near the ceiling. Beyond the shattered windows she could see nothing but the deep swirling of more endless shadows, not just a protective dome over the chapel, but a thick shell trapping the angelic army inside and blocking reinforcements.

Winter backed away. "You can't do this!" She eyed the trapped angels and the tightness in her skin disappeared. Without help, what could she do?

"What are you without your army?" growled the Acolyte as she stepped forward. The demonic armor vanished as the Acolyte took the form of Claire. "A simple human."

"Time for you to die," said the Eater. "Both of you to die."

"There will be no more running," cooed the sweet voice of the Wretch as she descended to hover to Winter's right.

Winter reached for Kaci's hand and pulled her close.

Kaci whimpered. "What are we going to do?"

Winter glanced back at the trapped angels and the vestiges of power in her vanished. "I don't know."

Then Rebecca was there beside them. "NO!" she screamed. "I won't let you do this!"

Everything moved at once. The Acolyte reached for Winter, her arm shrouding again with demons and slamming against a thin white shell. Winter's guardian. The one angel who had been with her for so long, feeding her thoughts and premonitions, connecting her to the larger angelic forces around her. But what could it do now? Alone?

The Eater rushed down the aisle from behind, arm raised to pound Kaci. But Rebecca raised both hands and the white shield slid around to protect them all.

The Wretch rose back into the air and came at them from above. Three brilliant white lights appeared, larger and faster than Winter had seen so far that night, and pulled the three chief demons away.

From above, a mass of demons, blacker than any human understanding, the purest evil, crashed through the ceiling and descended like lightning upon the white shell held in place by Rebecca.

Rebecca glowed as the demons struck, and Winter felt the power within herself mounting again. But the white shield flickered and collapsed. The flurry of demons tore at Winter's face. Strong shadowed arms wrapped around her, and Winter found herself being drawn toward the Acolyte. She beat and clawed at the demonic arms, but couldn't pull free.

The demonic cloud tore the vestiges of the white shield away with a shriek that didn't come from the demons, but from the pain and terror of an angel defeated.

Everything fell still. Winter could see clearly again. The larger, stronger angelic lights were now trapped with the rest. The Wretch had Rebecca pinned against the ceiling, and in front of the altar the Eater's strong arms held Kaci from behind. The Acolyte propped Winter up for a better view of Kaci.

"See how you fail," growled the Acolyte in her ear.

"No!" Winter shouted.

More shadows roiled in like black water from the windows and filled the crevices and aisles of the chapel. They swirled around the trapped angels, around Rebecca, around Kaci, and around Winter, pulsing, dancing, filling the air with a deafening revelrous shriek.

Then Xaphan emerged from the door to the tower. He smiled at the top of the steps like a general approving of the victory. Blood soaked his shoulder and arm, but he held himself as if it didn't hurt at all. He pulled the action on the gun in his hand and held it by his side, fixing his eyes on Kaci. Then he slowly descended the stairs.

Kaci screamed and thrashed at the Eater. Winter did the same, crying out for help that couldn't hear her, for intervention that wasn't coming, for more angelic forces that couldn't break through the barriers.

From within the black prison, the angelic presence suddenly materialized into recognizable beings, all reaching for Kaci, all wide-eyed and desperate. Their cries pierced through the demon shrieks and became the loudest sounds in the room.

The cries turned to words, clear and articulate to Winter for the first time. "Save the child!"

Xaphan reached the bottom and paced to within ten feet of Kaci. "Save the child!"

He glanced once at Winter, once at Rebecca, smirked, and then lowered his gun to point at Kaci's womb.

"Save the child!" The black prison cracked as the angels fought their captors. Hands reached out beyond the demons. "Save the child!"

Winter watched with her mouth hanging open. At any moment her nightmare would end and she'd awaken safe in her own bed in her own home, with her dad and mom, with everything that had gone wrong throughout the years leading her to this moment in time reversed into the perfect life she was supposed to have. Because what was the point of it all if in the last seconds everything failed?

Xaphan pulled the trigger. The boom filled the room. Silence fell as every demon held its breath in glee and every angel watched stunned. Kaci gasped, blood gushing from her abdomen. She cast a rapidly glazing look at Winter.

Xaphan pulled the trigger again. This time Kaci's chest exploded and she slumped in the Eater's arms.

59

Four Years Ago

Winter kept her head down as she walked through the chilly rain. At the first garbage bin she found, she tossed the medical folder inside. A few people passed her on the sidewalk with umbrellas over their heads. Some of them watched her, but most just passed quickly without looking up. The swoosh of cars kept Winter as far away from the road as possible.

Even if someone she knew were to drive by, she doubted they would recognize her. What must she look like? Bandages over her nose. A stiff walk from the pain in her side. Wet, dripping hair hanging in front of her face. Black pants and black t-shirt soaked to the skin. Thick brace on her forearm.

She gingerly crossed her arms and tried to walk faster, but her broken rib wouldn't let her. Each breath ached. With each hard step, a flash of fire spread through her chest.

Winter glanced up through her drenched hair and focused on the bridge. Nothing else really mattered. She could deal with a little discomfort until then.

It took an hour to reach the foot of the bridge. Winter gazed up to the top of the arch. The wet trusses glistened beneath the old lights. As she watched for at least ten minutes, only two cars crossed. This part of town had very little life left.

No one would see her. That was for the best. She had very little life left too.

In this, her last walk, she wanted to feel more, to experience the moment, the despair, the darkness, the rain. She kicked off her shoes and ground the heel of her foot into the concrete, savoring its roughness, and the intimacy of the rain.

Finally, she started up the bridge, up the footpath built into the side. She dragged her hand across the low wall that separated the foot-path from the road. The water tumbled from the wall, splashing over her hand and running down her wrist. The gentle rain sent rivulets down the path to caress her bare feet. A single car passed by, never slowing, filling the air with glittery mist.

As she reached the top of the bridge, she paused and stared at the bridge wall where Claire had stood. She studied the trellis that Claire had clung to. Winter moved into the exact spot she had once stood while trying to talk Claire down. She remembered when Claire fell, how Winter had rushed to the side in a vain attempt to catch her. She wasn't the only one. A police officer had tried too. People searched for Claire for days. The riverbank crawled with rescuers. She remembered it vividly, even though she hadn't returned to the spot until now.

But Winter? She was alone. She had always been alone, and now her aloneness had reached a deeper desperation. She no longer even had a place to sleep.

She had killed someone she had loved. Michael...His blood still stained her hands. The pain in her chest could have been the knife in her own heart.

She had killed Ryan too...

She had killed Claire...

She had killed her mom…

She had killed the baby…

God had killed Winter a long time ago. It just took until now for her to actually die.

She stood alone on the bridge. No one would reach out to catch her. No one would search for her. No one would care.

That's when Winter heard herself wailing. Her mouth hung open, and a deep guttural cry disappeared lifelessly into the steadily increasing rain. She let it finish and then shoved the rest of it down, stepping toward the wall where Claire had stood.

She grabbed the trellis and tried to heave herself up. Her rib protested and she screamed out in pain, but she pushed through it until she had a knee firmly on the rail. She paused to catch her breath, grabbed the trellis with both hands, and pulled herself up. Then she planted her feet and held the trellis with one hand.

The rain fell harder now, pounding on top of her head. Pounding against her heart.

She stood there, staring into the darkness below, facing the darkness within. What would be the point? What did she have left? She needed it to be over…

Winter screamed. She wept. She trembled. She ached. For the first time she finally let herself feel it all.

Her dad had left her long ago. Turned his back on her. Walked away. He didn't really love her then and he didn't love her now.

Her mom left her alone. God took her, just to hurt Winter. And now her mom lay rotting in the ground.

She had given her heart to Ryan, let herself love in a way she had never done before. When he died, so did any reserves of genuine love she had hidden away. How could she go on without a heart? How could anyone learn to love again after something like that?

Only Claire ever understood her. Without Claire, who could she talk to?

Being with Michael should have been a new beginning…a chance to rebuild all that had been torn down in her life. She had let him in. She had opened herself up. They'd begun to piece Winter back together. Then he smashed it all apart worse than before. But as bad as his betrayal was, there was no coming back from what Winter had done to him.

The only thing she'd truly been excited about in a long time was the baby. Maybe she could have given it the life she never had. Maybe she could have learned to have joy again through the heart of a child. But that was gone...gone like everyone else.

She screamed. She wept. She trembled. She ached.

Then it all stopped. The mourning of her life over, she turned her face to the rain and stilled herself. Her whole life had been leading to this moment. This is what God really wanted to happen. This is what he'd begun a long time ago, but she'd just been too cowardly to go through with it. All it would take was one step. One quick moment.

She let go with her left hand and stood holding nothing, arms slightly outstretched to either side.

Just one step. That's all it would take.

She eased her right foot off the edge and let it hover over the emptiness.

Just one step. And it would all be over.

Outside of Time

"No!" Winter screamed, but her voice seemed to bounce back upon itself, as if the atmosphere no longer permitted sound waves passage. She clawed out toward Kaci, her arms passing through the air with no resistance.

She had felt this sensation the year before when she had plucked Kaci from before the train. But something was different this time. Time had not just paused around her...all of reality stood frozen. At the train yard the physical world waited motionless as the spiritual world raged war around her. Now, even the demons holding her tight had ceased to move, the angels in their shadow cage transfixed with desperate arms still reaching for Kaci.

Winter gazed back at her friend, still slumped lifeless against the Eater holding her. Xaphan smiled at Kaci, gun still outstretched, tendrils of smoke motionless at the end of the barrel.

"We need your help, Prophetess," said a deep commanding voice.

Winter looked up to the man suddenly standing to her side. He wore gleaming silvery-white armor and held a helmet in his arm. At his side hung a curved sword, longer than she was tall, that shimmered as if poised to catch fire at any moment. His short silver beard matched the long hair tied behind his neck. Bright, ageless eyes, in a glowing face, watched her with a softness inverse from the hardness of his muscles. He looked down on her, easily two feet taller than she.

The horseman. The one that had stood at her side the year before when they escaped from the train yard. The one that had spoken to her on the road in Romania.

"What?" she asked, her voice weak and hoarse. She glanced back at Kaci and the tears fell.

"We need you to lead the army. Free yourself."

Objections and questions caught in her throat as she easily shoved aside the claws and arms that gripped her. She wanted to scream and attack the rider, but as she stood, she planted her feet and faced him with all the fury of eight years of hurt.

"Now?" she pointed back at Kaci. "Why couldn't you have come thirty seconds ago? It's too late! You're too late!"

The man's eyes flashed. "This is but one facet of war that rages with all the complexity of the most valuable diamond. It is a war you have already fought and are about to fight now. It is what has already happened and what will happen."

"No! How could God do this to me? I've done everything! I've lost everything! And now you want me to just leave her dead? Save her!"

The man shook his head. "I cannot. What has happened must always happen. It is the sum of what will happen and the result of the battle you are about to fight. The moments of time are painted in broad strokes that are laid down at different moments. Once the moment has been painted, it cannot be unpainted."

Winter clenched her jaw. "Who are you? What do you want from me?"

"I am Laban, the White Rider. And I desire simply for you to be what you were created to be. Our Prophetess, the one to lead the army, to command the battle, and to defeat the schemes of our enemy."

"I don't understand. We've already lost. She's already dead...the child is already dead. The prophecy is broken."

"Yet you have not commanded the army."

Winter wiped her cheeks, shaking with fury. "I still don't understand."

A twinkle shone in Laban's eye. "God is an infinite being. He exists at all times and in all times. He sees all of history and the future. He paints the paths of time and the fates of his servants from beginning to end, yet he paints as he wills. Sometimes he paints what is and then he paints what was. Sometimes he paints what will be before he paints what has been. And those who serve him, those who carry his presence and his power, can be his brushes."

"Are you saying we can go back and change things?"

"No. We can go back and begin things that have already happened and will happen. This is why the enemy will never win. The enemy, who knows not the infinite power of God, is a fish trapped in a bowl trying to outsmart birds who are free and watching the fish from outside the fish's reality. The army you must lead will fight outside of the constraints of time itself. It is a battle already fought but has yet to be fought. What has already happened must now happen."

"I have to lead an army outside of time? To fight a battle that's already been fought? You're insane."

"The insanity of man is but a flicker of thought for God. What humanity thinks is impossible, for God is simplicity. In the human realm of time, these battles have already passed, but outside of the human reality, the time for these battles is now."

Winter cast another glance at the lifeless body of Kaci. "What am I supposed to do then?"

"Lead the army."

"How? Where is it?"

Laban lifted his arms. Reality shifted as if Winter had been plucked from existence. The chapel and demons remained around her...Xaphan standing with his gun raised and Kaci slumped over lifeless...all just a mere reflection of the truth. Winter existed beyond the chapel, on another plane that intersected with the human realm, but could not be perceived.

All around her stood soldiers, bright faces and gleaming armor with dangerous swords at their sides. Just in front of her the other three horsemen astride their chargers. A fourth riderless horse, brilliant white, stood to one side.

"The four Watchers are here to be your commanders," said Laban. "Adom..." He indicated the first angel, red armored, scraggly red beard, astride a blood bay horse. "Sharok..." Clean shaven, golden armor, blond chestnut horse. "And Sors..." Black armor, dark braided beard, gleaming black horse.

Winter panned from them to take in the numbers of angelic warriors surrounding her in ordered ranks.

"How many?" she asked.

"Two hundred," said Laban. "An elite force of the finest warriors in Heaven, empowered with infinity."

"Why so few?

"These two hundred, at your command, are enough."

Winter nodded, feeling some of her frustration ebb away. "So, how does this work?"

"We stand now in the infinite, outside of human time. We can observe and be seen by neither humanity nor the spiritual world. We can study a single moment, or watch a century pass. All space and time are fluid beneath your feet. You merely have to think your destination and it will be done."

The chapel shifted slightly at Winter's thought, and suddenly there Xaphan stood at the foot of the steps, gun raised, but the first bullet had not yet been fired.

"We can change it!" Winter shouted.

"No!" said Laban, placing a hand on Winter's arm as Winter spun to run to Kaci. "You cannot change what has been done! You can only shape what has been!"

"I can't just leave her!" Winter glared at him and shoved him away. "You want me to command? This is it! Save her!"

Laban's hardened battle face crinkled into a dangerous snarl. Then he softened again. "I see I need to demonstrate."

Reality shifted around them. They were in the hospital at the foot of Davis's bed. Summer sat with her eyes closed in a chair by the window.

"We cannot save him," said Laban. "What is done is done. But it is our job to do what has already been done." He stepped closer to Davis. Reality blurred at his movement and Winter found herself at his side. "The bullet that struck his head entered a pathway of fatty tissue in his brain. It is the reason he survived. It is the reason he will live unharmed. This tissue in his brain is an abnormality that has existed since his birth. The miracle that saved his life began a long time ago, yet this miracle has not yet been done because we have not yet done it."

Reality shifted again. They stood in an old kitchen. For a brief moment Winter watched a young woman walk sporadically backward in a blur of motion before time halted on her sitting at a table, reading a book.

"Is this...?" Winter asked.

Laban nodded. "This is Davis's mother, twenty-three years prior to where we just were, according to the time of humanity. It has already happened, yet it is happening right now. She has only just learned she is with child." He stepped up to Davis's frozen mother and inserted his hand into her abdomen. "The abnormality that will one day save his life is now being painted."

Winter's heart fluttered. "Does this mean I can save my mom?"

At that thought reality shifted. Her mom lay asleep in Winter's old house.

"This is the moment the first cell of cancer formed," said Laban.

"Can you do something?"

He shook his head. "We cannot change what has happened."

"But this nearly killed me!" Reality shifted as her thoughts went to her mom. A much younger Winter stepped off a bus, her long, golden brown hair hanging limp on her back. Her friends called out to her from the bus as she walked up the sidewalk to the house. The young Winter paused and glanced at the driveway, to her dad's truck.

"Stop," said Winter. Reality stopped. She eased over to look her younger self in the eyes. "I remember this day. The day my world shattered. Is there nothing we can do?" she asked, casting back to Laban. The angelic army and the horsemen watched her closely.

"We cannot change what has happened," said Laban.

"But we can paint what has already happened?" she asked, looking past Laban's shoulder.

"Yes, Prophetess."

Winter spotted an angel standing among the ranks, watching her with a familiar face and suddenly she understood. She stepped toward the army, past Laban, past the other three horsemen, past the first two rows of angelic warriors. Everyone watched her in silence. Finally, she stopped in front of the familiar warrior. He had soft features and a firm jaw. His bright eyes met hers without flinching. He stood a head taller than she, long blond hair tied behind his back, yet he watched her with an eagerness that hung on her every movement.

"Hello," she said gazing up into his glowing blue eyes. "I know you. What is your name?"

"I am Magenel, Prophetess," he said.

"Magenel," she said, somehow knowing what it meant. "Shield of God."

"Yes, Prophetess."

"Will you be my shield?" she cast over her shoulder to her younger self. "Will you protect me?" She turned back to face him. "You will have to leave this army. You will have to join with my younger self and take the longer path of human time. You will have to fight alone when none of your brothers are there to fight with you. I need you. You must protect me when I cannot protect myself...and when I refuse to protect myself. You must also be my guide. When I am ready, make sure I can go and be where I need to be, the right places at the right time. Help me know what I need to do when I don't know it on my own. You are my premonition." She smiled at him. "You are my *sledgehammer.*"

Reality shifted around them briefly. Winter saw the underside of her old high school bleachers. Voices spoke behind her. She didn't need to turn, because she knew where and when they were. Her last thought had brought them to this moment.

"So, let me get this straight," said the voice of a much younger Winter. "Where everybody else is in a bumper car, my car has no bumper."

"Right," said Claire. "Or at least it can't be seen."

"...because I have solar sledgehammers all around me..." said Winter.

"...that are prepared to destroy any bumper car who tries to hit you," said Claire.

"Right," said the young Winter. Both girls started laughing, and the laughter trailed away as reality shifted back again and they returned to Winter's old house, the young, uninjured Winter still looking at her dad's truck.

Magenel firmed his lips and nodded. "I will be your shield."

He moved to step past her and Winter caught his arm. "I never said it while you were with me, but I want to say it now before you begin. Thank you."

He nodded again and walked out of the ranks, his fellow soldiers clapping him on the shoulder as he passed. He marched confidently by the horsemen as Laban watched on with approval. Magenel stood beside the younger Winter, looked back to the older Winter, nodded a final time, and then stepped into the temporal reality of Winter's past. When he did, he froze in time with his hand on the younger Winter's shoulder, gazing down upon her with the affection of an older brother.

Winter turned to Laban. "Now what do we do? When do we fight?"

"The battle is now. You have just begun. What Magenel does will bring you to this moment as a Prophetess. Without him, you will be lost. Well done."

"The battle is now?"

"The battle is you. You are the Prophetess. You protect the child. You defeat the enemy. If you are defeated before you even begin, then everything is lost."

"But how will I know what to do?" she asked.

"Simple," said Laban. "Remember. Follow the tracks of your own past."

Winter studied her younger self frozen in time with Magenel at her side. "My mother," she whispered.

Reality shifted. They stood in another hospital at the foot of another bed. Marie lay asleep, machines beeping and hissing around her. A nurse made notes on a chart and then walked from the room. Winter glanced back at Laban, and for the first time realized that the entire army had not followed. Only the Watchers were there, all four of them on foot. Laban stood closest.

"Where are they?"

"Here. Unseen," Laban said. "Seen if you wish."

Winter turned back to her mother and stepped up to the foot of the bed.

"I told you, you cannot undo this," said Laban.

"I know. You told me to remember and this moment is important." Winter peered around and wrinkled her brow. "Why is time moving?"

"It moves because you've told it to move." He waved his hand and the nurse walked backward into the room. He waved it back and she left again. "We are outside of time. We can see what we wish at whatever speed we want." He lowered it and let time tick at a normal speed.

"I wasn't here for her when she needed me," Winter said, clenching the bed-rail. "I came only at the end."

The machines began to beep faster. Marie thrashed in the bed and gasped. Nurses rushed in to restrain her.

"Her life is leaving her," said Sors, the Black Rider. "She is dying right now."

"She can't," said Winter. "I'm not here yet." She looked at Laban. "Help her. I'm not asking you to save her, but keep her alive…just a little longer. You must do it, because I've already seen it done."

Laban nodded, a gesture of respect more than acquiescence. "That is why you are our Prophetess. You know what has already happened and what must be done."

Three angels materialized, rushed forward, and put their hands on Marie. Marie's uncontrollable body settled down instantly. She opened her eyes and gazed up at the nurses. The machines stabilized into normal rhythms. The nurses chattered, something about paging the doctor, but Winter wasn't listening. Winter squeezed the foot of the bed and willed herself visible to only her mother.

Marie's eyes widened.

Winter spoke. "Hold on just a little longer, Mom. I'm coming. Wait for me."

Marie rolled her head to the nearest nurse and pulled at her.

"I have to wait for Winter," she croaked to the nurse.

The nurse nodded and adjusted the oxygen tube on Marie's nose. Marie watched Winter as the last couple of nurses made some adjustments on the machine and one by one they left.

Then Marie reached out to her. "Are you okay?"

Winter started crying. "I'm fine, Mom. You were right. God had something very special for me."

Marie smiled and shook her head. "You're not really here."

"Winter," said Laban. "You can't stay like this."

"I know," she said to him. "Mom, I love you."

"I love you."

"Wait for me."

Marie nodded again and at that moment the doctor and a nurse came in. Marie smiled up at the doctor. "I have to wait for Winter…"

Winter let herself fade back outside of time. "How long?" she asked Laban.

"I do not know," he said. "But time is not our master." He waved his hand and the scene blurred. When it solidified again, a younger Winter with short black hair wept at Marie's bedside. Magenel stood at the ready beside her.

"I can't watch this again," Winter told Laban. "We have to go. Call them back."

Laban nodded. He didn't speak a word, but the three angels holding on to Marie let go and returned to the ranks.

∞

Reality shifted and the world around them became dazzlingly white. The space between time. The space between existence.

Winter faced Laban. "I know what we have to do now. Since my mom died, it has been a constant battle for my soul, and the people I loved are the ones that suffered. We not only have to fight for me, we have to fight for them."

"We cannot undo what has already been done."

"I know!" The power behind her voice created an echo through the infinite that should not have existed. A rustle passed through the ranks of angels. Winter took a deep calming breath. "But if we don't try then we lose. I know now that there were forces at work in my life more powerful than I could realize. We are the force that fights for what is good and what is right."

"And the forces we will fight against?"

"Culsu. Mavka. Moloch. Xaphan. Maybe more."

The skin around Laban's eyes tightened. Another rustle passed through the ranks, not of fear, but of readiness and eagerness. Only Laban's eyes betrayed the danger.

"These are deadly demons," said Sors.

"We must attack immediately!" said Adom.

"We must wait for the right moment," said Sharok.

Winter nodded to them all. "Culsu has been trying to destroy me for a very long time. There's a reason she was able to deceive me so easily last year. We will begin with her."

The Watchers mounted their horses and positioned themselves behind her. "We are ready, Prophetess," said Laban.

"We go first to where Culsu entered my life." Winter shifted reality around them.

The interior of an abandoned warehouse materialized. Slightly in front of them stood a circle of people, all wearing black robes with hoods pulled over their heads so deep their faces were obscured in shadow. Demons clung to them like a second robe.

A large wooden X stood in a wide circle of glowing coals. Naked and strapped to the X, hung Alison. She screamed and wailed. Blood covered her skin from hundreds of cuts and demonic symbols carved into her flesh. Winter didn't want to think of all the things they did to her leading up to this point. As they watched, the ends of the X burst into flames. Alison thrashed against her bonds, her voice so raked and coarse it barely sounded human. The others just stood there watching and waiting.

Then a word cut through the air. A single word formed intelligently from Alison. "Culsu!" A deep roiling shadow rose up out of the coals, living and hungry. It swirled at the base of the X and wrapped itself around Alison until she could not be seen.

"Are we safe?" Winter asked.

Laban nodded. "We remain in the infinite. We will not enter until you command. We will not be known unless we enter."

"I don't understand," she said. "How are we invisible to the demons too?"

"We stand in the infinite, a state of existence where the Father dwells, where the fallen are not allowed, and where angels occasionally tread as needed to work out the commands of the Father. Demons and angels naturally abide in the spiritual realm, a place outside of humanity's perception yet still within the constraints of time and space. This is how Magenel protects your younger self. This is how Culsu manipulates her human prey. This is how we remain unseen. To be called by the Father to stand within the infinite is a privilege and an honor."

"What can we do here?"

"I do not know. Even I do not fully understand the mysteries of the infinite. I suspect we will be allowed to do whatever you command."

With that, Winter willed the scene in front of her to stop. Everything froze like a painting. She turned so she could address the entire army. As the intention to see the angels formed in her mind, suddenly they materialized in front of her.

"This is where it began," she shouted. "This is where Skotos tortured my friend Alison into calling upon Culsu. This is when Culsu began to destroy the people I loved and even tried to destroy me. This is where Culsu enslaved Skotos to Xaphan. This is the first enemy we fight. We must hunt down Culsu throughout time and stop her."

"Do we attack now?" Adom asked, his blood bay horse prancing.

Winter shook her head. "There's nothing we can do here. Alison made her choice. But I think I know where Culsu first met me."

Reality shifted. They were in Alison's grandmother's house. The younger Winter and Alison sat in the middle of the kitchen floor on either side of a small carpet with a pentagram woven into it. Candles flickered at each side. A Ouija board sat in the middle, and both girls gingerly held their fingers to the pointer.

Magenel stood just behind the younger Winter, leaning over her with his sword drawn, feet spread, ready to defend.

Culsu, an inky black mass still moving as if boiling, but now in a roughly humanoid shape, loomed behind Alison, stroking her hair with one hand and whispering into her ear. A long tendril snaked out from the other hand, touching the indicator. The indicator slid suddenly.

"Stop it," said the younger Winter. "You're moving it."

"No I'm not!" said Alison

"Prove it."

Alison looked at the board. "Can you give us a sign that you're really here?"

As the ritual proceeded, Magenel staring down Culsu and Culsu manipulating the Ouija board as if he were not even there, more demons appeared. They danced and floated around the room, pawing at both Winter and Alison, bowing before Culsu, and evading Magenel's sword.

"Okay," said Winter. "We need to help him. Send enough to keep the demons back, but do not attack Culsu. We don't want her to know our full strength."

Laban nodded. Five more angels entered and took up their swords beside Magenel. The demons gave them a wide berth now. Culsu watched them, still unconcerned, but interested and analyzing.

"That's not funny! Stop it, Ali!" shouted the younger Winter.

A couple of smaller, quicker demons skirted past the angelic swords and reached out to brush the young Winter's arm. As the angels moved to attack, they flitted away laughing, taunting.

"More," said Winter.

Five more angels joined the room. Culsu cooed into Alison's ear, red glowing eyes measuring each angel individually.

Alison leaned forward, her face absorbing the shadows and her eyes glinting with joy. "Are you Winter's mom?"

"STOP IT! Why are you doing this?" asked the younger Winter.

More demons arrived. The young Winter's voice ghosted from her mouth as the temperature in the room plummeted.

The angelic swords flew. The demons grew more bold and daring; some now fought with their own weapons…distorted things of torture. Still Culsu watched unafraid.

Culsu moved the indicator again and stood. She took a step toward the young Winter. The angels shifted to face the new threat. With one long arm Culsu kept a hand on Alison's back. With the other she struck forward, easily knocking away the angels standing guard and unaffected by their swords. She touched the younger Winter on the back. The younger Winter screamed.

"Enough!" shouted Winter and flashed her eyes at Laban with so much meaning he didn't hesitate before he led his horse forward into the battle.

Laban pulled out his flaming sword and advanced toward Culsu.

The younger Winter grabbed the indicator and Ouija board and hurled them across the room. As she did, Laban's sword fell, slicing through any demon stupid enough to stand in the way. The rest fled. Culsu slunk back into the shadows, red eyes trained on the horseman, and then faded away. The board and the indicator clattered to the floor.

Reality froze. Laban and the ten angels returned to the infinite. Magenel remained like a statue, sword still drawn, at the young Winter's side.

Laban reigned up beside Winter. "Culsu will know now that we are protecting the younger you. I'm not sure what she will do. But we must be careful."

"Agreed," said Sharok, easing next to Laban. "We must wait for the right moment."

Winter nodded. "We will follow, only intervening enough to keep my younger self safe. When the right moment comes, we will strike."

Reality shifted. They were in the halls of Trenton Hills high school. Time continued to stand still. The younger Winter faced Alison at the lockers, Claire just behind her. Magenel once again had his sword out at Winter's side. Directly behind Alison stood a much more solidified form of Culsu, sleeker and thinner, but with the same glowing red eyes. She had one hand on Alison's head in mid-stroke, eying Winter and Magenel with a cold, calculating stare.

"She suspects us already," said Sors.

"I'm afraid you're right," Winter said. "Culsu knows something is going on. But she won't act now. She will act soon. We must be ready. I'm bringing us next to our first truly important fight."

Reality shifted. Winter's bedroom.

"She's here," Winter said. She could hear her younger self crying in the bathroom. Winter blinked and time stopped, the walls of the house faded away until all that remained was a small square where the younger Winter stood in front of the bathroom counter and a mirror. All else now appeared as the sterile whiteness of the infinite…room enough for the angelic army to do its work, with a single moment in time isolated in the center.

Golden brown roots showed at the base of the young Winter's jet black hair. Dark shadows beneath her swollen and bloodshot eyes highlighted the gauntness of her cheeks. On the counter lay a towel, arrayed with stud earrings, several large needles, an ice pick, a pair of scissors, and a yellow-handled box cutter.

"Scissors are the emblem," Winter mumbled as she approached the red-eyed demon wrapped around her younger self and whispering into the younger Winter's ear. Magenel lay pinned to the ground beneath an abnormally stretched arm of Culsu, his sword just out of reach.

Winter turned a circle to address the army now surrounding the scene. "The previous fight was a minor skirmish. Culsu will be expecting us here. She is testing the protection around my younger self. You must keep me safe!"

Time resumed. The young Winter proceeded to pick up needles, whimpering to herself in the mirror as Culsu goaded her softly.

"Now!" Winter shouted.

The army collapsed in, stepping into reality. Culsu shrieked and struck out, releasing Magenel. Magenel rolled away and snatched up his sword, joining the ranks as they fell upon Culsu.

Culsu roared and other shadows arrived, demons joining the fray and easily held at bay by the skill of the angelic warriors.

The horsemen trotted in circles around the scene, remaining just on the edge of reality, unseen and barking orders to the angels.

Still the young Winter continued to mutilate her own body as Culsu kept one hand on her shoulder.

"My father!" Winter shouted. "Get him! Clear a path! This ends when he arrives!"

Sharok, on his blond chestnut horse accepted the order. He called a handful of soldiers to accompany him and they streaked like lightning, out of the infinite space and into reality beyond the house, in search of Steve.

Winter knew her dad wasn't far, but she did not realize until now the full strength of the demon. One small thing could cause the delay that would lose the battle. Culsu raged against the army, flailing almost desperately, but still clinging with one hand to the young Winter.

The young Winter took off her shirt, her torso veined in sticky trails of blood, like a demonic rash. She picked up the ice pick and leaned against the counter to pierce herself. As she twisted the ice pick into place, wincing in pain, Laban rushed in. His horse reared against Culsu and Culsu released the young Winter for a moment.

The young Winter put a hand on the counter to keep herself from collapsing, shaking her head and staring at herself in the mirror with a mix of disgust and surprise.

Culsu pressed back, both hands against Laban and his snow-white horse, shoving them away, sprouting more arms to reach out and strike at every soldier within reach. She turned and placed her two primary arms onto the young Winter's shoulders.

She reached for the scissors.

Winter clenched her teeth. "More!" she shouted.

The army surged. Culsu roared again. The three remaining horsemen pressed in. The young Winter placed the blade of the scissors against her wrist, tears running fast down her cheeks, mixing with blood to make long red streaks. She pressed and pulled, leaving a thin red line as two angels reached for the elbow of her scissor arm and pulled up to keep her from pressing any harder.

Culsu laughed and swatted them away. Then she leaned forward to whisper into the young Winter's ear. The young Winter repositioned the scissors, drew another scratch, and screamed.

Finally, the horsemen wrenched Culsu away, isolating and distancing the demon from the young Winter. As they fought beyond the bathroom, Winter watched herself helplessly, knowing the depth of emotional damage that had been done. Her younger self reached for the box-cutting knife. She flicked the blade out and pressed it against her wrists.

Winter leaned toward her. "Hold on!" she shouted, wondering if she could hear herself. "Just a moment longer! Just wait!"

Sharok and his soldiers returned, rejoining the battle against Culsu. A door closed downstairs. The young Winter slammed the box cutter down, checked the lock on the door, and turned to the shower.

Several feet away, Culsu growled in frustration, took another final strike at the angels beating on her, and then fled.

Adom moved to follow.

"No!" Winter shouted. "Let her go." She pointed to her younger self. "Help her."

Every soldier took a deep breath and relaxed, sheathing their swords. The horsemen dismounted, and every angel gathered around the younger Winter as she sobbed in the shower. Winter remembered that shower...the slow coming out of the fog of despair, the dwindling of any desire to end her own life. She had no idea what had happened around her.

Had it always been this way? Had Winter been the one helping *herself* the entire time?

When the young Winter's face filled with strength again and her tears subsided, the soldiers fell back into their ranks. Magenel put a fist to his chest and nodded in salute before stepping into reality.

Winter pulled away, back to the infinite.

"Culsu will not risk open battle again," said Sharok. "Not unprepared."

Winter nodded. "She was summoned by Alison and will stay with Alison. I think she only attacked me out of curiosity about why I was so protected."

"I agree," said Laban. "In the painting of time, other angelic forces have already intervened on your behalf. A tapestry is being woven."

Winter shifted reality forward. The younger Winter and Alison sat at a table in the food court of the mall with time standing still. Behind the younger Winter stood Magenel, poised and ready, but sword still sheathed. Culsu lurked behind Alison, clinging to Alison's back, arms wrapped around her and delving deep into Alison's chest. Culsu's forehead rested on the top of Alison's head.

In the shadows on the edge of reality, but phased differently than Winter and the army, were more angelic soldiers watching and waiting.

"See. The calling upon your life was recognized long ago," said Laban. "You were guided and protected by more than us and more than Magenel."

"Why do they look different?" Winter asked.

"These angels are still bound by time, yet they watch unseen from other spiritual forces. Empowered by the infinite, we can see them all and yet remain unseen by all."

"Are they in a different place than Magenel and Culsu?" she asked.

"Somewhat," said Laban. "For the angelic, the spiritual realm can be used in two ways. Magenel and the demon are in the spiritual now, a place unseen by humanity but seen by all other spiritual forces. The angels you see watching are in the spiritual unknown, invisible to the fallen."

"Oh," was all Winter could say.

"There is little for us to do in this moment, Prophetess. Our brothers keep the peace. Unless you wish us to attack."

"No. Not here." Winter shifted reality to the edge of a forest, street lamps only a few yards away. Alison stood over Philip, her dress torn and dirty as if there had been a fight. She clenched bloody scissors in her hands. Philip had one hand up as if to protect himself. His other hand clenched a deep bloody gash across his chest.

Culsu was so absorbed inside of Alison she almost couldn't be seen.

Winter shifted reality again. The angelic army had faded, invisible once more, and the horsemen watched her quietly. They didn't question her or offer suggestions...they waited as Winter scanned the tracks of her own past.

Prom. Alison and Culsu stood in an open space of the gym facing Claire. Stunned couples gave them a wide berth. The younger Winter and Ryan watched from one side. The bloody scissors lay on the floor.

Winter shifted reality. The blue Mustang raced below on the road. Black shadows clung to the roof. White mist trailed behind, fought off by the shadows. From the driver's window a bright white light emanated — Magenel fighting for the younger Winter. From the passenger window oozed a darkness blacker than the sum of all hate and despair — Culsu with Alison.

Winter turned to the horsemen. "Sharok...three miles down the road this car will collide with another and fly off the road. Go there now. Prepare the site. Be ready when the battle arrives." Sharok nodded and vanished. She felt, rather than saw, one-fourth of the angelic forces phase away with him. Winter turned to the next horseman. "Sors…two miles beyond the crash site is another car carrying innocent people. Go to them and protect them. Keep them alive." Sors nodded. He and another fourth of the forces phased away. Winter faced Laban. "Somewhere beyond that is a vehicle with a couple in it that must arrive at the right time to give my younger self help. Make sure they do." Laban nodded. He and another fourth phased away.

Winter gazed back down at the car. "The rest of us will join the fight here. The fight for my life and the fight for Ryan."

Adom stepped to her side, sword out, eyes flashing, his blood bay horse stamping. "We await your orders, Prophetess."

Winter nodded. Time flowed below them as they stepped out of the infinite into the spiritual unknown. With a mere thought, Winter sped off like a streak of lightning. To her other side other streaks flew through the air, Adom larger and tinged with crimson. Winter paused above the car to watch as her army phased into the spiritual now and crashed into the shadows, scattering them like a cloud of dust. The angels already present surged forward and joined Winter's army.

With a flicker of thought, the outside of the car faded away behind the infinite, leaving only the seats visible, the three people in them, and Culsu already in a fierce battle with Magenel for supremacy. Culsu arose from within the body of Alison, first her head emerging, then shoulders, dozens of arms, and torso, leaving only her legs embedded.

Alison was shouting at the younger Winter, gun to Winter's head. The younger Winter cried and clung to the steering wheel. Ryan sat wide-eyed in the back seat, as Magenel's bright sword flashed quick enough to keep all of Culsu's arms away from both him and the young Winter.

Winter moved to position herself between Culsu and Ryan.

"Prophetess!" shouted Adom, pulling in front of her and stopping her. "You cannot! If Culsu were to see you then our advantage would be lost. You must at least stay in the unknown and let *us* fight the battle!"

Winter grunted and jabbed her finger at him, for the first time noticing that her skin glowed. "His life is in your hands!"

Adom's eyes widened briefly and then he nodded. "Yes, Prophetess." He streaked into the back seat, brandishing his flaming sword.

At the sight of the horseman, Culsu screeched. The demons rallied back. The car swerved. The engine roared. Angels and demons swirled around every side like a bubble, unaffected by matter or speed, as if they fought in one place while the real world moved around them. The swords of Magenel and Adom moved so fast the blades could not be seen. Yet they could barely keep Culsu at bay.

Winter watched, feeling helpless. She blinked and let the fullness of reality return to her vision, though all matter remained translucent to her. She could still see the fury within the car, the terror on her own younger face, the malice on Alison's face, the confident fear on Ryan's face.

Headlights in the distance. The other car approached the faithful turn where this chase would end. Sharok and his forces waited at the turn and at the bottom of the hill. Sors and his forces encapsulated the oncoming car.

Winter could stop time, she could leave, she could fast forward. She didn't want to relive this scene...but she had to.

The younger Winter drove too fast to make the turn. She took the inside route of the road to lessen the sharpness, bringing her into the oncoming lane and unable to see the approaching car. The two cars met half way. The younger Winter corrected back to the outside. The other car did the same, but the young Winter had over corrected. The Mustang fishtailed almost sideways when they collided. The oncoming car struck the back end of the Mustang, spinning the young Winter back the other direction one-hundred-eighty degrees. The tires caught against the pavement and the car flipped, crashing onto the roof.

Tires. Roof.

Tires. Roof.

Then the car flew off the edge of the road into the air, still flipping toward a tree.

"Stop!" Winter yelled just before the car struck.

Everything halted. Every angel, her entire army, the three horsemen, every demon, and Culsu, all froze in time. Winter stood alone in a higher level of existence, another layer of the infinite that only she could enter somehow.

She floated toward the car, descending through the air as easily as walking upon solid ground. Once next to the car, she willed everything outside of her portion of the infinite to disappear until only Ryan remained.

His eyes were clenched. His hands spread out as if to brace himself. One of the arms bent unnaturally, broken already in the crash. Blood trickled from his face from the flying glass.

Winter went to him. She reached out and touched his arm, mending the bone with the power still surging through her. She brushed his face, wiping away the blood and cuts. Then with her hand still on his cheek, she brought him into the infinite with her.

He gasped and opened his eyes. "Winter! What's going on? Am I dead?"

Winter bit her lip. "No. But you will be soon."

"I don't understand. How is this possible? Where are we?"

"I can't explain completely, but it's really me and we're in a place where time doesn't matter. I can't keep you here. And...and I'm sorry I can't save you."

He smiled at her. "It's okay. I'm ready."

Winter's chin trembled. "But I'm not. I have missed you more than you'll ever know."

He reached out and wiped the tears flowing down her cheeks. "It's not your job to save me. I'll be okay, but you have to let me go."

"I know I do. I just..." Words failed her. She grabbed him with both arms and pulled his face to hers, kissing him in the precise way she had fantasized about for six years. "I loved you," she said, resting her forehead on his.

He laughed and pulled away. "I love you now," he said. "I don't know what this is, or where I am, but I know you're not my Winter. You're the Winter who survives. You're the Winter who gets to move on."

Winter shook her head. "I'm the same."

He gave her a soft smile. "No. You have to let me go. You have to love someone else. I think you already do."

Winter began to cry again. "I know...I just needed you to know. I needed to say goodbye." She kissed him again. "Goodbye." Her voice choked and the last syllable barely audible.

He smiled and brushed her hair. "Goodbye."

Winter stepped back, reaching out to him with both hands, and released him back to reality. Time resumed. Ryan flew away from her outstretched arms and the car slammed into the tree. She floated away backward from the crash, covering her mouth with both hands, knowing he was already gone.

Over half of her angelic army fought together now, bolstered by the other warriors that had been assigned to watch the younger Winter. A small group remained with the other car, keeping the severely injured driver alive.

The demons clinging to the Mustang fought with desperation, the battle pulled away from the car into the air, a flurry of weapons and streaks that even with the power coursing through her, Winter struggled to see clearly.

Only Culsu remained, fighting off three horsemen as she climbed out of the broken body of Alison in retreat. With one last flicker of her shadowed arm, she touched the front of the car and flames lept up.

The three horsemen drove Culsu away. The battle still raged above. The young Winter yelled out of the window for help that wasn't coming.

Winter searched around for someone, anyone. She raced back to the other car and grabbed the first angel she could reach. "I need you!"

He nodded and followed her to the blazing Mustang. Winter pointed to her struggling younger self, trying desperately to get the door open while Alison shrieked in the background.

The angel took the cue and materialized himself into the form of a human man, rushing down the hillside and grabbing the door. After several attempts to wrest it open, he succeeded. As the young Winter crawled out onto the ground, weeping, the angel dematerialized and returned to Winter's side.

"Thank you," she said.

He nodded and eyed the battle driving Culsu further and further into the distance, but stayed by her side, sword drawn.

Laban galloped up to them on his white horse. "The rescue vehicle will be here in a moment."

Winter pointed to Culsu and the horsemen. "Help them," she said.

Laban nodded and streaked away.

The younger Winter now clawed her way up the embankment. The car blazed behind her. Alison's screams died away. In the distance a car engine approached. As it rounded the curve and the driver spotted the inferno, it screeched to halt.

Young Winter reached the top of the embankment as a woman rushed toward her. A man slid down toward the car.

Culsu had disappeared. The demons above were gone or destroyed. As the army converged back toward the wreck and the horsemen gathered around her, Winter shifted them all from the spiritual realm to the infinite.

∞

Laban urged his mount forward. "I'm afraid Culsu knows more of our real strength than we should have allowed."

Winter stared at him. "That was harder than I imagined it would be," she said quietly.

Laban's face softened. "Know that he received his reward."

"I know." She took a deep breath and took in all four horsemen. "I'm fine. We have to keep following Culsu."

Winter faced away from the horsemen toward the blank whiteness of the infinite and concentrated. Around her, images of reality appeared like scenes from a movie. She moved them, slowly at first, then increasing to an impossible speed. She shuffled through every moment of every location, time flitting around them, all at once in a blur, like a kaleidoscope of existence. To one side every moment of her own time from the wreck forward, each second individually and all seconds at once. Beside that, all the moments of her dad's life.

As Winter flicked her eyes from one set of moments to the next, she added more people. Stacy. Claire. Shannon. Michael. Madam Morial. Kaci. Davis. Summer. Peter. Ayden. Graham. The lives of each converging in the infinity for Winter to peruse at will, searching for the single earliest moment where Culsu might reappear.

Finally, a shadow crossed one of the lines and Winter froze them all, pointing. "There. With Claire." Claire's reality expanded to fill the space around them as Winter pulled herself and the horsemen into the spiritual unknown on the street outside of Claire's house. A dark shadow hung over the roof, like an isolated storm. Black mist oozed from the walls.

"There are many demons here," said Sors, his black horse shaking its mane.

"Including Culsu. Look." Winter pointed to a set of red eyes just beyond a window.

Sharok leaned forward in his golden saddle. "Culsu is powerful, but she is a manipulator. Now that she knows the strength of us, she will not risk more open battle…not without preparation."

"Agreed," said Laban. "She prefers to work from the shadows, and this can be to our advantage."

"We must strike when she is weak," said Adom.

"Can we go in?" asked Winter.

"We will do as you command," said Laban. "But I do not recommend this. To stand in protection of someone is one thing, but to take the offensive is another. The enemy would retaliate and there would be open war."

"We cannot avoid open war," said Adom, raising his fist. His crimson horse pranced.

"No," said Sharok. "But this is not the time for it, nor is it the place."

"Culsu has made a stronghold here," said Sors. "If we attack her stronghold it will weaken us so that we cannot fight the more important battles later."

Winter studied the house a moment longer, recalling all the horrible things that happened to Claire there and knowing she still could do nothing to help her friend. Finally, she nodded to the horsemen and let reality slide by for a few hours, a smear of colors, until Claire exited the house on her way to school. Alone.

"See," said Adom. "Culsu hides in the shadows."

"She poisons the heart of this girl, to destroy her from the inside," said Sors.

"Claire," said Winter. "Her name is Claire. She was my friend."

"Then Culsu has found a way to make you weak," said Sors.

Winter spun on the black rider. "My friends are not my weakness!"

Sors stared at the ground and Laban urged his white steed between them. "We have little concept of friendship. We are creatures who love and defend by instinct. Companionship is our nature. Companionship by choice is beyond our understanding."

"Then know this," said Winter, clenching her fists. "Claire was my friend by choice. My choice and hers. So we *will* defend her…her and any of my other friends."

Laban nodded. "It will be as the Prophetess commands." He drew his sword. "Do we enter the house?"

Winter faced Claire's house again, the windows still oozing black mist. "No. You're right. We cannot go there now. We'll have to search the timelines for Culsu to emerge."

Reality shifted, a blur of time and location with Claire always at the center as if the universe moved and transformed around her. Winter paused in the restroom of Trenton Hills high school. Claire stood alone facing the mirror, crying to herself. Winter let time play normally and Claire reached into her backpack to pull out a pair of scissors before creeping toward the furthest stall.

Winter paused reality and cast over her shoulder to Laban. "Send someone into the cafeteria to notify Magenel so that he can make sure my younger self comes here."

"I will do as you command," said Laban. "But you must also know that your younger self is not yet regenerated. She has no immediate connection to the spiritual. Magenel can try, but your younger self may not hear."

"Send someone anyway," said Winter as she stepped closer to Claire. "I found her for a reason. So maybe it'll work."

"Culsu is not here," said Adom.

"Claire is poisoned," said Sors. "She seeks to destroy herself."

"Then we keep looking," said Winter.

She let reality slide by until her younger self came in searching for Claire, and then let reality blur again as they traveled further through Claire's timeline. Winter paused reality randomly to check, but never saw Culsu emerge from the house. Finally they found Claire leaving the house for the last time, as she escaped to Winter's house to run away.

"Culsu's not with her," Winter said. Winter shifted reality until the younger Winter and Claire had climbed out of Winter's bedroom window. "Send a horseman with a detail of soldiers to follow them in the spiritual now," she told Laban. "If Culsu shows up, I want her to know that we're watching. They are not to engage with Culsu without all of us. We will follow from the infinite and intervene if needed."

"It will be done, Prophetess," said Laban.

Sharok and twenty warriors stepped out of the infinite and took up positions around Winter and Claire alongside Magenel. Once they were in place, Winter phased through reality along Claire's timeline again.

A shadow formed and Winter stopped. "Here."

Before them waited a small two-story house, painted white and green. Little statues decorated the water-logged lawn. Rain poured down in floating sheets. Young Winter and Claire stood dripping on the porch, talking to an elderly man at the door. Clinging to Claire, shrunken as if hiding, lurked the shadowy presence of Culsu. Sharok and Magenel flanked either side of the young Winter as the twenty soldiers fanned out around them.

Winter stepped closer and peeled away pieces of reality, stripping the house bare of its walls and furniture, so that she could clearly see the playing field. A brief flicker of thought advanced reality and the two girls stood now inside the elderly couple's house. Winter released time to slip by normally again.

Claire disappeared around a translucent corner, leaving the young Winter dripping in the foyer. The elderly woman pointed Claire toward the restroom and then entered the kitchen with her husband. Claire took a step and paused next to a utility shelf in the hall. Culsu stroked her head. Claire reached down and snatched up a pair of scissors, then spun back to the kitchen. Claire shoved the man in the shoulder. He stumbled through the kitchen and fell.

The younger Winter ran in, followed closely by Magenel and

Sharok. The diminutive, shirking form of Culsu hissed at them from Claire's back.

"Not here in front of these people," Winter said as she let reality slip again and found her younger self walking in the rain. Magenel and Sharok still flanked her, with the twenty angelic warriors spread in a defensive formation. Claire pulled up in the elderly couple's car. Culsu had vanished.

"Where did she go?" asked Winter.

Laban shook his head. "She hides and waits."

"Then we keep looking."

Winter shifted reality, watching her younger self and Claire slide down the drainage ditch and climb into a low-income neighborhood. They walked until they came to an alley where they slept next to a dumpster.

Occasionally Winter would see Culsu lurking in the shadows, following the two girls, but never staying visible long enough for the angels around the young Winter to pull Culsu away and engage.

Once Culsu watched openly as gang members accosted the younger Winter and Claire, each gang member carrying their own personal demons on their backs. But as soon as Winter thought about ordering the entire army to attack, the demon fled again.

Winter continued to follow the two girls. Day broke. The girls approached the Old Trenton River bridge. At the top, they sat with their backs to the dividing wall between the foot-crossing and the road.

As sirens wailed and the police converged, Culsu finally emerged from the shadows and descended upon Claire, latching onto her in full force. Sharok, Magenel, and the rest of the warriors around the younger Winter took defensive stances as Culsu hissed at them, sprouting a tentacle-like arm for each angelic sword.

"Keep Claire from the ledge at all costs," Winter said to Laban.

Laban nodded. He took another twenty warriors and stepped into the spiritual now, positioning themselves beyond the edge of the bridge in mid-air to create a protective barrier that Culsu could not pass.

"Be ready with more," Winter said to Adom and Sors. "We don't want to reveal our full strength yet, but I will do what must be done."

Adom and Sors nodded to her and positioned twenty warriors each around themselves to wait the order to enter.

Culsu roared as Laban, Sharok, and their angels surrounded her. The demon suddenly swelled and towered over Claire and the younger Winter as shadows streamed out of the air and were added to her mass. More tentacle-like arms sprung from her back.

The two girls stood upon hearing the commotion at the base of the bridge, finding both sides blocked by police. Two police cars raced up toward them. While the younger Winter watched with wide eyes as the cars slid to a halt, behind her Claire backed up to the railing.

The officers jumped out, hands on their weapons. "Hands up!"

Claire scrambled onto the ledge. "No! Leave us alone!" Culsu grinned, laughing with a deep, purring rumble.

With a flicker of thought command from Winter, Laban led the first attack, pressing Culsu back away from the edge. But since their last encounter, Culsu had grown stronger and faster. The twenty warriors with Laban could barely keep back Culsu's flailing arms. Only Laban seemed to make any headway.

As the younger Winter rushed to the edge to stop Claire, Sharok, Magenel, and the other twenty warriors attacked Culsu from the rear. Culsu raged against both fronts, drawing more shadows out of the air, red eyes flashing.

The seconds of real-time ticked by. There wasn't much time left. She could hear her younger self talking with Claire through the melee of the battle raging invisibly around them. Several times Culsu made to grab at the younger Winter, but Magenel always cut the tentacle away. He barely seemed the same warrior that Winter had picked out of the ranks. His armor gleamed brighter, his face shone more intensely, and a power filled him that rivaled that of the horsemen.

It didn't take long before Culsu realized the warriors were more concerned with the younger Winter than with Claire, and her eyes widened as she tried even harder to reach her. But the harder Culsu tried, the more ferocious Winter's warriors became. Especially Magenel.

"I'm pregnant," Claire said, her words cutting through the battle sounds to reach Winters ears as clearly as if she had heard the words for the first time.

"Stop," Winter said out loud and willed everything outside of the infinite to stand still. She turned to the crimson rider, Adom, still at her side. "Earlier, I found myself alone in a part of the infinite. I'm not sure how it happened, but I think it was a layer that only I could enter. I want to do something similar here. I want to create a layer of the infinite where Culsu and the angels are in the physical space they are in now, but in the time of the infinite. Is that possible?"

"I do not know, Prophetess. We are not permitted to control the infinite, but perhaps this ability has been granted to you."

"Then I'll try," Winter said. "If it works, I and the rest of the army will stay here unseen. I want you to step into the space I create, but to remain connected with me. I have some things I want to say. You will be my voice."

Adom nodded. "As you wish, Prophetess."

Winter stared directly at Culsu and concentrated. She reached out to feel the infinite, searching for some sensation she could latch onto. It was there, like strands of silk. The fabric of the infinite became clear to her and she grabbed it with the same mental movement she used to manipulate time.

Winter folded the new layer. The spiritual battle resumed, but the physical world stood perfectly still. As soon as Culsu noticed the change, she hissed and tried to flee, but the warriors blocked her escape. Adom stepped into the new layer and held up his hands. Laban, Sharok, and their warriors disengaged and formed a tight perimeter around the demon. Culsu studied them, pulling her tentacles tightly around herself.

"Why are you here?" Winter asked from outside the new layer of infinity, unseen by Culsu.

"Why are you here?" Adom repeated.

Culsu trained in on him, though she still flicked her glowing red eyes around at all the other warriors. "I was summoned."

"Yes. But the one who summoned you is dead. Why are you still here?" Winter asked.

Adom repeated.

"Curiosity. The horsemen do not show themselves for no small reason."

"Then why are you destroying this girl?"

Adom repeated.

"For fun. Why do you protect the other?" Culsu's eyes flicked to the frozen younger Winter. "Three horsemen I see, the fourth is not far. Yet there is a power greater in control. What is behind the veil still? Why is this girl so important to you?"

"That is none of your business," Winter said. Adom repeated.

"Curious," Culsu said to Adom. "How far will you go? Protection has not been afforded a human like this since the old days of the prophets. Is she to become another?"

Sors stepped up beside Winter. "This goes too far, Prophetess. Culsu cannot know so much."

"Leave Claire now or you will be destroyed," Winter said. Adom repeated.

Culsu cast around at the forces surrounding her, measuring. She looked back at Adom. "What strength lies behind the veil? Do I dare test what I do not know?"

"Go! Now!"

"I will find out who this girl is. I will sate my curiosity."

"Go!"

Culsu lifted her arms from Claire. Laban and his forces parted to let her drift out over the river. She wore a sinister smile on her face.

"My work was complete in this girl long ago," said the demon. "She will destroy herself whether I remain or not." She pointed a finger at the young Winter. "This one I will have next." Then Culsu turned and fled.

As the warriors and the three horsemen returned to the infinite and reformed their ranks, Winter stared at Claire, the brokenness on Claire's face so complete that nothing would ever change it. Claire's hand rested on her abdomen. The younger Winter cried and lifted her hand toward Claire.

Winter remembered that moment. She remembered all these moments of broken-heartedness, and the feelings returned each time she relived one. She really couldn't escape what had already been done.

"There's nothing you can do," Laban said.

"I know, but I don't have to watch."

Winter let reality slide beyond Claire's fall and her younger self's reaction. She found the moment where her younger self leaned over the opposite side of the bridge, waiting for Claire's body to emerge and then let time resume as normal. Her younger self still cried and Winter realized she cried too. As she wiped the tears from her cheeks, she gazed at Laban, wanting to beg him to do something, anything, that might change the way she felt.

Laban's face softened. "If you will permit us, we will honor your loss."

"Anything," Winter sobbed at him, wishing she didn't sound like a blubbering idiot.

He nodded and turned. As he did, the entire host followed him, stepping into the spiritual now, and spreading out across the bridge in two lines. The younger Winter pulled away from the edge and glanced around at the chaos of rescue vehicles that were arriving. Then she drifted down the bridge, between the angelic lines, like a lost orphan. As she passed, each angel saluted her with a small bend of the waist and a hand against their chests. Magenel marched chin up at the younger Winter's side, parading as an honor guard.

The horsemen, however, turned to the older Winter. They dismounted and stood in line before her. Winter shifted her gaze from her younger self to watch the horsemen move closer together until they stood nearly shoulder-to-shoulder, each with his eyes locked on her. Then in unison, they drew their swords, held them point down with one hand, and placed the hilt against their chests.

Winter held her breath, heart stuttering for a beat.

"You have suffered much, Prophetess," said Laban as all four of them lowered their chins. "You have lost many that you love for the sake of the kingdom. We know it is not easy to have lived these things once, yet you live them twice. We are honored to have you command us."

Winter wiped another tear from her face and smiled. "Thank you. I'm not sure I've made any difference in the world."

Laban's wizened eyes narrowed as he looked up. "If there is one thing I have learned from all my years of service to the Almighty, it's that no one ever knows the far-reaching extent of their lives. I am confident you have made a difference and you continue to make a difference now."

"But if I can't change anything..."

"You must change things, and with each battle you do change things. Imagine if your life events had gone any differently. Imagine if we were not there to help your younger self out of the wreck or to fight for your younger life in front of the mirror. Your life would have ended in those moments. But you are the Prophetess...you have already seen what has been changed. Now you must see what might have been so that you will know the change is necessary."

"I can see what might have been?"

Laban nodded as the horsemen sheathed their swords. "The Almighty sees all possibilities. He has granted you the ability to control the infinite and with that you have the ability to witness the could-have-been. Look and see, and you will know that we do indeed effect change." He waved his hand to the opposite side of the bridge.

Winter faced that direction again and shifted reality to the moment when Claire climbed onto the ledge. Then with a sideways thought, she saw it as if the angels had never been present.

She watched Culsu wrap her arms around Claire and touch the younger Winter with long shadowy tentacles. Claire reached down and took the younger Winter's hand, pulling her up. Both girls stood on the bridge, hand in hand, staring at each other. As the officers held out calming hands toward them, they both took a side step off the ledge.

Winter shifted back to the actual, and saw herself leaning against the ledge after Claire had jumped alone. Culsu fled into the distance and the army of angels surrounded the younger Winter.

"See," said Laban. "You have made a difference."

Winter let the insecurities drain away. If she made a difference here, could she save Kaci? Could Kaci's death be merely one of multiple possibilities? Perhaps fighting in the infinite had a deeper purpose than she realized. It wasn't an exercise in futility by creating events that had already happened, but an exercise in shaping reality from a tragic timeline to one of hope. Though she had already lived it and knew what needed to be done, still the battles had to be fought. When she finally reached the end, perhaps different choices could be made.

"Right," said Winter, ready to move forward again. "Let's go."

With a flicker she sent reality flying around them, following her younger self through a blur of time, searching for more pivotal moments that needed intervention, where she suspected intervention had already occurred. She saw herself sitting at the edge of the river with Michael. She watched as her younger self awkwardly tried to reconnect with Stacy. She watched as Shannon reached out to the younger Winter, talking with her, inviting her to dinner with the Morial family, and her younger self reconnecting with Michael after months of isolation. She watched herself attend the Wiccan bonfire in order to grow closer to Michael.

A flicker of red in the shadows...

Winter stopped the stream of time on the backyard of the bonfire behind Madam Morial's house. "There," she said pointing into the forest beyond the clearing. "Do you see?"

"I see her," said Laban. "Culsu watches from the shadows."

"If we attack, she will flee again," said Sors.

"Agreed," said Adom. "She watches too carefully. Even Magenel has not seen her."

Behind the younger Winter stood her guardian angel, sword sheathed, but wary. Small demons frolicked around the bonfire, teasing the Wiccans but avoiding the angel completely.

"Here the advantage belongs to Culsu," said Sharok. "These fools call upon forces they cannot possibly understand."

"Culsu is not finished with this family," Winter said. "So we must do what we can to help. But not here. Let's keep moving."

She shifted time again. Her younger self continued to grow closer to Michael, hanging out at his apartment, going to a concert together. Winter blushed when her birthday night of passion suddenly leapt in front of them. She blurred past that moment and others like it, even though the angels around her did not react in the least. Still, she'd rather not have her past mistakes parading in front of an audience like an adult movie.

Winter finally paused time for a moment when she noticed herself kneeling before her mother's grave. "We're missing something," she said. "Culsu is not following me."

"Are you sure Culsu continues against you?" asked Laban.

"Of course I'm sure. But..." Winter flicked time forward in a leap to just a year ago, sitting in an apartment with Shannon, mere days before Shannon's murder.

"So, what is this evil spirit doing here?" the year-ago Winter asked Shannon.

"Alison, I think," said Shannon. "That's when it first showed up. It plagued Alison, it plagued Claire and Michael, too. And it plagued me. You don't know what my mom and I had to go through to get it to leave me alone." Shannon held up her arms and pulled back the sleeves to reveal ugly scars across her wrists. "I did that. With scissors, just to stop the voices Culsu whispered in my head."

"Culsu never left their house," Winter said from the infinite as she paused time again. "It's not following me, it's avoiding me. It's trying to get to me through Michael."

"Culsu works in the shadows. She manipulates and schemes," said Sors.

Winter lept backward in time and returned to the cemetery four years earlier. She flicked the infinite sideways until they found Michael at the same moment in his apartment. Winter and the horsemen stepped into the spiritual unknown outside the apartment and let time tick by.

"She's there," Winter whispered, pointing to a curtained window.

"How can you be so sure?" asked Laban.

"Because I feel her in my scars." She cloaked the infinite onto the scene so that everything but Michael and the demon stroking his head appeared translucent.

"Do we enter?" asked Laban.

Winter shook her head. "Not now. We'll have one shot at this before Culsu vanishes back into the shadows. She won't resurface until she starts looking for me specifically again. That's why she goes after Shannon. That's why she binds herself to Xaphan. One shot. And I think I know when."

Winter shifted reality to the moment where she sat with Michael in the living room of her dad's house. Culsu was not there, but knowing now what Michael dealt with beneath demonic oppression, Winter could easily see the shadows upon his face and the torment on his heart.

"I'm pregnant," said the younger Winter, glancing up at him and biting her lip.

Silence. Michael stared at her for a long time, his face blanching and his jaw slowly falling open. He eased back into the couch and looked away.

"Say something. Michael?"

"Are you sure?" he whispered.

"Yes. I took two tests."

"And it's mine?"

"Of course it's yours. What kind of question is that?"

Michael frowned. "Are you going to keep it?"

"Yes. We can do this, Michael. There's no reason to be scared of it."

"We?"

A flush crept across the younger Winter's face. "Yes, we. I'm not asking to get married or anything, but we've got something good here between us."

"What do you want from me?"

"I don't know. Just keep being Michael. My Michael. Help me. You just said you would...no matter what the problem was. Well, this is the problem. We're both responsible. If you break up with me, fine...but don't take it out on this baby, okay?"

Michael leaned forward and put a hand over his face. "Yeah...um. Okay. Look, I just need to think."

"That's what I'm afraid of."

He put his hand down and locked eyes with her, Culsu's influence more evident than before. "You know me. I'll do the right thing, right? I just have to clear my head."

Young Winter nodded, her face darkening red. "Fine. Go clear your head. But I need you to help me figure this out."

He stood and nodded. "I'll..." He shuffled toward the door without looking at her. "I'll call you tomorrow."

Young Winter followed two steps behind. "Michael…"

He barely cast a look over her shoulder at her as he walked out. "Tomorrow."

Winter paused reality and glanced at Laban. "He didn't call the next day. I didn't see him again for another week. But that's the moment Culsu strikes. I had to see this moment again to be sure."

"Yes, it is evident that Culsu has darkened his soul," said Laban. "What do we expect when we arrive?"

Winter stared at her frozen younger self, remembering the heartache and agony that was to come. "Hell." She faced the horsemen. "We're about to enter the most violent battle for my life. When I shift the infinite to that moment, we cannot afford to be discreet or to hold back any reserves. Culsu must be stopped. There is no other way. When my younger self goes to see Michael, we must be there with our entire strength if necessary."

The horsemen nodded as one. "It will be done, Prophetess," they intoned.

Winter turned away, took a deep breath, and shifted the infinite. The younger Winter walked up the sidewalk to Michael's apartment as Stacy drove away. She disappeared inside, but Winter peeled back the substance of reality so they could see through the walls. She stepped closer, still within the infinite…close enough to easily hear the younger Winter calling out for Michael. As she did, the army circled the scene as the four horsemen organized their ranks and prepared for the battle.

Michael approached, walking hunched over down the sidewalk with his hands in his pockets and his head down. Culsu clung so deep inside of him, that only her twisted face could be seen rising above Michael's head.

"What are you doing here?" Michael asked the younger Winter as he entered the apartment.

Culsu gazed down at her with a murderous hunger. As soon as he saw the demon, Magenel drew his sword and stood between them.

Culsu glanced at him once and then focused back on the younger Winter.

"We've had something good going on. I didn't want it to stop," the younger Winter said.

"Now," Winter said to Laban, who had stationed himself to her right. "Show yourselves. Just the horsemen."

The horsemen stepped out of the infinite into the spiritual now and took up positions beside the younger Winter and Magenel.

Culsu hissed as Michael crossed into the kitchen. She twisted to better face the horsemen as they flanked the younger Winter. "Why do the horsemen protect the girl?"

"She is not to be harmed, demon!" snarled Laban.

"You cannot stop me! I have so blurred this boy's thoughts that even if you remove me, he will still do my bidding. It is not in your power to interfere with human choice!"

"Fine!" Michael shouted. "I don't want the baby!"

"Then you don't want me!" screamed the younger Winter.

Michael slammed his beer down on the table and narrowed his eyes.

Culsu laughed. "There is nothing sweeter than taking unborn life…ripping away what could have been before it even begins! I will have the girl and her child too!"

The horsemen drew their swords. "We will not allow it!" said Laban.

Out of Michael's back sprouted four long demonic arms. They flailed at the horsemen, and the horsemen advanced to fend them off easily. Magenel stepped back closer to the younger Winter, arms out as if to shield her. Culsu studied them, calculating the strength of the horsemen and analyzing their defenses. Winter brought the rest of the army into the spiritual unknown now, holding out a steadying hand.

After a moment of skirmish, Culsu withdrew her thrashing arms and leaned over to whisper directly into Michael's ear. "If she won't kill it. You should." Culsu smiled back at the horsemen.

Michael collapsed into one of the dining chairs, put his head between his hands, and screamed. "Just shut up!"

The younger Winter stepped back and bit her lip, thinking he was screaming at her, completely oblivious to the spiritual forces around her and the demon manipulating Michael. "I want to be with you, Michael," she said more softly. "Do you want to be with me?"

Michael tilted his head to glare at her, his eyes flashing with Culsu's poison and the younger Winter took another step backward.

"Don't you see?" asked Culsu. "He's in my complete control. Nothing angelic can stop him from following my commands."

"Michael?" the younger Winter asked.

Culsu leaned back to Michael and whispered. "Kill the child. Kill it now!"

"I can't..." The words seemed to drag from his mouth.

"You can't? You can't be with me?" asked the younger Winter.

"Do it!" roared Culsu.

"I can't..." He pressed his hands flat on the table.

"You can't be a father!" said Culsu. "Say it!"

"I can't be a father."

Culsu glanced back to the horsemen, smirking. "Now a seed is planted that you cannot stop."

Michael picked up a pair of scissors lying on the table.

"Now!" Winter shouted to the horsemen from the unknown and they descended upon Culsu like holy fire.

The battle had begun. Culsu swelled bigger and more powerful than any one of the horsemen alone. Her reach stretched throughout the room, easily fending off their swords before they could even come close.

As the younger Winter tried to leave, flanked by the protective sword of Magenel, Culsu slammed all four horsemen backward at once and moved to block her path. Michael advanced toward the younger Winter with the demon. Culsu clutched Magenel with all four arms and tossed him through the air, beyond the walls.

Winter sent in the rest of the angelic army. They crashed into the spiritual now with all the force of a hurricane, but their initial attack broke upon Culsu's arms like a crashing wave.

Michael punched the younger Winter in the face, sending her sprawling toward the ground.

"Again!" screamed Winter, desperate to save Rebecca if there were any way possible. She stepped into the now herself, wrestling the urge to join the fight.

"What is this?" roared Culsu. "Who is this child?"

Winter glanced down at herself and found the body of a child...*Rebecca*. With so much thought toward the baby, she had somehow taken on the child form of Rebecca when stepping out of the infinite.

Culsu's eyes bulged and Winter pressed the advantage. She directed the angels and the horsemen by thought.

Rally, use the infinite, approach from two sides, shield the younger me.

Most of her directions were sent as impressions or emotions, interpreted by the army perfectly. A protective dome formed over the younger Winter as two separate forces swirled around to approach Culsu from different sides, bolstering the horsemen as they continued to push against the flailing arms of the demon.

Culsu roared, and the black smoke of thousands of demons flooded in to join her. As the demons engaged the angelic army, Culsu shoved forward with her long arms and smashed through the dome over the younger Winter.

Michael began to kick and stomp on her.

"No!" shouted Winter.

Magenel returned like a meteor through the room, sword a fiery whirlwind that sliced the arms of Culsu back long enough for the dome to reform.

The younger Winter connected a kick against Michael's knee and he stumbled back. When he did, the horsemen positioned themselves between him and her. The other demons pelted the angelic guard as the younger Winter crawled through her own blood for the door.

As Culsu continued to fight against the horsemen, she pulled out of Michael and let him continue on his own. He walked calmly past the angels, grabbed the younger Winter from under the dome, and began to beat her again. Culsu laughed as the angels fought to stop him, but they could do nothing.

"It is not yours to hinder human free will!" Culsu cackled.

As the younger Winter lay curled on the floor, Michael backed away and retrieved the scissors.

"You know," he said, his voice cutting through the battle sounds in the room. "If I let you go, you'll turn me in for this."

"Please," croaked the younger Winter.

Michael returned to her, kicked her once, and then rolled her onto her back.

Forget him! Winter sent out to the angels. *Help HER!*

He straddled her and raised the scissors. A dozen angels broke away from the fight and rallied around the younger Winter. Magenel slid onto the ground with her. As the scissors came down, all the angels poured their energy into her at once. She raised her arms and caught his wrists.

He leaned forward, and when he had teetered far enough, she brought up both thighs and sent him flying into the door.

Culsu lifted into the air, more arms emerging, still holding the horsemen at bay. She jolted around the room, knocking battling angels away from her demons, then settled back onto Michael.

The shield of angels still surrounded the younger Winter, pouring into her enough strength to crawl to the kitchen and pull herself up against the counter.

Culsu growled and Michael growled with her. Together they charged toward the younger Winter.

With a quick pulse of thought, every angel in the room descended upon Culsu, piling atop her and hiding both her and Michael from view.

"Leave me alone!" screamed the younger Winter, shaking a kitchen knife at him.

Culsu burst outward. The angels scattered for a moment and then re-converged.

"I can't let you leave," Michael said, stepping out of the fray as Culsu released him again so she could fend off the relentless angels.

"Why are you doing this?" cried the younger Winter as she stepped back. "I thought you loved me..."

"I'm doing this because I love you."

"Just let me leave. Please."

Culsu burst out of the angels again and claimed Michael more firmly. He straightened with her presence. As her extra arms and her demonic reinforcements fought against the angels, Culsu gazed down upon the younger Winter.

"There's just something about you..." Culsu and Michael said in unison.

"Michael! What's wrong with you?" the younger Winter screamed.

Then Culsu took over, giving demonic speed to Michael and knocking away the knife from the younger Winter. As the many arms of Culsu knocked back the angels and horsemen a third time, Michael punched the younger Winter in the side. She screamed and almost fell. Then his other hand came back around, human and demon hand as one, and struck her in the face.

She spun. Her knees buckled and her feet slipped. She slammed her head against the counter and landed on the floor.

"Enough!" Winter yelled.

Every angel, every horseman, every demon, ceased fighting and looked at her as if her command were law for them all.

"It is too late, girl! Whatever you are, you are too late!" Culsu shouted back at her.

Michael brought the scissors up over his head and jerked them down to the younger Winter's chest, with the full strength of Culsu behind the blow.

Winter phased through the infinite and grabbed their arms before they reached halfway, the power within her more than enough strength to hold Culsu and Michael back. Man and demon strained against her. Culsu leaned forward to stare into Winter's eyes mere inches away.

Then Winter released the child form of Rebecca and let her true self be revealed. Culsu hissed, her eyes widening with the first signs of fear the demon had ever shown.

"You have no idea who you're dealing with," Winter seethed.

At the sight of Winter's true form, every demon in the room fled. Culsu released Michael and jolted backward. Before the horsemen could close in for the kill, Culsu slipped away and disappeared.

Winter stood and faced her army, all huffing but still strong and still whole. As she listened to her younger self screaming and the knife thumping into Michael's chest, Winter trembled with each strike. Once the sounds quieted, Winter gazed down at her younger self, now crawling across the floor toward her phone. Michael lay lifeless with the kitchen knife in his chest.

The memory of that moment had haunted her for the past four years. Though everyone said it was self-defense, a part of her would always deal with the guilt. Now reliving this horrible event, she couldn't help but wonder if there had been another way...

Laban put a hand on her shoulder and gently turned her aside. He didn't have to say a word. His soft touch and knowing eyes lessened her aching heart. Maybe she wasn't guilty after all.

They stayed, silent and watchful, in case Culsu returned, but no demon dared...not even Culsu. Still, Winter let time flow normally for just a little while, and followed her younger self as the next few hours unfolded.

The police and ambulance arrived to find the younger Winter curled on the floor in a small pool of her own blood. They carried her to the nearest hospital where she woke up to the news that ripped every last shred of hope from her soul...the baby was lost.

Winter felt tears in her eyes again and placed a hand on her abdomen. The pain of losing the baby never really went away. It still hurt. More so than killing Michael. More so than losing her parents, losing Ryan, or losing Claire.

Sors dismounted to join Laban still standing at her side. "Even the unborn fly to the Father. You will be reunited one day."

Winter nodded and smiled up at him. "Thank you."

Steve came into the hospital room. Winter couldn't stand to hear the conversation again, so she slid time faster. Her younger self became belligerent, demanding to be released and refusing the help of the hospital. After being released, the younger Winter wandered toward the Old Trenton River bridge.

Winter tried to shift reality to follow, but the infinite trembled and refused.

"We are not allowed to go to that moment, Prophetess," said Laban.

"Why not?" She faced him and planted her feet. "There are questions I want answered."

He shook his head. "That moment is being tended by others. It is the convergence of many spiritual forces in the ultimate bid for your soul. It is the work of our brothers, not us. Even Magenel will not be allowed to intervene."

Winter clenched her teeth. "I will not intervene. I only wish to observe."

Laban shook his head. "It is not permitted."

Anger boiled up within her, but she turned away and took a deep breath. "Fine." She flicked the infinite a different direction and flew past at a faster rate than she intended, blurring through the summer and young Winter's recovery. She would have liked to have paused on the moment she heard the voice of God, but didn't want to back up. Besides, she probably wasn't allowed there either.

∞

Winter stopped the infinite at the moment where her younger self checked into the dorm freshmen year. The younger Winter wore a baggy Jack the Pumpkin King t-shirt and let her black hair swing to hide most of her face. Magenel still followed her, but shone more radiant. A bright white light emanated out of both of them, like a glowing film along their surfaces.

"Something is different. What is that glow on us?" she asked, suddenly forgetting the bridge.

"It is the Holy Spirit," said Laban. "This is your regenerated self. It is both an indwelling and a connection. Magenel is strengthened by it. He is no longer a part of our command. He has been appropriated for other purposes…to protect the Prophetess. There are many evil forces preparing to come against you. The power within your younger self is sufficient."

"Do they still need our help?"

"If necessary. Many spiritual forces converge around you. We are not the only ones who will come to your aid. Our brothers stand at the ready…entire legions, yet we are the only ones empowered by the infinite. The Spirit gives your younger self dreams and warnings. God himself is willing to pour out his infinite power into your vessel. This is you being trained to be a Prophetess and being prepared to lead the army."

"Can I give myself warnings now?"

"As long as you are not seen. It is important for you to understand the risk you took being seen by Culsu as your true self. We cannot risk others knowing what you will become. I fear the attacks against your younger self would be catastrophic. Therefore, we should aid only when necessary, and you should exercise restraint in how you interact with your younger self."

"Our intervention may be of no use," said Sors. "The Prophetess is connected now directly to the Spirit."

"As is Magenel," said Adom. "He has grown powerful."

"Yes," said Winter. "But I know my younger self then. I didn't always listen to any of those things. But I may listen to myself."

"It would not be wise," said Laban.

"I don't plan to be seen." Winter shifted reality and found herself in a theater-style classroom. "I will use Magenel." Winter stepped briefly out of the infinite into the spiritual unknown and approached Magenel standing behind her younger self. Magenel greeted her with a salute. "I need you to be the bridge between me and her."

"How, Prophetess?" he asked.

"Place a hand on her and a hand on me. Transfer my thoughts and memories to her."

Magenel narrowed his eyes. "What will that do?"

"It will help her to understand and to listen," Winter said. "Try it now."

Magenel nodded. He placed a hand on Winter's shoulder and his other hand on the younger Winter at the base of her neck. The younger Winter jerked up and scanned the room. She lifted her hand and watched the minute movements of her fingers.

Winter thought the word *pen* and young Winter turned to her neighbor just before a pen fell to the floor. Winter thought the word *danger* and young Winter spun quickly to the door at the back of the room. Winter nodded at Magenel and he broke contact with both of them.

"Do you understand now?" she asked.

"Yes, Prophetess."

"We will try again shortly," Winter said. She shifted reality, leaving Magenel and her younger self behind, and solidified later that same day in her dorm room.

Magenel nodded to her as she approached and reached his hands out to touch her and the younger Winter. She poured out information through the angel…Kaci knocking at the door, the details of the conversation that was about to be had. As the young Winter left the room with Kaci and Summer, Winter broke the connection.

"What use is this?" asked Sors

"It is teaching my younger self to listen."

"How much will you do?"

"As much as is needed," Winter said. "I want to try one more." She shifted reality and found the moment of her arguing with Mrs. Pritchett over a failed grade. When she stepped out of the infinite, Magenel saw her immediately. "Again," she told the angel.

He nodded and reached to her and her younger self simultaneously. Winter thought about Laurie and Jennifer. She tried to convey the right emotions and the right information. Her younger self glanced around nervously, but didn't seem to understand.

Winter broke the connection and shook her head as Magenel followed the disoriented younger Winter out of the classroom. "It's not working. She doesn't understand. I need a more direct way to warn her about Kaci. I need to do it myself somehow."

Laban shook his head. "Remember the danger, Prophetess."

"I know. I have an idea." Winter shifted reality and found herself that same evening asleep. Magenel stood guard at the foot of the bed. "God used to give me these vivid dreams. Maybe I can use one and warn her about Kaci." She stepped up to herself and reached out tentatively. "I'll take another form like I did before. If she sees me, she'll see Rebecca." Winter closed her eyes and touched the forehead of her younger self.

When she opened her eyes, she stood inside the dream…a dream of school apprehension and failed tests. Winter pulled the dream in the same way she manipulated the infinite, and formed the upper room of the tower. She formed the image of Kaci lying almost dead on the floor. Her dreaming self looked down upon Kaci's body and screamed. The younger Winter cast around desperately and locked eyes with Winter.

Then the dream pulled away as the younger Winter awoke screaming in the night. Winter backed away from the bed quickly, but just before she stepped into the infinite, her younger self saw her.

"That was too dangerous," said Laban. "You are too strong with the power of God, even then, even when you were not aware of it."

Winter nodded and froze time. "I know. I think I know a better way." With a flicker of thought she pulled Magenel into the infinite. "Magenel, I need you to take my memories. Absorb them all and keep them ready. When my younger self needs them, tell her what's about to happen. Scream it in her ear. Do whatever you have to do to get her attention. Can you do that?"

Magenel shook his head. "I'm not sure I have the power."

Winter took a deep breath and her skin stretched. Tiny bands of light emanated from her pores. "You will. God has given me the authority to give you this ability."

Magenel's eyes widened as Winter stepped toward him. She reached up to the tall warrior's face and clenched it between her hands. Magenel gasped, and with a pulse of searing light Winter's memories poured into the angel.

They flashed before her mind's eye like a fast-forwarding movie. Her enhanced mind processed each moment individually, sending strobes of emotions through her chest. Some moments she kept private, while others she imprinted onto Magenel, enough information that he could keep her younger self informed when she needed it. A few moments were so important that she enlarged them, making them more sharp and detailed than the others so Magenel would feel the urgency.

Moments like the attack on Laurie Dunaway, Peter's wreck, Skotos at the protest, the importance of the chapel, the botched meeting with the FBI, the silo, and Kaci in the tower. Most importantly she imprinted the identity of Xaphan so strongly that Magenel would know to send her younger self warnings whenever he approached.

She didn't stop there. The memories flowed. How to find Agent Gains, how to enter into another person's memories as Magenel did now, talking to Logan, trailing Sophie and entering Sophie's office, Mordensfield, saving Sadie from being kidnapped, the man in the silver and black mask, the shootings, the forest, the tree.

More. She needed to give him more. Finding Shannon, confronting Culsu, finding the logbook, Romania, the train yard, the collapse of the administration building, rescuing Kaci from the first kidnappers, getting out of Xaphan's house.

Winter broke away. Magenel squinted in pain.

"Tell her," she said. "Help me remember when I need it, both the memories and new information. Use Ayden if you have to, especially when I stop paying attention. As I grow in my connection to God, I will need less and less of these from you, but always be ready in case my younger self misses something."

He nodded. "Yes, Prophetess."

She waved a hand toward the horsemen. "Look for us during the hardest times. We will be there to help."

"Yes, Prophetess."

Winter transported Magenel back to the moment she had stolen him, then she faced the horsemen and willed her army to materialize. "The battles to come will be much more difficult than the small skirmishes we have already encountered. We will not only be dealing with one powerful demon, but several." She pointed to her younger self. "The power growing in me even then is enough to handle many of the battles, but there are moments when we must get involved. Legions of the enemy stand ready. They will fight legions of your brothers. We must be a dagger among swords. Quick. Decisive. Victorious. We strike and move on, leaving the details to your brothers and to the power of God in me. Use the infinite as a weapon. Step in and out, weaving through moments, to evade the enemy and claim the advantage."

"And where does it end, Prophetess?" asked Laban.

Winter bit the inside of her cheek. She knew where it needed to end, but didn't know how to explain it yet. "It ends when we all arrive back at the chapel in the final moments."

She spun back to the blank infinite and shifted reality until they floated high above the old president's house at the back of campus. Her younger self and Kaci were walking from the house toward the silo. Magenel stood just behind young Winter, leaning close to her ear, whispering. Warning. For the first time Winter saw the two powerful angels on either side of Kaci, each just as strong or more so than Magenel.

In the near distance a cloud of demons approached. They clung so thick to Xaphan's van that the vehicle could hardly be seen. In the middle of the mass, a sinister presence waited...a deeper, darker demon than Culsu. Winter let events unfold beneath them in real time as her younger self and Kaci entered the silo. Just before the demons arrived, Winter gave out orders.

"Each horseman takes one-fourth of the forces." She pointed to the field where she knew Kaci would try to escape. "Laban, position yourself there. Protect Kaci at all costs. The rest of you position yourselves around the house. Wait in the unknown for my signal, and remember to use the infinite as a weapon."

As Winter continued to hover just above the house, the army dispersed.

The van arrived, and along with it the legion of demons. They dispersed, flocking toward the silo like flies toward rotting meat. Flashes of light strobed around the silo, other angels rushing to the younger Winter's aid.

Xaphan's men began walking around the house, brandishing their weapons. One crossed toward the silo. Xaphan watched from inside the van, the demon attached to him towering high into the sky.

She had seen that demon before, a long time ago, in one of the first visions she had ever had. It was a grotesque black creature, scaly and bony, that grinned with long pointed teeth.

The younger Winter and Kaci burst out of the underbrush around the silo, heading toward the van, unaware that Xaphan waited inside. As they neared, he exited. The other men closed in, rushing with their weapons brandished. Demons swirled around them like bats.

Winter sent a pulse-thought out to the army. *Now!*

The division from the right of Kaci and Winter fell on the demons, flashing in and out of the infinite, attacking with precision strikes that scattered the demons in panic. The two girls ran back toward the silo, the younger Winter instinctively leading in the clearest direction away from most of the demons. More demons rushed in to block, reforming around one of Xaphan's men in front of the girls.

Kaci and young Winter stopped. Kaci bolted toward the field as the younger Winter sprinted back around the front of the house again through the clearer path. The angelic division nearest the silo engaged the knot of demons there as the division to the right of the house trailed the younger Winter, still flashing in and out of the infinite and cutting a clear swath as more angels formed a tight circle around her.

Winter watched Kaci run. A thick cloud of demons chased her, along with two of Xaphan's men. The angelic division waiting in that direction hit the demons head-on, keeping Kaci clear long enough to create separation between her and Xaphan's men and to allow Kaci's own angelic bodyguards to secure a perimeter around her. The men slogged through the tall grass as angels flashed in and out of the infinite to wrap their legs in spiritual bonds.

Xaphan watched the fight, arms crossed. Winter wasn't sure how much of the actual spiritual battle he could see or sense, but the demon towering over him eyed the battle carefully. Suddenly the group of demons fighting by the silo broke away and chased after Kaci. The angelic division they were fighting gave chase. Another group of demons rushed after them, and soon multiple dogfights erupted over the field, as Kaci continued to labor through the grass, trying to escape.

The demon Xaphan leaned forward over the man Xaphan, a

gleam of recognition on its grotesque face, and Winter knew it had spotted one of the horsemen. As if summoned, more demons materialized and rushed after Kaci, filling the air above the field like a plague.

Winter sent another pulse-thought out. *Everyone! Help Kaci!*

The two remaining angelic divisions flashed through the infinite and joined the fray.

Still Kaci ran.

Something shuffled below her. Winter glanced down and spotted her younger self climbing out of a window onto the roof above the porch. She sat there watching Kaci. "Come on, Kaci," the younger Winter whispered. "Run!"

Xaphan saw her. He turned to watch and the younger Winter locked eyes with him. Then she searched around desperately for a way to escape.

Suddenly, as Winter hung in the air watching the battle unfold, she heard her own voice echo in her head…both real and memory at the same time. An unspoken question, that came to her almost as if it had been shouted.

Now what do I do? It was her younger self crying out for help.

As Winter watched the scene, she could see the clear path behind the house where none of Xaphan's followers or demons waited, and she knew what must be done, because she remembered doing it.

Winter concentrated on her younger self and shouted. "The forest!"

Without hesitating, the younger Winter ran the length of the porch roof, gingerly dropped to the ground, and sprinted for the forest behind the house.

Winter stared back toward Kaci, the sky black with demons and more being called in by the second. Already the demons outnumbered her small force at least four to one. She knew they couldn't win this battle here. Now seeing how many demons had been called to ensure Kaci's capture, Winter wondered if the demon

Xaphan already knew Kaci's true identity even if the man did not.

Withdraw, Winter pulsed out to the army. In a blink, time stopped. The army stepped into the infinite and reformed around her. They watched her expectantly as she pivoted to face a blank space of the infinite. She took a deep breath to clear her head. The next delicate moments needed perfect timing. Here at the silo, the demons might assume the angelic army came to protect the younger Winter, but if they arrived too soon at the bell tower, the army might give Kaci away.

Winter shifted space and time around them without saying a word. The upper room of the bell tower formed, walls mostly transparent as she faded them into the infinite. Inside the room, Kaci stood fully clothed before Xaphan. Two of Xaphan's black-robbed followers held her firmly by the arms. Bruises already covered Kaci's face and blood trickled from the corner of her mouth. Xaphan clenched the crooked knife in his hand, poised for the next part of the ritual. The room was black with demons, all big-eyed and salivating.

Winter felt sick, knowing what they were about to do to Kaci. But it had already been done and she could do nothing to prevent it now. Interfering before her younger self arrived might prove far worse. As much as Winter hated it, she shifted time past the ritual, pausing once the younger Winter approached the tower from the outside. Xaphan had Kaci hastily stuffed into the dumbwaiter as if some invisible force had tipped him off.

Winter pointed to Kaci's broken and mangled body. "Make sure she stays alive." Without a word, a dozen angels rushed to Kaci's side and joined Kaci's two badly beaten guards who struggled to keep demons away.

Winter shifted the scene for the rest of her army to follow her younger self working her way through the chapel and up the stairs. Xaphan and his followers had just finished lowering the dumbwaiter when the younger Winter reached the door where Xaphan waited. As she turned the knob and entered, Xaphan spun to face her. The demon attached to him loomed in her direction. Demons rushed forward momentarily, and then retreated as Magenel flashed his deadly sword. He stood beside the younger Winter, eyeing the demons who flinched and cajoled at him.

"You're late, prophet," he said. "Honestly, how do you expect to even have a chance of defeating me if you never show up on time?"

"Where is she?" asked the younger Winter. "Where's Kaci?"

For a brief moment, the demons rushed in as one. Magenel fell beneath the horde. Xaphan laughed. The younger Winter put a hand to her stomach and swayed briefly.

Winter held a steadying hand out to her army as the two talked below. "Not yet," she said.

An energy pulsed out from the younger Winter like rays of light that pushed the demons back. She glowed with a power more pure and more intense than any angel.

"WHERE IS SHE?" The younger Winter's voice reverberated from the bells hanging above. Bats scattered. The clocked ticked another minute.

Xaphan stopped laughing. A shadow of doubt crossed his face and vanished. The demon attached to him smirked. His followers shuffled their feet and watched their master. The demons scurried away to hide in the shadows.

The power in her younger self kept the demons back, but at any moment they would rally and attack. As the conversation unfolded, Winter kept one eye on the broken body of Kaci and the angels working to keep her alive through the translucent floors.

"I need a small force to position themselves lower on the stairs," Winter said. "In a moment when she exits, she will be followed by all the demons and all of Xaphan's followers. They must think she goes down. Make sure the angels are seen and that the angels lead them into the main part of the chapel."

Sharok nodded his golden helmet. "I will see it done."

"The horsemen are not to be seen this time," she added.

Sharok nodded again. "As you command." He moved off, and a detail of angels followed him toward a lower section of stairs where they waited in the spiritual unknown to step into the now.

"As for the rest of you," Winter said, pointing toward Xaphan. "The demon attached to him is powerful. More powerful than my younger self can handle. It will take full possession of him and she will not be able to stop it. I don't know what other forces will come to her aid, but you must fight the demon and keep her safe."

The other three horsemen nodded. "As you command." They moved off, splitting the army into four additional divisions, and positioned themselves around the tower in the unknown, ready to move in.

Winter herself floated down to stand beside her younger self to watch the final moments of the conversation unfurl.

The younger Winter pulled out a small digital recorder and made a show of pressing the stop button.

"Ready!" Winter yelled to the forces. They all drew their swords and assumed attack stances.

The younger Winter held out her cellphone and took a picture. "Thank you," she said with a small curtsy.

Xaphan bellowed. Bats scattered and swirled through the room, perfectly in sync with the swirling fury of the demons. Xaphan leaned forward and launched his knife.

Winter grabbed her younger self's shoulder at the same time, willing her to move, and the younger Winter did at the last moment.

As the younger Winter blinked at the wobbling knife, Xaphan yelled, "KILL HER!"

"Now!" shouted Winter to her army.

Everything moved at once…

The younger Winter spun and fled back to the stairs.

Winter shouted at Magenel, "Take her up!"

Magenel grabbed the younger Winter as she took one step down.

Then she turned and ran up.

The angelic army crashed in at the same time, scattering the demons and infuriating the demon attached to Xaphan. Xaphan's followers rushed out of the room chasing the younger Winter, taking with them a flood of demons that sped away from the fury of the angelic army.

The task force lower on the stairs materialized. As the demons came out, the angels turned and fled down the stairs. The demons took the bait, rushing after them and pulling Xaphan's followers with them.

Xaphan himself stood in the middle of the room, huffing as his demon raged against the angels. Winter wondered once more how much he knew of the unseen battle around him.

Then the younger Winter came back in.

"No!" Winter shouted at her and Magenel. But it was too late. Xaphan seemed to have anticipated her return and crossed the room in two long strides, backhanding her to the ground, knocking her several feet away.

"You'll learn your place, prophet!" he shouted.

The angels converged around her. The demon on Xaphan struck out with more power and fury than Winter had seen from even Culsu.

"I know my place!" shouted the younger Winter as she stood to face him. "It's right here! Where's Kaci?" Swords flashed with brilliant light all around her as the demon on Xaphn tried to cut her down. The younger Winter stood there, unafraid and unaware.

The demon slammed with both fists in, and angels flew through the air as if thrown by an explosion. As the demon grabbed Winter by the throat, so did the man. He lifted her into the air as she thrashed with her feet.

"Now, you're beginning to understand," Xaphan said, both man and demon. "I can see it in your eyes. You fear me now. No mortal can stop me—especially you." He flung her across the room and her body whiplashed around one of the bell chains.

As she fell to the ground, the army re-converged around her, forming ranks. The demon plowed through them, barely slowed, throwing angel after angel through the air.

"Death is coming for you, Winter!" Xaphan shouted as the demon flung another group of angels through the air. "I AM DEATH!" When he knocked away the last guard, both demon and man slammed a foot into the young Winter's stomach. She flew through the air and crumpled onto the pool of Kaci's blood in the center of the pentagram.

"Prophetess!" Laban shouted. "They cannot defeat it alone! The horsemen must intervene!"

"No!" Winter shouted back. "Wait a little longer. Use the infinite!"

"Now we will end this," Xaphan said.

The scattered angels returned, this time flashing in and out of the infinite. Magenel recovered and braved the demon directly at the young Winter's side. As the demon swiped, Magenel caught the blow directly with his sword and leaned in. The man shoved the younger Winter on to her back. Magenel spun away and laid his hand on her to reconnect.

Xaphan the man raised his knife. "Tell your god I'm coming."

Magenel pulled on the young Winter's shoulder and she rolled out of the way just as the knife struck the floor. Magenel took her hand and guided it to one of the candles, and she smashed it into Xaphan's side.

The robe ignited. The man shrieked. The angels rallied and surrounded him, reinforcements pouring in from the unknown. The demon shrieked. Both man and demon stumbled back. As Xaphan ripped off the robe, the beast recovered itself and flung angels out of his way.

Young Winter tried to rise but slipped in the blood. Xaphan rushed at her with the knife held high. Then light flooded the room from below.

"This is the FBI," came a loud voice from the garden below. "We have the place surrounded. Come out peacefully, and no one will get hurt."

Wood splintered below. Gunshots. Xaphan cursed.

The younger Winter stood with blood dripping from her clenched fists. "You lose."

Xaphan yelled and rushed her again, the fury of the demon so powerful none of the angels could stand in its way. Still, the younger Winter stood defiant. Unafraid.

Voices floated up from the stairwell and Xaphan stopped again. Then he bolted for the door. He glared back as he exited, pointing the knife at the younger Winter. "This isn't over."

As he disappeared toward the roof, the younger Winter collapsed onto the floor and balled into the fetal position. Magenel knelt with both hands on her. The demons fled, and Winter's angelic army phased back into the spiritual unknown.

Agents rushed into the tower room and gathered around the younger Winter. A small pain went through Winter at the sight of Agent Gains. She watched him talk to her younger self. Saw him relay Kaci's description and condition into his radio. The younger Winter stood, casting around the room as Gains continued to talk. Then she spun on him.

"I need to find her!" she yelled.

Winter gazed through the translucent floor to where the angels were still sustaining Kaci below. Time was running out. She knew it then. She remembered it now.

Agent Gains and the younger Winter started clawing against the back wall at the removable panel to the dumbwaiter.

Winter looked to Kaci again. "I have to help them."

"You can't be seen, Prophetess."

She narrowed her eyes at Laban. "Kaci is dying. I need as many of you as possible to keep her alive. I'll take care of the rest." Angel wings rushed away as her army vanished and reappeared below.

"I need a knife," she said to Laban.

"You only need to will it."

Winter gazed to her clenched fist and a small dagger appeared. With a quick thought she phased across the infinite to stand in the hall outside the room. Then she dragged the knife deep across the palm of her hand, and quickly drew a downward-pointing arrow on the wall.

Winter willed the blood to enter the physical realm, at least enough for her younger self to see it. She spun back and found her younger self staring at the mark...just as she remembered. Winter released the blood to fade back into the infinite.

The younger Winter ran across the room and turned to follow, taking three steps at a time.

Winter phased herself into the next room and drew a bloody X on the dumbwaiter panel.

Younger Winter burst in and paid no attention to it, wrenching the panel free.

The bells rang. Below, hundreds of angels gathered around Kaci, more than just her army but still not enough. Even from there, Winter could feel Kaci's life failing.

Winter phased and drew another arrow.

Young Winter saw it and ran out of the room again.

Winter phased to the next room and drew another X. This time the younger Winter understood and continued down the stairs.

Another X.

Young Winter was practically falling down the stairs now.

Finally in the room with Kaci Winter wrote the word "Here" on the panel, and the younger Winter ran in to wrest the panel away, tearing the tips of her fingers in the process. With Agent Gains's help, they found Kaci and pulled her out.

"Stay with her," Winter told a myriad of angels, hers and hundreds of others, "until the paramedics have her stabilized."

Laban dismounted and came to her side. "May I, Prophetess?"

He held out his hand. Winter slowly let him take her injured hand. He wrapped it with both of his and released it after only a second, and the gash in her palm disappeared. "You have much courage," he said.

Winter just nodded at him, her heart still focused on the body of Kaci now being taken out of the room. She paused time and shifted the army into the infinite. The tower scene faded away.

∞

"What do you know about that demon?" she asked. "It's so strong."

Laban tilted his head as if she should know. "That is Xaphan, the demon from which the man took the name. They are practically one now. He is a principality, one of the first to rally to Lucifer's cause during the first war. The archangels themselves cast him out."

"Is our army powerful enough to stop him?" Winter asked.

"I do not know."

Winter shifted the infinite, letting time pass in large swaths around them. She stopped one early morning, inside the younger Winter's dorm room sophomore year.

Winter and Laban stood in the middle of the room, watching the younger Winter and Kaci sleep, while their three guardians stood vigil.

"She's right there beside me," Winter said, "and I don't even realize how important she is yet. I have to warn myself. Maybe if I call out to myself in the right way, I'll think it is Kaci calling."

"Do you have memory of this?"

"No. Not really. But I have to try." Winter placed a hand on her younger self and closed her eyes. She watched the younger Winter's dream unfold...a prophetic warning of things to come, given to her by God himself.

In the dream the younger Winter ran through the woods with Summer, Ayden, and Peter, though Ayden's and Peter's faces were distorted and unrecognizable. They fled from the Eater, until they finally came to a looming cliff, where a tree appeared.

At that point Winter willed herself into the dream, once again assuming the form of Rebecca. As Winter entered, a piece of the infinite came with her and the dream broke. Everything fell silent. The wind and rain of the dream froze in time.

She stepped out from behind the tree and the younger dream Winter turned to face her, and Winter remembered she'd originally thought the little girl *was* the Sandy she searched for. Perhaps she could use that...

"I'm right here," Winter said. "Right beside you. Wake up and see me."

Her dream self didn't seem to hear. "What?"

Winter huffed and tried to rebuild the dream herself. Maybe she could form images her younger self would understand. But when she tried to make clues materialize, the ground lurched. Light streamed in as the power of the infinite ripped the dream to pieces. The dream Winter fell to the ground and the infinite poured through, tearing apart the cliff and tearing apart the ground until only the tree remained.

"Who are you?" screamed the dream Winter. "Who are you?"

Winter couldn't control the power. The dream was too delicate and the infinite too strong. Only the dreamer could stabilize it. She had so much to tell her younger self. If only she would take control of the dream and help...

"Help me," she said, allowing the infinite to carry the words to her dream self. The infinite tore the tree apart. Only the light remained. Her dream self covered her face, not understanding that she had the power to fix it. "Help me," Winter said again. "What are you waiting for?" The infinite grew even stronger, tugging at Winter, pulling her away. "Help me!" she called again with a final plea. But it was too late. The dream had disintegrated.

As her younger self jumped out of bed and grabbed a pen and

notebook, Winter shifted back into the infinite and turned to Laban. "Why couldn't I control it?"

"These dreams are not yours to control," he said. "The dreams come from the divine. They are given to your younger self. You can enter them, but you cannot change or control them. To try would only destroy the dream, as you have seen."

"So how am I supposed to help myself find Kaci if I can't be seen or I can't control her dreams?"

"You are the Prophetess. Only you know."

Winter huffed and crossed her arms. "I can enter the dream, but not change it." Then she widened her eyes. "I have an idea."

She shifted the infinite to the moment her younger self had the next dream. The younger Winter had her head propped against her hand, fingers in her hair, blankly staring at her World Lit final exam, already watching the campus shooting unfold inside a vision.

Magenel stepped aside as Winter reached out to her younger self and entered the vision.

Once again, the vision reacted to her presence. Things froze where they were. The images of the shooter and the bodies dissolved, leaving the Union a hollow shell where the dream Winter lay on the floor.

Winter positioned herself in a hallway just out of sight, trying to keep the infinite at bay and allow the dream to proceed without interruption. She ran the plan through her head again, hoping she could emulate a child properly and bring her younger self to the right conclusions about Sandy's identity.

She laughed a child's laugh. The laugh echoed through the vision of the Union. Her dream self looked up, searching for the source, and then stood.

"Hello?" asked her dream self. She faced where Winter hid, and Winter ran down the hall so as not to be seen just yet.

At the next corner, Winter laughed again and waited for her dream self to spot her. When the dream Winter rounded the corner to the hall, Winter ran again.

"Hey! Wait!" the dream Winter called out.

Winter laughed again. "Let's play hide and seek!" She paused at the next corner long enough to see her dream self come around the previous corner. Then she started running again. "Can you find me?" she shouted and laughed again. Winter chewed the inside of her cheek, hoping the ruse would be enough.

"Wait!" the dream Winter shouted back. "Where are you?"

Winter shifted herself briefly with the power of the infinite until she stood right behind her dream self. The dream wobbled momentarily, but held.

"Where are you?" dream Winter yelled in the opposite direction with her hands cupped around her mouth.

"Right next to you, silly." Winter stepped out of the dream. She briefly saw the original dream resume at her exit, inserting the image of Xaphan right behind her dream self as the dream Winter spun around.

As the younger Winter jerked awake in her desk, Winter frowned and stepped back into the infinite. "I'm not sure she understands."

"She is beginning to," said Laban, now mounted and in line with the other horsemen, the army invisible again.

"Yes," said Winter. "I remember. But all the pieces are not in place yet."

Winter shifted the infinite and watched herself, halfway stepping into the spiritual unknown to observe time as it flowed, but still invisible to both humans and spiritual beings.

She watched her younger self return to campus in the restored BMW, driving for the first time since the wreck with Ryan. She shifted to the next morning and watched herself walk to the Union for breakfast. For a brief moment, she thought her younger self had seen her, and Winter stepped further back into the infinite. She shifted again and watched herself through the glass doors of Carmichael hall as her younger self studied during a freshman dorm meeting.

"You're searching, Prophetess," said Laban.

"Yes."

"For what?"

"For the right moments to help myself find the connections."

"Use your memories, Prophetess."

Winter nodded. "I had a breakthrough at the Union once, talking with Peter. That was my first clue to the AFRC, which led me to Mordensfield." She shifted reality to that morning and found herself walking through the Meadow with Summer. "Maybe if I nudge myself just right..."

She stepped out of the infinite, this time into the spiritual now, not assuming a full form, but with enough of her spirit touching reality that her younger self could see a presence. With a flicker of thought, Winter flew around the Ancient until her younger self noticed. Then she flew toward the Union and pulled back into the unknown just before reaching the door.

It worked. The younger Winter followed.

Winter nodded, satisfied. "This will lead me to Sophie, which will lead me to Mordensfield." Reality shifted to the night she learned about the town. Her younger self drove back to campus after a failed attempt at spending time with her friends.

Winter felt the stab of the same pain from that night...seeing her friends in relationships, happy. And now knowing that no matter what happened on this long infinite evening, no matter how she felt about Graham...it would probably never be.

The younger Winter approached the Raven. Sophie would be exiting soon. Winter remembered following her, but her younger self wasn't slowing down.

Winter shifted to float in the backseat of the car with her younger self, and then she spoke from the unknown, letting her words pierce through the spiritual now and into reality. "Sophie," she whispered.

The younger Winter twisted and looked directly through her.

Eyes wide, she spun back to the road. "What do I do now?"

"Sophie," Winter whispered again.

"Great. Now I'm hearing voices," said her younger self. "Listen, whoever you are. Either I'm crazy or you're real. Either way, that answer means nothing to me. I need a little more than that, please."

Winter clenched her teeth. She had to be judicious with her words so as not to reveal herself. "Sophie."

"Seriously, stop it, you creepy disembodied voice. I mean it. Shut up. You're not helping."

Was she really this stubborn and clueless two years ago? "Ryan," she said this time. That'll make her stop.

The younger Winter slammed the brakes and screamed. Then she began to hyperventilate. A horn honked behind them and the younger Winter pulled the car to the side of the road. Then she laid her head upon the steering wheel.

"Sophie," Winter repeated.

"Leave me alone!"

Sophie exited the Raven. Her younger self wasn't even paying attention.

"Sophie."

Finally, the younger Winter lifted her head, rubbed the fog from the windshield, and spotted Sophie.

Winter stepped back into the infinite and immediately released time to speed by in great swaths.

"You are still searching," said Laban.

Winter nodded. "Xaphan and Culsu hid in the shadows. In the end it was my search for Kaci that drew them out. I have to follow myself closely so we don't miss the right moments."

As her younger self and friends discovered Mordensfield and Sandy, Winter watched closely for any signs of a demonic following. But the demonic shadows that always danced just beyond reach were the only ones she saw. She watched herself and the others drive to Mordensfield and check in at a motel.

Winter stopped the flow of time, spotting something strange. Her younger self dreamed a unique dream. An invisible spiritual line connected the sleeping Winter to a man dressed all in black who stalked toward the motel from the parking lot.

"Curious," said Laban. "I have never seen a tethering like this."

"I remember this," Winter said. "I have to help. She doesn't know he's coming."

"It would seem she does," said Sharok.

"No. She sees, but she doesn't understand that it's real."

"What will you do?" asked Laban.

Winter took a deep breath and stepped into the spiritual now, assuming the form of Rebecca. She backed into a dark corner at the end of the motel wing by the stairs. As the man crept up the stairs, he ducked into a maintenance room near the elevators. All the lights on the balcony winked out.

Winter could still see the thin spiritual tendril connecting her younger self to the man. She willed herself to sync with the tendril spiritually, in hope the man could not see her but her dreaming self could. She had to find a place somewhere between the spiritual now and the infinite before it worked.

As the man crept past, she called out. "Winter."

The man continued forward, but the spiritual tendril paused, pulling against the man and stretching slightly. Then with a snap, the tendril broke free.

"Winter," she said again.

The end of the tendril took shape. The golden spiritual mist formed Winter's own face. It turned slowly, bobbing with the tendril like the head of an elongated snake.

Winter stepped out of the shadows to face the spiritual visage of her younger self. "Wake up."

Immediately, the golden tendril vanished. Winter shifted reality with a flash of thought, sliding sideways to join her younger self in the hotel room. Her younger self sat up in bed, casting around frantically. Magenel stepped to Winter's side in the spiritual now, ready to receive instructions.

Winter shook her head. "It's too much. It's too fast. I need to do this myself." She reached out and took the head of her younger self between her hands and dumped as much info into her as she could.

It took only a second. The man would enter within moments. The younger Winter jumped up and followed Winter's instructions perfectly, positioned behind the door as the man eased it open.

"By Summer," Winter said to Laban. "Make sure the bullet goes astray!"

Laban positioned himself just as the younger Winter grabbed the man from behind. The gun fired. It hit the alarm clock as planned, gently guided by Laban.

Summer screamed.

The man crumpled backward over the younger Winter's knee and slammed his head into the ground. They fought over the gun; the man cursed. She kicked his gun arm and then kicked his face. He rolled aside and came back up swinging the gun to face her.

"No!" Winter shouted, pointing to the gun. Magenel was there, fiery sword instantly thrust through the barrel of the gun just as the man pulled the trigger.

Click.

The momentarily stunned younger Winter launched forward and struck the man in the face. He stumbled out onto the balcony and ran away.

Winter pulled herself and the horsemen back into the infinite where the rest of the army waited. She grunted in frustration. "That was careless," she confessed.

"It's not easy getting involved in your own timeline," said Sharok.

Winter took a calming breath. "But we're almost there. We have to be there at campus when the shooting starts. We have to save as many lives as possible."

Adom nodded. "Then we should go."

Winter furrowed her brow. "Not yet. I want to see something first. Again."

The horsemen gathered around, and Winter shifted reality until they were at Mordensfield Elementary the next day.

She stepped into the spiritual now, careful to put on the form of Rebecca in case her younger self or any demon spotted her, and stood at the door to the classroom.

It was exactly as she remembered it…and it ripped her heart just like it had the first time. Most of the desks were turned over onto the floor. Abandoned backpacks hung dry-rotted in the cubbies against one wall. Black patches dotted the floor…old blood stains left behind.

"Four kids died here. They were seven," Winter said softly. "I committed their names to memory." A tear rolled down her cheek. "Lucy Asbury…Jason Long…Amanda Green…Billy Warren." Winter pointed to a slightly larger blood stain in the middle of the room. "That's where the teacher died to protect Kaci. Her name was Connie Morgan."

"It was a day of great evil," said Sors as the horsemen dismounted and came to her side.

Winter spun on them. "Where were you? Four innocent children lost their lives that day. Parents' lives were broken. Where were you??"

Adom shook his head. "The attack was strong and quick. We were not ready."

"No!" Winter shouted. "I want to know where were *you*? All four of you! Were you even here?"

Laban firmed his lips. "Kaci was being watched. The prophecy concerning the child was known to us, even if the strength of the enemy was not. Of course we were here. We are the watchers of such things."

"Then why didn't you do something?"

Laban pulled off his silvery-white helmet and held it under his arm. "We did. I gave Connie the courage to do what she did. I held her hand as her life left her. I stood guard to make sure little Kaci wasn't seen."

"I fought the ancient demon Moloch when he took us by surprise," said Adom, removing is crimson helm. "I watched while my brothers battled over the lives of the other children. I watched as they were defeated."

"I cleared the path for help to arrive," said Sharok, removing his golden helm, "I rallied a legion of my brothers to descend so that Moloch would not claim more."

"I wept over each child. I mourned their passing," said Sors, removing his black helm. "We were here, Prophetess." His face fell into a dark sadness, and Winter turned back to the classroom to hide the regret on her face.

But the fire still burned within her. "Why would God let something like this happen? Don't tell me he didn't know. Don't tell me he couldn't prepare enough angels to stop it. All of this…" She waved her hand in an open gesture meant to indicate more than just the room. "…must be some kind of game to him, isn't it? He could stop it. He can always stop it. But he doesn't." She spun back and stepped up to talk directly to Laban. "Why?"

"Because who can believe in his goodness if there were no evil to be the comparison? Who would choose to love God if there were nothing to choose from? You've learned these lessons before, Prophetess."

"I don't care! He could have saved these kids!"

"Do you see the pattern of eternity? You do not and neither do I. But what I have seen is this. Billy Warren's father was an alcoholic, like his father before him, and his grandfather. Billy saw the backside of his father's hand many times. The pattern of eternity foretold Billy's death at the hands of his father. His father would spend the rest of his life in prison, which would have only been five years until he took that life by his own hands. Billy's mother would enter a deep depression that would isolate her for years. She would remarry multiple times, but in her grief would seek out men who would abuse her. Billy's older sister would become addicted to many drugs and eventually give her life to prostitution to pay for her habit. In the end, drugs would claim her life.

"This is the pattern of eternity written by sin and the brokenness of humanity left unchecked by God. A pattern that did not come to pass because God ordained that Billy would die here, not at his father's hands. The pattern changed to one of God's design. Billy's father became a broken man. They moved from this town and he gave up alcohol. The family sought counseling at a local church, which would lead to the salvation of father, mother, and sister. The father would not go to prison and take his own life, instead he would become an elder in his church. The mother would start an outreach to other mothers who have lost their children to sudden and violent acts. The daughter will marry a man soon who will become a youth pastor, and she will one day lead others to rescue young girls from the world of prostitution.

"You call it a game to our Father, and perhaps it is. But the game is this…that the enemy seeks to weave a pattern of misery and destruction by using humanity's own sinful nature, yet God seeks to change the pattern to one that turns humanity to the truth and gives them hope. They play this solemn game, but only God sees all patterns and all possible patterns. So what the enemy means for evil, God will turn for good.

"His good work is always there in the patterns if you look for it, Prophetess. I gave you Billy's patterns; shall I give you the others? Shall I give you your own?"

Winter didn't know what to say. She had learned all those things before, but standing here again at this classroom brought back the old indignity. She took a deep breath and turned again to look at the blood stains. "And where is God now? Why is he not fighting with us?"

Laban actually laughed. "Prophetess, perhaps you are too tired. You are not thinking clearly in this place."

Winter couldn't help but crook a grin and cast over her shoulder. "What?"

"The full presence of God is too great and too pure. It would destroy you. But do not fear, because a part of his presence is in you! Where do you think your power comes from?"

Winter shook her head and laughed. "Sorry. You're right. This place is too emotional. Perhaps we should move on."

"Your younger self approaches," Sharok said.

Winter heard footsteps further down the hall beyond an intersection. She pulled herself out of the spiritual now and into the edge of the unknown just as her younger self, Summer, Davis, Peter, and Bevaldi, in his wheelchair, turned the corner. Winter lingered for a moment as they approached and then stepped completely back into the infinite.

"Where we go next, we go to save lives," she told the horsemen as they mounted and put their helmets back on. "Let us remember those children by saving others. A terrible thing happened on campus two years ago. Many people were shot." She looked up at Laban. "I will trust that the power of God in my younger self will be sufficient to fight without our help this time. We must help as many of the injured as we can. That's our next task...not a battle, but a rescue. Can this army do that?"

Laban crooked his head. "It is perhaps what we do best, Prophetess."

"Good," said Winter as she shifted reality around them until they gazed out upon the Meadow. "This is where most everything happens. Spread out, and be ready."

The army materialized around her and the angels quickly dispersed.

Winter pointed to Adom. "I also need some angels in the Union."

Adom nodded and galloped away with a detail of angels in tow.

Winter pivoted a slow circle, surveying the preparations. "Any moment now."

She stopped when she saw the Ancient. It swayed violently even though no wind blew. Every leaf turned in unison like a giant swarm.

She remembered this...it was a vision she saw, but how could she see it now too? Winter gazed to the right and saw her younger self at the edge of the Meadow, watching the tree.

Then the giant tree bent forward, the thickest limbs bending like rubber, and gently brushed the ground. The younger Winter drifted toward the tree, never taking her eyes off its mesmerizing motion. Dirt swirled into the air where the tree hit the ground.

Winter eased forward to the spot being cleared away, knowing what she would see...knowing who they represented. Once again it broke her heart to think of Kaci. The thoughts consumed her, more raw in the realm of the spiritual than she had ever experienced in real life. The dust cleared and the bones gleamed through clearly.

No matter what she did or how hard she tried, she'd never be able to stop the pain. Kaci was dead now. Shot in the chapel. Winter would have to live with that for the rest of her life. She felt herself drifting out of the spiritual now into reality, but she didn't care. She just wanted to have Kaci back.

"What's wrong?"

Winter glanced up and saw her younger self kneeling in front of her. Winter wiped the tears from her face and pointed to the bones, not really knowing what to say. "They're dry."

The younger Winter reached out and Winter took a step back.

The bullet ripping through Kaci's chest... "You have to make them live."

"How?" asked the younger Winter. "What do I do?"

"Prophesy to them, Winter. Speak to them. You have to teach them to live again."

"I don't know what to say."

Kaci's dead eyes as she slumped in the Eater's arms. "You have to help them! Please!"

"Who are you?" asked the younger Winter.

Winter took another step back and shook her head. How could she ever explain?

Her younger self finally gazed down to study the bones. She reached out and brushed them with her finger. Suddenly tears streamed down her face. She looked back up at Winter. "What do I do? I'm not good with puzzles...tell him that!" She tilted her head to the sky. "God, I'm not good with puzzles! Just tell me what to do, please!"

Winter took a small step toward her and reached out. Maybe she could tell herself a little more. Maybe she could guide her a little more directly. Then again, would she have made it to this point if she had known more? Could she even handle knowing Kaci would die anyway? No...it would be too much. She took a deep breath to respond. "It's the puzzle that makes you strong enough to handle the answer."

The younger Winter stared at her. "I can't!"

"You must."

"What's going on here?" came Ayden's voice from behind the younger Winter.

Winter glanced up and found Ayden flitting her eyes back and forth from the younger Winter to her, and to her horror Winter realized Ayden could see her too.

The younger Winter turned to Ayden. "Can you see her?"

"The girl?" asked Ayden.

The younger Winter narrowed her eyes back, and Winter's pulse quickened. She took two steps back.

"No, wait!" said the younger Winter.

"Who is that?" asked Ayden.

"Prophetess!" called out Laban from behind her. "Evil approaches this place!"

"I'm sorry," she told her younger self and Ayden. "You must be strong now." Then she turned and fled toward Laban, who had positioned himself beside the administration building.

"Come back!" yelled the younger Winter.

After a moment, Winter realized the two girls were chasing her. She sprinted past Laban and turned the corner at the back of the building and then stepped completely out of reality to join the angels in the spiritual unknown.

As her younger self and Ayden came into the parking lot behind the administration building, Winter eased over to Laban's side and turned to watch Dr. Cook walk to his car.

At the corner of a building on the other side of the street stood a man in a baseball cap. Logan. Sophie stepped up beside him. The younger Winter watched them, but behind Logan and Sophie, Winter could see something else approaching. A dark cloud of demons rose from the ground into the sky, swirling and chattering with excitement, easily twice as many demons as her little army. At the foot of the demons came the man in the silver and black mask, a massive, hulking demon attached to the human beneath.

Speaking into her silent thoughts, Laban said, "This man is consumed. The ancient demon, Moloch, whispers into his ear. This is the same that took the lives of the children."

"It will start here." Winter peered at the other bystanders around the building. "See if you can get them out of here."

Laban nodded. Immediately he and a detail of angels swirled around the bystanders, urging them to leave. Most of them did, veering off into the buildings.

Winter faced Dr. Cook as the Eater emerged from around the corner of the building. Someone stood beside him. An angel, though not one associated with her army.

The angel glanced briefly at Winter and then focused his complete attention on Dr. Cook, placing one hand on his shoulder.

Patterns, Winter thought, and then forced herself to close her eyes just before that first explosion of the shotgun.

Chaos erupted. Demons descended. People screamed. The shotgun continued to boom. Other angels not part of her army swarmed in and began battle. With mere flickers of thought, Winter sent her own angels to tend the fallen.

Campus security arrived at the parking lot, but the man and his demons had moved on silently. Then the fire alarm sounded, sending thousands of students into the Meadow. Security went into a panic, not knowing where the shooter had disappeared to, but Winter could still see his cloud of demons battling with the angels not far from there, near the chapel.

Winter shifted herself through reality to stand in the Meadow near the chapel and waited. The Meadow finally filled with students, and then the Eater emerged. He casually walked into the Meadow and turned up the sidewalk toward the Union, the shotgun strapped to his back and a semi-automatic rifle in his hands.

Winter followed. With each blast of the gun, someone fell. With each fallen body, a flicker of thought sent an angel to their side.

Patterns. She would do what she could...

Whether the victims died or not, Winter continued to send her angels to help. She didn't know how many would live because of her army or how many would be allowed to die regardless. It was all part of the pattern.

The man in the silver and black mask ascended the steps and entered the Union, but left a bloody scene in his wake. Thankfully there were enough of her angels for all of the fallen. The most seriously injured had more than one angel at their sides.

Winter watched through translucent walls of the Union as people fell to the Eater's gun inside, and were immediately tended to by Adom and his detail of angels. She watched her younger self, Ayden, and Peter flee from the building. She watched Davis struggle with the killer. Then the killer stalked after the younger Winter toward the music building. A flicker of thought sent any remaining idle angels there.

She surveyed the scene, wishing she could do more. So many injured. So many dying. The nearest angel held his hands on a wounded girl, his face grim and concentrating.

Behind Winter, a screech of tires signaled the Eater's escape with Summer and Ayden. Sirens wailed in the distance.

"Prophetess," said Laban, who was still nearby. He was always nearby. "There is little more we can do for them. Their fate belongs to the Father now."

She turned a slow circle. There had to be something more she could do. There had to be a way. Then she stepped out of the infinite, fully into reality, in the form of Rebecca.

"Prophetess?" asked Laban.

"It is my turn to help," she said and knelt beside the young girl nearest her, probably a freshman, with the grim angel still concentrating to keep her alive. The girl lurched from the pain of a giant hole in her abdomen, her skin pale and clammy.

The angel kneeling next to the girl glanced up and shook his head.

Winter took a deep breath and touched the girl's forehead. She didn't know what she did, but she felt the power of God within her drain into the girl. The girl gasped and lay still. Alive. The wound had not completely healed, but she would survive...Winter could feel it.

She stood and moved to the next victim and struggling angel. Another girl. Hemorrhaging from the neck. Winter touched the wound and it sealed. The pale-faced girl, soaked in her own blood, lay still and began to breathe normally.

Winter studied the field. At least fifty lay on the ground with angels at their sides. Others crawled or hobbled toward safety with angels as their escorts. Winter didn't know how many victims were in the Union.

As she gazed around, she could only think about saving as many as possible. Some might be already dead. Some would survive on their own. But how would she know the difference?

As if the thought had been projected to her army, an angel peered up and met her eyes. He knelt beside a guy lying face down, blood saturating his back. The angel lifted his hand into the air.

Winter went to him and laid her hands on the guy's back. He shivered and then began to breathe in a steady rhythm. Winter cast around again. Other angels were rising high on their knees, lifting their hands.

She went to the next. Another girl. Awake and alert, but her face as pale as the infinite. She saw Winter approach and tried to reach out, but winced from the pain of a gaping hole in her side. Winter knelt and placed her hands on the wound. The girl watched, mouth wide open. After a moment, the girl's eyes widened and her hands dropped to where the wound used to be.

Winter moved on to the next. And the next. Letting the power of God flow through her and bring as much healing as possible to this killing field.

As she stood from the last victim, Laban waited at her side. "There are others in the Union." Winter nodded and shifted reality until she stood in the Union among the bodies.

These were worse than in the Meadow. Some had multiple wounds. Some had been shot in places that were clearly mortal. All of them lay motionless on the ground. Each body had an angel beside it, but most of those angels just knelt with their heads down and their eyes closed, mourning the passing of the soul in front of them.

"Am I too late?" she asked softly. Every angel heard her and looked up.

Only four rose up on their knees and lifted a hand. Winter went to each, doing what she could, even though the wounds might be too much. Perhaps it was their time. If not, then she would give them what she could to keep them alive.

After tending to the last victim, she stood and faced the other horsemen, who had gathered while she worked. Around her, floating in the spiritual now, waited the entire army, their work complete. All watched her for the next command. "We must go to the forest," she said.

The horsemen nodded and Winter shifted the infinite sideways until trees flew by. She stopped at a horrible scene. Winter remembered being there, but seeing it from the infinite made her heart beat cold.

As the rain fell upon their heads in heavy drops, kneeling on the ground in a row were her younger self, Ayden, Peter, and Summer. Their hands were taped behind their backs. Sagging upon his knees at the end of the line sat the paralyzed Bevaldi. A massive hole had been dug into the ground before them. Xaphan stood near Bevaldi, holding a pistol casually at his side. The man in the silver and black mask towered over the younger Winter with his shotgun leveled at her face.

Aside from these details, Winter now saw what she couldn't see then. The menacing form of the demon Xaphan loomed out of the man's body and watched with ecstasy. Moloch, rising strong and impassive, clung to the Eater. Thousands of much smaller demons swirled around their feet, bowing to the prince demons. Others hung on the captives, pawing at their faces. Above them a net of demons formed a dome, like the one Winter had seen at the train yard, that flashed as angels tried to burst their way through.

The younger Winter opened her eyes, and they glowed brilliantly with a power Winter had never seen from this side. It was as if miniature suns illuminated her entire face from within, only allowed to escape unhindered from her eyes.

The demons near her all fled and screeched as if seared by fire. The Eater hesitated, halfway lowering his gun, as Moloch momentarily recoiled.

"It's not my time yet," the younger Winter said.

The demon Xaphan swelled and roared. The man screamed, "KILL HER!"

Winter froze time at that moment and took a long look at the demons and the angels above. "Listen closely," she told the horsemen. "The horsemen are not to be seen at all this time. Half of the forces are to use the infinite to flash in and out and cut a swath through the demons so that they can escape, using only as much force as necessary. The other half need to go above and help the other angels break through the dome. When the other angels arrive, we let them take over."

"Understood, Prophetess," said Laban.

Winter released time. "Now!"

"It's not my time yet," the younger Winter said again. She pulled her hands free.

Winter rushed to Bevaldi's side and placed her hands on his shoulders.

The younger Winter reached around and grabbed the shotgun just as the Eater pulled the trigger.

The gun exploded in his face.

Winter poured power into Bevaldi as she had done to the injured in the Meadow.

"GO!" Bevaldi yelled. His legs moved. He planted his feet and stood, spending the power she transferred to tackle Xaphan.

"Run!" shouted the younger Winter, and the captives took off.

Angels bored a hole through the demonic army for them, strobing in and out of the infinite and battering like a jackhammer. They were so fast and so precise that the demons fell into chaos.

As the captives disappeared into the darkness, Bevaldi continued to fight against Xaphan. Finally, Xaphan overpowered him, and he knocked Bevaldi to the ground as the power drained from the crippled man. As Xaphan leveled his pistol at him, suddenly an angel not of Winter's army appeared at Bevaldi's side. The angel nodded once at Winter and focused all his attention on Bevaldi.

Xaphan fired. Winter clenched her eyes at the sound, and the next thing she heard was Bevaldi's body falling into the pit.

When Winter looked again, Xaphan peered into the darkness after the escapees. The Eater stepped to his side and Xaphan handed over his gun. "Do not fail me again. And if you do I will blow your head off...so you might as well do it yourself." The demon Xaphan loomed over Moloch, and Moloch recoiled.

The Eater made no visible reaction to the threat, but took off running into the forest. Then in the silence and the patter of the soft rain, Xaphan turned to stare directly at Winter. Winter held her breath.

"I don't know what you are," he said. "And I can't see you. You were there in the tower and you are here now. I can feel your energy. Hear this. My master will burn this world and all the people on it. Stay out of my way lest you burn too." Then he fled into the darkness.

The horsemen stepped up to her side and they watched with her.

"How did he know?" she asked.

"The power of the demon is great," said Sors. "It feels the power within you and the power of the horsemen. He will sense us coming."

Then Winter remembered the tree. "We have to go help them."

"The power in your younger self is sufficient," said Laban.

She blinked at him. "And what if it's not?"

As he stared unblinking at her, Winter shifted reality until they hovered in mid-air in front of the tree. She heard the others crashing toward her below. She heard the shots from the Eater booming after them like thunder.

"I have to do something," she said and moved to step out of the infinite.

"Prophetess, wait," Sharok said.

Winter paused, on the edge of the spiritual now. Her younger self and the others broke free from the underbrush and slid to a stop as they faced the cliff in front of them.

"What now?" floated Peter's voice toward them through the rain.

The younger Winter searched around frantically until her eyes settled on Winter herself. Winter panicked and pulled more firmly out of reality as the younger Winter led the others to the base of the tree.

As they reached the tree, the Eater emerged and eyed them. Peter, Summer, and Ayden all cowered behind the tree as the younger Winter planted herself in front.

"Come, Prophetess." Laban lifted his hand toward the top of the cliff. "Come see the sufficiency of the power God gives you."

Winter floated behind him until they were far enough away and high enough to look back. A gasp caught in her throat.

The wind blasted in a vortex around the tree, catching the rain and wrapping everyone in a tight shell of wind and water. The younger Winter stood inside the shell, feet planted, light shining from her eyes, skin glowing from an inner radiance, with only Magenel for protection.

The Eater, spurred forward by Moloch, entered the vortex, and the tree lurched. The swirling wind closed in tighter, faster, roaring like a tornado.

As the spiritual wind howled, the hordes of smaller demons with Moloch scattered into the forest like rats from the light. Moloch continued to cling to the Eater, but rode him like a banner in a gale as the spiritual force tore at his skin.

Above, the demonic dome crumbled. The other angels rushed in and the rest of Winter's army stood down from the fight. The new angels did not engage with the younger Winter as Winter had expected. Instead, they gathered around at the ready, cutting down stray demons. Some surrounded Peter, Summer, and Ayden, giving them courage and strength. Otherwise, every angel, whether of Winter's army or not, simply stayed out of the way of the display of God's power coming through the younger Winter.

Still the Eater moved into the vortex. The ground trembled and lurched. The younger Winter held her hands out for balance.

The Eater lifted his gun.

In that instant the tree broke free from the ground. The vortex reached a new dynamic, spinning fast and fluidly like a giant wave, constantly adapting in all directions, wrapping the tree in a watery sphere. Water flowed violently into the crater left in the wake.

The Eater had managed to cling to a mere sliver of ground at the edge of the floating tree, bolstered by the powerful arms of Moloch. He swung his second hand up and lifted himself.

The younger Winter rushed forward and pulled at his hands. Magenel's sword flashed against Moloch, the demon easily ten times the guardian's size. The Eater grabbed the younger Winter, trying to fling her from the tree. She twisted from his grasp and flung herself backward, helped by Magenel. The Eater climbed even higher, now with his elbows on the ledge. Moloch loomed hungrily. Younger Winter kicked at the Eater. He grabbed her ankle. She kicked his face, and he pitched back over the ledge, one hand coming free and one hand still clinging to the dirt. The momentum swung him slightly under the ledge.

The tree dropped, crashing back to the earth, and crushing the Eater in the ground.

For a moment the tree groaned and swayed. Rain-soaked leaves fluttered through the air. The swirling vortex broke like a bubble and showered onto the ground like ordinary rain. The light left the younger Winter's eyes and she backed away toward the tree as angels rushed in to take posts of protection.

"Do you see?" said Laban. "The power which God pours through his Prophetess is sufficient."

"But I am not sufficient," Winter said.

"You are not required to be."

"Look!" shouted Adom. "Moloch escapes!"

"Let him go," Winter said, glancing back to Laban. "This victory is sufficient. Last year I forgot what it meant for God to be sufficient. I was…lost or distracted. I don't know."

"It was a lesson you needed to learn."

"But I wasn't listening."

"You did eventually."

"And how did I get there? How did I not die being stupid? Was it us? This army? Now?"

She shifted the infinite away.

$$\infty$$

Winter stopped the scenes of reality flashing past to watch her younger self with Ayden easing through the corridors of the school's coliseum. "See, we're going the wrong way. How did I not know the right way?" Winter stepped out of the infinite, through the unknown and the now, into reality, before the horsemen could stop her. Without consciously thinking about it, the form of Rebecca fell upon her again.

The younger Winter spotted her and stared.

Winter simply put a finger to her lips and pointed for them to go up instead of down. Then she stepped back into the unknown where the horsemen had gathered. "If I have to guide myself, I will," she told Laban.

"Be careful not to rob yourself of the lessons you needed. Let God weave the patterns."

"What if we're supposed to be a part of that? Maybe this is the way the pattern goes. Maybe we help to weave it."

"Perhaps," said the white horseman.

Winter grunted and shifted reality around them until the FBI safe house appeared before them.

Alison stepped out of the door, her face half burned away. Except it wasn't Alison at all. Inside the anonymity of the infinite, Winter could see the form of Sophie underneath. Culsu wrapped around her like a thick blanket and projected the image of Alison onto Sophie's skin. Beneath the facade, Sophie walked as if a zombie, pale and emaciated. Behind them, the building teemed with the shadows of demons swarming in and out.

"There's Culsu," Winter said. "We should do something. She knows about me."

"And what would you do?" asked Laban. "Engage in another

open battle? Culsu has grown stronger since we last encountered her. A legion of demons follow at her command. This is not the right time. She may know what you become, but she doesn't understand what you are. Culsu is clever. She will not attack again until she understands."

Then the younger Winter burst through the door. Magenel followed behind, looking frail and tired, his sword drooping in his hand.

"What's wrong with him?" Winter asked.

"Your connection to the power of God is weak," said Laban. "Look. Observe how thin the spiritual line is now compared to before in the forest. The battle in this place has been intense, and without a stronger power to call upon, Magenel fights emaciated."

"Why?"

"The power of God is strong, but so is the nature of sin. When a believer's focus is troubled, the flesh begins to win."

The younger Winter swung her gun forward, assumed a ready stance, and eyed Culsu.

Culsu turned.

"Alison?"

"I've seen enough," Winter said with a huff. She shifted reality again, a blur of shapes and color. "Is there anything we can do? Can I send more soldiers to help Magenel?"

"When you were younger, the battle for your life was a battle fueled by the grace of God and by the faith of others. Now that the power of the Holy Spirit resides within you, the battle is fueled by your faith. It doesn't matter how many you send. As long as your faith is weak, so they will be."

"Then what about Ayden? She has the gift, too, and her faith is new."

"Perhaps."

Winter halted reality outside of the Union one day after Christmas that same year. The younger Winter and Kaci walked toward the steps where Ayden and Nadeen waited.

Winter paused time and glanced around. Behind the horsemen, usually phased just beyond her sight, her army materialized, awaiting her orders. Who should she choose? She eyed the front line until she came upon a soldier with reddish hair, almost the same color of Ayden's. She smiled. "You. What is your name?"

"Neshamah," said the soldier as he stood forward.

Winter nodded. "Come with me, Neshamah." She led him through the infinite and into the frozen reality. Then she reached out and touched her younger self and clenched her eyes. After a moment she turned to Neshamah. "I just gave myself enough to nudge her in the right direction since she's no longer listening to Magenel. You must protect and guide Ayden. Place your hands on me and I will give you my memories to help."

Neshamah nodded. "As you command, Prophetess." He placed both hands on either side of her head, and Winter concentrated on pouring all her memories of the past two years into him. When she finished, he nodded again and stepped to Ayden's side, then crossed completely into reality and froze just as Magenel stood frozen beside the younger Winter.

Winter released time and watched for a moment as her younger self stopped on the sidewalk, pulled her coat tight, and turned to go back to the parking lot. Ayden, Neshamah close beside her, turned to follow.

Winter stepped to Laban's side and watched. "Since my faith last year was not enough to always hear, then Ayden will make sure I get where I need to be."

"A wise decision, Prophetess," said Laban. "Where do we go next?"

Winter bit her lip. "What happened must happen. I cannot intervene. Those lessons were necessary to realign my faith where it needs to be. That means there's only one place to go next. Romania."

The infinite soared around them as visions of reality flickered past. Forests, cities, and an entire ocean. When Winter stopped, nighttime overshadowed a gravel road. Her younger self lumbered toward distant city lights.

"This is where we help," she said to Laban. "This is where *you* must help."

Laban narrowed his eyes. "What is your command?"

"You must speak to her. Try not to be seen. But you must tell her what she needs to hear. Then we will bring her through the infinite and take her home."

"What am I to say?"

Winter just shrugged. "Say what I need to hear. Say whatever God tells you to say."

Laban stared at the younger Winter and led his horse out of the infinite, past the spiritual now, and physically into reality. His brilliant white charger gleamed in the starlight as it stepped boldly upon the road behind the younger Winter. At the sound of the horse's hoofs, the younger Winter slowed and began to turn to it.

"Do not turn around," Laban said to her.

The younger Winter pivoted back to Giurgiu, holding her hands up. "Who are you?"

"One who has been watching. You must continue walking; you have a very long way to travel."

She started walking, and Laban urged his horse forward again.

"What do you want? I have nothing, so you're wasting your time," she said.

"I want nothing from you but your ear. I come as a messenger from God, to give you a warning, to give you advice, and to speed you along your way."

"Listen, I know I've been screwing up lately, but I've made my peace with God about it." Her voice trembled with fear. "Things are going to be different...I promise. Please don't hurt me."

Laban laughed, a deep rumble like thunder, casting a quick glance to Winter herself watching from the spiritual now.

Winter just rolled her eyes at him.

He turned back to the younger Winter and shook his head. "Take my warning, Prophetess. You are going into a battle which you cannot fight and cannot win. The enemy has strengthened itself. If you face this enemy with the flesh, you will be destroyed."

"Then what am I supposed to do?" she asked.

"This is my advice. Do not fall into the trap laid for you again. Do not be tempted to rely upon your own strength. You cannot face the legions prepared against you, but the Warriors of the Lord can. An army is being prepared for you to command. They will fight this battle."

"What? Are you insane? Are you talking about an angel army? You can't be serious." She moved to glance over her shoulder.

"Do not turn around!"

The younger Winter obeyed and kept moving forward. "You've got the wrong person. I can't command an angel army. There's no way…"

The rumbling laughter erupted again as Laban cast his thoroughly amused look back to Winter herself. Winter threw him her best glare, but it only stoked his amusement.

When he finally stopped laughing at her, he turned to the younger Winter. "You humans are amusing to watch…always reaching for things not yours, but never claiming what is already given. You have been given this authority and this task, Prophetess. Claim it, but be warned not to reach for things not yours."

The younger Winter only nodded.

"And now, to speed you along your way," said Laban with a knowing nod toward Winter herself.

Winter stepped forward in that moment and clasped her younger self on the shoulder from within the spiritual now. She paused time and shifted reality around them all, using the infinite to bend time and space. After depositing herself on the road where Graham would soon approach, she let time resume.

Without waiting, Winter shifted reality again. She knew where to go. "Now we must fight again," she said aloud to no one in particular. She could feel the army arranging itself, preparing. "Only a few battles left, and this is one of the most important."

Reality halted at the abandoned train yard. Time moved around them, but they stood in the spiritual unknown, invisible to the hordes of demons. As Winter rotated to inspect the enemy, for the first time she actually saw the strength of the legions that had assembled for this night, and understood why things had almost gone horribly wrong.

The army, still visible to her, shuffled in uncertainty. She eyed them, but their faces only showed confidence and eagerness.

"I remember this night well," she said loud enough for all of them to hear. "I can tell you that another army of your brothers, one even greater in number than you, is approaching. It is not our job to fight these hordes, though the demon Xaphan and the demon Culsu will both be here tonight. This is not the final battle. The power of God inside my younger self will hold most of it at bay. The other army will do most of the work. Our mission here tonight is to protect Kaci...no matter what. If we are seen, then so be it. If our strength becomes known, then so be it. Kaci is in more danger now than she has ever been, and *we* must be the ones to fight for her life."

Winter felt the power of the other army approaching. Judging by the faces of her army, they did not. Perhaps it was the power in her again. Were her eyes glowing right now?

She pointed straight up. "Look! Look beyond the hordes! Your brothers are getting ready."

They tilted their faces up, and when they faced her again, many of them smiled the knowing smile of victory.

"Listen closely to me. Use the infinite. It has been given to you to work outside of time if necessary. You can do what your brothers cannot. With this we can keep Kaci safe."

On top of the hill in front of the train yard, a car approached and then stopped. The younger Winter and Ayden stepped out and gazed down upon the train yard.

"Get ready!" Winter yelled at her army as the demonic mass around them chanted rhythmically in anticipation of the younger Winter's approach. "Horsemen, take the army and find Kaci. Analyze the enemy. Look for weaknesses. But do not engage yet. I will join you shortly."

Her army disappeared as the younger Winter and Ayden ran down the hill. Angels from the other army swarmed to their sides. Demons charged forward. Magenel and Neshamah cut a swath before the two girls, and together with the other angels swirling like a protective drill, no demon could touch them.

Winter pulsed out a thought. *Magenel. To me.*

Part of his essence soared forward in a streak of white that stretched from her younger self until it cascaded upon her, though he still fought at the side of her younger self. Winter stepped into the spiritual now and looked at herself and the angel, speaking directly to the essence that connected to him. *Culsu is here. Xaphan is coming. Kaci is in danger. We will do what we can. Fight! Fight like you've never fought before!* He nodded and Winter locked eyes with herself for a moment, and then pointed to the door where Culsu held Kaci captive. *Lead her,* she told Magenel.

Winter pulled out of reality briefly and shifted to stand in front of the door. What lay inside was stronger still. An army of Culsu's own design. She could feel it just as surely as she could feel her own army, orbiting the horde, searching for weaknesses. But it couldn't be helped. Kaci was inside. Her own army would have to intervene one way or another, but first she had to bring her younger self here. With a flicker of thought a knife materialized in her hand, and she dragged it across her palm like she had done before in the tower.

The younger Winter rounded the corner. An organized legion of demons stood between her and the door. The angelic army around the younger Winter crashed in, but the legion held its ground.

Magenel! Winter called out again. Part of his essence came to her again, streaming forward and passing through the horde as if they were nothing. *Don't let them stop me. Bring me here!* She turned and wrote the word "Here" in blood on the door and then phased out of reality.

His blade flew in a blaze to cut the path, as the angelic army struggled to keep the bulk of the demonic legions from crashing down. Twice demons reached out and took hold of the younger Winter and Ayden, and each time Magenel and Neshamah hewed them away. The two protector angels from Winter's own army fought with a skill worthy of twenty angels from the other army. Still, the demons were too strong.

But *her* army was the elite. A flicker of thought brought them streaking back. *Now! Clear the path!* Her army joined the fray, shifting in and out of the infinite with such speed that the demons howled in fear. It wasn't long before the demons retreated back to leave a wide perimeter away from the angels.

The younger Winter and Ayden reached the door.

"Can you see anything past the door?" the younger Winter asked Ayden.

"No. But I'm still getting used to it. Can you?"

Winter shook her head. "But this is the place. Ready?"

Ayden straightened herself and nodded.

The younger Winter grabbed the knob, twisted it, and pushed the door open. What waited inside were demons of a different caliber than the ones outside. They watched with cold, intelligent eyes…calculating, patient, and full of a deeper sense of evil. The ones at the opening pawed at the two girls, as if trying to tempt them.

The younger Winter clenched her fists, and suddenly her eyes began to glow. She stepped forward. The demons moved aside, fading slightly as if they stepped out of reality and offering nods of twisted respect to Magenel and Neshamah.

"Do we follow, Prophetess?" asked Laban. "These are dangerous superior soldiers. They are for the enemy what we are for the

Kingdom. The fight will be bitter."

Winter shook her head. "Not yet. Not here. For now we wait in the unknown. Kaci will be coming soon."

Winter shifted herself to float above the scene so she could watch through translucent walls, and it didn't take long before Kaci emerged from a side door. Demons clung to her, hanging from her back and riding on her legs. At their presence the demonic legions cheered, jeering at Kaci unseen.

The younger Winter soon followed, chasing Kaci through the train yard. A train whistle cut through the air.

Winter shifted until she waited near the spot where Kaci would emerge to approach the tracks. "Ready!" she shouted to her army. They responded with a loud roar. Kaci rounded the last boxcar. Demons flanked her on all sides. "Now!"

Her army struck the unsuspecting demons, but thousands more demons had come in to join the fun. They not only hung off of Kaci, but clung to the younger Winter's legs in numbers too great to count. They overran Magenel despite his skill. Above, demons had formed a blockade to keep the other angel army out. If Winter's army didn't succeed, then there was nothing to be done.

Despite the army's attempt to wrest the demons away, Kaci's drug-induced despair kept her moving toward the train tracks.

"Prophetess! We cannot stop her!" shouted Laban.

The younger Winter inched around the boxcar. "Kaci!"

Kaci didn't turn. She didn't move. She stood by the tracks, waiting as demons pawed at her sides while so many others kept the angelic army at arm's length. They needed help. They needed more time.

The younger Winter slogged forward, dragging her demon-wrapped legs to ebb foot-by-foot closer. "Kaci! You have to listen to me! This isn't you...this isn't what you want to do...trust me, it's not the answer."

Kaci looked toward the approaching train, with no indication she heard the younger Winter at all.

"More!" Winter shouted to her army. "We need more! Horsemen, free the other army!" She pointed up, and the horsemen galloped through the air to attack the blockade.

"Kaci! Please!" shouted the younger Winter. "Even if you do hate me, even if you never want to see me again, don't do this! You're not yourself. Fight it! Don't listen to whatever it is in your head!"

The demons continued to jerk against the younger Winter's legs, nearly causing her to fall. She cried in pain, but continued to fight to get closer to Kaci. Now beyond the boxcar. Now crossing the open space. She reached out...

"Think of Peter," she said. "He loves you...not me. I'm sorry I haven't been the kind of friend you needed. I'm sorry I wasn't there when I should have been. But Peter will be there, for the rest of your life. Remember him...please!"

The train threatened...the chug of the engine and the rumble of its presence. Winter glanced up at the horsemen, still fighting to free the other army. She had to do something quick. Something drastic. They were losing.

The younger Winter took a step forward, slowly closing the gap. "Kaci, please..."

The train was nearly upon them. The whistle shouting in a long continuous blast for them to move. The demons crept up alongside Kaci, caressing her with their long fingers.

"Kaci...don't..." said the younger Winter.

Winter shook her head. She had to do something. The angels fought, demons fell, but there were ten more to replace each one. The horsemen made progress above, but too slowly. The train was there, demons riding in glee upon the front. Time was up. Time. They needed time.

She had the infinite. She had all the time in existence.

Kaci cast one broken-hearted look at the younger Winter, and then took a long step into the center of the tracks.

"STOP!" screamed the younger Winter.

At the same time, Winter reached out with her mind and snatched the fabric of the infinite, folding it into a pocket of time halfway between reality and the infinite. She grabbed every demon within the immediate radius, every angel, and even her younger self, and pulled them into the pocket. Time froze with Kaci extending one foot in front of the train, but every demon and every angel remained in a state of temporal motion. Now her army had the time they needed to make a difference.

With the sudden change, the demons looked around in panic, and the weaker ones immediately fled.

That's all the advantage her army needed. In the confusion, they crashed in between the younger Winter and Kaci like an avalanche. They fell upon the demons with a renewed fierceness that sent the evil creatures scattering in all directions. The angels twisted the demons out of the air, flinging them into the distance, casting them through the barricade where the other army could take care of them. The angels ripped away the demons clinging to the younger Winter, freeing her to move.

The demons screamed and tried to fight back, but the elite army pressed their momentum. The army filled the space between the younger Winter and Kaci, pushing back in all directions, and created a clear path through an angelic tunnel. With the demonic forces held back, Kaci's two protector angels finally succeeded in ripping the demons away from Kaci and casting them into the main battle.

Winter stepped up in the form of Rebecca next to her stunned younger self. "Winter!" she shouted.

The younger Winter peered down at her, her eyes wide.

"They can hold them back for a moment, but you must save her!"

She nodded, glanced at the shimmering tunnel and the chaos above, and ran. As she drew closer to Kaci, the demons screeched in frustration. Then she was there, wrapping her arms around Kaci and pulling her away from the train.

At that same moment, the horsemen broke through the barricade and the other angelic army rushed down. Winter shoved the demons and her younger self back into regular time, and with a pulse of thought her army stepped out of reality into the spiritual unknown as the other, much larger army finally took over.

Laban pulled up beside her. "We are not overrun by strength, but by numbers. The other angelic army is great, but when these demons rally they will be difficult to defeat. And the strength of Culsu's elite forces is not yet accounted for."

"Then we must make sure the other angelic army is not stopped. We must be there to lend our strength when and where they falter. Can you do that?" Winter asked. "If we stay hidden and use the infinite, then we can make a way for my younger self to escape with Kaci."

Laban nodded. "We will keep the path open for them. We will make the way."

At that moment, powerful black streaks like inverted lightning flew through the air. They struck the angels in large groups, slamming them far into the sky.

"What is that?" Winter asked, stunned.

Laban frowned. "It is Culsu's army."

Within seconds, they had slammed the entire angelic army back out of the reformed blockade. Nearby, more of Culsu's elite army approached, with Culsu herself in their midst. Ayden crawled before her like a dog and Peter held a shotgun to Ayden's head, with one of the darker elite demons clinging to his back.

Winter pointed back to the barricade. "We have to get the other angels back in! We can't fight these demons alone. Find the weak spot! Do something!"

Laban shot off, himself a streak of lightning, and began to probe the perimeter of demons again. The other horsemen did the same.

Winter watched her younger self talking with Culsu, wondering if she'd have to intervene again like she did at the train. She cast back toward the horsemen as they continued to probe the perimeter. When she looked back, the younger Winter and Culsu were circling, getting ready for their showdown.

Hurry! Winter pulsed out to the horsemen.

The slick black lightning demons clung to Culsu and waited at her feet. In front of Winter stood Magenel and Neshamah, swords drawn and determined.

Culsu swung her arms forward, and a division of her demonic army attacked. Magenel and Neshamah became a blur as they encapsulated the younger Winter and fought the shadows off. The demons soared back to Culsu, and then after a brief pause, Culsu launched them again, faster and this time with more numbers.

The younger Winter swung her arms forward, eyes and skin glowing, and at her command both Magenel and Neshamah launched forward to meet the demons.

How the two angels held their ground, Winter couldn't tell, but in the blur of motion and frenzied attacks from the demons, Winter could at least tell that the two angels flashed in and out of the infinite, tripled in strength by the power of God coursing through the younger Winter. Now facing five demons alone, now behind them hewing at their backs, now several feet away spinning into five more.

The elite demons of Culsu's army could not keep up. They screeched in frustration and slashed their swords into empty air where one of the angels had been a moment before.

Culsu stretched out her arms, and more of her demonic army rushed to her side.

Winter gazed around and found her own army at the ready...the horsemen still attacking the perimeter for weak places. At her scrutiny, the army stepped forward. "As many as necessary, keep them protected," she said.

To a soldier, they all nodded. Ten angels streaked off to soar around the younger Winter, just as Culsu launched a second attack that circumvented Magenel and Neshamah. The demons slammed onto the younger Winter, and the ten angels went to work keeping them away.

Culsu roared in frustration, and in that roar was a call to retreat. All of her demons backed away from the angels and clung back upon their host.

"How are you doing that?" Culsu asked, not to the younger Winter, but to Magenel and Neshamah. They stood their ground, fire flashing from their eyes, and glittering as if electricity ran across their bodies.

The younger Winter took the question as if to her. "I'm not," she said.

Magenel, Neshamah, and the other ten angels phased partially out of reality to reform around the younger Winter, but invisible to the demons.

"Where are they? Where are they?" Culsu screamed, casting around frantically in a complete circle. Her demons repositioned to watch every direction, eyes darting around and alert.

"You've lost," said the younger Winter. "This is a fight you cannot win, and you know it. I'm taking the others and leaving." She stepped backward toward Peter, Kaci, and Ayden.

"I have not lost!" shouted Culsu. She stretched out her hands and the entire force of her elite army gathered around her, swirling, absorbing. Culsu grew with their strength as they melted inside of her like a giant demonic mass. She grew, towering twenty feet high. The fire of Hell glowed from her face and she took a step forward. "I am the Acolyte," Culsu said in a deep thundering voice, both a roar and a screech. "I am the Right Hand of Hell."

The younger Winter took another step backward. The angels tightened in around her.

Hurry! Winter pulsed out to the horsemen.

It is no use, came Laban's response. *The net is too strong. You must send the others to help us.*

But when Winter looked, what was once ten angels around her

younger self had become thirty. The rest stood nearby in the infinite, ready to jump in. She couldn't ask any of them to leave. Not yet.

From far above, like a streak of black lightning, fell a hundred demons of Culsu's army, unseen to the angels protecting the younger Winter. They slammed in, scattering the angels. Magenel was flung through the air. Neshamah lay on the ground, struggling to get up. The others either had been knocked away or were being led away in battle. More of Winter's army entered, but with each one, ten more of Culsu's demons engaged. They really were outnumbered. Culsu had been hiding her real strength the whole time.

"I have taught you sorrow," Culsu said with another step forward, still growing. "Now I will teach you despair." The last word hung in the air, morphing into an ear-piercing screech that became her entire army screaming at the same time.

The younger Winter wobbled back, covering her ears, and then fell to the ground beside the screaming Peter, Kaci, and Ayden.

Magenel still couldn't get to her.

Neshamah had been dragged away.

The other angels were struggling to survive, and she had no more in reserve.

How much longer should she wait?

Laban! she cried.

Have faith, Prophetess. What has happened will happen.

Winter bit her lip. What did happen? Was it something else…or was it *her*? She stepped forward as Culsu bent down to stare in her younger self's face. Then Culsu reached for her head.

Winter reached out and almost…

Flash. Something shocked Culsu and she recoiled. Winter cast around and found all of her angels still accounted for and engaged elsewhere. What was that?

Culsu reached out with two hands this time. Flash. Culsu roared in the younger Winter's face.

Then Winter saw the glow in her younger eyes again. Something like a shockwave erupted from the younger Winter, sending Culsu's demons sprawling away from the angels. Magenel rushed to her side. Neshamah and the other angels reformed ranks.

Then a second later Winter heard Laban. *The wall is broken! God's power has breached it for us!*

From far away, Winter could see a side of the demonic dome crumbling. The angelic army cascaded in like a flood, streaking toward the younger Winter, who now stood on her feet, planted and staring down Culsu. The demons had resumed the attack, this time with their full numbers. Strengthened by the power coming from the younger Winter, the angels easily kept them back.

"Whatever power you wield is nothing compared to God's. Whether he fights for me or not, you will lose." The younger Winter took a step forward, and Culsu backed away while thrashing futilely at her. "But today…God fights."

Winter only stood back and watched, mouth open. The power in her younger self really was strong enough.

At the young Winter's words, the larger angelic army reached her. They swirled around, ripping away the demons trying to reach her through the smaller army, and then shot off to battle the Acolyte. Their momentum slammed fiercely, and Culsu's army fled. In the end, even Culsu could no longer stand the onslaught. She fled into the darkness, releasing Sophie to collapse upon the ground. As the other angelic army gave pursuit, Winter's forces stepped back into the spiritual unknown.

The younger Winter urged her friends to flee, but even as they hobbled away, the demon Xaphan loomed in the distance, surrounded by a million or more demons interlocked in a perfectly disciplined dome of shadows.

Winter shifted reality, sliding her forces through the train yard to a position ahead of the fleeing younger Winter and the others. "Stay out of the dome," she said. At a flick of her thoughts, the train cars became translucent and Winter watched Xaphan's approach.

Man and demon were nearly indistinguishable. The demon Xaphan leaned forward with cold, calculating eyes. The demon Culsu rushed to join the protection of the dome, chased by a blur of angels who crashed upon the demons like water upon a rock. All of Culsu's forces joined her, leading the pursuing angels in wild spirals and dives that ended with the demons inside the protective dome and the angels repelled by Xaphan's demons.

"Winter!" Xaphan called, his voice echoing through the night. "You have something of mine."

At the merest gesture, two branches of demons flew out of the dome, arching into a great crescent to surround the younger Winter. A few moments later, the younger Winter and the others came through the last gap between the boxcars, and the demonic arms slammed together to form an impenetrable wall.

"Stay back!" Winter shouted to her army as the two arms connected a mere thirty feet in front of them. "Horsemen, we will have to get in there to get them out. The other angels won't be able to break through. They are not strong enough. They can't fight both Culsu and Xaphan."

"These demons are dangerous, Prophetess," said Sors.

Winter spun on him. "So are you! I don't care if you're seen. I don't care what it takes…find out how to breach that wall!"

Sors nodded and the horsemen eased to the wall, careful to stay in the spiritual unknown so they could inspect its integrity without fighting.

Xaphan's dome crept closer. Between the wall and the dome, his demons made strategic strikes to lead the other angels away from the younger Winter. It wasn't long before there were no more angels to protect them. Even Magenel and Neshamah had somehow been wrested away and expelled beyond the wall.

Xaphan walked around the last boxcar into view, his dome of demons writhing and slinking around him, easily repelling any angel that came close.

The younger Winter and the others fell to the ground. The wall in front of Winter's army stretched upward and curved toward Xaphan. As it connected with Xaphan's dome, the demons rearranged and strengthened the entire dome with a uniform thickness, impenetrable to the angels.

"Laban!" Winter shouted over the screeches of the demons.

"We are trying, Prophetess!" he said.

Sophie screamed as Culsu's soldiers fell upon her. Culsu emerged from her position in the wall, eyes glowing red, and reclaimed Sophie. After a moment of thrashing on the ground, Culsu projected the image of Claire again and stood.

Winter felt helpless. She remembered feeling helpless then and she felt even more so now. Somehow help had gotten in before. What was different? What did she need to do?

Thousands of demons fell from the outer wall of the dome to fill in the empty space, descending upon young Winter, Kaci, Peter, and Ayden as they huddled together.

"Laban!" she shouted again. "Hurry!"

"There is no weakness, Prophetess! We are not strong enough!"

"We have to do something!"

"Only God has the strength. If he does not intervene..." Suddenly the demons inside screeched, and Laban turned to Winter with a twinkle in his eyes.

"What?" she asked.

The horsemen galloped back to her, each of them seeming to grow in size and strength.

"What's happening?" Then she felt it too...the burning, tightening of her skin, the glow that came from within, the rumbling in her ear, all of which meant only one thing...God intervened.

Laban shook his sword. "Prayer! God is giving us new strength for this task!"

Winter spun to face her entire army. The rumbling whispered the right sequence of commands into her ears. "We break in and we get them out! Half of you are the tip of the spear. Strike here," she pointed to the wall, "seven wide and make the path. The horsemen follow. As the horsemen push back Xaphan and Culsu, the second half of you are to make the others safe. Give them the time and protection they need to escape! Understood?"

They acknowledged with a booming whoop and rearranged according to her instructions as Winter stepped out of the way and faced the demonic wall.

"Stand ready!" she shouted.

Another booming whoop.

The younger Winter and Kaci sat up and clung to each other, and Winter felt the final surge of power they needed to break through. "NOW!"

They crashed into the wall and it crumbled like a failing dam. At the breach, her army flashed in like lightning, ripping demons away and pulling them into the air in violent swirling combat. Their ferocity sent a shockwave of panic through most of the unsuspecting demons.

In seconds, a corridor had been won. The horsemen thundered in, and behind them came the second half of the army. They shored up the corridor and pushed against the horde to keep the path clear.

Adom and Sharok leapt their steeds over the younger Winter, Adom rearing at Xaphan and Sharok rushing toward Culsu. Laban and Sors slid to a halt on either side of the younger Winter.

With the newfound power given to the angels, neither Xaphan's army nor Culsu's could find an advantage. They roiled in confusion and frustration, some fleeing from the battle. The breach in the wall had grown until barely any wall remained, most of the demons either scattering or taking their chances against the less powerful angels as the larger angelic army rejoined the fray.

The younger Winter stood now, holding on to Kaci. Ayden stood with her and helped Peter up. They rushed toward safety beyond the buildings and to the hill where Winter's car waited. As they approached Winter's vantage point, the younger Winter glanced up and saw Winter in the form of Rebecca standing there.

"You!" the younger Winter shouted. "You did this? Who are you?"

"Winter!" shouted Ayden. "We don't have time!"

Winter phased more firmly into the unknown before the younger Winter turned back.

Back in the battle, Xaphan and Culsu retreated now that their armies had scattered like gnats. With a flicker of thought, Winter sent out the command to withdraw.

∞

In the infinite, the horsemen returned to her side.

"We have revealed our strength," said Adom.

"The enemy will prepare accordingly," said Sors.

"We have lost the element of surprise," said Sharok.

Winter eyed Laban, his face etched with a deep concern. "What do you have to say?" she asked.

"All they say is true, yet we knew this moment would come. Culsu already guessed much of our strength. Perhaps Xaphan already knew. I am more concerned over that which I did not know would come."

"And that is?"

He frowned even deeper. "Your younger self has now been granted the ability to see beyond the veil. If we step out of the infinite into the spiritual now for even a moment in her presence, she may be able to see us."

Winter nodded. "Yes. This was always meant to happen. I should have told you."

Laban took a deep relaxing breath. "Prophetess, you did not deem it necessary...indeed it was not. But it was unexpected."

Winter eyed all four horsemen. "We must be more cautious with our presence, though we'll do what has to be done. My younger self must not know all that we are doing. Xaphan has retreated, but he'll return even stronger. We have to lay down a foundation to make sure he fails. Yes, we've revealed our strength. Yes, he'll prepare accordingly. And yes, we've lost the element of surprise. But there's one thing he does not know about…me. I've already fought this battle once, and we go to fight it again soon. When the final battle comes…" She bit her lip, thinking about Kaci, still trying to work out a way to save her. She took a deep breath and continued. "When the final battle comes, this time there will be two of me."

"The ways of the Lord are indeed strange," whispered Adom.

"Maybe," said Winter. "But it's the only way." She looked at Laban. "Does the army need rest?"

He shook his head. "The infinite is pure. When we enter the infinite our strength returns."

Restoring energy surged through Winter, too. She straightened and inspected the army, now noticing just how refreshed and ready they appeared. "Then let's go."

Reality shifted. Winter simultaneously followed the timelines of herself and Kaci, blurring the scenes together in a constantly evolving mashup. The wedding and its preparations. Finding and moving into the apartment.

Winter slowed things down to the natural pace and watched the unloading at the apartment. "We have to be watchful," she said. "Xaphan will come from different directions at once. He'll attack here and at the school. I need patrols in both places so we arrive at the right time. He may try other things too that I never knew about. So I want perimeters around the apartment, the school, Peter's job…Everywhere any of them will be, send a large enough detail that can report back. No more hiding in the infinite. We stay vigilant and visible. I alone will wait from the infinite where I can receive the reports instantly."

"It will be done, Prophetess," said Laban.

"I want at least one horseman here at the apartment at all times."

"Yes, Prophetess. I will stand guard here myself."

"And I need scouts. We need to find Culsu, Moloch, and Mavka, before we battle the demon Xaphan."

"Mavka has not been revealed to us yet," said Sharok.

"Another dangerous enemy," said Sors. "Perhaps more so than the other two."

"She is coming," said Winter. "In human form, she calls herself the Wretch."

The horsemen nodded and then divided the army. The army separated and stepped from the infinite, and it wasn't long before Winter found herself alone in the white expanse. She projected reality around her, scanned the images of time herself. She had only gone a few days when Adom materialized in front of her.

"Prophetess, there is trouble…two weeks from the time you are watching."

Winter immediately shifted time in a broad swath. "Where?"

"At the school."

Then Laban materialized. "An attack is forming at the apartment."

"Of course," Winter muttered. "The school attack is a diversion for the other, but we have to be at both."

Winter paused the shifting of reality over the Meadow. A black cloud hung over the administration building, writhing with anticipation.

"Vultures," said Adom. "They are awaiting death."

"Yes," said Winter. "One-third of the army is to join Laban watching Kaci. Bring the rest here."

"Yes, Prophetess."

A heartbeat later, hundreds of warriors and two more horsemen stood beside her.

She glanced up to the horsemen. "Have the army stay out of sight as best you can. I don't want my younger self seeing so many at once, but they need to stay in the spiritual now. I want the enemy to know we are here." She pointed to the religion building. "I need one of you to attract the attention of my younger self. She needs to be ready. Help her save as many people as possible. I have other things to do, so I'm trusting in you."

Adom nodded. "It will be as you command, Prophetess."

Winter shifted reality away from her army. The Meadow blurred beneath her feet as she soared away alone. She phased through the wall of the administration building and stopped in Dr. Streffield's office.

Winter took a deep breath, assumed the form of Rebecca, and stepped fully into the office.

Dr. Streffield immediately stood. "Who are you? Where did you come from? What's happening?"

Winter stepped toward him. "I am not of this world and I came to help. I will disappear in a moment, so you must listen quickly."

His eyes widened, but he didn't speak.

"You have information on your computer that Winter needs."

"How do you know that?" he asked.

"The time for stalling is over. You cannot wait anymore. She has to have that information. Quickly. We have only minutes."

"I don't understand," he said.

"A flashdrive. Save it onto a flashdrive now."

"Now?"

Winter phased through space, suddenly inches from his desk, her hair blowing backward with the speed. "NOW!"

Dr. Streffield jerked open his top desk drawer and fumbled in it, tossing stuff on the ground. Panic etched its way across his face. Finally, he found a flashdrive and plugged it into the side of his computer.

"What's happening?" he asked as he clicked the mouse.

Winter firmed her lips. "You don't want to know."

Dr. Streffield's face paled. "Do I need to call in a warning?"

Winter shook her head. "There is no time. You have to get this information safe first. We have only moments."

"Hello," cooed a sing-song voice.

Winter spun to see the Wretch standing in the center of the office, her long blonde hair covering her naked body as water pooled onto the floor. She tilted her head and watched Winter with her pale eyes.

"I was hoping I would meet you soon," said Mavka. "My brothers and sisters have told me of the power of the Prophetess."

Winter heard Streffield's typing stop so she spun on him. "Keep working."

Mavka fixed her gaze on Streffield and glided toward him.

"No," Winter said, stepping to block her.

"No?" Mavka asked. "I am here to take him. Will you stop me, child?"

"I will do what I have to do," said Winter, her mind poised to call her army to her side.

Mavka narrowed her eyes and whispered. "Shall I test my strength now?" she said as if to herself. The demon sighed and then rose up to fly through the ceiling.

"What was that?" Streffield asked.

"A demon," she said, turning back to him.

He yanked out the drive and thrust it at her with a trembling hand. "Here. Take it."

Winter backed away, shaking her head. "No. You have to give it to her."

"I thought you said there isn't enough time."

"There isn't. Grasp it tightly in your hand."

Dr. Streffield wrapped his fingers around it and squeezed.

"No matter what happens next," Winter told him, "do not let it go until you put it directly into Winter's hands."

He didn't have time to respond. A sudden and ear-shattering boom tore the room apart.

Winter stepped away from the explosion back to the infinite, wishing she could do something, but her younger self waited below to help. Instead, she shifted reality, flitting time forward slightly, until she arrived at the apartment moments before Kaci and Peter were taken. Laban saw her coming and met her in the spiritual unknown.

"I feel my brothers at work," Laban said.

Winter nodded. "There will be work here soon. Are we ready?"

Laban guided his horse to her side and Winter felt the presence of the angelic forces gathered around and watching. "We are ready, Prophetess."

They waited silently as time ticked normally, and within just a few minutes a black cloud of demons approached from the horizon. It hovered in the distance behind the apartment for several minutes and then slowly crept through the forest toward the apartment. The demonic cloud paused about a hundred yards away and descended into the trees.

All was still and silent. Winter eyed Laban, who watched unflinching. The soldiers waited as still as statues behind her.

Then out of nowhere, six men rushed around the apartment and into Peter's and Kaci's unlocked door. Kaci screamed. Peter shouted. Then the men exited…three dragging the unconscious Peter, and the other three escorting the still struggling Kaci. The demons descended and picked apart the angels surrounding Kaci and Peter.

"Do we engage, Prophetess?"

"Not yet," Winter said, narrowing her eyes.

The men dragged Peter and Kaci in two different directions. Winter peeled away the substance of reality so she could watch their progress in both directions. She saw the hulking demon waiting near the getaway car.

"Moloch is here," she whispered.

"Yes," said Laban. "His vessel may have died, but the demon lives on."

Finally, Winter's black BMW slid into the parking lot. It was time to engage. As the younger Winter, Ayden, and Graham exited the car, Winter relayed instructions to Laban.

"Half the soldiers with Ayden," Winter said. "Half with my younger self. Now!"

The angels split up and crashed into reality, swirling and rushing into the forest in both directions. The demons that had been hanging back scattered and fled to warn the others, but were quickly cut down by Winter's forces.

Winter glanced at Laban. "You and I will confront Moloch. We cannot have him getting involved in this."

"Moloch is strong."

Winter shifted them through space toward the demon. "We don't have to fight him or defeat him. Just distract him."

All around them, Winter's elite angelic army battled the weaker demons, taking care of the spiritual threat while younger Winter and Ayden fought the physical. Winter and her angels passed young Winter and Ayden, and Winter solidified herself as Rebecca in front of Moloch, just out of his reach.

The demon narrowed his eyes, lowering his horned head. "Your deception is weak. I see you, Prophetess. Do you defy me again?"

"I will defy you always," Winter said. "Look around you. My army is defeating yours. You have lost your advantage."

The demon huffed long tendrils of black smoke. "Do you think I have not the strength to defeat these winged pests?"

"Do you think you have the strength to defeat the power inside of me?" With a flicker of thought command from Winter, Laban circled behind the demon and materialized.

Moloch bellowed and spun to keep an eye on both of them. "I do not fear the horsemen!"

Laban drew his sword and it flared with fire. Winter and Laban both stepped forward, and the demon backed away.

Behind her, two men dragged Kaci through the brush toward the car. A moment later two gunshots rang out. The men screamed and fell to the ground. Kaci fled back into the forest.

Winter didn't flinch. She simply stepped closer to Moloch, letting the power swell within her. Then her angelic army arrived and converged around Moloch, surrounding him.

"Look around," said Winter. "Is this the fight your master wants you to have? You are nothing alone!"

Moloch bellowed again, crouched, and then launched himself into the air. He vanished after only a few feet.

Winter took a deep breath and smiled at Laban. He sheathed his sword and nodded.

"Moloch, Culsu, Mavka, Xaphan," said Laban. "We are not strong enough to defeat them at once."

"Then we have to defeat them one at a time," said Winter. "No more waiting. We must search out and destroy them."

"Agreed," said Laban.

"A third of the army stays with Kaci at all times from here on out, unless recalled. Appoint one horseman. I'll need the rest with me. I'll meet you in the infinite momentarily. Be ready."

Laban nodded.

Winter sped time away from him to that same night and approached her younger self struggling to sleep on the couch in Kaci's empty apartment. Beside the younger Winter, Magenel waited and watched the older Winter. He didn't speak, but he stepped to one side as she drew near.

Winter acknowledged him with a nod and then placed one hand on her younger self. A gentle nudge from Winter pushed her younger self over the edge and into unconsciousness. Winter fell in with her, pulling her younger self to the dream she needed. She painted a picture of Tishbe University destroyed. Every building around the Meadow lay in piles of rubble, bodies of the dead lay in rows. She painted the destruction throughout Cherithville and even the world, showing her younger self exactly what would happen if they failed.

The dreaming younger Winter stood in the middle of the Meadow, gazing into the distance. Winter materialized behind her in the form of Rebecca.

"It's more than you know," she said.

Her younger self spun around. "Who are you?"

"That's not important."

"Why not?"

Winter frowned, frustrated that her younger self remained so fixated. "Please. Focus on what is at stake. This hasn't happened yet. It's all up to you. His plans go beyond this place to the entirety of the world, but it's your choices that will determine whether or not he succeeds. No matter what happens, you can't let her or the baby die."

"I'm leaving to find Xaphan and stop him. What else am I supposed to do?" the younger Winter asked, kneeling on the ground to face her eye-to-eye.

"You already know. "

The younger Winter narrowed her eyes. "Who are you?"

"You have to finish this," Winter told her. "And in the end, you will have to finish it alone." She gave herself a sad smile, knowing her younger self didn't realize the deep truth in that statement.

Then she released the dream while her younger self still called out for answers. She stepped back into spiritual now, cast a look at Magenel and then stepped into the infinite to find Laban and the other three horsemen waiting for her.

"Culsu is the weakest of the four," Winter said. "We will find her first. It's time this demon paid for what it has done to me and my friends."

The infinite shifted, and visions of reality passed by. Winter focused on the demon, and soon Culsu soared before them, flying through the air. Winter let time stand still and studied the frozen Culsu for a moment, seeing the determination in her red demonic eyes.

"She is alone," said Adom. "I do not understand."

"She has been waiting for Xaphan to call her back," said Winter. "With Mavka and Moloch on the move, Culsu has been commanded to return. She's flying back to Sophie, and she senses that my younger self is with Sophie now. Look at the eagerness in her face."

"These demons are taking human hosts so they can attack within the physical world," said Sors.

"An abomination!" cried Adom.

"What do you command?" asked Laban.

Winter lowered her chin. "Destroy her."

And then they were out of the infinite, in real time, surrounding the demon. Culsu shrieked but didn't engage immediately. Without other demons to rally to her side, she fled at the speed of light. The angels easily kept pace, closing ranks around her and probing for openings in Culsu's defensive arms.

The battle raged as they sped through the sky, surrounding Culsu in a globe of angelic light. The horsemen circled, casting out orders. The warriors pushed in, hacking at the arms and finally reaching her body. A dozen angels pierced her side with fiery swords at once.

Culsu screamed and fell from the sky. The angels fell with her, continuing their assault. Finally, they pummeled to the ground, and once Culsu had her feet, she ran.

The horsemen ran along her side, but Culsu now found demons to draw to her aid. One by one, the angelic soldiers engaged other enemies, giving Culsu more room to run. An abandoned power plant lay ahead. A cloud of demons swirled around it. Small demons, but outnumbering the angels two-to-one. They scattered as Culsu approached, but with a loud cry, they rallied to her side and sped toward the angels.

The angelic army handled the new threat easily, but Culsu still could not be caught. She vanished into the building, and through the translucent walls Winter watched her rampage throughout the room. As the demons surrounding Culsu united to push back the angels, Culsu murdered every human in the room. First, sending shards of glass into one, then possessing a second and ripping the arms off the third. Cain Golia fired gunshots at the possessed man, shattering his chest. Culsu released the dead man, wrapped her fingers around

Cain's head, and Cain turned the gun upon himself.

The wrath of Culsu fell so swiftly Winter didn't have time to save any of them. Culsu spun to the back room, extending arms out of her back to fend off any angels that breached her demons. She opened the door, and paused.

The younger Winter stood there facing the demon, guarding Sophie. Culsu moved in. Sophie screamed.

"No!" the younger Winter shouted. "You can't have her!"

Culsu paused again and then eased forward once more. The younger Winter extended both arms to push Culsu back, but Culsu easily slid her backward. The demon laughed.

The younger Winter's eyes began to glow. The angels brightened in strength. Culsu's laughter turned to anger as the strength of the angels halted her advance.

Then Culsu broke away, scattering into a million shadows, swirling around the room, and descending upon Sophie.

As the younger Winter fled into the main room, the angels finally shoved away the weaker demons. The angels took positions around Winter and waited for Culsu.

The younger Winter hid behind a work table as Culsu entered, fully in control of Sophie, and now wearing the form of Claire.

Wait, Winter thought out to her army. *We have to get my other self out of here.*

The angels stood down and moved to surround Culsu, standing in the spiritual now but half in the infinite, enough to be seen but not enough to be touched. Culsu studied them. She spotted the horsemen behind the ranks and shouted. "Winter!"

Winter waited on the edge of the infinite, not yet ready to step in or be seen.

"Why are you hiding? I know you're here," Culsu said, still surveying the entire army. "We have much to talk about since we last spoke. You are a curious puzzle. I'd like to know more about what you are."

Culsu moved deeper into the room and the angels shifted to keep Culsu perfectly in the center of their circle. Culsu fixed her eyes on the horsemen and roared, "Show yourself!" She turned a full circle, eying the soldiers more venomously. "It doesn't matter how much power you bring against me, I will destroy you this time. I've been waiting for you. I knew you would come again. Does it help you to know that Sophie's in here with me? Screaming to get out? She feels the pain, you know. Anytime something happens to me, Sophie is the conduit for all that pain. This is why you will fail. Your compassion is your weakness. You wouldn't want to hurt her, would you? I shall enjoy ripping your skin off, and not even the entire horde of Heaven can stop me!"

Winter had heard enough. She stepped fully into reality, fists clenched, skin tight, and eyes glowing. Claire smiled at her. "There you are."

Suddenly, the younger Winter stood up, eyes closed tight, and started walking straight toward Culsu.

Culsu pivoted to face her. "What is this? Another trick?"

As the younger Winter passed by the nearest angels, they swirled, swords extended, creating a solid bubble around her.

"What are you doing?" asked Culsu as she backed away from the approaching flurry of angels. The rest of the army phased fully out of the spiritual now and closed in unseen.

Culsu spun circles in panic, searching for the army, glancing from one Winter to the other. "Where are they? Show them! I will not be tricked!"

Then Culsu roared and pummeled against the cloud of angels around the younger Winter. White flashes filled the room as the angels deflected each blow.

The younger Winter turned toward the exit. Culsu followed, still unable to penetrate the cloud.

"NO! I won't let you escape me! Not this time!" She cursed and shouted. The angels flashed with each deflected blow.

"NO!" Culsu leaned in close to the younger Winter. "You're mine! You're mine!"

The younger Winter stopped, turned around, and opened her eyes.

Winter phased through the infinite to stand right beside herself in the spiritual now, where Culsu could see the both of them. Culsu stumbled back, eyes bulging.

"We'll meet again," said the younger Winter to Culsu. "But I want you to remember this moment right now the next time you think your power could ever be stronger than the power God pours into me." She balled her fist, drew it back, and aimed for Claire's face.

Winter pulsed out a command to her army, and a hundred angels wrapped around the fist and slammed into Culsu like a hammer.

Culsu, the body of Sophie, and the form of Claire, flew across the room and slammed into the far wall.

As the younger Winter left, Winter crossed to stand over Culsu. Her army gathered around, sword tips toward the demon. The horsemen stood two to either side of her.

When Culsu recovered and gazed up, she screamed, a screech of terror and panic. "What are you? What are you?"

"I told you we would meet again," Winter said.

"This is impossible!" shouted Culsu. She reached out with four arms to strike at Winter. The horsemen moved to intercept, but the arms came up short as they hit an invisible wall not caused by any angel present.

Winter held a steadying hand to the horsemen. The power racing through her from God was beyond anything she had ever felt. Her skin stretched tighter than ever. She took a step closer to Culsu.

"You will leave Sophie and never return to her." Her voice resonated throughout the room.

"She is mine!"

Winter took a deep breath and let the power flow through her, nothing of her own, but her body as the conduit. In that moment, her mind was completely connected with the Holy Spirit…her thoughts in perfect sync.

"Get off of her," Winter said, not as a suggestion or request, but as a command that could not be refused.

Culsu screeched and writhed as she rose into the air, leaving Sophie unconscious on the ground.

"You are defeated and will be chained," Winter said calmly. At those words, ethereal bands wrapped around all of Culsu's limbs and around her neck.

Culsu thrashed against them, screaming in pain.

"You will be bound to Hell, never to return."

Culsu's shrieks reached a new feverish pitch. The ethereal chains seemed to pull and stretch her. Light emanated from the infinite, to encapsulate the demon in a bright shell. And then Culsu was gone.

Winter collapsed. The power had so taken hold of her, that her body could barely respond on its own.

Laban quickly dismounted to help her stand again, concern etched on his face. "You are human. You were never meant to contain so much raw power from God."

Winter pushed through the fatigue and straightened. "I'm fine."

"Winter?" asked Sophie.

Winter knelt beside Sophie on the ground. A trickle of blood flowed from Sophie's head, but her eyes looked up at Winter with clarity.

"You're free now. Completely," said Winter.

"Completely?"

"Culsu is gone."

A smile crept on Sophie's face. "Thank you…"

"I didn't do it. God did. He has a plan for you, and I suggest you use your new freedom to find out about it."

Sophie nodded. "How?"

Winter stood and backed toward her army. "You already know where to start. I'm sure you'll figure the rest out just fine." She and her army stepped back into the infinite.

Without waiting, she turned to the horsemen. "Culsu is defeated. I should have had Mavka and Moloch bound in the same way when I had the chance."

"The pattern weaves, Prophetess," said Laban.

"Yes. I need to find them again, but I'm not sure where to start."

"These demons are deep in the council of Xaphan," said Sors. "More so than Culsu."

"They may be near to him, waiting his commands," said Sharok.

"Find Xaphan and we can draw out the others, one at a time," said Adom.

"Prophetess," said Laban, "remember to follow your memories."

Winter closed her eyes in thought, searching her memories for places she may have encountered the demon Xaphan again.

"Xaphan's mansion," she said, looking forward to a blank space of the infinite. "Xaphan was there, but so was Mavka."

She filled the space with images of reality blurring by in mixed times and locations. Finally, she settled on Xaphan's mansion from high above. A hazy shell of demons hung over it. Reality soared around Winter and the horsemen until they were in the middle of the entrance hall.

The grand staircase rose up before them as they stepped into the spiritual unknown. Divine power coursed through her, and with an outstretched hand to the horsemen to remain unseen, she stepped completely into reality and planted her feet, this time as herself, not Rebecca.

"Xaphan!" she called. "I'm here! I'm waiting for you!"

The silence grew thick as demons swirled in, surrounding her but not daring to come close. Some watched eagerly, some cowered. But they all knew her.

The demon Xaphan rose first from the floor, like the head of a giant serpent, wider than the staircase, grinning teeth longer than Winter was tall. A moment later, the man came out of the secret door and the demon retracted to settle around him as a perfect skin. Demon and man calmly paced to the front of the stairs and faced Winter.

He cocked his head to one side. "Interesting."

"This ends tonight."

"I'm not sure that it does."

Winter gritted her teeth. "I won't let you hurt anyone else."

He held a casual finger out to her. "Tell me…how is it that moments ago I found you in my office? I saw you with my own eyes fleeing through my escape passage. But now I find you here, and obviously no longer fleeing."

Winter pursed her lips and curled her fists.

"How do you plan to stop me? Did you bring your horsemen with you?" His face twisted into a sneer. "I have summoned the princes of Hell to my side, more powerful than your puny horsemen."

Winter pulsed out a command and her army materialized. The horsemen stepped to her side.

"And now your playthings appear. While they stand here idle, my princes are at work." He snarled and spoke quickly. "The prince Mavka pursues your doppelgänger now. She will take away your rest. The prince Moloch hunts your friends and family, and you will weep bitterly when he is done. The prince Culsu guides my followers in the preparations that will kill millions of innocent people. And with my work, I shall be named chief prince of Hell, and you shall feel my fire, Prophetess. Can you defeat us all?"

A flicker of thought sent two horsemen and a third of the army after Mavka. Then Winter took a deep breath. "Culsu is gone. She is bound. The others will be bound as well." Winter raised an eyebrow, lips curving in a slight smile. "Did you not know?"

Xaphan's nostrils flared. He reached out with both arms and the demon inside him doubled in size, extending its arms to slam into Winter. Hundreds of demons descended, but they all crashed into a bright white shield. The resulting recoil sent a shockwave through the house, knocking paintings from the walls, exploding lights, and rattling the chandeliers.

Winter stepped forward, ready to bind Xaphan right then, as her army engaged the demonic horde.

Xaphan growled and struck out again, stronger, bigger, more powerful. The entire body of demons surrounding his home rallied to plummet onto them, but any that survived her army were met by the same white shield around Winter.

The power coursing through Winter flowed stronger than she had ever felt. She could sense it boiling in the two horsemen behind her, her army around them fighting the demons, and even the horsemen and soldiers who now battled Mavka in the forest.

It could be over. It should be over.

Xaphan struck again. And again. Each blow recoiling through the building, shaking the walls and trembling the foundation. Mortar flaked from the ceilings and walls. Demons began to flee. The chandelier in the entry hall crashed to the ground. Smoke billowed into the room.

Winter continued to walk toward the demon. Just a little closer. She reached out her hand, focusing the power to grab Xaphan, ready to place the chains on him.

Fear crossed Xaphan's face, both the face of the man and of the demon. Deep, trembling fear shivered through the remaining demons, scattering them like bats to leave Xaphan alone. And then…

Xaphan ran.

The man turned and bolted for the back door, demon screeching in panic. Winter's heart drummed and she reached out quickly with the power to grab the demon. Both demon and man fell backward, but the bond was too hasty. There wasn't enough strength to keep them long. The man pulled free from the demon and continued to run. The demon stood, jerked against the spiritual bonds and snapped them in a shower of sparks. With a shiver and a quick tornado-like spin, the demon disappeared. Winter grunted and rushed forward, but the man was gone as well.

"Prophetess," Laban said, and she turned to him. "This place is falling. A fire rages below. You have taken your human form, so you must remove yourself now."

Then she remembered. "Erickson! He's here, trapped. I have to get him out." She phased herself to the hallways beneath the mansion. Thick smoke floated against the ceiling. She ran through it, fully in reality, coughing as the smoke burned her lungs. She ran past Xaphan's office, past another adjoining hall, following a spiritual magnetic pull until she finally came to the right hall.

Thick iron doors lined the walls, each with a small rectangle cut into the bottom. A sturdy lock and knob waited for her when she found the correct door. Winter gave the lock no thought, but grabbed the knob and pulled. As she did so, she finally remembered to step out of the physical space and put on the form of Rebecca.

Erickson, pale and emaciated, his eyes wide with madness, rushed at her. But he stopped short when he saw her fully, disappointment on his face.

Winter frowned and stepped inside. "You need to escape."

"What have you done with her?" Erickson asked. "Where is she?"

Winter shook her head, not sure who he spoke about, and eased closer. "They have tainted you. But I will free your mind." Winter reached up and touched his forehead.

Erickson took a deep breath. The madness in his eyes disappeared. His shoulders straightened. Then a look of pain came over his face and he turned to one side and vomited.

"It will get better," Winter said. "There is only one person who can take the darkness away completely."

"Who?" he asked as he straightened and wiped his mouth.

"You already know. You just have to admit it to yourself."

Erickson glanced behind her to the hall. "What do I do now?" he asked.

"Escape," Winter said. "And then get to work. They still need your help."

Erickson nodded and then ran past her into the smoke-filled hall.

Winter stepped back into the spiritual unknown and shifted reality to find the rest of her army with Mavka, hoping she wasn't too late to chain the Wretch once and for all. But as reality flew by, her army met her halfway. She pulled them into the white space of the infinite.

"What happened?" she asked.

Sors shook his head. "Mavka is strong, Prophetess. We cannot contain her alone."

"It will take the divine strength within the Prophetess," said Adom.

Winter grunted in frustration. "They'll be coming after Kaci and me more than ever. We have to get to them first! Setup a perimeter to intercept them. Half with my other self, half with Kaci. Now!"

The horses pranced at the urgency in her voice, and her entire army immediately disappeared. Winter found herself alone in the pure white and quiet of the infinite. She took a deep breath, listening to the air rush in and out of her lungs. She could hear her drumming heartbeat slow to a calmer rhythm. Any moment one of the horsemen would return...

The air changed, filling with a charged spiritual energy that didn't come from her or directly from the infinite. She spun around expecting to see someone else behind her, as if eyes had been staring at her from far away, half hoping one of the horsemen had returned. Instead, she saw shadowy figures, with her in the infinite but shifted away from her as if the figures were in a different temporal point within the infinite itself. The figures faced each other about thirty feet from Winter, talking to one another in muted, garbled voices. It was a girl dressed all in black facing a man in white.

Winter eased a little closer, straining to hear them.

"And then what?" asked the girl in black, the voice muffled and jumbled as if the face were beneath a pillow. Still, Winter recognized something familiar about the shadowy girl and muted voice.

"And then you'll understand," said the man as he backed away…backing toward Winter. "Go. Get the answer you want." He turned to walk straight toward Winter.

Winter caught her breath and glanced around as if she could hide.

"Wait!" said the girl. Winter definitely recognized her. Was it…*her?*

"Yes?" asked the man as he half turned back.

"Um…thank you," said the girl. *Her.* Another, future, Winter.

"You're welcome," said the man. He continued walking, and within two steps his shadowiness fell away and he became crystal clear. He had dark olive skin and bright brown eyes. His black hair was pulled back and his dark beard reached just to the top of his chest. He wore blue jeans and a t-shirt. He winked at her as he walked past. "Shouldn't you go check on Kaci?" he asked.

Winter bit her lip and nodded. *That voice…* And then he vanished.

She looked back, but the future vision of herself had disappeared as well. Immediately, a sense of urgency fell upon her. She didn't know if the feeling of being caught doing nothing spurred her forward or if something truly needed her attention, but she did what the man said and drew images of reality so fast around her that all the colors blurred into an indistinguishable shade of brown. The images soared, drawn to Kaci like a magnet at some point in time near where Winter had just left her army. She wasn't sure where time might actually land, only that she needed to let God take her to the right moment.

She landed in the clouds high above a hospital and could sense all four horsemen nearby with the entire army, which meant both her slightly younger self and Kaci were below. And if they were both at the hospital, it meant time had progressed to the first week of April.

This happened only a month ago, she thought as she soared around the building, searching for any hidden demonic presence. She couldn't sense any. She descended into the building and found Laban standing in the spiritual unknown, watching over Kaci. The other three horsemen were elsewhere, patrolling…watching.

Kaci lay in an exam room of the ER. Her face was pale but harboring a smile. She was safe. Peter waited with her. So did the one-month younger Winter. An ultrasound technician moved a probe over the still-alive baby.

Winter felt another pang of guilt. She had to find a way to save them, but how? What happened would always happen. She couldn't change that…or so Laban kept saying. But wasn't this why she had the gift of prophecy? To protect Kaci and the child?

Laban acknowledged her with a nod and she returned the gesture. "Any news?" she asked.

"No, Prophetess. Neither Mavka nor Moloch have found us, and none of our scouts have found them. All is well and quiet. However, I hear whispers from my brothers that Ayden Shields and Greg Erickson have fought many demons far from here."

"That was the plan," Winter said softly.

The ultrasound tech spoke now, giving Kaci and Peter the news that they were having a baby boy. Soon after the tech left and a doctor came in, the younger Winter stood to leave.

Winter moved to the end of the hall from her other self and waited. She had to do something. She had to try again to warn her younger self. She had to tell her more. But what? How much could she dare to reveal directly?

Winter stepped into reality just enough so that her other self could see her. She took the form of Rebecca again. When her younger self glanced her way, they made eye contact and Winter crooked her finger for the younger Winter to follow.

Winter led herself through hallways of the hospital, always staying out of reach and shifting through the infinite a little if her younger self came too close. They arrived in an empty wing and Winter stopped to wait for her younger self. When the younger Winter rounded the corner, Winter led her into an empty patient room and stood at the foot of the vacant bed.

The younger Winter slid to a halt after sprinting in. "Who are you?"

Winter needed to answer the question this time, but how? How could she explain any of this? How could she give a warning that would make sense? She knew what the other Winter thought...knew her younger self suspected her of being her own unborn daughter. She was right, though not in the way she thought. Still, she deserved to know at least who she saw, even if it was only an illusion.

"A little girl never loved. Never held. Eternally in the arms of God," she told her younger self. It was enough. The younger Winter's hand dropped to her abdomen and tears welled up in her eyes.

"But how?"

The question she couldn't answer... Winter bit her lip. "It doesn't matter how. I am here now like this because you've needed me."

The younger Winter took a small step forward. "You've been helping me?"

Winter nodded.

The younger Winter burst into tears and fell to her knees, gazing upon her with streaming, glistening eyes. "I am so sorry...I wish I could have..."

"What is done is done," Winter said. "What has been done was meant to be done and cannot be undone. There's nothing you can do to change it, and you shouldn't anyway. Your past has led you here. Without your past you could not face the future. And what you do here today and in the near future is what you were always meant to do. I have seen it and soon you will see it too. It will happen, has always happened, and is even happening now." Winter realized she might have said too much.

The younger Winter rubbed her eyes with the heels of her hands.

"What am I supposed to do with that?"

"Be encouraged. You may not understand why or how, but things are as they should be. Keep going. You're almost there."

"Is that the only reason you came?" asked the younger Winter. "To tell me to keep going? After everything that's happened, all the times you've refused to talk to me, you're doing this now? What else is there? Why are you really speaking to me?"

"You have to save Kaci and the child. You have to do whatever it takes. Don't..." Don't do what? How could she explain? What could she say that could make a difference? "Don't leave her. Ever. Every moment from now until Xaphan is defeated, stay at her side."

The younger Winter nodded. "Okay. I'll try."

"And you need to tell Graham how you feel. Tell him before it's too late. I know you. I know your thoughts. I know you will keep your feelings bottled inside and you'll miss something good right in front of you. You need to let your heart love again, even if it's for a short time."

"How do you know?"

"Because I'm a part of you." Winter's heart ached to be back in Graham's arms. "Tell him."

"And what if he doesn't feel the same?"

Winter laughed. "He does. You're just too stubborn to admit it to yourself."

"I don't know if I can," said the younger Winter.

"You will. You've already done it. You just don't know it yet."

At that moment, Laban arrived behind the younger Winter. Winter caught his grim face and knew he came to summon her. Magenel noticed too and grabbed for his sword. Winter knew what was about to happen. If she could change anything, maybe she could start with this...her dad.

The younger Winter sensed something too. "Don't go," she whispered. "I don't even know your name."

Winter gave her a soft smile. "Yes you do."

"But I'll never see you again…"

"You will. I promise. Just not here." Winter backed away from her younger self.

"I need you," sobbed the younger Winter.

Winter shook her head. "Not anymore. You're almost ready now. Go. Tell him." She stepped fully into the infinite white and found her army waiting for her in orderly ranks.

Laban urged his horse forward. "A scout has located the demon Moloch."

"I know," Winter said, feeling the pit of her stomach drop. "I know."

The infinite shifted at Winter's thought until her army stood on the street where she used to live.

The house still stood intact in the night. Her dad's truck sat in the drive as she had last seen it. Beneath a streetlight several houses away waited another vehicle that Winter recognized as one the ones that had pursued her and Graham away from the explosion. Her younger self had not arrived yet. That was good. Maybe she could fix this before anything happened.

In the dark yard, watching the house with ape-like muscular arms stretched out to either side as if to embrace the structure, stood the hulking form of Moloch. His long black face had an almost bovine quality from the side. Flies swarmed around him in a thick cloud. A breeze wafted the stench of rotting flesh.

Winter clenched her teeth and ran toward him, anger flashing, shame numbing her chest. "No!" she screamed. "I won't let you!" As she came within mere feet of him, she clenched her fists and prepared to launch it into his face.

Moloch turned to her in a blur. One giant arm swung around, hammered into her shoulder, and easily drove her into the ground.

And then the horsemen were there. Laban pulled her back to safety on foot as the other three engaged Moloch on horseback. Unlike the multi-armed elusive Culsu, Moloch fought with brute strength, grasping swords and swinging groups of angels through the air.

Winter panted as she lay on the ground. Laban swung into his saddle and joined the battle. Moloch spun around as the horsemen circled him, and the angel army reformed to encapsulate the demon in a glowing sphere.

"Prophetess!" Laban called to her. "We have him!"

Winter knew what needed to be done. Moloch had to be bound immediately. If she had known Moloch was responsible for her dad's death, she would have done so at the tree or behind the apartment. If she had, maybe things would have been different. She let the anger of the what-ifs course through her and stood.

Things could be different now.

Moloch continued to pound against her army, and they fought back valiantly, keeping him contained. But in the end they would never be powerful enough to defeat any enemy...not in the way these demonic princes needed to be defeated. That power only came from God.

God could have easily endowed Laban or any of the angels present as a conduit for that power. For that matter, he could have appeared himself or enacted some other divine intervention of his choosing. But for these battles, for this time, *she* had been chosen as the conduit.

Winter stood and cleared her mind, emptying herself of herself and allowing the rumble that signified the power of God to fill every cell of her body. Again her skin stretched and pulled, and now she understood what that meant. Her finite human body was never designed to contain the pure unbridled power of God. The more he poured into her, the more likely her body would tear apart. If she ever experienced the full presence and power of God while in her human body, she would die.

Moses had to hide behind a rock to experience the full power of God, and he still came down from the mountain with his face glowing. What would happen to her if this kept up?

Winter stepped confidently forward, not of her own strength, but in the infinite power she had been connected to. The angels parted to allow her to pass into the containment field.

Moloch turned defiantly to face her and spoke with a deep, resonating bass. "And it shall be that the doom of Moloch will come from a child."

Winter raised her hand and the power flowed through her ready to bind Moloch with chains. Whether the thought to do it came from the power or the power obeyed the thought, she couldn't tell, but the thought and the power were inseparable. And neither thought nor power belonged to Winter.

"You are defeated and will be chained," Winter said, her own voice strange to her ears as if it flowed along the currents of a raging river. At those words, ethereal bands wrapped around Moloch's arms and legs and pulled tight.

"I may be bound, child Prophetess, but my deed is done. You will suffer even as I suffer," boomed Moloch.

"You will be bound to Hell, never to return," Winter said, and a brilliant ball of light swirled around Moloch. The light grew until he could no longer be seen, and then it vanished.

Moloch was gone, but it was too late.

"Where is he?!" Winter heard her own voice yelling from the street.

She turned to see her younger self there standing near her black BMW. Graham stood beside her, pulling her back toward the car.

The power drained from Winter. Her heart pounded and cold sweat broke out on her skin. "No…"

"Dad!" yelled the younger Winter, looking up at the house.

Winter spun and looked up too. "NO!" Then with a flicker of thought time froze.

Laban stepped to her side in the stillness. "You cannot undo what has already been done."

Winter felt her face contort. "Shut up! This is my fault! We've seen Moloch twice already! If I had bound him then, this wouldn't have happened!"

"Whether by Moloch's supervision or another's, this would have always happened. It is part of the pattern."

"No! I will not watch him die again, do you hear me? I will not!"

Laban pursed his lips and backed away.

Winter wept at the silhouette of her dad in the window, knowing deep down she could do nothing even if she wanted. She shifted reality around her until she stood in the room with him. An angel waited by his side, ready to escort his soul. Winter reached out with a fresh surge of power and brought her dad into a bubble of the infinite where she could unbind him from time.

"RUN!" he was yelling as Winter released him from the time-lock.

"Dad..." she whispered.

His head jerked toward her and his eyes widened with panic, even though his bruised and swollen face could barely move. One eye had nearly swollen shut, and when he spoke, he could barely make his lips meet. "I don't know how you got here so fast, but run. Get out of here!"

Winter shook her head as the tears rolled. She knelt next to him and grabbed his face with both of her hands. A swirl of light surrounded him, and when it disappeared, his body was healed and the ropes had fallen from his hands.

"How..."

She shook her head again. "It's hard to explain. But look..." She pointed out the window to her younger self. "That's me. In the past."

Steve's mouth fell open. "How is that possible?"

Winter shrugged. "This is what I was meant to do." She reached out to embrace him, and the tears came so fast her breath caught in her throat. "I can't..."

He stroked the back of her hair. "You can't what?"

"I can't save you," she croaked.

He gently pushed her to arm's length and stared her in the eyes. "A few moments ago I was ready to die. All I wanted was for you to be safe. Nothing has changed. If you can't save me, that means you came here to tell me goodbye."

Winter's chin quivered. "Dad..."

"You're safe. I don't know how this has happened now, but you really have become an amazing woman. I am proud to be your father. We had our rough moments, I know, and there's not a day that goes by that I don't regret each one. But I am so proud of you."

Winter couldn't help herself. She climbed into his lap and held on to him tight. "I love you," she said into his shoulder.

"I love you."

Winter wept against him for a long time. Here in the infinite, she could cry as long as she needed. Eventually, she quieted, and Steve eased her away again.

"You have something to do. You can't stay here forever." He kissed her forehead. "Go. Be amazing. Be what you were always meant to be." He pushed her enough so that she had to stand. Still she reached out to him. For a brief moment he touched her fingers in return, and then he faced the window and the younger Winter.

Winter shook her head furiously. "No...Dad, I can't..." She took a rushed step toward him, but when he held up his hand she stopped.

He glanced at her. "I'm ready."

She ran to him anyway and hugged him again. Then she backed away with her hand over her mouth. He faced the window again, and in that moment Winter released him back into the frozen reality.

She couldn't bear to watch. Without restarting time, she simply stepped completely into the white expanse of the infinite as time resumed. Once there, she fell to her knees and wept again, alone in the expanse. Minutes ticked by according to her own internal clock. Eventually her army gathered quietly around her. The horsemen dismounted and stood in a circle around her, backs to her, swords drawn and points down in front of them. They never spoke; they never hurried her.

She didn't know how much time had passed according to human measurements, but it felt like at least an hour. That same hole in her heart that had opened the first time she saw her dad die had reopened, but at least this time she'd gotten to say goodbye.

She rubbed her eyes dry and stood. As she planted her feet, the horsemen sheathed their swords and turned to her.

"We're almost to the end now," she said.

Laban nodded. "While you were here alone in your grief, we stayed to guard your younger self. A horde of demons arrived after Moloch's demise. They pursued your younger self vehemently. Other angels came to her aid, but were not enough. Your younger self was too distraught to call upon the Father's power. So we intervened and assured her escape."

Winter nodded. "Thank you. That's exactly what was supposed to happen. But no more chasing demons. This has to end now. We have to go get her."

"Get who?"

"Me," Winter said. "We have to get *me*. Together we will finally stop Xaphan." She brought them partially out of the infinite and they hovered over the forest where they could see the cabin not far away. "Things happen here, but we must not intervene. Xaphan has to think he's won." She thought a brief moment about Davis and about the abnormality painted in his brain so that he would survive. "We will find myself a few hours later at the hospital. Only then will everything and everyone be in place."

Winter shifted time and reality again, stopping in the hospital room with her younger self. Magenel, battle-weary but alert, stood just over the younger Winter's shoulder.

After a brief moment of indecision, Winter shifted again to Davis's room a little while later, where Summer sat in a chair by the window staring teary-eyed at the slightly younger Winter, who sat in a wheelchair with her bandaged leg stretched out and bandages wrapped around her shoulder. This was the moment she remembered. This was when it happened.

Winter held a hand to the horsemen and stepped partially into reality and into the conversation between the other two girls.

"My heart…has been ripped out of my chest," Summer said with a trembling chin. "I feel like I'm living my worst nightmare. It hurts like I'm having a heart attack, but for some reason I just won't die. Don't you dare tell me it'll be all right. You have no idea how I feel."

The slightly younger Winter sat up straight and wiped her eyes. "I love you, Summer, but don't you ever say I don't know how you feel. Of all the people in this freakin' place I'm the *only* one who knows exactly how you feel. You've had your heart ripped out once. It's happened to me five times. Five times! And Xaphan just killed my dad. I don't even have a body to cry over. At least Davis is still alive. It sucks, I know. But at least you still have him."

Summer looked away from her.

The younger Winter softened. "I don't know how, I don't know when. But when I say it's going to be all right, you can believe me. I've lived it and I know. More than that, I can feel it."

Winter finally stepped completely into the room in the corner by the head of Davis's bed, and allowed herself to be fully in reality, seen as Rebecca by everyone. "It *will* be all right," she told them. "He will live."

Summer jumped out of her seat. "Who is that?"

"You can see her?" the other Winter asked.

Summer nodded.

"What do you want?" the other Winter asked, turning back to her.

"You have to save Kaci. You have to go now. Time is up. This has to end," Winter said.

"As you can probably see, I can't," said the other Winter.

"You will be able to in a moment."

"How?" asked her other self.

"How is not important," said Winter. "All that is important is why. You have to save Kaci and the baby. If you don't, millions of people will die."

Ayden rushed in, Neshamah just behind her. "Winter, I have to talk to you." She paused when she saw the form of Rebecca. "It's her…"

"What?" the other Winter asked Ayden.

Ayden turned to her. "I know where Kaci is. I just had a vision. Graham went to go get Peter. We have to figure it out and go."

"What kind of vision?"

Ayden took a deep breath. "A round room."

The other Winter's eyes widened.

Graham came in, and Winter's heart pounded. She bit her lip, wishing she could rush to him. Peter came closely behind him and they both stopped short when they saw Winter in the form of Rebecca.

"Who's that?" Graham asked.

"She's, um…I'll explain later," said the other Winter. "We have to find a way to get out of here."

"I will help," Winter said.

A nurse came in, with a stern look on her face. "Only two people are allowed at a time. Some of you will have to go."

The other Winter snarled at the nurse and pointed to Davis. "Listen, we were all there when he got shot and he may not last much longer, so just give us ten minutes, please!"

The nurse narrowed her eyes. "Ten minutes. But keep it down!"

"Ayden had a vision?" asked Peter after the nurse left.

"A round room," said Ayden.

"The bell tower," said the real Winter. "Xaphan took her back to where it all began. She's there now."

"Then we have to get there," said Graham.

"But Cherithville is two hours away," said Summer.

The other Winter turned to the real Winter. "You said you could help."

Winter nodded. "But only you."

Silence filled the room, and after a moment Graham broke it. "No. I'm going too."

The other Winter shook her head. "You can't. I was always meant to finish this alone." She panned them all. "We all knew that."

"You won't be alone. We will do this together," Winter said.

Graham reached out and grabbed the other Winter's hand. "I can't let you."

She smiled softly at him. "You have to. There was no one to save me when I needed it. So I'll be there to save her." She turned back to Winter. "What do I do?"

With a flicker of Winter's thought, two angels materialized out of the infinite. First they went to Magenel and clasped him on the shoulder. In an instant, the fire returned to the guardian angel and his face lit up with renewed energy. The two new angels, Magenel, and Neshamah all stepped to the other Winter's side and put their arms around her. White energy swirled through the room, surrounding the other Winter and healing her wounds. Once she had been made whole, Magenel stood by her side at the ready, and the other two angels came to stand by Winter in the corner of the room.

"Stand," Winter told her other self. "Your clothes are here." With another flick of thought, she summoned a set of her favorite clothes from the suitcase still in the trunk of her drowned car. They passed through the infinite instantly, and appeared clean and neatly folded beside the wall.

The other Winter slid her ankle out of the extended footrest and placed it on the floor, and then flexed her shoulder against the bandages.

"Help me," she said to Graham as she yanked the arm catheter out.

The other Winter slid the sleeve of her gown up and yanked at the bandages on her arm and shoulder. Graham pulled out a pocket knife to help. After freeing her arm and leg, the other Winter stood out of the chair and Graham pushed it out of the way. She reached for her underwear and skinny jeans.

"You picked out my favorites," said the other Winter.

Winter gave her a sideways smile. "I know you. I want you to be comfortable."

Once the other Winter had her pants on, she grabbed the black peasant top. "Turn around Peter."

Peter looked away as the other Winter yanked off the gown and slid the shirt on quickly.

"Peter," said the other Winter.

Peter turned back, eyes to the floor.

The other Winter sat in the wheelchair to pull on her socks and black combat boots. "I'm going to save her. I promise. I'm going to save both of them. When I'm done, you'll be safe for good. Just promise me one thing."

"What?"

"Don't ever let them go."

Peter looked her in the eyes. His chin trembled and he wiped a tear from his cheek. "I won't."

"Summer," the other Winter said. "I don't know how it'll happen or how long it will take, but it *will* be all right. Davis is going to live. Just promise me you'll marry him and be happy."

Summer sobbed and nodded quickly.

"Ayden," the other Winter said. "I don't know how long this will take. Keep them safe for me. And when it's all over, I hope you have the normal life you've wanted."

"I will," Ayden said, her voice tense.

Once the other Winter finished tying her boots, she stood and faced Graham. "I'm not sure what to say to you."

"You're saying goodbye," Graham said.

The other Winter reached around her neck to clasp her locket into place. "Maybe. I don't know. I just wish we had more time. For what it's worth, I love you, and I think I could love you for the rest of my life."

"If that's true, then come back."

"I don't know if I can."

"Try. Promise me you'll try."

Winter felt punched in the stomach as the other Winter nodded and kissed him. She remembered that kiss. She remembered the promise. Now, she wasn't so sure any more...

The other Winter backed toward the corner where Winter waited. "I *will* try. I promise. Look for me," she said, never taking her eyes off of Graham.

"I'll never stop," he said.

The other Winter finally let his hand drop. She took one last long look at all her friends. "I'm ready," she said without turning.

Winter grabbed her hand. With a flick of thought she brought her other self and Magenel through the infinite, passing through time and space in an instant, and materialized in the Meadow on the campus of Tishbe University.

As Winter released her other self, she backed into the spiritual unknown where her army gathered around, waiting for instructions. As she watched her other self pick up stones from beneath the Ancient, a host of new angels materialized and joined the army.

"What's going on?" she asked Laban.

Laban smiled. "These are the angels who were assigned to help your other self. But in this moment, we will all fight as one."

More angels came. And then even more, filling the Meadow with brilliant glistening soldiers as far as she could see.

"How many?"

"As many as needed, Prophetess."

For the first time since she entered the infinite, since she watched Kaci die, Winter felt a ray of hope. Maybe they could win after all. Maybe they could bend the rules of time and actually save Kaci and the baby. Maybe the prophecy wouldn't fail. Maybe...

She felt her eyes flashing and her skin tightening. At the same time, the army, a hundred times its original size, rippled to full attention, falling into orderly lines at the command of the horsemen.

Winter gazed toward the tower. A nearly solid mass of shadows surrounded it. All of Hell seemed to have been emptied. It would take every soldier here to break through.

Her other self already jogged toward the chapel, unaware of the magnitude with which the spiritual forces around her prepared to fight. But that wasn't her task *then*. She was only meant to save Kaci and save the child. Her burden *now* was to fight the horde and defeat Xaphan. She failed the first time. This time she planned to rewrite the rules...

Winter faced Laban. "Listen closely. I need those demons contained. No more come and none of them escape. It will take most of these angels to do that. The elite must follow my other self and make sure she gets to Kaci. Once Kaci is rescued, the elite will engage Xaphan and keep him busy. As my other self is escaping, the rest of the army must surround her until they are safe. Understood?"

"Yes, Prophetess," Laban said.

"I will draw out Mavka alone and bind her. Then we will take care of Xaphan."

Laban nodded. "It will be done, Prophetess."

She gazed toward the chapel and saw her other self standing before the doors. It was time.

"Now!" she shouted and immediately shifted herself through the infinite to stand just behind her other self, the horsemen on her heels.

The doors exploded inward with a surge of divine power that poured into the other Winter. As the other Winter stepped into the room, the horsemen and the original elite army swirled in to engage the demons inside.

Above, the other angelic soldiers surrounded the legions of demons around the tower, engaging them in furious combat that no mortal could see.

As her other self fought inside, Winter shifted through the infinite and landed in the top of the bell tower, where Xaphan prepared his knife and Kaci lay struggling against the ropes on the altar. Mavka stood at his side. Winter needed to slow them down. She needed to buy time for her other self and the army to climb the tower.

Winter stepped out of the infinite, using Rebecca's form one more time. "No!" she shouted.

Xaphan stopped and stared at her with hate and shock. The demon attached to him leered forward. Mavka floated into the air, glowing a sickly green.

Other demons rushed toward Winter, but she stood her ground. As the demons struck her, they repelled backward in a brilliant flash of white.

Then the demon Xaphan engaged. It laughed with a low growl, and reached out with an open claw. The blow slammed Winter, knocking her to one side.

Xaphan took up his knife again and this time raised it high over his head.

Winter shifted through the infinite and grabbed his arm. He roared and the demon spun to strike at her again. Mavka flew to her other side, flailing with her long claws. The power in Winter was strong enough to keep them at bay, but she had to separate the demons before she could chain them. Her other self needed to hurry to take over protection of Kaci. She needed her elite to pull the two demons apart.

Xaphan the man struck her with his free hand and Winter fell back into the waiting arms of Mavka. As the man faced her, the demon grew to fill the room with his presence, opening his massive jaws as if to swallow her whole.

"I don't know what you are, but I will not be stopped by some kind of trickery," Xaphan said.

"It is no trick," Winter hissed. She let the power fill her

completely as she had done with Culsu and with Moloch, concentrating on the demon Xaphan and ignoring the tight grip of Mavka. "You shall be chained," she said, her voice sounding as if coming from a tunnel. White bands suddenly clasped onto the demon Xaphan's arms.

Mavka shrieked, released her, and fled. The demon cowered against the wall, holding her hands out as if they had been seared.

Xaphan, both man and demon, laughed as one, a rumble filled the room and shook the walls. The demon pulled against the white bands and they shattered in a rain of light particles.

Demon and man merged again and opened their mouths to speak, two voices, in perfect unison. "No human vessel can channel the power to defeat me." They swung together, two arms, two fists, and pounded Winter to the ground. Xaphan rushed forward as if phasing through the infinite himself, and backhanded her. She flew across the room and slammed into the wall.

Xaphan snatched up his knife, twisted back to Kaci, and raised it high. Winter opened herself to more power than she ever had. The pure divinity poured so forcefully through her that this time her skin split in hairline tears along her arms and legs, and her insides burned like fire. She cried out from the pain, but phased through the infinite to stand between Xaphan and Kaci.

As the knife came down, Winter grabbed his arm. The demon struck against her, but this time too much power raced through her for him to breach. The man glared, straining with all his strength to bring the knife down, huffing inches from her face.

They both trembled...Xaphan against the loss of his strength, Winter against the power tearing her insides apart. One of them would give out first...but Winter didn't have to outlast him, she just had to endure long enough for...

The door on the other side of the room exploded, and the other Winter stepped in. The hordes of demons in the room gathered into a singular mass, banding together in strength. The walls shook and the floor vibrated. A bell tolled. Winter's elite army rushed in, swirling and snatching up the mass of demons.

Xaphan jerked away from Winter, roared, and launched the knife through the air at the other Winter. Mavka rose to attack, but angels wrapped their arms around her, pulled her toward the window, and blasted her out.

The horsemen arrived and reared against Xaphan, as the knife soared from the other Winter, back through the air to embed in his shoulder. As he stumbled, the horsemen pressed forward, swords flailing against the attacks of the demon Xaphan.

Winter reached for Kaci even as her other self did the same. They pulled at the ropes together, and the strands fell away like cobwebs. Then the other Winter rushed Kaci out of the room.

As the other Winter and Kaci turned to descend, Xaphan slammed the horsemen aside to give himself room to move. "Winter!" demon and man bellowed as he rushed toward the door.

Winter phased through the infinite and stood in his way.

"Out of my way, girl!"

"No," sneered Winter, and then she released the child form of Rebecca and planted her feet as her real self.

Both demon and man reeled backward. The horsemen grabbed the arms of the demon, stretching out both demon and man as one. A hundred more elite angels surrounded Xaphan with swords pointed.

"No!" Xaphan screamed. "This isn't possible!"

Winter took a deep breath and let the divine power fill her so much she thought her heart would burst this time. She could see beyond the structure, beyond the atmosphere, beyond the veil of Heaven itself. She saw the shining city. She saw the glory of God radiating from the center. And around all of this, she saw an angelic creature, worm-like and made entirely of holy fire. It weaved through the air, keeping watch. When the fire being spotted her, it eyed her with an intelligent, eager face.

Winter knew what needed to happen next...

"This ends now." Her voice thundered like a crashing wave.

Xaphan screamed and thrashed against his bonds, and then just as suddenly, he relaxed. Both demon and man smiled. "Your bonds cannot hold me."

"They don't need to. They need only stop you long enough for Kaci to escape and the fire to fall."

Xaphan laughed. "Do you believe she will leave this building alive? You may have chained my princes, but I have released them again. They have been hiding in the shadows, waiting for you. They are waiting for her now below." His laugh became a cackle. His eyes flashed the fire of insanity. "All of Hell is released for me!"

Winter felt the power drain from her as her heart ran cold. Culsu...Moloch...back? She couldn't change it...it was still happening...

She cut her eyes to the horsemen. "Save her!" Then she shifted through the infinite to the chapel below, just in time to see Culsu, Moloch, and Mavka advancing on her other self and Kaci, all possessing humanoid shells and wearing their chosen faces, but all demon. Winter materialized as Rebecca beside her other self and Kaci. "NO!" she screamed. "I won't let you do this!"

The three demons attacked. Culsu came first, and Magenel intercepted, his blazing sword a solid light through the air to keep the demonic tentacles away. Moloch barreled toward them down the aisle. Winter held up her hands and let the divine power flow through her. A spiritual shell surrounded them, and the two demons could not penetrate.

Then the horsemen arrived...only three of them, Laban still missing. Winter could feel his power contending with Xaphan above. Sors attacked Moloch, muscular demon striking at the black rider. Adom, on his blood bay, charged against Culsu, slicing at the flurry of her arms. Sharok circled around Mavka, each probing the other for weaknesses.

But a legion of demons, hundreds of them elite and blazing like lightning, fell from above. The sudden pressure against the barrier broke Winter's concentration. What little power she had been able to open up to suddenly vanished as her mind gave in to the panic.

It was happening again…she couldn't change it…

Though her army had arrived in full force, the sheer numbers of the enemy broke through their defenses. The elite demons went for Magenel first and brought him to his knees. A heartbeat later, the demons had disarmed him. A small band of demons latched on to the other Winter and pulled her toward Culsu. They ripped away the connection between Magenel and the other Winter, and Magenel screamed with pain as they dragged him toward a black cage hanging near the ceiling.

Another band of demons ripped away Kaci's angels and jerked them to the cage, which now teemed with defeated angels.

Inside, Winter's army was overrun. From outside, she felt the power of the other angels struggling, barely containing the never-ending supply of demons, unable to penetrate to help. She and her army were alone…and she couldn't change it.

Culsu slammed Adom to the ground, and a hundred elite demons forced him to the cage. Sors fell. Sharok fell. Each was carried to the cage, unable to overcome the darkness inside the chapel. Above, Laban succumbed to Xaphan, and demons pulled him toward the cage, too.

Then Culsu wrapped her tentacles around the other Winter and dragged her backward. Moloch squeezed his arms around Kaci and pulled her toward the altar.

Mavka grabbed Winter with a wet grip like blocks of ice. She flung Winter through the air and pinned her against the ceiling.

Winter couldn't change it…This was exactly what happened last time.

Thousands of demons danced around the room, cheering in victory. Xaphan emerged from the tower door, blood soaking his shoulder and arm. Demon and man smiled over their victory. They fixed their eyes on Kaci. With ready gun to the side, Xaphan slowly descended the stairs.

"Save the child!" cried the angels to her from the cage, but Winter couldn't break free from Mavka's icy grip. She couldn't reach the power. She couldn't change it. What had been done must always be done.

Xaphan reached the bottom and paced to within ten feet of Kaci. "Save the child!"

Xaphan glanced once at the other Winter. Then he smirked up at Winter against the ceiling.

"Save the child!" the angels cried. Even the horsemen bellowed. "Save the child!" But they couldn't quite break the prison…not without her.

She couldn't change it…it had already happened this way…

She could stop time, but it wouldn't help. She could seize every angel and demon in the room and pull them into the infinite, but it wouldn't stop the inevitable. She could use the infinite to free her army for another sortie, but they still couldn't win. What happened must happen. It had already happened, and she could do nothing about it.

Despair filled her and she stopped struggling. She could only be still and watch. Again.

Xaphan lifted the gun and pulled the trigger. Silence filled the room as every demon held its breath and every angel watched stunned. Blood gushed from Kaci's pregnant stomach. Winter felt her heart break all over again.

Xaphan pulled the trigger again and this time Kaci's chest exploded and she slumped in Moloch's arms.

Then Winter halted reality. She couldn't let time keep moving forward like this any longer. What was the point? Why be allowed to command an army like this if she couldn't save Kaci and save the child? It didn't make sense. Now it was over. It had happened again, with nothing changed

What would become of her now? How long did the army stay under her command? Was this it?

Winter peered down to her other self, gone already, ripped into the infinite to command her army on the futile journey that would lead her right back to the same place with the same outcome. She looked over to her army, still trapped in the bands of demons, but now fuzzier...disconnected. No longer *her* army.

Yet here she remained, still in control of time, still a part of the infinite. Was there something else for her to do? Had she missed anything?

Winter shifted reality around herself, out of the hands of Mavka and into the white expanse of the true infinite. Instantly she felt refreshed and energized. The minuscule cuts in her skin where the raw power of God had torn through were healed.

She stood there, thinking, turning aimlessly, hoping for some guidance. The silence of the infinite pressed upon her. The clarity of the whiteness made it seem as if she could see forever and yet nowhere at the same time, as if she stood in the center of a giant crystal.

It should be lonely, and yet she didn't feel alone. Footsteps approached from behind, and she turned. Where nothing had been a moment ago, a man now faced her. He had dark olive skin and bright brown eyes. His black hair was pulled back behind him and his dark beard reached just to the top of his chest. He wore blue jeans and a plain t-shirt, and his hands were in his pockets.

The man she had seen earlier...She had watched this happen from the outside...

He smiled at her. "Hello again, Winter."

"Who are you?"

"Don't you recognize me?"

Winter's heart fluttered. She didn't know whether to embrace him or fall on the ground. All she could do was stand and stare. "Am

I dead?"

The man shook his head. "No."

"Then why am I here?"

"Because there's still one more thing for you to do," he said.

"What? I did everything, didn't I?"

He chuckled. "Yes. You did very well. I'm proud of you. I couldn't have asked for a better Prophetess. You know, there's never been one quite like you before."

"Then what did I miss? I don't understand."

He took a shuffled step closer, and leaned toward her with a knowing look. "There's one place you didn't go, remember?"

"But Laban said I couldn't."

"No. *He* couldn't." The man motioned to either side. "But he's not here any longer. It's just you."

"You mean, I can go there without them?"

"You can go wherever you like." He shrugged a little and his eyes twinkled. "And stay as long as you like."

"And then what?" asked Winter.

"And then you'll understand." He backed up. "Go. Get the answer you want." He turned to walk away.

"Wait!" Winter reached out to him.

He half-turned and raised his eyebrows. "Yes?"

"Um…" She couldn't think of why she had stopped him. She had the answers she needed. She just needed to say… "Thank you."

He smiled and nodded. "You're welcome." Within two steps he had vanished.

Winter stared after him for only a moment, and then she shifted the infinite and stepped into the spiritual unknown, four years ago, at the Old Trenton River bridge. She hovered in the air, gazing at the bridge from high over the river, and then stopped time and lowered herself toward the scene unfolding below. The rain hung like jewels suspended in the air.

In front of her, two figures stood on the rails of the bridge. One she recognized as herself, barefoot, bandaged face and arm, soaked completely by the rain. The other wore a hooded raincoat. Angels surrounded the unknown figure, and a small, embattled cloud of demons clung to the younger Winter. Magenel stood to one side with his sword tip on the ground, waiting patiently and expectantly.

Different angels fought against the demons clinging to the younger Winter. Above and below the bridge, an entire host of angels had gathered simply to watch the scene.

She never told anyone what happened on the bridge that night. Not even Kaci. But this moment, these few precious minutes of her life, were perhaps the most important she had ever lived.

She returned now for only one thing. Only one question had gnawed at her all these years. Deep in the pit of her stomach she thought she knew the answer, but here in this moment she could finally find out for certain.

Winter floated through the air until she hovered right next to the rail, face to face with the stranger. A mere touch of her thought and the hood became translucent, and for the first time she could see the person's face clearly.

Despite her gut feeling, Winter still gasped. Now she understood. It all made perfect sense. She knew exactly what had to be done.

Slowly she backed away from the scene, the plan already unfolding in her mind, perfect and daring. She stepped back into the infinite for a brief moment and then phased through time to the hospital.

There she floated through the air and watched two other versions of herself in Davis's hospital room, preparing to attack the tower. When they both vanished, she froze time and floated down.

The first thing she did was phase Ayden and Peter into the infinite. They gaped at her with their mouths open.

"What's going on?" Ayden asked.

"There's not a lot of time to explain. Kaci is going to need both of you soon, and I have to get you there."

"You found her?" asked Peter

Winter nodded. "I'm saving her."

"What do we have to do?" he asked.

"Get her to safety." Winter shifted the infinite and phased them through reality until they stood in the Meadow, mere minutes after her younger self had just stormed into the Chapel. "Wait here until you see her, then get her out as quickly as you can."

"What about you?" asked Ayden.

"I have something else to do." She stepped back through the infinite and returned to the hospital room. This time she went to Graham.

She stood for a moment in front of him, studying his sad face. Then she reached out, grabbed his hand, and pulled him into the infinite.

He stared at her with wide eyes. "Winter…what's going on? Where are we?"

She smiled a sad smile at him. "This is a place where time doesn't matter. I had to see you again, one more time."

His face fell. "You're not coming back then."

She shook her head. "I don't think I can."

"Then why are you here?"

"Because I love you." She put a hand to the side of his face. "I want to live my life with you. And I don't know how it might work, but we might be able to do something like that here."

"What do you mean?"

She leaned forward on her toes and kissed him.

The world exploded in her mind. Minutes felt like real minutes. Hours felt like real hours. Years felt like real years.

They dated, watched movies, ate meals out. After a year, they married, a small ceremony with a few friends at the courthouse. Graham carried her over the threshold of their first apartment, insisting he haul her up the stairs and almost dropping her on the landing.

Graham took a job with the government, working cyber-security. Winter finished her degree and began working at a women's shelter. She drew upon her past experiences to help other women out of abusive relationships.

After three years, Winter gave birth to a son. She named him Noah. He was a feisty boy, all energy and imagination. They left the apartment and bought their first house. Shortly after Noah turned four, Winter gave birth to another son, Steven. Though not as full of imagination, he analyzed everything with a sharp mind. He also cuddled with Winter on the couch for hours while they watched TV…a momma's boy through and through. A year and a half later, Winter was surprised to find herself pregnant again. A girl. They named her Elise. Elise lived in a dream world, and loved to dance and play with animals.

As Graham and Winter approached their tenth anniversary, he received a promotion to director. They relocated to a new city, and Winter decided to stay home for a while with the kids.

Noah grew up to look just like his father. He found a career in advertising, married, and gave Winter and Graham two grandchildren. Steven became a pastor, and eventually joined the faculty at a seminary. He also married and gave Winter and Graham four grandchildren. Elise went to veterinarian school, but dropped out to pursue her passion in dance. She married a professional dancer and gave Winter and Graham two more grandchildren.

Graham finally retired and they moved again, this time to a small country home away from the city. After years of learning to garden and hanging out with other aging grandparents, they finally became too old to do much. Grandchildren grew up and brought to them great-grandchildren. Ten great-grandchildren became sixteen. And when Winter turned ninety-two, and Graham turned ninety-six, the oldest of the great-grandchildren brought them their first great-great-grandchild…a daughter named Winter.

The kiss ended. Winter pulled back from Graham, feeling the

silent tears streaming down her cheeks, his cheeks glistening with tears of his own. They had lived a lifetime in that kiss. Minutes felt like minutes. Hours felt like hours. Years felt like years.

Here in the infinite, they could live forever in a moment.

"Was it real?" Graham croaked.

"I don't know," Winter whispered.

"What happens now?"

Her chin trembled and she could barely speak. "Now...I have to go."

"And what am I supposed to do?"

She wiped his cheeks. "You've lived one life with me already. I want you to go live another without me. Promise me you'll be happy."

"I can't promise that."

Winter pursed her lips. "Promise me you'll try."

He stared at her for a long time. "I will try," he croaked.

She nodded quickly and kissed him again. Before he could say anything else to stop her, she gave a flicker of thought and sent him back through the infinite to the hospital room, as if he had never left.

Then Winter returned to the chapel.

Outside of reality, in her own personal form of the infinite, she walked down the aisle, through the demonic horde, to where Kaci slumped lifeless. She glanced to the version of herself being held back by Culsu. Absolute heartbreak on that face. She looked up to her other self in the form of Rebecca pinned against the ceiling by Mavka. Defeat and despair on that face.

It only took a flicker of thought to move time backward. Xaphan held the gun out. The angels stretched against their bonds. Kaci was still alive.

Winter stepped between Kaci and the gun. There was really only one thing she could do...only one course of action. She had to change it. And the power she needed to change it would tear her body apart.

She spread her feet and took a deep breath. Then she cleared her mind and opened herself to the raw divine power God poured into her. The first surge stretched her skin, her vision sharpened, and she could hear the rumble of the power of God in her ears.

With that surge of power, she grabbed everything but Kaci in a time-lock. The other two versions of herself stretched toward her until they connected and were absorbed. Now there was only one of her. Now it was really time to end it. She stepped back into reality, back into her own time, and left the infinite behind.

Four Years Ago

As Winter stood, arms out, face to the rain, one foot hovering just on the edge of taking that fateful step, a car slowed down behind her and stopped.

A door opened. "Hey!" cried out a young woman's voice through the patter of the rain.

Instinctively, Winter put her foot back on the rail and grabbed the trellis. She half turned her head toward the intruder. "Leave me alone!"

"You don't want to do this! Please, just come down!"

"You don't even know me! How do you know what I want?"

The young woman stood at her side now, looking up. Winter could tell the girl was near her own age, maybe a little younger, but the shadow beneath the hood of her raincoat hid her face.

"I know you want to live," she said. "Otherwise you would have jumped already."

"I could jump now." Winter swung her foot over the edge.

"No!" shouted the young woman. "Just not yet. Hear me out

first."

Winter grabbed the trellis with both hands and turned a little to better face her. "Who are you?"

"That doesn't matter. Listen, I don't know what you've been through, but it must have been horrible for you to come here tonight."

Winter leaned against the trellis and clenched her eyes, uninjured hand dropping to her abdomen. The emptiness inside of her ached.

"I just want you to know that there can be something better."

Winter shook her head. "There is nothing left for me."

"You don't know that. You've got this entire life ahead of you. If this is the worst that it gets, the only thing left is for it to get better. Think about it. If you can get through this…"

"I *can't* get through this."

"Yes, you can," said the woman. "Maybe not on your own. But you can."

"What do you mean, not on my own? I've always been on my own. I'm all alone. That's the problem. Everybody I love has either left me or died."

"Sure. Because that's what humans do. But God doesn't leave."

Winter snorted. "What do you know of God? He's the one that's done this to me. He's the one that hates me. He's been pushing me to kill myself for years."

"No, he hasn't."

"You don't know!" Winter shouted.

The woman held up her hands. "You're right. I don't know. I don't know anything about you. But I know my God, and my God loves me. He cares about me. There have been some horrible things in my life. I've been broken just like you, but God was there. He's always there."

"Not for me…"

"He will be if you let him."

"If he wants to be there for me so badly, where is he now? Huh?

Where is he?"

The woman reached out but stopped short of touching Winter. "I stopped, didn't I? I'm here."

"That doesn't mean anything."

"Doesn't it? In the loneliest moment in your life, the girl who is always alone, in this moment…tonight…you're not alone. Not only that, but the person here with you is trying to convince you that God has something more for you."

"What more could there be?" asked Winter.

The woman shook her head. "I don't know. But maybe all of this misery you've been through…maybe it's so you can help someone else later. Maybe somebody in the future needs you, but you can't help them if you end it now. There's something special about you, I can tell. Don't throw it away."

"Special?"

"Yes. God has something unique and awesome planned for you. You just have to let him show you the way."

"Why would I let God do anything?"

"Did you ever stop to think that maybe he's been there the whole time? Maybe he's been trying to get your attention, but you've been trying to hold on to too much control? Give God a chance…a real chance. You'll see that I'm right."

Winter shook her head. "I can't do that. It's too late."

"It's never too late." The woman faced the rail and grabbed the opposite trellis of Winter. She put one knee up and scrambled to her feet, clinging to the trellis with both hands. Then she slowly turned, placed her back against the trellis, and clung to it with both hands near her waist.

"Are you crazy?" screamed Winter.

The woman laughed. "Crazy? You did it first."

"What are you doing? Get down!"

"I want you to know that you're not alone. If this is what it takes to convince you, then here I am…standing on the bridge for you.

Together. What do you want to do next?"

"Why?"

The woman tilted her head. "Because someday you may have to stand on the bridge for someone else. And that person shouldn't be alone either."

"You're insane!"

"You're right." The woman's voice trembled. "I'm terrified. I'd love to climb down. So what's it going to take?"

"Take for what?" asked Winter.

"What's it going to take to get you to climb down with me?"

Winter bit her lip. "God proving you're right."

"What would God have to do to prove himself?"

Winter's chin trembled. She started to cry again, her warm tears mixing with the cold rain on her cheeks. "He can start with my dad apologizing and actually telling me he loves me. And mean it!"

"Is that all?"

"It'll never happen!" Winter screamed. "He hates me!"

Another vehicle approached. The woman cut her eyes and Winter glanced over her shoulder. Steve was there, his truck parked by the other car, jumping out and leaving the door open.

"Go away!" Winter shrieked and faced the river again.

"Stop!" Steve shouted. "I need to talk to you!"

Winter clenched her eyes.

"I'm sorry," said Steve. "I'm sorry for everything. I don't blame you for wanting to jump, I blame myself. I'm sorry I left you all those years ago. I'm sorry I didn't do more to help you spend time with your mother before she died. I'm sorry I made excuses to work late. I'm sorry I avoided you. I'm sorry I was too absorbed in myself to see what I was missing. I'm sorry about Ryan. I'm sorry about Claire." He could barely speak now, but he stood closer to her and she could still hear him through his raked tears and the gentle rain. "I'm sorry about Michael and the baby. I'm sorry for what I said at the hospital."

"Dad…" she croaked.

The woman stretched out across the rail and grabbed Winter's hand while still clinging to the trellis.

"It doesn't matter what happened between your mother and me, you are not her. You are your own self. I'm proud to be your father. I'm sorry I haven't done better, but I want to. Just give me another chance. I love you. I know I haven't always shown it, but I do. Please, just come down. We can start over and get this right."

The young woman squeezed her hand. "Do you believe me now?"

Winter slowly turned to the woman's soft small smile beneath the shadowed hood and the dripping water. "How?"

"Does it matter?"

Steve put a hand on Winter's leg. "Please come down."

Winter released the woman's hand and grabbed the trellis. She eased down to her knees as her dad held tightly to her ankles. By the time she reached the ground, both of them were weeping. Winter collapsed into his arms.

They clung to each other, kneeling in the rain. Winter sobbed in his arms. Steve stroked her hair and trembled. When Winter finally looked up to thank the woman…she was gone.

Present Day

With the overwhelming, terrible power coursing through her body, Winter freed Kaci from the time lock. Everything else she held in stasis so nothing could stop her. But Kaci needed to escape and Winter didn't know how much she'd be able to help her.

"Winter?" Kaci asked.

Kaci still struggled against the hold of Moloch, stuck in the physical world. Winter couldn't free her from reality, yet. She needed more of the power to pull Kaci from both, so she let more course through, and cringed.

"What are you doing?" Kaci asked, panic in her eyes. "Stop it!"

"I'm saving you," Winter said with a strained voice.

"You're killing yourself!"

"It's the only way, Kaci. I've seen it. The only way to save you is to change it."

"Winter, I don't know what you're doing…but there has to be another way."

Winter opened the gate to the power further. The skin on her face and arms split in minuscule red lines again. Out of those lines dripped slow drops of blood and streamed bright beams of light. She cried out again. Her insides boiled. Her mind held all the infinite knowledge of history. She couldn't make sense of anything. So much...so strong. With it she pulled Kaci partially out of reality, and Kaci fell through Moloch's arms to the floor.

"Winter!" Kaci scrambled back to her feet and reached out tentatively.

Winter squinted at Kaci. "I remember now. It was you. It was always you."

"What are you talking about?"

"That night on the bridge, four years ago. I was ready to end it all, but it was you who stopped me. You stood on the bridge with me and saved me."

Kaci clasped both hands to her face. "That was you?"

"Do you remember what you told me?" she asked. The power surged again and she whimpered.

Kaci reached out again, crying. She shook her head.

"You said I didn't have to be alone. You stood on the bridge for me because you said someday I may have to stand on the bridge for someone else. And that person shouldn't have to be alone either."

Kaci shook her head quickly, unable to speak. "No..." she croaked. "Don't..."

Winter let a little more power in. The cracks in her skin became open cuts. The light streamed through the room, casting sharp shadows on the walls. Winter screamed in pain, and Kaci cried, once again trying to reach out.

Winter took a deep breath and opened her eyes fully. "You were right. You were there for me in the loneliest moment of my life. In the loneliest moment in your life, in this moment...tonight...you're not alone." Her chin quivered. The power held her muscles so rigid, she couldn't wipe away the tears falling down her cheeks. "So this is me...standing on the bridge. For you."

"You don't have to do this," Kaci moaned. "There has to be another way."

"There was never another way," Winter said. "This is how my story ends. The way it was always meant to."

"Not for me...don't..."

Winter tried to laugh. "By saving you, I'm saving the world. That's not so bad."

"But who will save you?"

Winter shook her head. "Listen..." She cried out again with a fresh surge of power. Only one barrier left and it would tear her apart. The prophetic portal opened up and the rumbling of God's voice poured through her with words to Kaci. "There's not much time left. I have one final message for you. When this day is over, you will be at peace. God is defeating the enemy through his Prophetess and will safeguard you for the rest of your life. Raise your son in the ways of the Lord. Name him Isaiah, for through him God will bring revival to the world. As for you, you and Peter will live a long, peaceful life, blessed of God."

"But what about you?" Kaci screamed. "I can't lose you!"

"As for my Prophetess, declares the Lord, I will call her home and give her rest. Her path has been long and difficult, and now her reward will be great." Winter took a deep breath as the tunnel of the prophecy fell silent, but the power still poured in.

Kaci doubled over, hands on her face, crying uncontrollably.

"You have to go now," Winter said, her voice surprisingly strong and calm.

Kaci shook her head. "Not without you!"

"GO!" With a flicker of her thought Winter grabbed Kaci with the power and transported her to the porch beyond the shattered doors of the chapel. Winter turned her head and made final eye contact with Kaci. In that look, she gave Kaci all the things she wished she could have said. Kaci's body rocked as she sobbed. Then she put a hand to her belly, turned, and ran toward the Meadow.

Winter let the last barrier to the power break. Her cut skin opened into gashes. She felt as if it were ripping from her body. Her insides burned and boiled, the pressure threatening to blow her apart from the inside out. Her heart pounded too fast to hold out for more than a few moments.

With a flicker of thought, a great band of light swept toward the shattered door, catching up the splinters of wood, rebuilding them perfectly, and setting the door into place, locked and sealed spiritually. With another thought, a bubble of spiritual energy pulsed through the room, catching up every angel, and transporting them safely to the infinite. A third thought sent the bubble far out and then retracted it in, snatching every demon anywhere near the school, and dragging them into the chapel…millions of demons, all bound in one place. A final thought solidified the spiritual bubble onto the walls of the chapel, creating an impenetrable prison. All that was left was the fire…

Another surge of power coursed through her, but this time her insides ruptured. Blood gushed up through her mouth and spilled down her chin. Her heart seized, and all strength in her body failed. She had just enough left to make sure the spiritual prison stayed intact, and then the power drained out of her. Blood flowed out of the millions of gashes in her skin. She tried to breathe, but gurgled instead.

Time restarted.

For a brief moment, a cry of chaos and confusion rose up from the trapped demons. And then a single gunshot rang out.

Winter felt the punch in her back and the sting out of her chest. Her eyes fell dark and she collapsed.

Huddled snug beneath his arm and holding his other hand, Winter walked with her dad through the rain to his truck. The headlights gleamed through the haze. The windshield wipers beat at regular intervals. The door stood open, soaking the seat.

Inside, Winter pulled her arms tight around herself to conserve warmth and protect her rib. Steve sat there, staring at her. "I don't know what to do now."

Winter blinked at him. She knew exactly what to do.

They drove through the city, until they came to a neighborhood several miles from home. She had only been there once before, months ago.

Steve parked on the side of the street and together they walked, soaked, through the rain to the front door. Winter reached out and rang the doorbell, then huddled against her dad again.

Daniel answered. Ryan's father. His eyes darted, shocked, and then his face softened. He didn't speak. They didn't speak. He just opened the door wide and stood aside so they could enter.

Present Day

Winter's eyes fluttered and she parted them enough to see fuzzy shapes leaning over her. Her whole body was numb. Her heart would completely stop soon; the buzzing in her ears was nothing more than the life draining from her body. Her arm lay in a wet pool of her own blood. Warm still.

She blinked again and the shapes cleared. Demonic faces peered down on her. Four nearest, wearing human masks, but the demon clearly recognizable beneath the skin.

At her feet hovered Mavka, wearing a face she had never met, but knew it to be Dr. Simmons, now the Wretch. The naked, dripping demon glared down on her with white eyes and a blank expression.

To her left leered Moloch, wearing the face of the man who was once the Eater. His black eyes glistened with victory.

To her right was Culsu, still wearing the face of her old friend Claire. The Acolyte. Satisfaction painted her smile.

And above her head knelt Xaphan. Demon and man inseparable. He held a jagged knife in his hands. He grinned with all of his teeth and raised it high above his head, the point aiming for the center of her heart, only a few inches from where the bullet had exited.

Beyond all of that, beyond the chapel ceiling, beyond the sky, beyond the stars, beyond material reality, Winter saw the Kingdom of Heaven again. It gleamed white with a hope beyond any pain she could ever endure in this moment.

And around the city, flying like a majestic serpent, the angelic fire being still watched her. Eager. Waiting.

Four Years Ago

Winter held her breath. Daniel placed a handkerchief over her nose and mouth and plunged her into the warm water. Her clothes clung to her skin, and for a brief moment all went silent. It was the death of her old self. Leaving everything she had been behind. Giving it all to Christ, to transform into whatever he wanted it to be. The silence filled her with so much joy and hope that tears stung the corners of her eyes, even in the brief moment of being submerged.

The moment ended almost as quickly as it had begun. Daniel brought her up into the air. Into new life. Into a second chance. She knew all of those things had happened that rainy night a week ago, but actually going through the symbolic motions of starting over somehow made it all the more real.

She emerged to Daniel's smiling face, eyes full of tears. Beyond him on the stairs of the baptistery stood her dad, red-faced and trying to choke back his own tears, as he waited for his turn in the pool.

Applause filled the air. She gazed out at the people of the church. Hundreds of people. Someone cheered. Someone yelled. People rose from their seats, and quickly the entire church stood on their feet celebrating.

Winter put a hand up to cover her open mouth and looked back at Daniel.

"Lots of people have been praying for you for a long time," he said. Then he wrapped his arms around her and hugged her tight.

Present Day

The fire being watched and waited. Xaphan stood poised to strike down the knife. Her heart failed anyway. Her breath nearly spent. Her vision fading for the last time. She concentrated on the fiery angel and stared into his eyes.

"Come," she whispered.

Then the knife plunged into her heart.

Chapter 1

The Fire Falls

Peter and I gaped at each other as we stood alone in the Meadow. I wasn't sure what had happened just now. We had seen Winter disappear with the girl, then almost immediately Winter returned to drag us here.

After the initial shock, Peter glanced around, more desperate than confused. "Where is she, Ayden?"

I took a long turn to peer into the shadows around us, but didn't see her anywhere. "I don't know. But the round room I saw…she said it was in the chapel, right?"

Peter spun to face the chapel and I stepped up to his side. That's when we saw Kaci stumbling down the sidewalk between the buildings.

"Kaci!" Peter cried out and took off running.

I didn't hesitate to follow, but before we could get to her, she collapsed onto the grass just as she reached the Meadow. She cried out and held her pregnant belly.

"No. Please tell me you're not…" I said as we knelt at her side. Maybe I could have said it better, but delivering a baby was not on my radar.

Kaci shook her head, and then she sobbed again. The pain on her face was not all physical, and it confused me. So much crying...it couldn't all be from the baby. Then it hit me and I looked up toward the chapel. I could just see the porch from where we were.

"Where's Winter?" I asked.

Kaci groaned, this time grabbing her stomach with both hands. "The baby!"

Peter turned to me, panic-stricken. "Ayden. She's going into labor."

"Then call 911," I said.

"My phone is back at the hospital, I can't."

I felt my back pocket for my phone, and realized that I had put it down too. My heart ran cold and I shook my head at Peter.

"We have to do something," Peter said.

"I know. Just let me think..." I leaned back with my hand on the ground and landed on something hard. I grabbed it and couldn't believe what I held.

"It's a phone," I said.

"What? Here?"

"Do you want to call or what?" I asked, tossing it to him.

He stared at it for a moment, while Kaci clenched her teeth and rocked back and forth. "This isn't just any phone. It's Winter's phone," he said softly.

I grabbed Kaci by the shoulders. "Where is she? Hurry! I need to help her!" I might have shaken her a little, too.

Kaci took one hand and pointed to the chapel. "Please! Get her out!"

As Peter began to dial for an ambulance, I nodded and sprinted to the chapel. When I mounted the stairs, I could tell something wasn't right. I expected some dark energy to try to stop me. It wouldn't be the first time. Greg and I had already encountered more than enough Satanic strongholds.

But all the dark energy I could feel here was somehow trapped inside. I tried the door, but found it locked. More than locked. Sealed.

I beat on it and kicked it, but my fists couldn't quite get to the surface. What had Winter done?

Then I heard the roar, like a giant wave crashed toward us or a massive windstorm swept through the air. It came from above, so I backed down the steps and peered up.

I wasn't sure what I saw. A meteor? A fireball? It was so much more. It was like lightning the diameter of a bus, with a length that didn't seem to end. Yet it was solid fire, pure and white, with red, orange, and blue flickering at its edges.

And it came fast.

I spun and ran as quickly as I could toward Peter and Kaci. "RUN!" I screamed. "RUN!"

Peter glanced at me, phone still against his face, then his head pivoted up. He immediately grabbed Kaci under the arm and tried to pull her to her feet.

I reached them and grabbed Kaci's other arm. Then we half ran, half dragged Kaci, through the Meadow toward the Ancient, trying to put as much distance between us and whatever it was crashing down toward the earth.

The sound grew and filled the air with a roar that shook the ground. I chanced a look back, and the fire really did look like some kind of meteor falling directly toward the chapel.

Even as I watched, the long tower of fire landed. The impact sent a flash of light that made me clench my eyes in pain. Then the shock wave lifted us off the ground and tossed us through the air to land another twenty feet away. Kaci rolled onto her back, screaming. The heat wave followed, a searing blast as if someone had opened a door to the Sahara desert.

I rolled over and ogled back. Every building surrounding the chapel blazed and crumbled before my eyes. And in the center of the impact, where the chapel should have been, smoldered nothing but a pile of rubble.

Chapter 2

The Mantle

I had to do something. I had to try. I had seen Winter do some amazing, unthinkable things. Most recently teleporting Peter and me over a hundred miles. She could still be there. She could still be alive. Then again, she could be somewhere else for all I knew. Maybe she'd walk out from behind the Ancient and surprise us all.

But Kaci said she was in the chapel, and feeling the power sealing that door...I knew nothing could enter or leave. Not even her.

I jumped to my feet and ran recklessly toward the inferno. The heat blasted against my skin, hotter than anything human flesh should be able to withstand, but somehow I knew I'd be all right. It hurt, and I'd have a good sunburn afterward, but God would keep me safe until then. If he allowed me into the furnace, it had to be for a good reason.

The buildings still crumbled around me. I had to wait for one wall to completely topple before I could pick my way through the wreckage to reach the chapel. I could barely see straight. The heat and the flames blurred everything in wavy lines. For every breath I took, I coughed three times. Despite all of that, somehow I had enough strength and oxygen to continue easing my way around glowing bricks and blazing wood. Even the charred grass glowed in places with bright embers.

I was protected, but what about my clothes? What about my shoes? Everything seemed to be okay for the moment, so I stepped through another burning pile, the flames tickling against my legs, and finally passed by the collapsing buildings to the rubble that used to be the chapel.

When I rounded the final pile, I thought I'd have to get my hands in the flames and dig her out, or at least search for her. But I was wrong.

She was there...alive, standing in the flames, arms outstretched. She spun as she danced, eyes closed and mouth open in the biggest smile I'd ever seen on her face. Small flames danced with her on the tips of her golden brown hair like beautiful flowers. I'm not sure what shape I expected to find her in, but I didn't expect to find her so...beautiful.

Then I saw someone on the other side of her, watching her intently, with the most loving grin on his face. I didn't recognize him. It didn't matter. When Winter finally stopped spinning, she spotted him and her face lit up even more. She rushed through the flames, wrapped her arms tightly around him, and held him in a long embrace.

That's when I noticed the man was not alone. He stood in front of something. It looked like a rounded box, roiling with a low flame as if the flame were the side of the box itself. The brighter flame making a circle along its side became a wheel. A bigger, more solid flame in front of the box moved in a purposeful, intelligent way. The stamping of a leg. The tossing of a mane.

The more I stared while Winter and the man held one another, the more the flames took shape before my eyes, until I could clearly see edges, muscle, workmanship, design. A chariot. A chariot and horse made entirely of fire.

When Winter finally pulled away from the man, she gazed a long time at the chariot. She walked over to the horse and stroked its neck.

The horse nuzzled her gently, and Winter laughed. The man stepped into the chariot and held his hand out to her.

I could see the big breath that she took. She reached out and took his hand, moving alongside the chariot to enter with him.

"Wait!" I yelled, rushing forward a few steps into the blazing rubble.

Winter turned to me. She laughed again and dropped the man's hand. Then she walked toward me.

"What do I do?" I asked. I'm not sure why I asked that, but then I realized I was crying and I didn't want her to go.

Winter reached around her neck and unclasped her locket. She grabbed both sides of the chain with one hand and held it dangling out to me. I held my hand out and she lowered it into my palm.

"You go on," she said with a warm smile.

I shook my head, still not knowing what to say as I clenched the locket in my hand tightly. "But…what do I tell the others?"

Winter laughed, and the flames in her hair flickered at the sound. She tilted her head to one side as if she were considering the question a little more carefully. "Tell them…I'm okay." She smiled that big smile she had while she was dancing. "Tell them I'm happy. My story wasn't always a happy one, but the story doesn't end here. It goes on. And so will yours. Maybe my story helped you through some things along the way. But you, and everyone else who knew me, need to live your story. Then maybe your story can help someone else. Just promise me this one thing."

"What?" I asked.

"Don't forget me."

I pressed my lips together and didn't speak. How could I ever forget her? For that matter, how could I ever go on like my life had not been changed in the most amazing ways? How could I not tell everyone I met?

She just smiled and took my silence for agreement. Then she turned back to the man waiting for her in the chariot. As she approached, he held out his hand again and she took it. She cast one final look at me as she stepped in beside him, then she gave him all her attention.

The flames roared in front of me, swirling in a sudden gust of wind like a blazing tornado. I shielded my face against the unexpected rise in temperature and thought maybe my protection had been taken away. But the flames settled back to their proper places.

And Winter was gone.

I don't remember much about climbing out of the burning rubble. I remember that firefighters were already arriving. Some of them stared at me, one even tried to pull me away, but I ignored them all.

I just kept walking, fist clenched, toward the Ancient. Paramedics were beside Kaci, helping her onto a lowered stretcher. Peter stood by, running his hand through his hair and rocking from foot to foot.

I kept walking. Fist clenched.

Peter saw me and ran to me. "Where is she?" he asked.

I bit my lip and kept walking. Fist clenched. Until I stood beside Kaci. Kaci looked up at me with big, frightened eyes. Peter stood on her other side, both of them trying to read my face.

When I opened my hand and let the locket tumble down the chain, their faces fell. When I put it around my neck, they both silently wept.

"She's okay," I finally said. "She's happy."

Chapter 3
Saying Goodbye

It had been six months since the fire. Officially they called it an "explosion" caused by a faulty gas line. Six buildings were destroyed in that fire, but already the school had nearly finished rebuilding. It hardly looked like the same place.

We gathered together beneath the Ancient on a quiet Sunday afternoon. It was the first time any of us had been back. One by one, we gathered around silently. I don't know who had arrived first, but no one spoke. Everyone just stared at the ground.

Peter and Kaci stood close together, with baby Isaiah held tightly against Kaci's chest, sound asleep. Peter rubbed Kaci's back gently. I kinda hoped the baby would wake up before I had to leave.

Kaci's parents stood near them. Chris and Beverly. They waited solemnly, with their hands clasped in front of them and their heads slightly bowed. Their demeanor betrayed why we had gathered more than anyone else.

Davis was there too, in a wheelchair. He still didn't speak as clearly and intelligently as he used to. You could see the frustration behind his eyes when he tried. He also still couldn't walk on his own, but Summer told me his physical therapy went well. All the doctors called it a miracle, and they all expected him to be completely back to his normal self. Eventually. He still had a long way to go.

Summer stood beside him, one hand on his shoulder, and Davis reached across his body to hold it. Though they missed their original wedding date, they were hoping it could happen before Christmas. No one took better care of Davis or stayed at his side more than she.

Between Peter and me stood a young woman I had never met. She had long, dark brown hair and soft Asian features. Of all of us, she was the only one already crying and wiping tears from her cheeks. Kaci had invited her. Stacy, she said her name was.

Beside Stacy stood a man I didn't know either. Someone else from Winter's past that Kaci had contacted. Kaci said it was a long story how Winter knew him, but that it wouldn't be right if he wasn't here. He worked as a pastor in Winter's hometown. Daniel, I think.

Graham lurked a little separated from everyone else. I hadn't seen him since Winter took me from the hospital. He had dark circles under his eyes and his scraggly beard began to grow out of control. He stood with his hands in his pockets and stared at the bench in front of us.

On that bench several pictures had been laid. Everyone had brought a piece of Winter…small glimpses into her life and expressions of how she had touched each one of us. We had come together one last time just for this. We had come to say goodbye.

"Um," Peter said when Agent Erickson stepped to my side, the last to arrive. Peter paused and cleared his throat. "We all know why we came. I'm not sure what to do. But I know we're all the family Winter had. Her mother and last of her grandparents died while she was in high school. She lost her father not long ago. She had no brothers or sisters. No extended family, really. As far as the world is concerned, there's nothing and no one to remember she even existed except for us. I thought maybe each of us could say a few words, and then we could share a prayer. I'll go first." He took a deep breath. "Winter saved my life multiple times and in more ways than one. She always spoke her mind and never pretended to be anything other than what she wanted to be. I have to admit, I didn't know what to expect the first time I saw her. It was a CLC party off campus. I kept stealing glances at Kaci, and Winter was sitting next to her…all in black, with all this scary makeup on." He laughed. "Honestly, I was a little concerned for Kaci's safety. But that was also the night of the wreck, and I found out later that Winter was the one who saved my life. We met for the first time just after I woke up in the hospital. I knew then that this was someone who could change the world. And she did…" Peter clenched his lips and his voice choked.

As Peter fell silent, Stacy jumped in. "It seems so long ago when I first met her. I don't really know any of you here, but I've known Winter for eight years. Things were bad for her back then, but you're right. There's was always something else there…something fighting for her and something trying to tear her apart. But she was always a good person. She was a great friend, even then. Sure we had our disagreements, but we were stupid teenagers, right? I wish…" She covered her mouth. "I wish we'd spent more time together lately…" A loud sob escaped from her and she shook her head. "I'm sorry…"

Daniel put an arm around her. "I don't know any of you either, but I know she loved all of you. When she came home and we would have a chance to talk, she would tell me all of these wonderful things about her friends here. It was my privilege to lead her and her father to Christ. It was my privilege to baptize them. And if Winter has meant anything to any of you, I hope that you'll make Christ as important to you as he was to her. That's what she would want."

A few moments of silence passed, and then Kaci's father spoke. "I remember when Winter came into our lives. Kaci came home talking about this strange girl with these abilities. I knew it was happening again. We'd heard about the prophets that had been involved when Kaci was little. We didn't understand it, but we knew that Kaci wasn't safe. But in college Kaci didn't want to run anymore, and when I met Winter in person at our house, I knew that she was the one who would stop it. We owe our lives to her. She was there for Kaci when no one else was."

"Freshman year, when we lived together," said Summer, "everyone said an angel and a demon lived together."

Everyone laughed softly.

Summer widened her eyes and glanced at each of us seriously. "People were scared of her. We had to divide the room and put all of her black stuff on one side and all of my pink stuff on the other. She couldn't stand my pink stuff."

Everyone laughed again.

Summer shook her head. "But I was never scared. She was different, but I could see her heart. She probably thought I was a total flake. Maybe I was a little." She wiped her eyes dry. "But I knew she was really just like me. Scared. Overcompensating. And lonely. We needed each other. Davis saw it first, I think. He saw right through her from the very beginning. I think the first time I heard her laugh was with Davis. She helped me realize that Davis and I were supposed to be together." She rubbed Davis's shoulder and he gazed up at her and smiled.

Summer fell silent, and the silence persisted while most everyone sniffled and wiped quiet tears. Davis probably wouldn't speak, and that was okay. Summer had spoken for them both. And Erickson wouldn't talk either...not exactly his style. That only left Graham and Kaci, both of which had earned the right to have the final word if they wanted.

That meant my turn had come. "I didn't like Winter when I first met her. I thought she was arrogant and dramatic and selfish." I shook my head. "Boy, was I wrong. How could she be arrogant when she probably had the biggest self-esteem problem I had ever seen? She had gone so long thinking she was completely unlovable, and all I did was hate her for it. Now I know she wasn't being dramatic at all..." I smiled and spread my arms to include everyone. "We all know it was real. Everything was so real, and Winter was the epicenter of all that weirdness. Honestly, I don't know how she handled it, but she didn't do it for herself. She did it for all of us. She never demanded anything for herself. I think she tried that one time, and it ended in complete disaster. Winter was really never allowed to be selfish…and that's what made her the most generous person I've ever met. The real reason I think I didn't like her is that we were just alike. She was just…further along on the journey than me. I hope one day I can become half of what Winter was to all of us."

I could have said more, but I had said enough. My heart pounded from trying to hold it together. Now as I bit my lip, my own tears fell. I looked at Graham, hoping to pass a cue to him to pick up where I left off. He stared at me with red eyes and a trembling face. I couldn't help myself. I ran to him and hugged him tight. He needed it. I needed it.

Kaci began to talk, and I pulled away from Graham and turned to her.

"I found out something just before…" she trailed off. No one needed her to finish that sentence. "I met Winter for the first time at the CLC. She was in the freshman small group I led, but what I didn't realize was that our paths had crossed several months before. I didn't recognize her because the night I first saw her it was dark, raining, and she had all of these bandages and streaking makeup all over her face." Kaci took a deep breath. "We had a meeting at the FBI field office in Trenton Hills the next day about me returning to Tishbe. They had found out Xaphan knew I was there, though he didn't know who I was. They wanted to move us again, but that was the night I decided to stop running. My parents were meeting me there and I had been driving all day from school. The GPS took me through a back road to save some time."

Beverly moved to Kaci's side and grabbed her hand.

"I came to an old bridge just before I entered the city," Kaci continued. "I saw her and stopped. Winter was standing on the rail of the bridge about to jump. I knew things were bad for her in high school…she told me about most everything, but she never told me about this. I don't think she told anyone."

Stacy sobbed loudly for a moment, and then covered her mouth with both hands.

"I was there for her," Kaci said. "I didn't know who she was, but she needed me. I held her hand." Kaci choked. "And I think that was the first time Winter understood that she wasn't alone. When her dad showed up, it was a miracle. I couldn't believe it, but I knew that she was safe and there was nothing else I could do. So, I got back in the car and I left while they clung to each other in the rain. I never even asked for her name..."

Kaci broke down crying. Her mother handed her a tissue, and Peter took the baby who began to stir. When Kaci composed herself she continued.

"I have thought about that night so many times over these years, and I never once thought it might have been her. I never told Winter about it...I never told anyone. No one was supposed to know we were in Trenton Hills that night." She let out a calming sigh. "Winter was there for me. When I needed her the way she needed me, she was there for me like I was there for her. I will *never* forget her."

When Kaci fell silent, I looked up at Graham. He grabbed my hand at his side and shook his head. He wasn't ready yet. He would be ready someday, and I'd make sure I was there for him when he needed to let it all out. It was the least I could do for him. It was the least I could do for Winter.

We all stared at the photos for a long time. There was a photo of Summer and Winter in their dorm room four years ago. A photo of Kaci with Winter just after the engagement party. A selfie of Graham and Winter at the wedding. A picture of Davis and Summer with Winter, eating lunch at the Union. A picture of a younger Winter, with three other girls; one of them was Stacy. A prom picture with Winter and a cute boy beneath an arch of balloons. A picture of Winter, her dad, and Daniel, all dripping wet in white robes. And a larger version of the picture still in the locket around my neck...thirteen-year-old Winter with her mom. I brought that one.

We waited there, and no one wanted to say anything else. No one wanted to break the quiet fellowship we had in that moment.

Finally, Peter spoke, his voice hoarse. "Maybe someone should pray now."

"I'll do it," said Daniel. He stepped forward and bowed his head. We all did the same, and then he prayed, a gentle, simple prayer, thanking God for our friend.

When he finished, everyone cast around at each other uncertainly.

Peter pulled Kaci close. "We're going to go get some food at the Raven, if anyone wants to join us."

Everyone smiled, even Graham, and agreed. I glanced across to Agent Erickson, and he gave me a knowing look and a backward nod of his head.

I nodded and walked to Peter as the others gathered together, smiling and hugging, and preparing to relocate for lunch.

"I've got to go," I said.

"More weird stuff to check out?" Peter asked. Kaci frowned.

"Probably," I said. "The FBI keeps us pretty busy. They have occult specialists, but they've never had a team like us. We've lived this stuff. There's still a lot of dangerous activity out there. We have to stop it before someone else gets hurt...before there's another Mordensfield Elementary, or another Sandy, or another Xaphan."

"But why you?"

"I'm the only one who can." I studied the pictures for a moment, then turned back. "Winter was uniquely qualified for her task. I'm uniquely qualified for this one."

Erickson stepped to my side, and Peter acknowledged him with a nod. "Right. Make sure you two come see us next time you're in town."

I looked down at Isaiah in his arms and smiled. As I rubbed the baby's soft cheek with my finger, I said, "Of course I will."

Peter hugged me, and before I had barely released him Kaci did too. I smiled at them and backed away, Erickson already in stride and leaving.

"Bye," I said.

"Goodbye, Agent Shields," said Peter.

As I caught up with Erickson, I couldn't help but think how different things had turned out than what I expected. I never wanted to get involved in this kind of stuff. I didn't want to be friends with someone like Winter. I wanted a fresh start and something normal. But I'm beginning to realize more and more that it's not always about what I want out of life. I don't really know what I want, but as long as I let God take the lead I'll be exactly where he wants me to be and I'll become exactly who I'm supposed to become. He's the one who writes my story and I'm okay with that.

Winter's story may be over now, but mine is just beginning.

He has made everything appropriate in its time. He has also set eternity in their heart, yet so that man will not find out the work which God has done from the beginning even to the end.
Ecclesiastes 3:11 (NAS)

Winter

BOOK ONE

0

It was August already. The summer had gone by faster than Winter wanted it to. Her ribs still ached if she twisted the wrong way, but her nose had healed just fine and she was finally beginning to feel normal again.

Move-in day was only a couple of weeks away. She had spent the past two days packing things in her room, ready to load them in the trailer occupying a generous portion of their drive.

As Steve pulled his truck back into the drive, a productive day of college shopping behind them, Winter felt a small pang of nostalgia.

"I'm not sure I want to do this," Winter said, looking at her dad as he parked in the garage.

"Listen," he said. "Parkway is just on the other side of town. Anytime you want to come home for a weekend or have dinner, or anything…just let me know. It's…what? A twenty-minute drive? If that."

Winter sighed as she opened the truck door. "I know. I feel like you and I are just getting started the right way. I don't want to ruin that."

Steve unlocked the house door and ushered her in. "This will be a good step for you. Community College will help you figure out what you want to do with the rest of your life. You can't live with me forever."

"I know."

"And, you've got a bunch of classmates going, so there will be people you know there."

"I'm not really friends with them…"

"But you will be. You've got those two girls from church that graduated from North Trenton you'll be in the suite with. I think it's a great opportunity. It's not like you'll be hours away from everyone you know."

Winter flopped down on the couch and dropped her shopping bags at her feet. "I know. Sorry. Guess I'm just getting nervous. Besides, you need me. I shudder to think of this place becoming an old man's bachelor pad."

Steve laughed as he walked into the kitchen. "I'll be fine. Don't worry about me."

Winter frowned in his direction. She wasn't so sure.

"Listen," Steve said, emerging from the kitchen. "It's already after five and we have small group Bible study in a little over an hour. How about I go pick up a pizza real quick?"

"Sure," Winter said as she stood. "I'll just be getting ready."

As he left, Winter sank further into the couch and stared at the blank TV. What was she so worried about? Parkway Community College would be a great new start for her. Things could be different there. She could start over.

"Winter," said a man's voice.

Winter leaned forward and turned. "Yeah?" From the window she saw her dad's truck drive by. She jumped up off the couch. "Is someone there?"

The room answered her with silence. She rubbed a hand through her hair. Maybe she just needed rest. Maybe the stress of getting everything ready for college toyed with her mind. But just to be certain, Winter walked through every room downstairs and even stuck her head in the garage.

She was alone. Which meant she must have imagined it. Then as she returned to the living room, it happened again.

"Winter..." The voice came from upstairs.

"Who's there?" Winter called out. No answer. She rushed to the kitchen, reached for a knife from the butcher block but stopped short as her heart ran cold. Never again...

Instead, she grabbed a pan from the cabinet and the phone from the wall. Then she eased upstairs, trying to be as silent as possible, listening for any sound of an intruder. But the house still sat eerily silent. Was she going crazy?

She checked the spare bedroom and closet first, then she checked her dad's room and bathroom. No one.

"Winter..." This time the voice seemed to come from her own room.

"Who is that?" Winter screamed. She started to call the police, but for some reason stopped after dialing the nine. Curiosity replaced her fear. Excitement raced through her veins. She lowered the pan a little and crept toward her room.

She eased through the door and looked carefully around, but the room was empty. She went to her bathroom door and shoved it open. Also empty. Slowly she walked inside to check the shower, but stopped when movement on the mirror caught her eye.

White streaks swept across the surface spelling her name. *WINTER.*

"Winter…" said the voice again, louder now. Closer. In her room for certain.

She spun. "Get out!" But she still saw no one there. Back in her room, she flung open her closet and checked under her bed. Nothing. Standing in the center of her room, she spun in circles, waiting for the voice to speak again. Why hadn't she called the police yet?

"Winter…"

"What do you want?" she yelled. "Who are you?"

"You know who I am," said the voice softly.

Did she? More excitement coursed through her than fear. She didn't want to run from the voice, she wanted to run after it. She didn't want to find the man to get rid of him, she wanted to embrace him. She couldn't understand why she felt like that, but every time the voice spoke her heart fluttered.

"What do you want?" she asked again, more gently.

"I need you to do something for me," said the voice, still and lovely. "Something only you can do."

Winter shook the pan, but only because a part of her thought that would be the right thing to do. Then she lowered it completely. "What?"

"Go to Tishbe."

"Go to Tishbe?" she asked. "I don't even know what that means!"

"You will."

She had to know more. She had to have all the answers. She had to be certain. "Who are you?"

Silence. Was she going crazy? How else could she explain hearing voices like this?

"Tishbe...Tishbe..." whispers floated in the air. Soft whispers. Almost imperceptible. "Tishbe...Tishbe..."

"Stop it!" Winter screamed. She ran from the room, but the whispers followed her.

"Tishbe...Tishbe..."

She fled down the stairs into the living room, tossing the pan and phone onto the coffee table and covering both ears with her hands. She curled up on the couch and clenched her eyes, trying to make it stop.

"Tishbe...Tishbe..." The whispers were still there. Always there. Penetrating through her hands, just at the edge of her hearing. Always. "Tishbe...Tishbe..."

She stomped her feet. She hummed to herself. She rocked back and forth. She cried.

"Tishbe...Tishbe..."

The minutes passed. Too many to count. The repetition of the word boring a hole into her mind.

"Tishbe...Tishbe..."

A door closed behind her, the only new sound she had heard since the whispers started. At the sound of the door, they finally silenced.

"I'm home," her dad called.

Winter stayed on the couch, ears covered and eyes tight, praying the whispers wouldn't come back.

Suddenly, her dad was there. "Winter, what's wrong? Did something happen?"

She gazed up at him, and the trapped tears behind her eyelids fell down her cheeks. "I...I don't know..."

He placed the pizza box on the coffee table as he sat. "Tell me. What's going on?"

Winter turned away. She looked at the coffee table and to the box of pizza. Her eyes fell on the rectangles of paper on top of the box. "Is that the mail?"

"Yeah," he said.

The piece of mail on top was a full-color picture of the largest live oak tree she had ever seen, standing in the center of a wide green lawn with buildings in the background. Over those buildings loomed a majestic clock tower. In the center top was a maroon logo of a bird with the initials TU.

Beneath it…the name "Tishbe University."

Winter snatched it up. "What's this?"

"I don't know. It came for you. Your mom went there for a while."

Winter stared at the brochure and read the words at the bottom carefully, her heart pounding in a way she had never felt before. The words read, "It's not too late! Register now!"

She bit her lip and narrowed her eyes. "Dad. We need to talk."

READ WINTER'S STORY AGAIN IN CHRONOLOGICAL ORDER

Twelve Years Ago
(prior to **Prophetess**)

Prophetess (Book 2) – Chapter 0

High School
Year 1

Winter (Book 1)

Chapters - 2, 4, 9, 12, 15, 18, 24, 27, 30, 33, 38, 41, 44, 51, 54, 57, 62, 65, 68, 72, 74, 77

Year 2

Prophetess (Book 2)

Chapters – 2, 5, 7, 10, 12, 15, 18, 21, 24, 28, 33, 35, 38, 41, 44, 47, 50, 53, 56, 58, 60, 62, 64, 66, 68, 70, 73

Year 3

Acolyte (Book 3)

Chapters – 3, 6, 9, 12, 15, 18, 21, 25, 28, 31, 34, 37, 40, 43, 46, 49, 51, 54, 57, 60, 63, 66

Year 4

Mantle (Book 4)

Chapters – 3, 6, 9, 12, 15, 18, 21, 24, 27, 30, 33, 36, 39, 42, 45, 48, 51, 54, 57, 59, 60 (immediately after the Infinity Chapter), 62 part 1, 62 part 3

The Summer Before College
(Found at the end of **Mantle**)

Winter – Chapter 0

College
Year 1

Winter (Book 1)

Chapters - 1, 3, 5, 6, 7, 8, 10, 11, 13, 14, 16, 17, 19, 20, 21, 22, 23, 25, 26, 28, 29, 31, 32, 34, 35, 36, 37, 39, 40, 42, 43, 45, 46, 47, 48, 49, 50, 52, 53, 55, 56, 58, 59, 60, 61, 63, 64, 66, 67, 69, 70, 71, 73, 75, 76, 78, 79

Year 2

Prophetess (Book 2)

Chapters – 1, 3, 4, 6, 8, 9, 11, 13, 14, 16, 17, 19, 20, 22, 23, 25, 26, 27, 29, 30, 31, 32, 34, 36, 37, 39, 40, 42, 43, 45, 46, 48, 49, 51, 52, 54, 55, 57, 59, 61, 63, 65, 67, 69, 71, 72, 74

Year 3

Acolyte (Book 3)

Chapters – 0, 1, 2, 4, 5, 7, 8, 10, 11, 13, 14, 16, 17, 19, 20, 22, 23, 24, 26, 27, 29, 30, 32, 33, 35, 36, 38, 39, 41, 42, 44, 45, 47, 48, 50, 52, 53, 55, 56, 58, 59, 61, 62, 64, 65, 67, 68

Year 4

Mantle (Book 4)

Chapters – 0, 1, 2, 4, 5, 7, 8, 10, 11, 13, 14, 16, 17, 19, 20, 22, 23, 25, 26, 28, 29, 31, 32, 34, 35, 37, 38, 40, 41, 43, 44, 46, 47, 49, 50, 52, 53, 55, 56, 58, the Infinity Chapter (found after 59), 61, 62 part 2, 62 part 4

Ayden's Point of View
(After chapter 62 of **Mantle**)
Chapter 1, Chapter 2, Chapter 3

ABOUT THE AUTHOR

Keven Newsome began his writing career at the young age of ten by creating fanfiction of his favorite video game. He only wrote four pages, though, painstakingly in King James English since that's how they spoke in the game. It was horrible and he promptly abandoned his writing career forever. Thankfully, some years later, fourteen-year-old Keven disagreed with that hasty decision and discovered writing could actually be fun. Since then he has authored five novels, published four of those, and written and published several short stories. He has also recently returned to his favorite video game and become an award-winning fanfiction author on Wattpad. The four books of his Winter series, *Winter, Prophetess, Acolyte,* and *Mantle,* together have been finalists for seven awards and winners of three of those. Originally from south Mississippi, he and his wife live a nomadic ministry life, followed relentlessly by the collective cries of his fans to finish writing his next book already.

http://kevennewsome.com
https://linktr.ee/knewsome.author